When It Began

Two Brothers. Two Girls. One Shared Dream.

Denice Perkins

S & G Publishing Designs

Published by S&G Publishing Designs

Edited by LZ Edits

Cover by GetCovers - Cover design services

Interior Design by S&G Publishing Designs

First edition 2026

Perkins, Denice. When It Began. Contemporary Christian Novel. S&G Publishing Designs

ISBN: 979-8-9852792-7-6

Library of Congress Control Number: 2026912941

The Great Commission

Matthew 28:16-20

16 Then the eleven disciples went away into Galilee, to the mountain which Jesus had appointed for them. 17 When they saw Him,
they worshiped Him; but some doubted.
18 And Jesus came and spoke to them, saying, "All authority
has been given to Me in heaven and on earth. 19 Go therefore
and make disciples of all the nations, baptizing them in the name
of the Father and of the Son and of the Holy Spirit, 20 teaching
them to observe all things that I have commanded you; and lo, I
am with you always, *even* to the end of the age." Amen.

***

My prayer is to follow Jesus' instruction and lead others to Him.

Contents

Part One

Robert

Robert

Chapter 1

The Dream

Robert Jackson's parents, both teachers at his high school, stood with his siblings from their seats behind the graduates when his name was announced. Heat rose up his neck and onto his face as the applause, whoops, and whistles from family and friends increased. He prayed nobody noticed his embarrassment. On the stage, he accepted his diploma, and his mother's camera flashed.

Captured. Thanks, Mom.

Back in his seat, he absentmindedly watched his classmates cross the stage. His parents often said they dreamed of his college graduation, but he dreamed of something else entirely. He wasn't looking forward to shattering their dream, but he would have to soon.

When the ceremony ended, Robert followed his classmates outside. On the lawn in front of the high school, where the mascot's statue stood beneath the waving U.S. flag, his mother had already chosen the perfect spot for pictures.

"Son, which college offer did you choose?" his father asked.

Shuffling his feet, Robert drew a breath. "I think I would do well in college, but I'm not goin' to go. I want to help make our town better for the families livin' here." He pulled off his graduation cap and ran his fingers through his dark auburn hair.

His dad's eyes narrowed. "Mighty big dream. Do you have a plan?"

Robert met his father's hazel-eyed gaze, like his own, head-on. "I've accepted a job with Bard's Buildings to learn construction and home remodelin'. After gettin' my contractor's license, I'll study to become a realtor and start my own business, fixin' up run-down houses and sellin' them at fair prices. It won't cost you a dime, no tuition, books, or room and board."

His mom frowned, then opened her mouth, but Solomon, his younger brother, clapped him on the back before she said a word.

Solomon winked. "Let's get to the church graduation party. I talked to Emelia. She's hoping you'll be there."

"We'll discuss this more later, son. We're proud of you." Dad handed Solomon the camera. "Take a picture of Mom and me with Robert in his cap and gown first. Then we'll get the other shots your mom wants before you boys head out."

Solomon snapped a photo of Robert in his cap and gown with their parents, then a shot with his favorite teacher. The teacher returned the favor by taking a picture of Robert with his whole family. His mom captured the serious poses first, then some of her children being their silly selves. With everyone laughing, their parents shooed the boys off to the church's graduation party.

Robert and Solomon stepped into the Fellowship Hall of the Northside church of Christ. While Solomon joined some friends, Robert scanned the crowd until he caught sight of a familiar figure. Her long, dark brown hair cascaded down her back, and even without seeing her face, he knew it was Emelia. His feet moved before his thoughts caught up.

She turned just as he reached her, and their gazes locked. Her chocolate eyes made his chest tighten. When his mouth, usually so sure and brusque, refused to cooperate, he stuffed his hands in his pockets.

Emelia smiled. "Congratulations, Robert."

He swallowed. “Congrats, Emelia.”

She laughed softly and extended her hand. He hesitated a second before lacing his fingers through hers. “Where we goin’, Em?”

“You’re always hungry,” she teased. “Let’s get some food.”

The youth minister’s prayer gave him a moment to settle himself. When Emelia let go to grab a plate, the sudden emptiness of his hand startled him. He followed her in line, filling his plate absentmindedly. They found a quiet corner table and set their food-laden plates down. Once they settled, he reached out again.

“Let’s pray,” he said in a steady voice.

She raised her brows but offered both hands. He wrapped his hands around hers and closed his eyes.

"Lord," he whispered, “thank You... for everything. And for Em. In Jesus' name, amen.”

"Amen," she said, her fingers twitched slightly in his palms.

He'd finished, but he held her hands a moment longer.

“Em?”

She tilted her head. “You’ve never called me that before. Why now?”

He took a long, slow drink of iced tea. “Because you matter to me. We both graduated today, and I don’t want this summer to be the last time we spend together.”

Her eyes widened, her breath hitched. She looked down, then up again. “You’re special to me, too. I’m staying. I’ll be studying business and accounting at the community college. Are you going away?”

“Nah, I got a job with Bard’s Buildings, learnin’ remodelin’.” His voice lifted with hope. “And you’re stayin’.”

Her lips parted in a quiet smile. “So, we’re both staying.”

Her restless fingers picked at the chips on her plate. He placed his hand on hers. She stilled.

“I’ve got a dream,” he said. “Want to hear it?”

She met his gaze. “I do.”

“I want to fix up homes. Start my own business one day. Get a real estate license. Take houses people gave up on and make them livable again. Families need that. Our town needs that.”

Before she could reply, Solomon dropped into the seat beside him, hair falling over his brow. "If he lets me, I'm jumpin' in the second I graduate."

Emelia laughed gently, eyes flicking between them. "I forgot how alike you look. Only a year apart?"

"Eleven months," Robert said. "Remember when Mom dressed us alike?"

Solomon groaned. "I've tried to forget. But thanks for ending that phase. You did us both a favor."

Her laughter bubbled over. "You two speak and act so differently. No offense, Solomon, but I think Robert's more handsome."

Solomon grinned. "None taken. Beauty is in the eye of the beholder." He grabbed his plate. "Robert, ask her out." Then he was gone.

Robert leaned toward Emelia. "You blush pretty," he said softly.

She ducked her head, hair shielding her face like a curtain.

"I'd really like to take you out. Tonight, if you're free."

She peeked up and tucked her hair behind her ear, revealing the soft pink in her cheeks. "I'd like that."

Chapter 2

The Push For College

Over the next several weeks, dinner at the Jacksons' grew thick with silence and sidelong glances. Then one evening, Robert's father pushed back his chair and fixed a hard glare on his son.

"Are you serious about this young lady you're dating?"

Robert sat straighter, his heart kicking up a notch. "I am. I believe she's the one. I'm not ready for more than datin' yet, but I'm prayin'. I've placed our future in God's hands."

His father's chair creaked as he leaned forward, his voice sharp. "If you want a future with means, construction won't cut it. You need college. Engineering. Stability. Please tell me she's not the reason you're passin' on school."

Robert's shoulders sagged with a sigh. "We've been through this. Bard's gave me a raise and offered me an internship. I'll be workin' toward my contractor's license. I accepted the promotion and the responsibility."

His dad scoffed. "So your whole future relies on sweat and hope? Go. To. College."

Robert pushed his plate aside, his appetite gone. His eyes flicked to his mother, silently pleading. But her tight-lipped frown gave him nothing. He stood and grabbed his keys from the credenza.

"Young man! Where are you going?" his mother called out as he opened the front door.

"I don't know." He closed the door behind him.

He drove aimlessly past Emelia's house, around the quiet town square with its storefronts shuttered for the day. His stomach rumbled. A drive-thru burger joint filled the void. He parked at the park near the town square, found an empty bench by the spring-fed waterfall, and sat heavily.

He bowed his head. "Lord, please forgive me for my disrespect. If I'm wrong about this path, if college is Your will, please show me. I see promise in this job. I feel alive building somethin' real. Emelia's sharp with money, and my mentor believes in me. I want to live according to Your purpose. Please guide me."

The sound of the water soothed him. He watched it tumble over the rocks, then lifted his eyes toward the evening sky.

"My parents think I'm makin' a mistake. If they're right, please show me, Lord. In Jesus' name, amen."

He tossed his trash, climbed back into his car, and headed toward Emelia's house. Unannounced. He stepped onto her porch, wiped his damp palms on his jeans, and rang the bell.

Emelia's father opened the door, his eyes narrowed. "Emelia didn't mention having company."

Robert met his gaze, voice steady. "No, sir. I didn't plan to come by. But I'd like to talk with her, if that's okay."

The man studied him, brows drawn. "Wait here."

The door banged shut behind him, leaving Robert alone. He shifted his weight and ran a hand through his hair. Her father's stern face still burned in his mind. Pacing the porch, he caught movement. Emelia stood in the doorway.

She smiled, though her brow creased. "You're upset."

Robert stopped pacing. "Can we talk? Go somewhere?"

"Let me ask my parents." Her voice was gentle as she stepped inside.

He followed and sat where she pointed, his legs bounced, and his hands clenched. Voices floated from the back room. Emelia's was calm, her father's rose. Robert couldn't make out words, but the tension pressed like a weight on his chest. He closed his eyes.

Lord, does he think I'm not enough? If college is the way to build the kind of life Emelia deserves, I'll do it. I want to earn her father's respect. Please guide me. In Jesus' name, amen.

He opened his eyes as Emelia returned.

"I'm ready. But I need to be home by ten," she said, tucking her hair behind her ear.

Robert nodded and glanced past her. "Mr. Norton, I'll have her home on time. Thank you."

Her father's voice followed. "Where are you taking my daughter?"

Robert answered without hesitation. "To the park. To walk and talk. Then for her favorite ice cream, then home."

Her father gave a single nod. Robert reached for Emelia's hand, and together, they stepped out into the summer evening.

Robert drove in silence, the low hum of the engine the only sound between them. He pulled into the small lot beside Waterfall Park, closer to Emelia's house than the one on the south side of town. Before he could open his door, her voice cut through the stillness.

"I've heard about you," she said quietly, her eyes locking onto his. "You date girls just long enough for them to fall for you, and then you walk away. I thought I was different. I thought you cared."

His chest tightened. "I do care. The last thing I want is to break up with you."

Her expression softened, but a shadow lingered in her gaze. "Okay. Do you ever kiss a girl?"

A smile tugged at his lips. "I've never wanted to until you. If I kiss you, it'll be because I love you and I'm ready, then only with your permission."

He stepped out, grabbed a small pack from the back seat, and circled the car to open her door. She hesitated a beat before taking his hand, their fingers laced together. She stared at the path ahead.

"I don't want you to kiss me unless you love me. Forever love me. If you're not sure, please don't. My heart couldn't handle that."

Robert stopped walking, and she stumbled. He caught her, his hands steadying her.

"Em," he said gently, "I would never lead you on. You and I, together, is the only thing I'm sure of. I'm not goin' anywhere."

Her breath hitched, and a smile crept in. "I was scared. But if you're sure, I'm sure."

He held her a moment longer, reluctant to let go of her warmth. "Thank you," he said quietly. "You don't know how much that means."

He pointed toward a secluded picnic table in a corner of the park. "I want to talk about the future with you, our future. If something doesn't feel right, I need you to say it. I don't want to make decisions that won't make you happy. You won't lose me by being honest."

At the table, Robert pulled out a spiral notebook and a pen from his pack. Emelia looked at them curiously.

"Why'd you bring those?"

He exhaled slowly. "You know an abridged version of my dream. You are better than I am when it comes to money and details. I was hopin' you'd help me figure out if my business idea makes sense."

He searched her expression but couldn't read it. "My parents want me to go to college. They think it's the only way I'll have anything to offer you. I want to build something solid with you. I don't want to let you down."

She opened the notebook, fingers brushing the page. "We'll figure it out. Together."

Her smile lit up her face, and golden flecks danced in her chocolate eyes. Robert swallowed hard. That sparkle stole a little more of his heart every time.

They scribbled, talked, and pondered—two versions of the future: one grounded in the work Robert already knew, the other in the unfamiliar terrain of part-time college and a full-time job. They both agreed his current path felt more promising, but they'd research further, run numbers, and set goals before deciding anything long-term.

When she finally set the pen down, Robert placed his hand over hers. "We're planning our future. Is a future with me what you want?"

She leaned her head on his shoulder. "It makes me happy."

He wrapped an arm around her and held her close. "I want a future with you," he whispered.

Then, gently pulling away, he added with a smile, "Let's pray before we get ice cream."

Joining hands, they bowed their heads until their foreheads touched.

Robert started. "Lord, we come before You tonight, trusting Your hand in all things. As we begin shaping our future, guide us to honor You in every step. Help me grow, help me prove I'm ready, help me protect this woman You've brought into my life..."

Emelia's voice joined his, soft and reverent. "Thank You, Lord, for this man who seeks You first. Help me be steady, patient, and kind. Help me be the woman he needs. Bless the choices we make together."

A hush fell over them, warm and sacred. Robert finished, his voice thick with emotion. "We know You are always with us. Forgive us. Lead us. Yours is the kingdom, the glory, and the power. In Jesus' name, amen."

Their eyes met again.

"I'd love to see you tomorrow, take you to dinner." Robert grinned. "Let's get ice cream while there's still time."

She nodded, fingers squeezing his in reply.

Chapter 3

Love's Quiet Beginning

Robert walked Emelia to her door, their fingers entwined. With a quiet smile, he placed the notebook in her free hand and opened the door.

"I'll see you tomorrow, Em," he said, his voice low and steady.

She stepped into the entryway but didn't close the door. He caught her hand, their eyes meeting for a long, quiet moment. With a soft sigh, he let go. Lingering in the doorway, she watched him slide into his car and didn't shut the door until it disappeared down the street.

Still holding the notebook, she bowed her head.

Thank You, Lord, for the quiet strength of Robert's presence. He hasn't kissed me. He hasn't said the words. But I know we belong to each other. I love him. Please give me the strength to hold those words close until he's ready to speak them. Thank You for giving me such a good and faithful man. In Jesus' name, amen.

The entryway lights spilled into the living room, where her parents sat side by side on the couch. Her shoulders slumped.

"You don't have to wait up for me," she said, her voice edged with unease.

Her father stood and crossed toward her. "We always wait up. You're our daughter, and your safety is never something we take lightly."

Her mother joined him, eyes soft but serious. “Robert radiated anxiety when he arrived. And you were clearly nervous. That alone gives us reason to ask questions.”

They offered hugs, but Emelia’s guard was rising, bracing for the inevitable interrogation.

She followed them to the couch and sat in the space they carved out just for her, between them, with Robert’s notebook cradled tight against her lap. Her mother turned her calm yet piercing gaze on her.

“What happened tonight?”

Her father crossed his arms. “If that boy breaks your heart, we’ll have words. I promise you that.”

Before she could answer, her mother’s gaze fell on the notebook.

“Why do you have that?” she asked, pointing. Her tone held more concern than curiosity.

Emelia lowered her eyes and gave a cautious smile. “It’s Robert’s notebook. I’m helping him outline his business plan. It’s still early and will take time, but he’s committed to building it from the ground up, slow and steady. We’re working through two possible models.”

Her dad raised a skeptical brow. “You could’ve mapped all that out at the dining room table.”

Emelia held the notebook tighter like a shield. “Some things are personal. What we talked about tonight didn’t need extra ears or well-meaning advice. I love you both, but I’m ready to start shaping my own future.”

Her mom leaned forward. “You’re starting college next week. That notebook means a lot more to you than business plans.” After a pause, her voice was quieter. “How serious are things between you and Robert?”

Then her father’s voice cut through, the worry spilling out. “Are you kissing that boy—or more than kissing?”

Emelia stood, shaking her head. “Why would you even think that? The only physical touch Robert and I have is holding hands. Tonight, he steadied me when I tripped in the park. That’s all. He didn’t let me fall.”

She smiled at the memory, then met their eyes.

"I was nervous tonight because I thought Robert might be pulling away. But I asked him directly if that was his intention. He said no, absolutely not. He wanted me involved in his decisions because he hopes they'll shape our shared future."

Her father frowned. "He's talking about a future with you and hasn't even kissed you? Does he love you?"

Emelia felt heat rise in her cheeks. "He hasn't said it. And I don't think he will, not yet anyway. But I know he loves me. He told me he wants to kiss me, but only when the time is right and with my permission."

Her mom raised her eyebrows. "That notebook, does it include plans for college, too?"

"It does for me," Emelia said, firm but respectful. "As for Robert, that's something we're figuring out together. College isn't the only road to success, and it's not guaranteed to be the right one for everyone. His parents are pushing him to enroll, but that's their voice, not his. Yours won't be added to the pressure. We prayed over it tonight, and we'll keep praying."

Her father ran his hand across his mouth, his frustration evident. "If you're keeping plans from us, don't expect our support."

Emelia nodded. "I'm not hiding them. But it's not my place to reveal everything. Once we've made some firm decisions, I'll ask Robert to sit down with both of you. I believe he wants your blessing. He's planning a life with me."

She turned before any more words could be spoken and retreated into her room, heart full and weary.

Inside, she sat on her bed and wrapped her arms around the notebook, the symbol of their shared dreams, fragile but real. The only thing missing tonight was his voice saying, *I love you*. And maybe the brush of his lips across hers. But he had spoken volumes about a future. Their future.

She closed her eyes and whispered to God again.

"I don't want to be patient. Please let this unfold faster than we expect. I love him, and I'll continue to pray this. Help me be satisfied with his promise of our future. In Jesus' name, amen."

A knock interrupted her thoughts.

"Are you decent? May we come in?" her father asked.

Please, no more questions tonight, she prayed, setting the notebook gently on her nightstand.

"Yes, come in," she called softly.

Her parents entered with genuine smiles and embraced her with arms of comfort and love.

"Don't forget to say your prayers," her mom murmured.

"I love you both," Emelia said as she held them close. "I won't forget."

"Good night, baby girl. Sweet dreams," they said together.

She smiled, her heart lighter. "Good night. Sweet dreams."

It had always been this way, a nightly tradition, steeped in love and God's presence. But things would change, and she would change with them. One day, she and Robert would create their own ritual, one rooted in faith and tenderness.

She let her thoughts roam to the park, to his touch, to the quiet depth of his smile. Her heart hummed with gentle longing.

"I want a future with Robert," she whispered.

She closed her eyes and pictured his face—the softness of his gold-dusted hazel eyes, the long, straight nose that fit him just right, and his smile, sincere and a little crooked, which made her feel like the only girl in the world.

She changed for bed, then knelt beside it.

"Thank You, Lord, for my loving parents. Thank You for Robert, a man after Your heart. Forgive me where I've failed and help me readily forgive others. In Jesus' name, amen."

Emelia was slipping beneath her covers when the ring of the kitchen phone sliced through the quiet. She threw on her robe and dashed down the hall, her heart racing—not from fear, but from hope.

She snatched the receiver from its cradle. "Hello?"

"Hey," Robert said, his voice tender. "I'm sorry if I woke you."

Just hearing him was like finding the glow in a starless sky.

She looked up and saw her dad standing nearby. With her palm over the handset's speaker, she whispered, "It's Robert. I'll be quick."

He nodded. "Construction means early mornings. For his sake, keep it brief. I'll see you in the morning."

When her father disappeared down the hall, she slid her hand from the speaker. "You didn't wake me."

"I just wanted to say goodnight to my girlfriend one more time."

Her cheeks flushed, the sweetness of his words coating her like warm honey.

"Thank you," she said.

He chuckled. "I haven't said it yet."

"Robert."

"Goodnight, sweetheart."

Emotion swelled in her throat. "Goodnight, my love." The words emerged without thought, yet they held the truth.

There was a pause, then he spoke, his voice deepened with warmth. "I'm stealin' that. Goodnight, my love."

"Goodnight."

The soft click of the line disconnecting tugged at her heart. She pressed the receiver to her chest, as if she were hugging Robert. She wanted just one more minute, one more shared heartbeat.

With her heart full of hope and dreams, she walked slowly to her room. Her smile stayed as she sat on the edge of her bed. They hadn't said *I love you*, not outright, but they'd claimed each other.

Tonight, Robert had given her two gifts more valuable than any kiss: the certainty of a future and the intimacy of being *his love*.

She curled beneath the comforter, the spicy scent of his cologne lingering in her memory, and the steady rhythm of his voice echoing in her thoughts. Her smile matched the fullness of her heart. Sleep came gently, carrying her into dreams lit by hazel eyes and shared promises.

Chapter 4

Am I In Love?

All the way home from Emelia's, Robert drove in silence, but her words kept replaying in his head. Then there was the way she listened, the steadiness in her eyes that seemed to catch him whenever his confidence slipped. The future felt closer, more real, and a little scary.

Turning off the engine in his driveway, he didn't move. Stillness surrounded him while the porch light cast a warm glow. He rested his forehead on the steering wheel and prayed.

"God, why does this have to be so hard? Help me be a respectful son, a good example to my siblings, and the man Emelia needs. Forgive my sins and help me forgive others. Yours is the honor and glory. In Jesus' name, amen."

He lingered in the hush that followed, then forced himself upright. After one long glance at the front door, he climbed out of the car and went inside. The soft click of the keys landing on the credenza was the only sound. When he turned, his parents waited in the living room.

"You guys don't have to wait up on me anymore," he said, voice low, chin tucked, eyes drifting downward.

His mother gave a small wave toward the couch. His father, sitting beside her, spoke gently but firmly.

"Son, when you stomp outta here, leavin' without sayin' where you're goin' or when you'll be back, yes, we have to wait up for you. We love you. We need to know you made it home in one piece."

Robert sat slowly, scrubbing his hands through his hair, then letting them fall limp in his lap.

"I'm sorry I left like that," he said. "It was disrespectful, and I worried you. I'll apologize to Solomon and the girls. I don't want to be the brother who teaches them what not to do. I want to be the kind of man you raised."

His mother leaned forward and placed her hand over his. "I'm thankful you recognize your mistake. You are forgiven. We love you."

A smile tugged at the corners of his father's mouth.

"I'm proud of you," his dad said. "Apologizin' to your siblings will show them something worth lookin' up to. You're a good son and a good brother."

His parents exchanged a glance, and his father's voice turned cautious.

"Are we correct to assume that you've decided against goin' to college?"

"I have," Robert said. "The only way I could is part-time, and I'm not doin' that. When I accepted the internship with Bard's Buildings, I signed a contract. One of the terms is full-time employment for three years."

He paused, then pressed through.

"After I get my contractor's license, I will work in that capacity. They know I want to rehab homes here in town, and they're fine with it. I won't be their competition because they do remodels for homeowners and new builds for bigger clients."

He stopped, feeling exposed under his parents' eyes. His father looked to his mother again. She nodded slowly, her smile tinged with sadness.

"My boy is grown now," she said. "Thinking and making choices for himself. We wanted something different, but we'll pray God guides you where you need to go."

Robert bowed his head. "I should've talked with you and Dad first. I prayed about it. I believe it's the right decision. But I'm sorry for disappointin' you."

His father said quietly, "Son, look at me."

He did.

"We should've been listenin'. Not just talkin'. We pushed too hard in a direction you didn't want."

A moment passed. His dad leaned forward. "Talk to us, boy. How did you spend your evenin'?"

The words '*Talk to us, boy*' weren't harsh from his father. They were filled with care.

"I went to Emelia's." Just saying her name eased something tight in his chest. "We talked things through. She's helpin' me create a plan for startin' my business. She was in DECA in high school and helped launch the school's retail store. Her job was to learn how to write a business plan and build one for the store."

He sat straighter. "She's good. She knows what she's doin'. She's helpin' me research startup costs to put a price on each step."

He looked between them. His father was unreadable, but his mother's smile widened and wrapped around him like a blanket.

"I'm not wearin' rose-colored glasses," Robert said. "I know I'll have to work full-time for a few years and build my business on nights and weekends. It's not an easy road, but it's a road I want to travel. And I have Emelia's support."

"You have Emelia's support," his father echoed, slow and deliberate.

Robert nodded, trying to swallow past the lump in his throat.

His father chuckled. "You're datin' Emelia Norton from church."

"Yes, sir."

"You were serious at dinner, and now her support matters to you. Are you 'I love you' serious about her?"

His mother wrung her hands in her lap.

Robert's mouth straightened. "I don't know yet. But I see her in my future. And I won't say those words or kiss her until I have a viable plan and a place for us to live."

He looked at them both.

"Mom, you were in college when you married Dad. And Dad, you were in your first year of teachin'. You lived with Mom's parents while she finished school, and you saved the down payment for this house. It worked for you, and I'm thankful."

Then, turning fully to his father, Robert said, "You told me I had nothin' to offer a girl yet. You were right. But I want to offer her a home and a future. I have a decent income now with a promise of increases."

They nodded. Slowly, quietly.

Robert stood, and his parents followed. His mother stepped to him, wrapping her arms around his chest. "Talk things through with us going forward, son."

His father joined them, holding them both close. "We'll pray for you and Emelia. And we'll support you however we can."

Their embrace anchored him. After a long moment, they released him, and he started toward the room he shared with Solomon.

Behind him, his mother's voice rose gently.

"Don't forget to say your prayers."

Robert stepped into his room and peeled off his clothes. Solomon, already in bed, turned toward him. "Long day, brother?"

Robert didn't meet his gaze. "Yeah. Very long." He tossed his dirty clothes in the hamper and pulled on a clean T-shirt.

"I thought Dad and Mom were going to let you have it," Solomon said, yawning. "The way Dad paced the house and their snippy voices all evening, I figured it'd be worse."

Robert faced him. "They had every right to be angry. I shouldn't have left like that. I still live in their house. They will always be my parents and deserve my respect."

He sat on the bed, serious now. "What I did at dinner was wrong. I already apologized. Don't use my mistake to justify disrespect. What. I. Did. Was. Wrong."

Solomon held up both hands. "I got it. Respect our parents. We all love them. It's nice to know that you're as human as the rest of us, though."

Robert rubbed his face. "But I'm the oldest. I should've been the example."

Solomon frowned. "You're acting like I'm the big brother now." He paused. "You know what Ephesians 6:1-2 and 1 John 1:9 say."

Robert nodded, listening as Solomon quoted softly: "'Children, obey your parents in the Lord, for this is right... Honor your father and mother.' And 'If we confess our sins, He is faithful and just to forgive...'"

Robert smiled, his expression softening. "We're blessed with godly parents. My mornin's close. Pray with me."

They knelt beside their beds. Each offered quiet thanks and asked forgiveness. Then they lay down. Within minutes, Solomon's breathing evened into sleep.

Robert lay awake, trying to empty his mind. But Emelia kept creeping in.

He slipped to the kitchen and lifted the receiver from the wall phone. Each spin of the dial brought him closer to her voice. He hesitated, then started to hang up, but he heard her voice.

"Hello?"

"Hey," he whispered. "Sorry if I woke you."

He heard muffled voices in the background, then Emelia's soft tone returned. "You didn't wake me."

He smiled. "I just wanted to say goodnight to my girlfriend one more time."

Their teasing flowed easily, each word familiar. Then she said it: "Goodnight, my love."

His heart caught. *My love.* "I'm stealin' that," he said. "Goodnight, my love."

"Goodnight."

He hung up, touched by her grace. "Thank You, Lord, for her love," he whispered, and returned to bed. The rhythm of Solomon's breathing lulled him to sleep.

Chapter 5

A Home?

Robert's alarm sounded at five-thirty. He dragged his tired body out of bed and gathered his work clothes. As he reached for the doorknob, Solomon stirred behind him.

He groaned. "I don't like your alarm one bit."

Robert shook his head, already halfway gone. "Hush. Roll over and sleep like every other mornin'."

"Have a good day, bro." Solomon's muffled voice came from his pillow.

After showering and dressing, Robert packed his lunch and grabbed a banana, a granola bar, and coffee for the road. He arrived first. Just the way he liked it. *On time is five minutes late.* His father's voice echoed in his head, grounding him as he finished his coffee in the quiet before his workday began.

Tap, tap, tap.

He turned toward the sound. Eddy stood outside the window, grinning. Robert nodded as he stepped out.

"Early as usual," Eddy said.

"Yeah. I refuse to be late."

They shared a quick laugh and headed into the house they were remodeling. Inside the kitchen, Eddy gestured toward the cabinetry. "These beauties are solid wood. We're only taking them out because the homeowners don't like them. It's delicate demo today. No sledgehammers."

Robert frowned. "If they don't want 'em, why be delicate?"

"Because we salvage the good stuff. It goes to people who need it."

Robert nodded slowly. "Do these cabinets have a home?"

Eddy's smile faltered. "They do, but they won't be installed anytime soon. I'm helping an older couple fix up their place. But with my family obligations, progress is slow. I feel like I'm letting them down."

"You should've asked me," he said without hesitation. "Helpin' this community by giving run-down homes new life is why I'm here."

Eddy looked at him for a beat, then smiled. "You're an answer to prayer. Let's get these out in one piece. After work, you can follow me over and meet Jerald and Susan. We'll show you the place and talk through the needs."

"Sounds good." Robert gripped his screw gun and started in.

By noon, they had removed and loaded all the base cabinets. Over lunch beneath a tree, Eddy kept stealing glances at Robert. Eventually, Robert raised an eyebrow.

"Why are you lookin' at me like that?"

"There's a smile stuck on your face today," Eddy teased. "Something has shifted. With you and your girl?"

Robert's unguarded gaze drifted. Emelia filled his thoughts. "Yeah. I suppose it has."

Eddy chuckled. "That look, I remember it well. I've worn it. You're in love."

Robert's smile faded just a touch. "I think I am. But marriage. That's miles away. I still share a bedroom with my brother."

Eddy tilted his head, fingers brushing his chin. "Hmmm."

"Hmmm, what?"

"Taking these cabinets to the Carters might work out in more ways than one. There's a space in their home with a mostly finished bedroom and bath. If they're open to it, you could live there while working on the house. That might make it easier on everyone."

Robert perked up. "Maybe. I need to meet them first. See the space."

Eddy finished his water and stood. "Back to work."

Robert polished off the rest of his lunch and stood, too. The upper cabinets took more time and teamwork—one man to hold while the other removed the screws. Progress slowed.

"We won't finish these today," Robert said.

Eddy nodded. "We'll wrap up on Monday. Let's get the trailer loaded."

When the job site was cleared, they drove out of town, turned onto a gravel drive half a mile down a country road. The old house sat on a generous strip of land with a yard stretching two acres or more, bordered by pasture where a few cows grazed near a lone horse. The property showed wear and neglect, but something about it spoke to Robert.

Approaching the house, Eddy gestured toward it. "They need help. I just can't get here often enough to make much difference."

Robert nodded, taking in the duplex-like layout. Before they reached the door, it opened to a warm welcome from a couple likely in their late sixties.

"Eddy, you brought a friend," Jerry said, smiling. "Introduce us and show us the cabinets."

"This is Robert Jackson."

Jerry's brow furrowed. "Related to Mark and Betsy Jackson?"

"Yes, sir. They're my folks."

Jerry grinned and clapped him on the shoulder. "They're good people. They raised you kids right. Are you making them proud?"

"I hope so." Heat climbed his neck.

Sue playfully swatted Jerry's arm. "Stop embarrassing the boy, Jerald."

Eddy gestured between them. "Robert, meet Jerald and Susan Carter."

"It's a pleasure." Robert shook their hands.

Sue wandered toward the trailer, eyeing the cabinets. "These are nicer than the ones in my kitchen. Do you think... No, never mind. That's too much to ask."

"Ma'am," Robert said gently, "if they'll fit, I'd be glad to put them in your kitchen. They belong to you now."

Eddy chuckled. "I knew you'd say that. You've got a servant's heart."

Robert met his gaze. "It's her kitchen. She should get what she wants."

"I like this one, Eddy," Jerry said. "And I'm on to you. You want him to take this over, don't you?"

Eddy raised a hand, stopping Robert. "Let me speak with them privately. I'll get you an answer."

Robert nodded and stepped back toward the trailer. "I'll work on the straps."

He moved deliberately, but his thoughts drifted. *This is takin' too long. Emelia's gonna think I forgot her.*

He bowed his head slightly as he tugged a strap loose. *Please, God, let this work out. If I can live here, I can help. If not, I'll likely be no greater help to them than Eddy. I want to serve You. I want a future with Emelia. It's all in Your hands. In Jesus' name, amen.*

Robert finished with the trailer and tucked the straps into Eddy's truck, then leaned against it until Eddy returned with Jerry and Sue.

"You're in, if you want to be," Eddy said, clapping his back. "Let's unload these cabinets before I go home to an unhappy wife. She hates when I'm late."

They carried the cabinets into the unused side of the Carter home. Once finished, Eddy pointed out areas of the space while Robert explored. Water damage was mitigated, but repairs were sparse.

He sighed, taking in the exposed framing, concrete floors, and a cave-like bedroom. At least the bathroom fixtures were usable, and the bones looked sound.

As they finished, Robert shrugged. "That bedroom's like a cave with that dark paint and no windows. At least it has a floor. The bath works. What've you worked on?"

Eddy scratched his head. "I gutted the wet stuff and replaced the damaged framing. Their grandson fixed up the bedroom but left after his fiancée refused to live here. He didn't do right by them."

He pointed toward the bathroom. "Those fixtures were salvaged from our last job. I installed them myself. I'll come help you with anything tricky."

Robert nodded, hands slipping into his pockets. "I think I can make it work. Emelia won't want to live here yet. What do they need from me before I move in?"

"That's up to them. Probably just steady work and help with groceries and utilities. They're waiting to talk it over with you." Eddy grinned. "Time for me to earn points with Trudy. See you Monday."

When Eddy left, Robert surveyed the unfinished space again. *Is this home now?* His gaze lingered on the bare studs and concrete floor. *Lord, if this is the right step, make it clear. I want to help. I want to grow. I want to be ready for Em.*

He knocked at the Carters' back door. Jerry welcomed him inside and led him through the galley kitchen. Sue sat at a small table, smiling warmly.

"There's a cup on the counter and fresh coffee in the pot. Join us," she offered.

Robert nodded toward the wall phone beside the pot. "I'd love to, but I'm late pickin' up my girl, Emelia. May I use your phone first?"

"Of course," Jerry said with a chuckle. "We've already lost one helper over a girl. We'd like to keep you."

Robert lifted the receiver, then paused. Turning toward them, he said, "If I give you my word, I'll keep it. That's how I was raised. 'But let your 'Yes' be 'Yes,' and your 'No,' 'No.' For whatever is more than these is from the evil one.' Matthew 5:37."

Jerry and Sue exchanged a smile. "You are making your parents proud," Jerry said.

Warmth crept up Robert's neck. "I try. But sometimes I fail."

"We all do," Jerry said gently, then smiled. "Now, call your girl and bring her back for dinner. We want to meet her."

Robert spun each number, letting the dial's hum soothe him. Emelia answered on the second ring.

"Hello, Em. I'm sorry. I'm runnin' late."

"What happened?"

“I helped Eddy deliver cabinets after work. It took longer than planned. The homeowners let me use their phone. I didn’t want you worryin’.”

“Are you still coming?”

Her tone tugged at his heart. “I’ll be home in fifteen minutes. I’ll shower and come straight to you if you still want me.”

“I do. I’ll see you in about an hour?”

“Yes.”

“Please thank them for me. I’ll see you soon.”

“I’ll thank them for both of us. See you soon, Em.”

He replaced the receiver and turned back to the table where the Carters had been sitting. *Where’d they go?* Then he heard a TV playing in the next room.

Knocking on the door’s facing, he said, “Thank you from both of us. If I bring her for dinner, it’ll be around seven-thirty if that’s not too late.”

Sue waved him off. “Dinner’s in the slow cooker. We’ll relax till you get here. Go get your girl.”

Robert beamed. “Thank you. We’ll be here.”

Chapter 6

Our First Home

Fifty-nine minutes after speaking with Emelia, Robert knocked on the Norton's door. She opened it and stepped into his arms. After a quick embrace, she stepped aside to let him in.

"Dad!" she warned.

"It's fine, Em," Robert said, meeting her father's gaze. "Mr. Norton, I'm sorry I was late pickin' up your daughter."

Mr. Norton's expression was unreadable, forehead drawn. "Son, I understand you're planning a future with my daughter. I think you and I need to talk."

Robert nodded. "Yes, sir. May I meet with you tomorrow?"

Mr. Norton's face eased. "Meet my wife and me at the diner near the Southside church at nine for breakfast. Get Emelia home by midnight. That's generous, considering you were late."

Swallowing hard, Robert met his gaze. "I'll have her home on time. And I'll see you both in the mornin'."

Emelia tugged him out the door. "I'm sorry about my dad."

Robert opened the car door for her. Once she was settled inside, he hurried around to slide inside and hold her hands.

"We are planning a future. You're eighteen and start college on Monday. I'm nineteen, workin', but I don't have a place of my own yet. Your parents are right to be concerned about how serious we are."

His eyes fell to her hands resting in his. A future, theirs, flashed in his thoughts. A young woman, their daughter, stepping toward a door. A man, his image unclear, opened it for her. His big hand closed gently over hers.

Emelia's hands jerked free. "Robert, what just happened?"

Her wide eyes pulled him back to the present. "I...I saw myself in your dad's shoes. Our daughter was grown, and in a relationship." He rubbed the back of his neck, the hairs there prickling. "It freaked me out a little."

Emelia slipped her hands in his again, her smile soft but steady. "You see us married. For a long time. With children."

He gently squeezed her hands.

"I see you in every part of my life."

He let go, then backed down the driveway.

Emelia watched the landscape shift beyond the car window. Houses grew further apart, giving way to wooded areas and open fields. Her pulse ticked upward. Why are we leaving town? Robert hadn't said anything unusual yet, but something about him softly singing along with the radio, all relaxed and unhurried, nudged at her intuition.

She looked over at him. His face was relaxed, a crooked smile playing on his lips as he formed the words to the songs, like whatever lay ahead had already settled in his heart, or so it seemed to her. That smile. She knew it. While it made him more handsome, it often meant he was up to something.

"Where are we going?" she asked quietly.

When he glanced at her, his smile grew. "Eddy and I delivered cabinets to Jerry and Sue Carter this afternoon. They invited us to dinner. Sue said she has a roast and vegetables in the slow cooker. I hope you're okay with that."

Her stomach fluttered. Dinner with strangers? Not exactly what she'd expected. His crooked smile remained as he watched the road.

"Robert, your face tells me there is more to this." She kept her voice firm, steady. "How does a cabinet delivery become a dinner invitation?"

His smile faded. "I made a deal with them. That's why I was late. Their house is split like a duplex. They offered me the side that needs a lot of repairs, rent-free, in exchange for helping them restore it. We still need to work out groceries and utilities. But they want to meet you before we finalize anything."

Emelia sighed and blinked. She wasn't just along for dinner. She was stepping into his vision for the future.

"Are you serious?" Her heart skipped a beat.

"I'm completely serious. They're in their late sixties, and they need help. I want to help them. And I'm hopin' you'll be at my side." He hesitated, his voice gentling. "When I show you the side of the house where I'll live, you'll need to have some vision. Even if you hate it, I think I still have to help them."

She touched his arm softly. "This is the beginning of your dream. I will help and support you."

He turned down a gravel road and prayed aloud, his voice deep and soft. "Thank You, Lord, for this beautiful woman with a helper's heart. In Jesus' name, amen."

A lump rose in her throat. She hadn't expected that prayer, but it filled something deep in her. Maybe it was her value he spoke into the silence, or the steadiness in his faith. Either way, it mattered.

As they pulled into the driveway, her eyes scanned the yard. Neglect clung to everything. The grass needed cutting, and the house needed more than paint. Her smile faltered, but she said nothing.

When Robert helped her out, she leaned in. "Are you sure about this?"

He whispered into her ear, low and close, "Trust me, Em. I'm doin' the right thing. We can really make a difference."

She gripped his hand. "I trust you."

Before Robert could knock, the door opened. Sue smiled. "You kids hungry?"

Emelia breathed in deeply. The scent of roast and vegetables filled the air, comfort layered in every scent. "Dinner smells delicious."

She paused when Robert tugged her hand and slipped his arm around her waist. "Emelia, this is Jerry and Sue. And this is my girl." His voice held warmth and emotion.

Her cheeks flushed at the glint in his eyes. He seemed to stand taller than usual, chin lifted high. *He's proud of me.* Her heart fluttered beneath her ribs.

She shook Jerry's hand, then Sue's. Their warm welcome comforted her. Jerry brought the roast and vegetables to the table while Sue poured tea, and Emelia offered her best smile.

"I hope you kids like sweet tea," Sue said.

"We sure do," she replied.

At the table, Jerry reached for Emelia's hand to complete the chain of hands encircling the table. The gesture made her breath hitch as she bowed her head.

"Thank You, Lord, for bringing this young couple into our lives when we least expected it. Thank You for the meal before us and bless Sue's hands that prepared it. Please forgive our sins. In Your Son's glorious name, amen."

Jerry's words wrapped around her, soft and sincere. We were prayed for, she realized, and her heart swelled. We mattered to them the moment we walked through the door.

She had a million questions but held them close. Instead, she answered gently when asked and listened as Robert shared more about them. She watched Jerry and Sue as they told their story, heard the quiet ache in their need. When the meal ended, she understood.

They couldn't do this alone—Robert had stepped in.

She offered to help clean up, but Sue shooed them toward the back door.

"Come on, kids," Jerry said, handing Robert a can of bug spray. "There's still some time before sunset. You should explore the property. I use this around my cuffs and shoes. Keeps the ticks off."

Robert took it. "I'll spray you, Em. Then you spray me."

They laughed, spraying each other, then started down the path Jerry pointed out. The yard stretched around them. It was wild and worn. Winter would come fast. This had to be done and soon.

They walked until the woods gave way to the back field. A comfortable silence lay between them. At the edge of the trees, Emelia stopped and pointed to a log.

She sat first, and he joined her. When Robert wrapped his arms around her, she leaned in, resting her head lightly against his chest. His hand slid through her hair.

The moment wrapped around her, tender and new. She knew he'd never let himself be this intimate with anyone. Within her, joy and hope bloomed.

Please, Lord, she prayed silently. *I want him to kiss me. I want him to say he loves me. Please.*

Instead, Robert pulled back. "My love, we should walk back before we lose the light. I want to show you the house."

He helped her up. With his arm around her, he guided her through the woods, the field, the yard, and into the neglected side of the home.

Her jaw dropped at the skeletal walls and bare concrete. "Are you sure you can live here?"

He led her to the unfinished bathroom, which had working fixtures, and then into the bedroom. It was empty but finished. Sort of.

"My love, I know it's not perfect," he said. "There's a lot to do. Some of the work I'll need to finish, and some I'll need to fix. You don't love this dark bedroom, do you?"

She scanned the dark gray walls, white ceiling, and light gray plank flooring. "I don't like it much. There isn't a single window."

He nodded toward a doorway. "That leads to a walk-in closet with an egress window. But that's the only one. I'm gonna frame some windows in the wall between this room and the kitchen to bring in light. And with a lighter paint color of your choice, I think we can live with it."

She couldn't help smiling. "We can live with it. I get to choose paint colors? You're going to make this our home?"

He tucked his chin, suddenly shy. "If Jerry and Sue don't object, yes. I want this to be somewhere you'll want to share with me someday..." He swallowed. "...when we're married." His hand touched her hair against her shoulder. "I know that won't happen soon, but..." He breathed in and out. "Em, I love you. That's the only picture I can see."

Her heart soared. Her arms flew around him. "I love you too," tumbled out before she could even breathe.

When he held her, she felt her world change. Her body tingled. Her heart fluttered. Butterflies stirred deep in her tummy.

Then his quiet, steady voice met her ears. "May I kiss you?"

Answered prayer. Thank You, Lord.

She nodded, eyes fluttering closed. His breath brushed her cheek, then his lips met hers.

It lasted only a moment. But it was everything.

"Is this alright, Em?" he whispered.

She opened her eyes and caught the golden glint in the center of his hazel eyes. "Yes," she whispered, and her eyelids fluttered again.

When his lips met hers once more, everything softened. This time, he parted her lips and swept his tongue across hers. Their mouths explored, searching and learning as they pulled closer. Her body formed to his. Her legs forgot how to hold her.

He ended the kiss before she was ready. His arms supported her, keeping her close.

"My love are you okay?" he asked.

"Yes," she murmured, breathlessly. "More than okay." She buried her face in his chest, wishing the euphoria would stretch longer than a few heartbeats. But even as her body steadied, the ache for more lingered.

He let her go gently, and she took a slow breath. "I think maybe you lied to me."

His eyes widened. "I haven't and won't ever lie to you."

She narrowed her gaze. "You said you'd never kissed a girl before."

He stuffed his hands into his pockets. "We just shared my first kiss. I'd never done it before, but that doesn't mean I hadn't looked into how it should be done."

Her smile bloomed. "From what I just experienced, I'd say you looked in all the right places. Robert Jackson, you are a good kisser. But you may need to practice those skills to perfect them."

He gave her his signature crooked smile. "Mmm, I suspect it'll take me a lifetime of practice to perfect those skills." His gaze dropped to her lips. "Lots of practice."

The warmth in her chest surged again. "Would you like to practice one more time before we go say goodbye to the Carters?"

She didn't wait for him to answer. She stepped into him, and he folded her back into his arms. Their second kiss melted her just as deeply as the first. She held on, heart fluttering, until he broke the kiss again.

Through the open door, she glanced around the dark yard, her joy dimming. "It's going to be a while before we can get married, isn't it?"

He let out a breath, and his shoulders sagged. "I'm sorry, Em. It's gonna be a while. I'm not even sure how long." He stretched his arms wide. "This is a lot to wrap my head around."

She nudged his arms down, wrapping her own around one of his. "I'll be right beside you. I love you, Robert."

He kissed the top of her head. "And I love you."

They closed up the house and walked to the Carters' back door. When Jerry welcomed them inside, they followed him to the living room, Emelia staying close to Robert. The older couple sat on one couch. She and Robert settled on the other.

Sue's eyes found her. "Our grandson fixed up that bedroom, hoping his fiancée would agree to live here after they married. She refused, and he left us. We know Robert's willing and able to help us, but are you willing to live there with him after you're married?"

Emelia felt joy rise inside her. "I start college on Monday, but I'll be by Robert's side as much as I can when he's here. I want to make this our first home. I hope that's okay."

When Sue rose, Emelia met her halfway. Unshed tears glistened in the older woman's eyes as she pulled Emelia into a gentle hug.

"My dear, you and Robert are the answer to our prayers. This is a load we cannot bear alone. Thank you for rescuing us."

Emelia clung gently to her, moved by something larger than the two of them. *Thank You, God,* she prayed silently. *This is Your plan for us.*

When Sue pulled back, she brushed her tears away. "I'm sorry, dear. I didn't mean to be so weepy."

Emelia waved off the apology. "I'm thankful we can help. God is taking care of all of us."

She sat again beside Robert, who pulled her close.

"Em's right," he said. "Your prayers and ours were answered today, just in different ways." He hesitated. "Do you guys attend church?"

Jerry frowned. "Three years ago, I got sick. It was hard to get to worship. When I felt better, Sue injured her shoulder and needed surgery. She's doing better, but then the flood happened. I know none of that's an excuse, but it became easier to stay home."

Robert nodded. "I'm sorry for all the things that pulled you away. Em and I attend the Northside church of Christ. I could help you get to services on Sundays and Wednesdays."

Jerry's eyes brightened. "We used to go there. That's how we know your parents and watched you grow." He glanced at Sue, who nodded. "Yes, we'd like to get back to church."

Robert stood. "I'll need to buy some bedroom furniture. Once I've got that together, I'll move in, if you're okay with that."

Jerry stood, too, and offered Robert his hand. "The sooner, the better, young man."

They shook on it.

When Robert reached for her hand, Emelia stood beside him. "I promised your dad I'd get you home on time tonight. I'd better do that."

She looked at Jerry and Sue. "Thank you again for supper. I'll thank the Lord for you and pray for you tonight."

"Thank you, young lady," Jerry said warmly.

The older couple walked her and Robert to the door. Emelia noticed how they lingered outside, watching even as she climbed into the car. It wasn't until Robert turned onto the road that the Carters finally closed their door.

She placed a hand on Robert's arm. "I'm thankful you were late picking me up. You needed to be there with Eddy this afternoon to meet them. They need us."

Robert kept his eyes steady on the road. "God works in mysterious ways. They need us, and their souls do too. We need to pray we're up to the job He's laid at our feet."

"We will pray about it all. Together and separately."

Silence stretched between them. So much changed tonight. Smiling, she counted her unexpected blessings.

At the end of her road, Robert pulled the car over. "After I talk to your parents tomorrow, if they say it's okay, will you go furniture shopping with me? Eventually, it'll be our bedroom. I want you to like the furniture."

Her excitement bubbled over. "I'd love to go shopping with you for our bedroom furniture."

Robert chuckled. "Slow down, Em."

She caught her breath, then spoke her heart. "I know it can only be a kiss on the cheek, or maybe a soft touch on the lips, but will you always kiss me goodbye, starting tonight?"

Robert grinned. "My parents always kiss goodbye. Do yours?"

"They do."

"Then we should follow the example they set for us. I don't think they'll argue too much with us about it."

He put the car back on the road, then parked in front of her house. He got out and opened her door. She took his hand, leaning into him as he walked her to the porch.

"We could sit and talk since you're home early," he said quietly. "But I think it's better if I don't come in tonight. I need to talk to my parents about everything that's changed."

Holding her hands, the tenderness in his eyes made her heart skip a beat.

"I understand," she whispered. "I'll wait up for your goodnight call."

He tucked her hair behind her ear. "I want you to sleep well. Don't wait up. I'll see you tomorrow."

Her hands felt cold the moment he let go, but when he wrapped her in his arms and gave her a gentle kiss on the lips, warmth spread through her like sunlight.

"I love you, Em," he said, releasing her.

"I love you."

She watched him walk to his car. At the driver's door, he paused and turned back. "Tell your parents I'll see them at the diner at nine."

"I will." She placed her hand over her heart and watched his car until she lost sight of her love.

Chapter 7

COMMITMENT

Emelia sank into the living room sofa, the weight of the evening settling around her like a warm blanket. Her mother entered from the kitchen, drying her hands with a dish towel.

"My little girl looks like she had a big night." She sat beside Emelia. "Do you want to tell me about it?"

Emelia closed her eyes briefly, searching for words she could share. "I love you, Mom," she said softly. "But I'm not your little girl anymore." She exhaled slowly. "I'm Robert's girl."

Her mother tilted her head. Her smile faded, but her eyes stayed soft. "What do you mean by that?"

"I love him." Her voice held wonder. "And he loves me. He said it tonight. He kissed me for the first time. My future... It's with Robert."

She stared into the room.

"You've only been dating for three months," her mother said, concern knitting her brows. "How can you be sure it's love?"

"We've known each other practically our whole lives," Emelia replied, her voice firm but tender. "School, Bible school, church camp, youth group, every part of my growing up had Robert in it. I've watched him become the man he is. Loving him was easy. And this isn't infatuation, Mom. What we feel is real love."

She caught herself before saying more. The words bubbled just beneath the surface—ones she knew she shouldn't say. *We're adults. We can marry without your permission.* But she held them back. Robert wouldn't want that tension with her parents. Neither did she.

Instead, she said, "I don't want to argue. Please accept our feelings and respect our plans. Please, Mom?"

Her mother nodded slowly, her smile still absent. "I need you to understand our concern. You start college on Monday. Your dad and I want to see you earn your degree. Have you thought about how a serious relationship might complicate that?"

Emelia shook her head gently. "Robert supports my education. He believes in me enough to entrust me with managing our finances and helping him plan his business. He trusts me, and I trust him. He's not going to college unless we find a part of his business where it would truly help. He's not holding me back."

Her mother didn't speak, and Emelia continued. "We're not getting married anytime soon. There's work to do first. A house to rebuild. School to finish. But we know we're headed there."

Her mother's eyes widened, and her hands covered her mouth. "A house to rebuild."

"Yes." She nodded. "Robert is remodeling a house where he will live. His labor is his rent."

She touched her chin thoughtfully. "You may know the people who live there, Jerry and Sue Carter."

"I remember them." Her mother's brows drew down. "They haven't been to church in a long while."

"You'll see them Sunday." Emelia smiled. "Robert and I are bringing them to church."

A smile crept onto her mother's face. "Well, with a house to fix, is there any chance you'll wait until after college to get married?"

Emelia's mouth fell open slightly. "I hope not. I'm praying for next summer." Her gaze dropped to her bare left ring finger.

"I understand," her mom said softly. "I always hoped you'd be a little older before you fell in love. Your dad and I were older than you and Robert when we got serious. We still finished college after marrying, but it was tough. Balancing work, school, and a new marriage, it stretched us."

Her mom tucked a strand of hair behind her ear. "We want you to be happy. If Robert is the man who makes you happy, we'll support you *both*."

Emelia lifted her eyes. "So you and Dad aren't planning to be hard on him tomorrow?"

Her mother tilted her head, a smile tugging at the corners of her mouth. "I didn't say that. If he asks for our daughter, he needs to understand what a gift you are."

Emelia gasped, her voice full of awe. "You really think he'll ask for your permission to marry me?"

Her mom wrapped Emelia's hands in hers. "You're making plans. You've spoken of a shared future. Now you're saying you're in love. What else could this be building toward?"

Tears sprang to Emelia's eyes, and she collapsed into her mother's embrace. "Come pray with me, Momma."

Holding her, her mom stroked her hair.

"Momma," Emelia whispered, "I'm excited. And I'm scared. Leaving you and Dad to build a life with Robert is a lot. I love him so much. But everything is changing."

"I know, my girl," her mom murmured. "I know. Let's go pray together."

Robert parked in the driveway. Entering the house, he wasn't surprised to see his parents. He sighed, remembering their worried faces as he rushed through the house earlier, barely pausing to say he was heading to Emelia's.

He nodded and gestured toward the kitchen. "I know we need to talk. Tonight?"

Neither of his parents smiled.

"Yes, Robert. Tonight," his father said frankly.

They followed him to the kitchen. Robert filled a glass with water and sat at the table. His parents joined him. He took a long drink.

His father's gaze was steady. "We're concerned about your future. You're not attendin' college. You seem completely focused on Emelia. You've got a job, and we're thankful. You've vaguely mentioned a remodeling business. Where's your head, son?"

Robert glanced toward his mother. Her face was unreadable.

"I know I'm not walkin' the path you hoped," he said quietly. "And I'm about to give you more reasons to worry. Do you remember the Carters from church?"

His mom tilted her head and gave a faint smile. "I do, but it's been years since they've attended."

His dad frowned. "What do they have to do with anythin'?"

"I met them today. And it struck me. Their church family should've been checkin' on them, helpin' them. They stopped attendin' about three years ago. Jerry got sick. Some kind of circulation issues. He could barely walk until the doctors figured it out. Then he had surgeries to restore circulation in his heart and legs. Sue hurt her shoulder last year and needed surgery. And when the flash flood came last fall, the lower level of their house flooded. Why weren't we there?"

His parents' expressions fell. His dad's shoulders sagged, and his mom wrung her hands on the table.

"We should have been there for them." Her voice quavered. It sounded like she was holding back tears.

Robert straightened his spine. "I didn't bring this up to make you feel guilty. I just need you to understand that they need help. They can't keep up their home, let alone restore it. I'm gonna help. I'll be movin' into the damaged part of their house this week so I can be there to do the work."

His mom gasped. "You're moving out?"

"Yes, ma'am."

His dad leaned forward. "Can you afford rent, groceries, utilities, and everything that comes with living on your own?"

"My labor will be my rent. I'll help with groceries and utilities. I actually have a healthy savings account, but I doubt I'll need to touch it, not even for the bedroom furniture I'll need."

His dad nodded slowly, a faint smile rising. "I'm glad you've thought this through. Do you have the skills for everything that needs to be done?"

His mom leaned in before he could answer. "What does Emelia think of all this?"

Robert drew a deep breath and smiled. He spoke to his father first. "I don't have all the skills yet, but Eddy, my boss, has done most of the repairs so far. He's the reason I met the Carters today. We salvaged cabinets from the job site today, and I helped deliver them. He knows this work inside and out, and will help me when I need him."

Then he met his mother's gaze. "Emelia and I had dinner with the Carters tonight. We walked the property, and I showed her the house. She's on board. The Carters want us to make that part of the house our first home, and we want that too. They need help, and we feel led to be there for them. I believe God put them in my path."

His eyes misted. He blinked and looked down for a moment.

His mother's smile returned, faint, thoughtful. "I've heard a lot of we and us tonight. How serious are you and Emelia?"

Robert swallowed and wiped a hand through the condensation on the side of his glass, drying his hand on his jeans.

"Robert?" she said softly.

He looked up. "I'm meeting her parents for breakfast tomorrow. I love her. I kissed her tonight. I'm gonna ask their permission to marry her. Don't panic. It'll be a long engagement. I have a house to remodel first."

His dad shook his head, smiling with a glint of humor. "Thank God for a damaged house with built-in chaperones. You've given your mom and me a lot to pray over tonight. I think it's time we turn in."

They all rose. His mother hugged him tightly, pressing her cheek against his shoulder.

"Don't forget to say your prayers." She followed his dad down the hall.

Robert sighed, his heart full. *That went better than I thought it would.* He picked up his glass and headed to his bedroom.

Solomon's voice greeted him the moment he opened the door. "How did tonight's interrogation go?"

Robert said instead, "I might need your help tomorrow afternoon. I'm buying a bedroom set. I'll need help moving it to my house."

Solomon shot upright, eyes wide. "Your *house*?"

"Keep it down," Robert whispered. "Dad and Mom just went to bed, and I assume the girls are sleepin'."

"Okay, okay. You have a house?"

"Sort of. It's a whole story. I'll tell you tomorrow. I need sleep. I'm facing Emelia's parents over breakfast."

Solomon's eyes widened again. "You aren't asking..."

"I am," Robert cut in. "Please, let's sleep tonight."

Solomon chuckled. "I doubt you'll be sleeping much. One question. Did you say 'I love you'? Did you kiss her?"

Robert sighed. "Everyone's nosy tonight. And that's two questions."

"Come on, bro, give me something."

He nodded. "Yes. I did both."

Solomon grinned. "Since we've both read the same articles on how to kiss, tell me, did the techniques work?"

Robert chuckled. "A man's not supposed to kiss and tell."

Solomon laughed. "Ahhh. They worked. Thanks for not telling me."

Robert grinned and thumped him with his pillow.

"You're gonna miss me when you're gone," Solomon said, smiling.

Robert pulled his shirt off and tossed it in the hamper. "I will."

And just like that, the conversation ended. Robert finished dressing for bed and slid beneath the covers.

Chapter 8

May I Ask Her?

Robert's alarm buzzed sharply at seven Saturday morning. He rolled over and slapped it off, blinking up at the ceiling.

Solomon groaned from the other side of the room. "You've got to be kidding me. It's Saturday."

Robert sat up, rubbing his face. "Get over it, brother. I'm the one goin' to breakfast with his future in-laws and askin' for permission to marry their daughter."

Before Solomon could answer, a knock rapped at their door.

"Up and at 'em, boys," their father called. "Breakfast in thirty."

Robert grabbed his clothes and headed toward the bathroom. His dad met him in the hallway, brows furrowed.

"You sure about this, son?"

He looked his dad in the eye. "I am." He stepped into the bathroom and shut the door quietly.

By the time he dressed and headed to the kitchen, most of the family had finished eating. His mother handed him a steaming cup of coffee. "You've got a few minutes before you need to leave. Sit with us."

He slid into the seat beside Solomon, across from his sisters. Solomon got up to refill his mug, leaving Robert to face the storm brewing in Lexi's scowl.

"What'd I do?" he asked.

The older of his two younger sisters crossed her arms. "Other than your apology the other morning, Millie and I haven't seen you. Are you even our brother anymore?"

Millie mirrored Lexi's glare, lips trembling.

Solomon returned, eyes amused. "Whoa. What'd you do to them, Robert?"

Millie wiped at her eyes. "You're never around. We miss you."

Their mom laid a calming hand on Millie's. "Robert's building a life of his own. But he still loves you. And he'll find a way to make time."

Robert glanced at his dad, who nodded quietly. He raised his hands in surrender.

"You're right. I haven't been around like I should. And by next weekend, I won't be livin' here anymore."

Both girls gasped. Lexi jumped up from the table, ran down the hall, and slammed the bedroom door. The sound echoed through the house.

Robert set down his mug and walked after her. "Lexi," he said gently, palm against the door.

Her voice cut through the door. "Go away, Robert. That's what you're doing anyway. So do it!"

His forehead rested against the wood. "I'll always be your brother. And I'll always love you."

Footsteps padded toward him, and Millie flung her arms around him. "I love you too," she whispered.

He sat down on the hallway floor with Millie curled into his lap. "How about this? After breakfast with Emelia's parents, I'll come back here. You and Lexi can help me pick out a present for Em. Then lunch, just us."

The door creaked open a few inches. "Will you stay home with us after?"

Robert hesitated. "I can't, Lex. I have plans with Em."

He called down the hall. "Mom?"

She appeared, brows raised.

"Would it be okay if I bring Em home from church tomorrow for dinner? We'll spend the afternoon with Lexi and Millie."

Her smile was warm. "Emelia's welcome here anytime."

Robert turned back to the door. “Girls, I can’t give you today. But Em and I will give you tomorrow. Is that okay?”

Lexi eased out and sat beside him, leaning into his shoulder. Robert wrapped his arms around both his sisters and held them close.

They sat quietly until their dad stepped into view. “I’m glad you made things right with your sisters. But if you’re serious about this mornin’, you need to go. I’m sure you don't want to be late.”

Robert chuckled. "I know, Dad, on time is five minutes late. I'll be there early."

Robert kissed each girl on the cheek. “I’ll be back soon. Get ready for our date.”

Both girls stood, wearing sweet smiles now. He rose, gave Solomon a quick clap on the back, and hugged his parents before walking out the door. His heart was full, his nerves humming with hope tucked close to his chest.

When Robert stepped into the diner, tension coiled beneath his skin. His eyes swept the tables for the people he both dreaded and hoped to face, Mr. and Mrs. Norton. They hadn’t arrived yet.

He exhaled, shaking the tension from his shoulders. “A couple will be joinin’ me,” he told the server. “A corner booth, please.”

Once seated, he ordered coffee and orange juice from Martha, who wore a kind smile and a crooked name tag. She returned with his beverages and three menus. “Are you waiting to order until the rest of your party arrives?”

“Yes, ma’am.”

He stirred sugar and cream into his coffee with his eyes trained on the door. When Martha subtly waved in his direction, he followed her gesture and saw them. Henry and Peggy Norton walked toward him.

He stood, heart thudding against his ribs. He greeted them with an outstretched hand. They shook his hand, firm and formal.

Peggy slid into the booth, followed by Henry, then Robert took his seat. Once they were settled, Martha took their drink orders.

Their menus lay untouched when Martha returned with their coffees and waters, and raised a brow. "Do you need more time?"

"We don't," Henry said.

"I'm ready, too," Robert added.

She took their orders and slipped away.

"Thank you for meetin' with me," Robert said, offering what he hoped was a steady smile.

Emelia's parents exchanged a glance. Peggy nodded. Henry's voice softened. "Let's start on a friendlier footing. We've known you since you were knee-high. Call me Henry, and my wife, Peggy."

"Yes, sir."

Peggy smiled at him. "I had a long talk with my daughter last night. She filled me in on the seriousness of your relationship. I understand 'I love you's have been said and kisses exchanged."

"Yes, ma'am."

Henry leaned in, voice low but clear. "What are your intentions with our daughter?"

Robert reached for the strength he'd prayed for all morning. "I love Emelia," he said plainly. "I want to ask her to marry me. I'm not in a position to marry her yet, but I'm prayin' I will be within the year."

While Robert took a long sip of coffee, a heavy silence settled over them. Grasping for calm, he slowly drained his mug.

When Robert met Henry's unblinking gaze, Henry flatly said, "Spit the rest out, son."

"Refills?" Martha asked.

Robert slid his cup toward her, and she filled it. The Nortons hadn't touched theirs. He doctored it and set it aside. He looked up and met their gazes.

"May I have your permission to ask Emelia to marry me?"

Peggy smiled. "Emelia said that's what you'd be asking."

But when Henry shook his head, Robert's hope shattered like glass on concrete.

"She's only eighteen," Henry said. "She wants a business degree. And you've got no plans for college."

Robert stirred his coffee, the movement small but grounding.

"You're set on rehabbing houses," Henry continued. "Fixing them up and selling them. It's a noble idea, but it's a big one."

Lifting his gaze, Robert gave a nod. He needed to be steady. Honest. "Emelia knows my dreams. She believes in them. And I believe in her. I want her by my side as my wife, my partner in life and business."

"And what about her education?" Henry pressed.

"I'm remodelin' a home for us. Once I finish the essentials, I'll make a space for her to work and study. We know we need her education to succeed. Together, we'll build more than homes. We'll build a life."

Henry laughed. "You're three months out of high school, Robert. That doesn't make you a contractor."

Robert's ire rose, and he took a deep breath.

These people are gonna be my family. Lord, help me be even-tempered.

"No, sir. Not yet. I'm an apprentice. But in a year, I'll have the documented hours and skills to apply for my national contractor's license."

After a breath, he continued. "In Missouri, I don't need a national contractor license. Locally, not much is required. As long as I don't work in larger municipalities, which I'm not plannin' on, all that's needed is registration with the Missouri Secretary of State, then state and local tax identification numbers. If I have employees someday, I'll need to carry workers' compensation insurance."

When their meals arrived, Robert stopped talking. Plates of eggs, sausage, and pancakes for Robert and Henry, and a fruit plate with yogurt for Peggy. Robert smiled at Peggy's fruit and yogurt. Emelia would've chosen the same.

"Thank you," Peggy said, and Martha turned away to take an order.

Robert continued. "I won't start my own business yet. I've signed on full-time with Bard's Buildings for three years. Conner Bard's trainin' me and helpin' me earn my hours."

Peggy tilted her head. "If you don't need a license to work locally, why pursue one?"

He smiled. "Em and I talked about that. Long term, we want to help more than in Hillsburo. You've heard of Churches of Christ Disaster Relief Inc.?"

They nodded.

"If I'm nationally licensed, and homes need rebuilding after a disaster, we'll be equipped to serve. It's something we dream about. Serving together. Loving through our work."

Henry leaned back, eyes still sharp, but softer. "You're not just dreaming. You've done your homework. You know what you want and how to get there. You want to make it matter."

"Emelia said you want her to manage your finances. Is that true?" Peggy asked.

"I do. She knows my income and my bank balances. I trust her. The better her education, the better we'll manage. I believe in her."

His stomach growled, embarrassingly loud. He winced.

Peggy smiled. "Don't apologize. Eat."

They shared a meal, and they chatted. Even though the tension faded, the big question remained unanswered. When Martha brought the check, Henry reached for it without hesitation.

"Sir, I'd be glad to pay."

Henry shook his head with a smile. "My wife and I are treating our future son-in-law to breakfast."

Robert froze. "Your future..."

Henry stood, clapping his shoulder. "You heard me."

"I have your permission? I can ask her?" he asked, his voice tight with hope.

Peggy pulled him into a hug. "She loves you, Robert. I also see how much you love, respect, and trust her. I wish you two were older, but I trust in God's timing. We will keep you in our prayers."

When she let him go, Robert blinked, caught between awe and disbelief. "Thank you."

"She's expecting you this afternoon," Henry said.

"I'll be there between two and three," Robert said, his grin breaking free.

When he walked to his car, he felt like he floated there with the grin still glued to his face.

Thank you, Lord. Please let Lexi and Millie be ready when I get home. In Jesus' name, amen.

There was more to pray over, but first, he had a ring to buy. Emelia was waiting.

Chapter 9

Did He Ask?

Emelia had eaten, made her bed, showered, and dressed. Still, her parents hadn't returned. In the quiet, she went to the kitchen and started baking Robert's favorite chocolate chip cookies. He always devoured them at church dinners.

She'd just placed the first sheet in the oven when the front door opened. Setting the timer, she rushed to see her parents.

Neither smiled.

Her heart sank as she searched their faces for any sign of hope. Her father sniffed the air. "Smells like cookies."

"Chocolate chip," she said quietly. "Robert's favorite." She turned toward the kitchen.

Her mother gently caught her hand. "He loves you, Emelia."

She didn't turn. "I know that."

Tears welled in Emelia's eyes. She slipped from her mother's grasp, fleeing to the kitchen. Her father followed.

"My girl, why are you so upset?"

She sniffled and grabbed a paper towel. "You told Robert he couldn't ask me to marry him. Is it just because we're young?"

Her father leaned against the counter. "Permitting a man to marry our daughter reminds us the days you'll be at home are numbered. That's hard. We're going to miss having you here. We don't want to lose you, but it's clear how deeply you two love each other. So yes, we gave him our permission."

The timer buzzed. Emelia slipped on oven mitts and pulled the cookies from the oven, setting the tray on the cooling rack. She slid the next sheet into place and reset the timer. Her dad's words replayed through her mind, and her eyes grew wide when she realized what he had said. She turned and threw her arms around him.

Her mom bumped her husband playfully with her hip. "I was there too. I deserve some of that gratitude."

Emelia let go of her father and turned, wrapping her arms around her mother. A moment later, she stepped back, filled with joy. "You gave Robert permission to ask me to marry him!" she cried, spinning in a delighted circle around the kitchen. Her cheeks hurt from smiling so wide.

Her dad snagged a warm cookie from the cooling rack.

"Dad," she said, half laughing. "I baked those for Robert."

He grinned, unrepentant. "They're my favorite too. And you, young lady, have been my girl a lot longer than you've been his."

She handed her mom a warm cookie. "I'm your girl too."

She sank into a chair at the kitchen table, the thrill gradually fading. "I'm glad the wedding's still a ways off. I'm going to miss you both. Eat all the cookies you want. I'll make more for Robert."

The phone rang. Her mom, being the closest, picked it up. "Didn't we just leave you?"

Emelia watched her expression shift, curiosity stirring.

"Six thirty," her mom said.

"Yes, that's right," she added a moment later.

Her mom nodded a few times, then passed Emelia the receiver without a word. Emelia took it as her parents quietly left the kitchen.

"Hello," she said.

"Hey, Em."

"Robert."

"I told your folks I'd pick you up between two and three. My sisters and I have an errand first, and I was going to grab lunch with them, but they want you to come. Want to join us?"

"I'd love to." Her smile bloomed, brushing away all lingering curiosity.

"You've got some time. We'll be there as soon as we can."

She giggled. "I have a surprise for you when you get here."

"Really? I can't wait to see what it is. I love you, Emelia Norton."

Though the room was empty, her cheeks heated. "I love you, Robert Jackson."

"See you soon, my love."

"Goodbye, my love."

As she replaced the phone in its cradle, the timer chimed. She pulled one sheet out and slid another in, resetting the timer. After transferring the cooled batch from the rack and setting the warm ones to cool, she picked up a cookie and sat down again.

The bite was sweet, but sweeter still was the vision unfolding in her heart: a diamond sparkling on her left hand as she walked down the aisle in a princess-worthy gown, her father steady at her side, toward the man who helped her believe in dreams.

When Robert parked in the driveway, parted drapes revealed two eager faces. He sighed. They're ready.

Lexi threw open the front door. "Robert, we need to talk."

His brows knit. "About what?"

Inside, Lexi and Millie sat upright on the sofa and motioned for him to join them. "Girls," he warned, but sat anyway.

"You're buying Emelia an engagement ring, right?" Lexi asked.

Millie cut in, "Do you even know her ring size?"

He chuckled. "Yes, I want your help pickin' the ring. No, I don't know her size. Is that important?"

Lexi shook her head. "Typical man."

"What!" Robert stifled a laugh.

"Do you want to kneel on one knee and propose, only for the ring to stop at her knuckle or slide off?" Lexi asked, clearly unimpressed.

Robert's eyes widened. "Definitely not."

"Then get her ring size before we shop," Millie said sweetly but firmly.

"Call her mom," Lexi added. "Simple."

He hesitated. "What if Em answers?"

"You just had breakfast with her parents," Lexi said. "Tell her you forgot to ask her mom something. It was a big moment. You were nervous. It's believable."

She straightened. "Robert, you're smart. You can pull this off."

He stood. "I get it, girls. I need the info. I'll make the call. Pray for me."

"We will." They giggled. "And ask Emelia if we can pick her up for lunch."

He paused. "You want Em to join us?"

They nodded. "She's going to be your wife, which makes her our sister. You two are a package deal now," Lexi said, grinning.

Robert headed to the kitchen and dialed Emelia's number. Peggy answered with a teasing, "Didn't we just leave you?" but kindly gave him Emelia's ring size, six and a half. Relief and excitement surged through him. He had what his sisters said he needed before shopping.

When Emelia came on the line, her voice lifted his heart. He invited her to join them for lunch, and she accepted with a giggle and a promise: "I have a surprise for you when you get here."

His pulse jumped. "I love you, Emelia Norton."

"I love you, Robert Jackson."

After exchanging soft goodbyes, he let the moment settle as the line between them disconnected.

Back in the living room, he told his sisters, "Okay, girlies, her ring size is six and a half, and we're pickin' her up for lunch. Let's move."

Lexi and Millie beat him to the car, both sliding in on the passenger side, Lexi in front, Millie in back. Before starting the engine, Robert turned to face them. "I need you to promise me you'll keep a secret. Can you do that?"

Lexi frowned. "Depends on the secret."

"Fair answer," he said. "It's nothin' bad. I can't afford a ring from a fancy jewelry store. Eddy told me about a reputable pawnshop that sells nice rings at decent prices."

He hesitated. "We're going there today. It's technically a jewelry store, but I don't want it known that Em's ring came from a pawnshop. Can you keep that part quiet?"

Millie stayed quiet while Lexi tapped her chin. After a moment, she said, "If they sell jewelry, it counts as a jewelry store. We don't have to mention what the sign says, right, Millie?"

Millie smiled. "Since Lexi thinks it's okay, and that's what you want, then it's our secret."

Robert grinned. "Thanks, girls."

He started the car. His sisters' chatter filled the short drive with laughter and easy company. As soon as he turned off the engine, they bolted from the vehicle.

"Stop!" he called. They froze near the hood.

"I have to follow Mom's rules. Stay with me at my side, or at least in sight."

"We will," they chorused.

"Besides," Lexi added, "how would we see the rings if we weren't with you?"

The moment they stepped inside, Lexi and Millie made a beeline for the jewelry cases. Robert followed, easily identifying the case with the engagement rings and wedding sets.

A man about his age approached with a friendly grin. "Getting married?"

"Yeah," Robert said, glancing up briefly.

"What's her ring size?"

Lexi nudged Millie. "Told you so."

"Alexis," Robert warned.

The man chuckled. "Your sisters?"

He nodded. "Yes."

"I'm Jim. My dad owns the shop," he said, offering his hand.

"Robert," he replied, shaking it. "And these are my sisters, Alexis and Mildred."

Jim shook hands with both girls. "Smart move bringing them. A feminine opinion helps."

He turned to Robert. "See anything she might like?"

Robert studied the sets behind the glass. "You have engagement rings paired with weddin' bands for both. In your opinion, should I go for a set or just an engagement ring?"

Jim shrugged with a smile. "If you're lucky, and I mean really lucky, the man's and woman's bands fit both of you. That's rare, but when it does happen, sets are more affordable. We have two identical sets. Want to take a look?"

"Yes," Robert said, echoed quickly by the girls.

Jim retrieved the sets and laid them out. "Her size?"

"Six-and-a-half," Robert answered, eyes widening at the sparkle. "They're beautiful, but how much?"

Jim chuckled. "You've seen jewelry store prices. Relax, these are different. Half-carat diamonds, fourteen-karat gold. My dad marked them at two hundred each."

An older man stepped in behind Jim and clapped his shoulder. "I'm Jim's dad, Joe."

"This is Robert," Jim introduced.

Joe gave a warm smile. "Those sets have been sitting too long. If Jim can mix and match to fit you both, I'll give it to you for one-eighty. You seem like a good young man. We'll make it work."

He walked off, leaving Robert blinking in surprise.

He turned to Lexi and Millie. "Well? What do you think?"

Lexi giggled. "I'd take a diamond like that from the right guy."

Robert groaned. "No diamonds for you. Not for a few more years at least."

"I want one," Millie declared.

"You're both too young," he said firmly. "When you graduate from high school, you can start dreamin'. Until then, no sparkle."

Millie crossed her arms. "I'll be an old lady by then."

Robert and Jim laughed as Jim retrieved a sizing rod from under the counter. He slid the engagement ring onto it. "We have a winner. It's a six and a half."

He checked the woman's wedding band from the same set. It matched.

Turning to the man's ring, Jim asked, "What's your ring size?"

Robert shrugged, removed his class ring, and offered it.

"Try it on your left hand," Jim said. "The sizes can differ."

Robert slid it onto his left ring finger. "Feels fine."

"Point your fingers down and shake hard," Jim instructed.

Robert did, and the ring held.

Jim slid it onto the sizing rod. "Size ten."

He checked the men's rings. "This one's an eleven. No good."

The second set's ring stopped at ten. "Perfect."

Jim placed the matching rings—two six-and-a-halves and one ten—in a box, returned the extras to the other box, then to the case, and locked it.

Robert lifted the box so Lexi and Millie could see. "Do you think these are the right rings for me and Em?"

Millie ran her finger along the bands. "I love them." Lexi nodded.

Robert handed Jim two hundred-dollar bills. Jim returned a twenty. "Have them appraised. You'll be pleasantly surprised. Also, get the diamond prongs checked every six months or so."

"Why?" Robert asked.

"You don't want to lose the stone," Jim said. "This jeweler is honest, does great work, and won't oversell you."

He handed Robert a business card.

"Thanks for everythin'," Robert said, waving as he and his sisters left.

Back in the car, Robert said, "I don't care what they're worth. I'm just thankful I could afford rings I'm proud to give Emelia."

Lexi tapped her chin. "Still, you should know their value and have those prongy things checked."

Robert smiled. "Thanks for your wisdom, sis."

He pulled out the card and glanced at the address. "Glitter & Gold is in that shopping center on the corner. Let's head there now."

Robert pulled into the shopping center and parked near Glitter & Gold. Lexi and Millie followed him into the shop, the bell chiming overhead as they entered. He took the ring box from his pocket and approached the counter just as a man emerged from the back.

"How may I help you?" the man asked with a warm smile.

"I'd like these rings appraised and the diamond prongs checked," Robert said, opening the box.

"Jackson Owens," the man said, extending his hand. Robert shook it.

"I'm guessing Joe or Jim sent you. Years ago, I sold two identical sets to a pair of brothers. Tragic story—neither ever got to propose. They ended up at Joe's pawn shop. I doubt they've ever left the box."

Robert handed Mr. Owens the box. He turned it over to reveal the Glitter & Gold imprint. "Verbal appraisals are free. Written ones cost twenty-five. I'll check the prongs at no charge and let you know if repairs are needed."

"A verbal is fine. Please check the prongs," Robert said.

"I'll examine them now. You can leave with the set if all looks good."

The trio watched as Mr. Owens assessed the diamond's clarity, color, and the gold content of the band and prongs. He chuckled. "I only sell the best," he said, then jotted a number on paper.

"The prongs are sound, and the diamond is secure. Come by every six months for a check. It was nice meeting...?"

"Robert Jackson. And these are my sisters, Lexi and Millie."

He smiled. "Pleasure to meet you. I'll help you keep these in top shape. See you in six months."

As Robert began unfolding the paper, Mr. Owens advised, "Do that later, sitting down. The number might surprise you. Let me know if you'd like a written estimate."

Robert pocketed it, and once in the car, secured the rings in the glove box. "Let's go get Em."

From the back seat, Millie whispered, "I think that number's big."

"Girls, stop speculatin'," Robert warned. "I'll check it tonight and share tomorrow. But whatever it says, Emelia can't know."

They echoed, "It's our secret."

"Thank you," he murmured, grateful when their chatter shifted to lighter topics.

Thank You, Lord. Help them keep today's secrets for me. In Jesus' name, amen.

Chapter 10

Sisters

Robert waited on the porch for Emelia, not wanting to leave his sisters alone in the car. When he returned hand-in-hand with her, Lexi had shifted to the back seat beside Millie. After helping Emelia into the vehicle, he handed a paper sack to Lexi.

"Those are my favorite cookies. If you stay out of them, I'll share after lunch. If not, I'm eatin' every last one."

Emelia laughed. "He's serious. I've seen him polish off a whole batch at church."

Lexi set the bag between them, the scent of fresh-baked cookies filling the car. Robert slid behind the wheel just as Millie's hand reached toward the bag.

"Give it here," he said. "I should have known that was too much temptation for you, little one."

Millie huffed. "I'm not little. I'm eleven. That's double digits just like you."

Robert raised his brow. "Oh-kay." He and Emelia both burst out laughing.

They ate at All On A Bun, the hamburger joint they all liked. After lunch, Robert asked, "Are you girls ready to head home?"

Emelia smiled. "I'm enjoying time with your sisters. Why can't they join us for shopping?"

"We're hitting secondhand stores. I need some budget-friendly bedroom furniture. You girls want to come?"

"Yes!" they said in unison.

"We'll need to check with Mom and Dad first," he said. "This wasn't part of the original plan."

His face tightened, and Emelia leaned closer. "Something wrong?"

"Just being selfish," he murmured.

Lexi cleared her throat. "It's rude to whisper in front of people."

"You're right, Lex," he said, putting on a smile. "Let's ask Mom and Dad if we can have more time together."

At the house, Robert burst inside. "Dad! Mom!"

They came running. "Where's the fire?" his dad asked.

"No fire." Robert heaved a sigh. "Emelia wants the girls to come shoppin'. I won't take them if you need them home."

His mom smiled crookedly. "Solomon's down the road at Alex's. You and Emelia have the girls. I'll be thanking the Lord for a childless afternoon. I can't remember the last one."

"Go on," his dad said with a grin. "We're good here. See you tonight."

Robert left the house, silently praying, *Forgive me, Lord. I wanted time with just Em.* Still, he smiled as he reached the car. "You did the research, Em. Where to first?"

"There's a big secondhand store in the old nursery building, the one with the name still in big green letters out front," Emelia said. "I'm excited to pick out our first furniture."

He backed out of the driveway and headed that direction.

"I thought this was for my brother," Lexi blurted. "You're not even married."

"No, not yet," Robert replied. "But it'll be for our bedroom when we are. Would you like to go home?"

Lexi pouted. "No, but I don't want to lose you. She's taking you away from us."

"Alexis," Robert began, but Emelia gently touched his arm. "She's okay." Then she turned to the back seat.

"My brother James left for West Point two years ago. He only comes home four times a year. I miss him constantly. I know how hard it is to miss someone. Lexi, I'm not here to take Robert from you. I want you in my life, too. I've never had a sister. Would you and Millie be my sisters?"

Millie smiled. "I'll be your sister."

Lexi didn't smile. "You'll be my sister whether I like it or not."

Robert opened his mouth to chastise Lexi, but Emelia looked his way, and he shut it. "Thank you for giving me a chance, Lexi," she said softly.

"You're welcome," Lexi replied, her voice tinged with a little more warmth.

As they pulled into the old nursery parking lot, Robert glanced around the car and was surprised to find three smiling faces. *How did that happen?* He stayed quiet, not wanting to disrupt the peace, and took Millie's hand. Emelia and Lexi joined them, and together they walked inside.

The massive building was full of secondhand furniture. After browsing, Robert and Emelia paused at one bedroom set. She opened every drawer while he checked the joints and overall condition. Everything looked solid, and it was affordable.

Turning to the girls, Emelia asked, "What do you think of this set?"

Millie frowned. "Those boards look uncomfortable."

Robert laughed. "It's just the frame. I'll add a mattress."

Millie grinned. "Then I'll like it."

Robert removed the tags and walked up to the counter, where a woman named Mary, according to the badge pinned to her shirt, greeted him with a smile. "Buying this for you and your wife?"

He flushed. "We're not married. Not yet." He glanced back at Emelia and the girls. Then he whispered, "I bought her a ring this mornin'." His admission surprised him.

Mary nodded. "The bed in this set is a queen. We have a similar set with a king in the back. Do you want to see it?"

"Is it more expensive?" Robert asked. *I've always slept in a twin. Why would I need a king?*

"Twenty-five dollars more, I think. Mostly due to the larger bed. Let me verify."

While Mary flipped through her ledger, Emelia asked, "Have you paid yet?"

Robert wrapped an arm around her and gestured toward Mary. "She said there's a similar set with a bigger bed. That one is a queen. Do we need a king?"

Emelia's smile deepened, her eyes softened. "We might appreciate the extra space once we have children."

Robert's heart thudded at Emelia's mention of children. *Our children.* He braced himself against the counter, took a slow breath, and steadied his thoughts. "Ma'am, may we see the other set?"

Mary's finger paused on the page, her head lifting. "Yes, sir. The king set is thirty dollars more."

She turned to a nearby clerk. "William, can you take over? I'm showing them a set in the back."

William nodded, and Mary led them through a doorway at the back of the building. The king-sized set stood solid and stately. Robert, Emelia, and the girls inspected it carefully.

"Do you like this one as much as the other?" he asked.

Emelia traced the carved rosettes along the bedpost, her touch lingering. "I like this one better."

He had guessed her answer before she uttered it. Even if it had cost much more, he'd have found a way. Emelia would have the room she loved and the space they would need in the future.

He smiled. *Thank You, Lord, for makin' the difference only thirty dollars.*

Emelia turned. "Robert, look." She nodded toward where Lexi and Millie were admiring an old dressing table.

"That isn't in the best of shape," he said.

"But with some cleaning, glue, stain, and upholstery on the bench, it could shine again."

They faced each other and whispered, "Christmas."

Robert turned to Mary. "How much?"

Her lips pressed together. "We don't usually sell pieces in disrepair."

"I appreciate your honesty. My sisters are smitten with it." He glanced at Emelia, then back at Mary. "We'd like to fix it up for them for Christmas. I'll give you twenty-five dollars for it, as is."

Mary sighed. "Repaired, it would sell for four or five times that, but we're behind. I'll take your offer."

"Add that and the extra thirty for this bedroom set to my bill. May I use your phone to call my father? I need him and my brother to bring the truck and trailer."

As they followed Mary to the front, Robert overheard Lexi and Millie telling Emelia how much they adored the vanity. He smiled. They're gonna be so surprised on Christmas morning.

He spun the dial of the desktop phone and spoke with his father, who agreed to bring Solomon to help. Robert handed over the cash and pocketed his receipt. "We'll be back in fifteen minutes," he told Mary.

Turning to his family, he said, "Let's walk down to the creek and skip rocks while we wait."

Millie bounced excitedly. Lexi rolled her eyes.

He took Emelia's hand in one of his and Millie's in the other. "Lex, come on. It'll be fun."

Lexi dashed past them. "I'll skip a rock the farthest!" she called over her shoulder as she raced down the hill.

"We'll see about that, missy," he said with a chuckle.

After several joyful throws, Millie squealed. "There's Dad's truck!"

Lexi huffed. "Millie, you startled me. On purpose! All my perfect flat rock did was go plop. I could've made it skip at least seven times!" She pointed at Emelia. "You made me lose to her."

Robert caught Lexi's arm and turned her toward him. "Lexi, I love Emelia. Your rudeness to her stops now. I promised we'd spend tomorrow with you and Millie. That ain't gonna happen unless your attitude changes."

Lexi stomped her foot. "Everything's all about her. You bought her a whole bedroom set and ignored the vanity Millie and I liked."

He let go of her arm and blew out a breath. "I noticed you both loved it. But I needed furniture. Without it, I'd be sleeping on the floor with my clothes in boxes."

He looked away, pained. "Yes, I bought the set Emelia liked. After we're married, she'll share my room. Doesn't matter now. We need to meet Dad and Solomon. You're goin' home with them."

Emelia stepped beside him. “Lexi, please get Millie and go to your father. I need to speak with Robert.”

Lexi didn’t respond. Instead, she grabbed Millie’s hand and stormed off.

“She’s fourteen,” Emelia said gently. “And you’re her hero. She’s never had to share you. I understand what you can’t. You’re not a girl. Lexi and I are.”

Robert shifted uncomfortably.

“She’s dealing with emotions she doesn’t understand. And she was sweet to me today. Lexi likes me, or she wouldn’t have tried at all. You and I need to love her through this.”

Robert groaned. “You’re right. I need a break from Lexi and time with you. There hasn’t been a single moment all day when I could kiss you.”

Emelia giggled. “And there it is, the reason Robert is cranky.”

She grabbed his hand and led him up the hill.

In the parking lot at the top, they met his father, brother, and sisters, then entered the store. After quick introductions, William directed Mr. Jackson to the loading dock.

“Emelia, will you stay out here with the girls while we load the furniture?” Robert winked.

“Sure. I’ll let Lexi show me her rock skipping technique. I’ve never skipped a rock seven times.” She grinned.

When Robert saw Lexi smile at Emelia, he sighed in relief. The girls headed toward the front door.

Robert followed William and Solomon. When his father backed the trailer up to the loading dock and spotted the vanity, he asked, “Why’d you buy that?”

“Lexi’s been salty with Emelia all day,” Robert said. “She noticed Lexi and Millie droolin’ over it and suggested we fix it up for them.”

William shook his head. “My sister sold it to him for less than a quarter of its value.”

“We’ll restore it and surprise the girls at Christmas. Got an old blanket to cover it?”

“I saw a couple of old ones in the back of Dad’s truck.” Solomon lowered himself off the dock.

They tucked the vanity and bench between other pieces, covering them with the tattered blankets. Then, together, they secured the load.

"Lexi said you told her she had to go home with us," Dad said. "Should I handle her attitude, or do you want to?"

Robert groaned. "Being an adult ain't always fun."

Solomon laughed.

Robert glowered. "Watch yourself. You'll be here soon enough."

Turning to his father, he added, "I'm bringin' Emelia into the family. She says it's normal for teens to struggle with adjustments. She's right. It's on me to walk them through this."

His dad smiled. "You've got a good one. Hold on to her. Come on, Solomon, let's get this home."

Robert rejoined the girls out front.

"Let's go home, ladies." He smiled, watching them climb the slope up from the creek.

Lexi glared at Robert, frowning. "I thought you were mad. I thought I had to go home with Dad."

"I was frustrated. I haven't liked your behavior today. But I love both my sisters and want to take you home."

Lexi's lip trembled. "You're not staying, are you?"

"Lex, Millie was right. Those slats won't make for comfortable sleeping. I need to find a mattress tonight."

Lexi lifted her gaze to Emelia. "I'll be nice tomorrow. Please come to Sunday dinner and spend the afternoon with us."

"I like my new sister. Please come," Millie added.

Emelia beamed. "I already love you both. Let's make Robert watch a girlie movie after dinner."

Robert groaned, and the girls giggled as they headed for the car.

Chapter 11

Mattresses

Emelia stayed in the car while Robert walked his sisters inside to let his parents know they were headed to Joplin to find a mattress. Alone, she stared out the windshield, replaying the day in her mind.

Suddenly, her breath caught. "I told Robert we'd want a bigger bed when we have children," she said aloud. Her hands flew to her face. *Why did I say that? He'll have second thoughts now.*

The car door opened. Emelia sat up straight, dropped her hands to her lap, and forced a smile, hoping it masked her panic.

Robert returned the smile, then tilted his head. "Why is your face beet red?"

She groaned. "Because I said something at the store I shouldn't have. I'm sorry."

He touched his chin, gaze drifting toward the windshield. After a moment, he looked back at her. "I have no idea what you're talkin' about," he said, starting the car and backing out.

Emelia focused on her breathing, willing the panic to leave her body. The silence between them comforted her.

When Robert turned north onto the highway, he finally spoke. "Em, are you worried about saying we'd want a bigger bed when we have children?"

Her cheeks flamed again, heart thudding.

He reached for her hand. "Don't you remember what I said the other night? About imagining myself in your dad's shoes, and realizing how freaked out I'd be if our daughter were eighteen and in a serious relationship?"

He glanced at her and smiled. "My love, we've been talking about marriage. Marriage and children go together. I want our children. Maybe not right away, but I definitely want a family with you. That's why I bought the bigger bed."

"Marriage and children," Emelia whispered, eyes fixed on her bare left hand resting in Robert's.

He lifted it to his lips, kissing the back of her ring finger, then turned it over and pressed a kiss to the soft inside of her wrist. A shiver ran through her. Her breath caught. He kissed the place where a promise would live.

"I love you, Em."

"I love you, too."

The radio played softly as Robert navigated Range Line Road toward Croft Bedding. He pulled into the lot, parked, and hurried around to open her door. She took his hand and stepped out.

At the front of the car, he paused. "Wait here a minute. I need somethin'."

He unlocked the passenger door, slid inside, leaned over, then stepped out again, locking the door behind him.

"Did you get what you needed?" she asked.

"Sure did. Let's go pick out a mattress for our big bed."

She swallowed a laugh. *Thank goodness my parents didn't hear that.*

Inside, the salesman assumed they were married, and neither bothered to correct him. They laughed as they tested mattress after mattress, flopping onto each one like kids at a sleepover.

When they found one, they both liked, Robert asked the price, then dropped onto the nearest bed. "You've got to be kiddin' me."

"I can show you some clearance options," the salesman offered.

They followed him, trying out a few more beds side by side, giggling as they rolled from one to the next. Finally, they found another they both liked at half the price.

"Thank You, Lord," Robert said aloud.

At the counter, he paid in cash and arranged to pick it up after the weekend. Then he led Emelia back to the mattress they'd chosen and motioned for her to sit.

She looked up at him, puzzled. "Why did we come back here?"

His grin made her heart stutter, her blood fizz, and butterflies swirl in her tummy. When he lowered to one knee, her hands flew to her face.

She gasped. *He's proposing.*

The world around her faded. Her vision tunneled to Robert, on his knees, holding a sparkling diamond ring. Her breath hitched. More butterflies.

His smile radiated pure joy. "We know where our first home will be. We've furnished our bedroom and bought the mattress we'll sleep on, where our children will join us someday. The only thing missin' is our weddin' date, my love. Will you marry me and set a date for our life to begin?"

Tears welled instantly, spilling down her cheeks before she could blink them away. Her heart felt too full for her chest. *This man. This moment. This promise.* It was everything she'd prayed for, wrapped in tenderness and love.

He took her left hand in his. "May I put this on your finger, my love?"

"Yes," she whispered, her hand trembling. "Yes."

Her hand shook in his, tears streaming freely now. She swiped at them with her free hand as he slid the ring onto her finger, right where he'd kissed her earlier, as if he'd known.

"You're stuck with me now," he said, grinning so wide it lit his whole face.

He rose, pulled her into his arms, and kissed her thoroughly right there in Croft Bedding, with joy and a touch of mischief. She melted into him, heart pounding, soul joyous.

When she pulled back, she searched his eyes—her fiancé's eyes—and saw home.

He kissed her cheek. "Let's go eat," he said.

When Robert pulled into the parking lot of The Rafters, the nicest restaurant in Joplin, her eyes widened.

"I want to treat my brand-new fiancée to a special supper," he said.

"I've heard this place is expensive. Are you sure?"

"I'm positive, if they'll seat us without a reservation."

"You didn't make one?"

He grinned. "I bought your ring this morning, but I hadn't planned to propose. After everything today, and sharing all those beds with you, it just felt right."

She giggled. "I never imagined accepting a proposal in a mattress store, but it was perfect. Romantic. And it came from the best man I'll ever know."

His cheeks flushed, and she giggled again. He took her hand and led her inside. Her heart sank at the sight of suits and elegant dresses. *We're so underdressed. They'll never seat us.*

Robert approached the maître d' and spoke quietly. Emelia fought the urge to flee. After a moment, the maître d' approached her. "Ma'am, I hear congratulations are in order. May I see your ring?"

She lifted her hand, and he admired it. "It's beautiful. Let me show you to your table."

Robert took her hand, and they were led to a quiet corner table. The maître d' pulled out her chair and placed menus before them.

"I'll be right back with chilled sparkling cider and champagne glasses," he said, then disappeared.

Emelia opened her menu, then looked up, wide-eyed. "There are no prices. I'm afraid to order."

Robert smiled. "The menu's designed that way so you won't worry about cost. I've got this covered."

She traced the edge of the menu. *Their strategy isn't working. Not knowing makes me more anxious.*

The maître d' returned with an ice bucket and two crystal flutes. He poured a taste for Robert, who nodded, then he filled both glasses and left them.

Emelia took a sip, and the tart sweetness coated her tongue, bubbles tickling her throat. Robert reached for her hand.

"A toast?"

She nodded. "A toast."

"To a lifetime of happiness together," he said.

They clinked glasses and sipped.

"Do you know what you want?" he asked, setting his glass down.

"I do, but I'm afraid to order it."

"Don't be. Please, get whatever you want. I'm thinking crab-stuffed mushrooms to start. Sound good?"

She licked her lips. "You know I love crab." She glanced at the menu. "Are you okay if I order the prime rib?"

"Yes, my love. I meant it. Whatever you want."

She sighed, finished her cider, and pushed her glass toward him. *I can't control the cost, but I can choose to enjoy this moment.*

He refilled her glass.

"Thank you for lovin' me," he said, leaning in for a quick kiss.

They returned to her house before curfew. At the door, Robert asked, "Do you want me to come in when you show your parents the ring?"

She looked up at him. "Not tonight. I want this to be just ours for a little while."

He tucked her hair behind her ear, fingers trailing its length. "God blessed me with a woman who's beautiful inside and out. I'm so in love with you. I'll spend a long time on my knees thanking Him for you."

Her eyes fluttered closed as his lips met hers. She melted into his arms, heart full, body weightless.

The porch light flickered on, snapping her back to reality. Her legs felt like jelly, and she clung to him until she could stand on her own.

She stepped back, nodding toward the light. "Seems it's time for me to go inside."

He touched her cheek. "I'll pick you up for Sunday school in the mornin'. Good night, my love."

She turned the knob. "I'll be ready. Good night, my love."

She stepped inside and closed the door behind her.

Chapter 12

Engaged

Robert didn't see his parents when he came in, so he headed straight to his room. Solomon sat up in bed, then moved to Robert's.

"The girls wouldn't stop talking about the ring they helped you pick out for Emelia. Got a plan for your proposal?"

Robert rolled his eyes. "Those girls are gonna be the death of me. No, I don't have a plan."

Solomon's eyes narrowed. "Oh." He chuckled. "Your face tells me everything. You already popped the question."

Robert tried to keep a straight face but failed. He grinned.

"And she said yes." Solomon nodded. "So is there a date?"

"No date yet. I'm exhausted, and we've got church in the mornin'. I want to sleep, but someone's sittin' on my bed." Robert yawned.

Solomon laughed. "Alright, alright." He returned to his bed.

The room fell quiet, the soft hum of the ceiling fan the only sound between them.

After a moment, Robert said, "You wanna pray?"

"Yeah," Solomon said.

They knelt by their beds.

"Lord," Solomon began, "thank You for today. Thank You for Emelia saying yes. Help us be men who honor You with our words, our choices, and our love."

Robert added, "Lord, I want to love Emelia the way You love us with patience and kindness. Give us rest tonight and prepare our hearts for worship tomorrow. Forgive us our sins as we forgive others. In Jesus' name, amen."

"Amen," Solomon said.

The next morning, Robert realized he hadn't told Emelia what time he'd pick her up for Sunday school. It was only seven o'clock. He headed to the kitchen, where his mom was making breakfast.

"I'm sure gonna miss this in the mornings." He hugged her tightly. "I'm gonna miss you," he said, his voice catching.

She gave him a warm look as he reached for the wall phone.

"Who are you calling?" she asked.

"Emelia. I told her I'd pick her up, but I also need to get the Carters. I didn't think through the order."

His mom nodded. "Then you'd better call them both."

He spent the next few minutes on the phone. Thankfully, Emelia agreed to be picked up first, giving them a few quiet minutes together.

Alone. So I can kiss her.

The thought filled him with joy, and its importance caught him by surprise.

At Emelia's, he found her waiting on the porch swing. Meeting her halfway, he walked her to the car and opened her door. When he sat behind the wheel, he reached for her left hand.

He froze. The ring was gone. His breath caught.

Emelia lowered her chin and quietly unzipped the pocket of her Bible cover, pulling out the ring. Robert took it from her, his heart cracking. He held it between them, trying to steady the storm inside him.

"You said you wanted to marry me. If that's true..." He drew a breath. "Why isn't this on your finger? Are you ashamed to be engaged to me?"

He had never felt so small. *Is it because I didn't go to college? Are my choices makin' her second-guess us? Were my parents right?* The questions swirled as he stared at the ring that hadn't lasted the night.

Emelia's gaze stayed steady. "I'm not ashamed of you. I'm honored by your love. I told you last night I wanted to keep our commitment between us for a little while. Just ours. I couldn't do that if I wore the ring in front of my parents."

He rubbed his chest with a clenched fist, as if he could press the ache away. "Emelia, you're my treasure. I want everyone to know. My family already does. What am I supposed to tell them?" His chin trembled.

"I love you. I want to marry you. I just wanted to hold the promise close before sharing it. Please, Robert, I want your ring on my finger. I want to be yours, and you to be mine. Tell your family we're in love, and I'll tell mine the same."

Her eyes shimmered, and the tightness in his chest eased.

"I want this ring on your finger," he said quietly, "but I need a promise first."

She nodded.

"Promise me, if I slide it back onto your hand, you'll wear it proudly. No matter who sees it."

When she didn't answer right away, he dropped the ring into his shirt pocket, his heart splintering. He exhaled hard, then drew in a shaky breath. "Emelia, I love you. But this doesn't feel right. You should go to church with your parents. I need to pick up the Carters."

She didn't move. "Robert Jackson, you are not breaking up with me. You love me, and I love you."

She reached into his pocket, but he caught her hand. She leaned in and kissed him, firm and tender, the press of her lips calming the storm in him. When she pulled back, she dropped the ring back into his pocket.

"I want to be your wife. You want to be my husband. You know that's true. And you're going to put that ring on my finger so I can show it to everyone at church this morning."

She kissed him again, and the ache behind his ribs dulled.

"Are you going to take it off again?" he asked, still not whole.

"Not unless I need to."

"Why would it be necessary?"

She smiled. "You work construction. I'm going to be your partner. There'll be times when wearing rings isn't safe. And I don't want to lose the diamond or my finger."

"Oh." He nodded, smiling. "That makes sense. I can live with that. Otherwise, you'll wear it always."

"I will." She offered her left hand.

He slipped the ring back onto her finger and kissed it gently. "I love you."

"I love you, too."

Robert started the car and drove to the Carter home.

They were the first to see Emelia's ring. Jerry clapped him on the back. "Good job, kid."

Sue took Emelia's hand, admiring the ring with soft gasps before pulling her into a hug. "Congratulations."

Watching them, something in Robert eased. The knot that had sat in his chest all morning loosened. He held his chin a little higher.

By the end of worship, he'd lost count of how many people she'd shown the ring to. Each time she smiled and said, "Robert asked me last night," something in him settled deeper. She wasn't just proud of the ring. She was proud of them.

As they left the building, Robert walked her to his car, his hand resting on the small of her back. Before he could open her door, his sisters appeared.

"Can we ride home with you?" Lexi and Millie asked at once.

Robert smiled. "Girls, I'm taking the Carters home. You'll need to ride with Mom and Dad. My car won't hold all of us."

Lexi's face hardened. Her glare shifted to Emelia.

Robert stepped between them. "Lex, keep your mouth closed. I told you yesterday, this behavior won't fly. We're not breaking our promise to you and Millie. We're just taking the Carters home first."

Lexi spun around and bolted toward their parents. Right in front of a car.

Out of the corner of his eye, Robert saw the vehicle. He lunged, grabbing Lexi and pulling her out of the vehicle's path. They crashed onto the pavement, breath knocked from his lungs, heart pounding.

He held her tightly, trembling. His first instinct was to scold her, but the reality of what could have happened stopped him cold.

"Lex, I love you. You cannot ever do that again."

"I love you, too," she sobbed. "I don't want to lose you."

Solomon's voice broke through. "You still have a big brother at home."

Lexi lifted her head. "Yeah, I still have you. But that doesn't mean it's okay for Robert to leave."

Solomon gently pulled her from Robert's arms and into his own. "Sis, you scared Dad, Mom, and me."

He turned to Robert. "Brother Stephens slammed on his brakes, but as you can see, his car didn't stop in time. We're grateful you snatched her out of harm's way."

Solomon lifted their fourteen-year-old sister into his arms and carried her to their parents like a child. Robert followed, holding Millie's hand. Emelia and the Carters stayed by his car.

On his way back, Robert approached the vehicle that would have hit Lexi. He placed a hand on the driver's shoulder, felt the man trembling, then saw tears on his wife's face.

"Is Alexis all right? I'm so thankful you grabbed her." Brother Stephens took a breath to steady his voice. "I didn't see her. I tried to stop. There wasn't time. I'm so sorry." He looked down.

"Brother Stephens, she's scared but fine. You did nothing wrong. She ran out right in front of you." Robert gave his shoulder a gentle squeeze.

They exchanged a quiet nod, and Robert returned to his car. He leaned against it, exhaled sharply, and covered his face with his hands.

Emelia laid her hand on his back. "My love, she's okay."

He leaned into her touch, grateful for the comfort. "I know. But because of us, because I'm moving out, she was almost hit. What am I supposed to do with that?"

Two strong hands landed on his shoulders. Jerry's voice was steady. "You have good parents. They'll take care of Alexis. You and Emelia keep doing what's right."

Robert's throat tightened. "I almost lost my sister."

"We'll talk to her when we get to your house," Emelia said softly, her hand still moving gently across his back.

Sue stepped beside him, taking his hands in hers. "It scared you as much as it did her. But you saved her, Robert, hold onto that."

He nodded slowly, drawing in a few deep breaths to steady himself. The ache hadn't vanished, but its weight had shifted. He wasn't carrying it alone.

"I'm sorry," he said quietly. "Thank you. I'm okay now. Let's get you home."

Chapter 13

The Hard Part

After dropping off the Carters, Robert drove home with Emelia at his side. In the quiet between them, he prayed for his family's healing.

His mother opened the door before he reached it and pulled him into a tight hug. "Thank you for taking care of your sister today."

"Lex is angry with me and jealous of Emelia. How do I keep her from doin' somethin' like that again?"

She pulled back and met his gaze. "You can't. She is responsible for her actions. She knows she owes you both an apology, but I don't think it'll come today." She sighed. "She'll stay in her room today, except to eat dinner and go to church tonight. Your father and I want her to think and pray about what she did."

Robert nodded, and his mom stepped aside. "Emelia, will you help Millie and me put dinner on the table?"

"Yes, ma'am."

"My dear, you're becoming part of our family. Call me Betsy, and my husband, Mark. Maybe one day, you'll be comfortable calling us Mom and Dad."

Emelia smiled, slipping into the kitchen with his mom and youngest sister. Lexi was probably in her room, and movement came from the bedroom he shared with Solomon. That left him alone with his father.

"Robert, sit down."

He lowered himself onto the couch, eyes on the floor. "I'm sorry, Dad."

"Son, look at me."

He looked up, unsure what he'd find.

With a dip of his chin and a soft smile, his father said, "We're not upset with you. If not for your quick actions, Alexis would've been hurt or worse."

He shuddered as the moment replayed in his mind, fear and anger tightening his chest. "She scared me. If I weren't movin' out and hadn't fallen in love with Emelia, she wouldn't be actin' like this. One minute she's fine, the next she's causin' a scene. I don't know what to do."

His dad's smile faded. "We don't have easy answers. We're not thrilled you're movin' out, but we know it's part of your journey. We think Alexis needs a clean break and time to cope. I talked to the Carters. They're fine with you movin' in today."

Robert's eyes widened. "Today? What about my promise? Couldn't I still spend time with Millie?"

"Alexis is our priority, and we've talked to Millie. Though disappointed, she understands. Your furniture's on the trailer in the garage, and Solomon's packin' your things. We can move you between dinner and evenin' worship."

Robert flinched. "You said this isn't my fault, but it feels like you're kickin' me out."

His dad placed a hand over his. "We love you. We're not kickin' you out. We're movin' the timeline up for Lexi's sake. Have you decided to stay?"

He shook his head. "No, I'm committed to the Carters. You taught me to keep my word. I see your point about Lexi. I should be upset that Solomon's packin' my things, but he'll do a better job than I would. He knows what matters to me and will take care of it."

His dad smiled. "You and Solomon have always looked out for each other."

His eyes widened again. "I have a bed, but no mattress or box springs. I bought them last night and said I'd pick them up after the weekend."

"Where did you buy it?"

"Croft Bedding."

"Are you sure they're not open today? Call and check."

Resigned, Robert stood, pulled the salesman's card from his wallet, and went to the kitchen. To his surprise, the call was answered.

"Croft Bedding, how may I help you?"

He explained his situation and was told he could pick up the mattress anytime before five. Relieved, he hung up, but his shoulders slumped. *I never imagined last night was the last night I'd sleep in this house.*

His mom plated the ham while Millie pulled the silverware from the drawer, and Emelia took the steaming macaroni and cheese from the oven—the rich scent of melted cheese and butter filled the air. Robert turned to leave the kitchen, but the aroma turned him back.

A picture of his future filled his mind, years of carrying hot casseroles to the table for his beloved. For the first time since the accident, a genuine smile curved his lips.

He set down the dish and turned to Emelia. "Our plans for this afternoon have changed."

She placed her hand on his cheek. "Are you alright with moving out today?"

He shrugged. "I guess so. It was gonna happen this week anyway. I'll miss my family, but we have to start buildin' our future, and it won't happen here. Sometimes being an adult is hard."

She nodded. "I'm sorry."

"My love, it's not your fault. It's no one's. I think my parents are right. Lexi needs to know she can't change our relationship or where I live." He pulled Emelia close. "I love you."

"I love you, too," she whispered.

At dinner, Lexi and Millie sat across from Robert, Emelia, and Solomon, with their parents at each end of the table. Their father usually said grace, but today was different.

"Robert, since you won't be eatin' with us regularly anymore, please say our prayer."

His dad gave him a slight smile, his eyes glassy. Robert nodded, and the family joined hands.

"Dear Lord, thank You for my family. Help each of us feel loved and important. Thank You for this food and the hands that prepared it. Bless Emelia and me in our new commitment. Help us love and support those affected by it. Be with me as I adjust to life on my own. Comfort my sisters and help them find peace in my absence. Forgive us our sins and help us forgive others. With honor and praise, we pray in Jesus' name, amen."

He exhaled and looked across the table.

"Lexi, Millie, I want you both to understand, my love for you hasn't changed. Yes, I love Emelia and want to build a life with her. Yes, I'm movin' to the Carters. But none of that makes us any less family. I'm sorry it's hurtin' you."

Millie stood and rounded the table. "I love you, Bubba."

His heart warmed at the nickname she'd used since before she could say his name. He hugged her. "I love you, Millie."

When she returned to her seat, Lexi frowned at her. Millie crossed her arms and glared.

"Lexi, leave me alone! I don't care if you're mad at Robert and even madder at Emelia. I'm not. I love my Bubba and my new sister, and there's nothing you can do about it. If you don't want to be nice, fine. Emelia is nice to me."

Alexis pushed away her plate and pinned Robert with an angry gaze. "I hope I never see you again!" She stood and ran to her room.

Emelia swiped a tear from her cheek. "I'm sorry. I didn't mean to cause so many problems. Robert, please take me home."

Before he could answer, his mother covered Emelia's hand. "My dear, you've done nothing wrong. Mark and I will deal with Alexis. Her behavior is unacceptable and won't be tolerated. I'm sorry you had to see her this way."

Robert sighed. "Mom's right. I've never seen her act like this. We weren't allowed to be rude growin' up. I don't want you to go, but I'll take you home if that's what you want."

His father stood. "Sit, Betsy. See if you can convince our daughter-to-be to stay." He turned and walked down the hall to the girls' room.

When he returned with Alexis in tow, Robert stood by the door, his hand on the knob, and Emelia at his side.

"You'd better hurry before you miss your chance," his father said.

A contrite Alexis approached. "I'm sorry," she whispered, wrapping her arms around Robert. Tears streamed down her cheeks as she looked up at Emelia. "Will you still be my sister?"

Emelia smiled and pulled her into a hug. "I'd love to be your big sister."

Robert looked at his sorrowful sister. "Lexi, I can't bear the thought of losin' you. Do you realize you put yourself in danger today?"

She nodded, swiping at her eyes. "I do. I won't do that again."

Solomon entered. "Does anybody want me as a brother, or am I just chopped liver?"

Robert laughed. "No, brother, you are not chopped liver. I had to share a room with you. Trust me, even on your worst days, you never smelled that bad."

His mother chuckled. "Now that we've established your opinion of liver, can we please eat this ham before it's cold?"

The family sat around the table and enjoyed their Sunday meal.

The rest of the afternoon was a whirlwind. After unloading everything into his new room, Emelia directed furniture placement while Robert made the round trip to pick up his bedding set. As soon as the mattress was on his bed, he sent Emelia to church with his dad and Solomon.

Staring at his bare mattress, he sighed and headed to the big-box store for pillows, linens, and a comforter. Wandering the aisles, he filled his cart with a mini fridge, toaster oven, coffee pot, groceries, and anything else he thought he might need.

At the register, he sorted essentials from extras, apologizing to the cashier for the items he decided against buying. *At least I can make coffee, eat breakfast, and pack lunch in my bedroom-kitchen.*

Back at the Carters, he lugged everything inside. He set the mini fridge beside his dresser and placed the coffee pot and toaster oven on top. The fridge filled quickly with perishables. He unpacked just enough to prepare for work, leaving the rest in bags and boxes.

Exhausted, he considered going straight to bed, but hunger won out. I should at least see the Carters. Maybe they'll have some leftovers.

He knocked on the back door and was immediately welcomed inside.

Sue placed a hand on his arm, and he covered it with his own, grateful for the comfort.

"You've had a long day. I made a plate for you. I'll warm it, if you're hungry."

"Please. Or should I say thank you."

She pulled the plate from the fridge, covered it with foil, and placed it in the oven. "It'll be warm in about fifteen minutes."

Jerry motioned him to the table. Sue set a glass of water in front of him.

"Son, what time do you need to eat breakfast before work?" she asked.

Robert's mouth fell open, speechless. Jerry clapped him on the back.

"You came here to help us. Let us help you. We asked for help with groceries. In return, we'll make sure you're fed."

Robert nodded, swallowing past the lump in his throat. "You'd do that for me? I don't want to be more trouble than I'm worth."

"Robert, we know you'll keep your word. Emelia will help too. We'll provide what you need and keep our word to you. We want you to be family," Jerry said.

Sue smiled. "So, what time do you want breakfast?"

Robert leaned back, closing his eyes to keep from crying. When the wave passed, he opened them. "Is six too early?"

"Not at all. We usually eat around then."

"I bought some things I can heat in my toaster oven. If it's okay, I'll put them in your freezer."

"Bring them in—they might come in handy," Sue said with a half-smile.

He stood.

"Go on now," she said. "Your supper will be warm when you get back."

He grabbed a sack and loaded it with frozen breakfast sandwiches and toaster pastries from his mini fridge. Before heading back, he paused to pray.

"Thank You, Lord, for these people who've opened their hearts to me. Help me be worthy of their faith. I want to serve You. Please help me be a good servant. In Your Son's precious name, amen."

He returned to the Carters' kitchen. Sue took the sack and peeked inside. "This stuff doesn't look so bad," she said, handing it back.

She pointed to a small room near the back door. "Put those in one of the baskets in the chest freezer."

Robert flipped on the light and paused to admire the shelves lined with casserole dishes, canned goods, and jars of flour, beans, and pasta. My mom would love this room.

He placed the boxes in a basket, closed the chest freezer lid, and returned to the table just as Sue set down his warmed plate.

"Be careful. That plate is hot."

He bowed his head and offered a quiet prayer of thanks for the meal and for the loving generosity of the couple beside him.

While he ate, the conversation flowed, filled with thoughts and dreams of the future.

When he finished, he rose and washed his plate and utensils at the sink.

"We don't expect you to do that," Jerry said. "Sue and I usually wash dishes together."

Robert turned. "If my parents ever found out I didn't wash my dishes, they'd have my hide."

Jerry and Sue laughed.

"I can believe that about Mark and Betsy. They've always held you kids to high standards," Jerry said.

Robert's smile faded. "Please pray for my sister, Alexis. My engagement and movin' out have thrown her for a loop. She scared me today."

Jerry nodded. “She scared us all. We know you weren’t ready to come today, but your parents thought it was best for her." Jerry shrugged. "We agree. The situation is final now, beyond her manipulation.”

Robert leaned against the counter. “I hope you’re right. I’m worried about her.” He stared at the floor, replaying the near miss.

Sue placed a hand on his arm. “She’s a loved young lady. Before you crawl into bed, put her in God’s hands.”

She squeezed his arm, then let go.

“Yes, ma’am. I think I’ll do that now. Thank you for supper. I’ll see you in the mornin’.”

“Good night, Robert,” they called after him.

Chapter 14

Together

Emelia sat beside her parents at the evening service, her mind far from the minister's message. If Robert hadn't whisked her out of sight for a few stolen moments, she wouldn't have had a single kiss beyond the ones she'd given him in the car before church. *If my parents saw those, I'll be hearing about it.*

She grimaced, then smiled as her thoughts drifted to the kiss they'd shared in what would become their closet. Even a brief kiss from Robert made her insides melt and her blood run hot.

If Robert works on the house after work and on Saturdays, Sunday will be all we have. My classes start tomorrow, and he's not living at home anymore. Maybe Mom and Dad won't be too restrictive since the Carters are there.

Her thoughts spun, trying to picture the changes ahead. The scrape of a hymnal cover against the wooden holder snapped her back. Her mother nudged her.

"Emelia, where were you?" she whispered, brows furrowed.

Emelia grabbed her songbook and stood. Peeking at her mom's page, she found the right number and began singing. But her mind wandered again. Only the booming voice of the man leading the closing prayer pulled her back in time to say amen.

The service ended, and she followed her parents toward the center aisle. At the end of the pew, Alexis stood waiting. Emelia hesitated, unsure what to expect from the straight-faced teen.

Their eyes met. Alexis looked down. "I wanted to tell you again how sorry I am."

Without hesitation, Emelia reached for both the girl's hands. Her face softened. "Sis, I've already forgiven you."

Alexis pulled her hands free and wrapped her arms around Emelia, who sighed in relief.

"I saw you sitting with your parents and realized you're going to miss Robert, too."

"We all start school tomorrow, and with Robert working at his job and on the house, we won't see much of him. I already miss him. How about you?"

Lexi stepped back. "I miss him, too."

"Lexi, I miss my brother and your brother. I don't want to miss you, too. Will you give me a chance?"

Lexi nodded. "Yes." She gave Emelia another quick hug before running up the aisle.

Solomon turned, gave Emelia a strong nod and a smile, then took Alexis' hand. Emelia returned the gesture, her heart lighter.

Her road with the Jacksons wouldn't always be smooth, but in this moment, she knew it would be worth it.

Robert woke Monday morning to the blare of his alarm. *I'll have to thank Solomon for packin' that.* He chuckled. *It's probably the first thing he packed. He hated hearin' it.* His smile faded. *I can't believe I'm missin' our morning banter.*

He stood and stared at his bare feet. Digging through a box, he found his old church camp flip-flops. He smiled at the memories. Now, they'll get me from the bedroom to the bathroom until the floors are done.

After showering and making his bed, he headed to the Carters' back door and knocked.

"Come on in, Robert," Sue called.

He stepped into the kitchen, greeted by the comforting scent of bacon, eggs, and hashbrowns. "Thank you for breakfast," he said.

"Grab three plates from the cupboard and silverware from the drawer below. Set the table, please," Sue said.

"Yes, ma'am."

Jerry's voice came from the hallway. "Was that Robert I heard knocking?"

"It was me," he replied.

Jerry frowned. "Did you knock when you lived with your parents?"

Robert met his gaze. "No."

"We told you last night, you're family now. Your key works in all the doors. Stop knocking and come on in."

"Are you sure I won't invade your privacy?"

Jerry chuckled. "Son, we don't run around naked in the public areas of our home. We'll protect our privacy. You just come on in."

His face heated. "Yes, sir," he squeaked.

Jerry and Sue laughed, and Robert joined in, the tension easing from his chest. He'd left his childhood home behind, yet this couple made him feel like he belonged, like he'd found a new home.

After breakfast, he packed his lunch and headed to work. While he and Eddy worked side by side, Robert's thoughts drifted to Emelia starting college, and Solomon and the girls back in school. Not only am I in a new home, but everyone's schedule has changed. *God, help me through these changes.*

"Hey, Robert." Eddy's call snapped him out of his thoughts. "You disappeared for a minute. Help me get this door out?"

"Sorry." Robert grabbed one end of the door. "This is a pocket door, right?"

"Yeah. Why?"

"Do you think I could put this in between my bathroom and primary bedroom?"

"A pocket door could work. Let's save this one. Let's put it in my truck instead of the dumpster. When did you move out there?"

"Yesterday." Robert sighed. "Everything's changin' so fast, I don't think my heart or my head have caught up."

"You must've found a ring on Saturday. Word at church is Emelia's left hand has a new sparkle."

"It does. She'll have homework now. Since I live in my homework, I'm not sure we'll see much of each other."

They loaded the door into the back of Eddy's truck, then the remaining upper cabinets onto the trailer. Eddy turned to Robert. "And you miss her already."

"I'm pretty pathetic." Robert groaned.

Eddy smiled. "Not pathetic. Just in love."

Robert nodded. "Yeah."

After work, they unloaded the cabinets and door into Robert's half of the house. "Nice bedroom furniture," Eddy said. "Emelia helped you pick it out?"

"She did."

"Where are you starting?"

Robert flipped the bathroom light. "Thought I'd start where you left off. I'm prayin' Emelia will have time Saturday to look at tile with Sue. Since this'll be Sue's space later and Emelia's for a while, I want them both to like it."

"Talking to both of them before plans are made, that's smart."

"I spoke to Sue last night. Sue's gonna shop with me. I'll run it by Emelia tonight."

"I'll help you install the door. I'll bring my family's schedule tomorrow so we can figure out a time."

"Thanks, man." Robert clapped him on the back.

As Eddy reached the door, Robert called after him. "Hey, I've never done tile before. Can you give me a list of what I'll need? If you've got time Saturday, I'd appreciate a tutorial."

Eddy turned in the doorway. "I'll have the schedule tomorrow. We'll figure it out."

When the door closed, Robert looked around the house. Salvaged cabinets stacked in the open room, doorless bedrooms, unfinished bathroom, bare concrete floors. He sighed. *What have I gotten myself into?*

He bowed his head. "God, I don't know enough to do most of what's needed. I need Your help. Thank You for a roof over my head, for the people willing to help, for Emelia, the Carters, and my family. Forgive my sins as I forgive others. In Your Son's name, amen."

He walked to the Carters' back door, raised his hand to knock, then remembered Jerry's words. He opened the door and stepped inside, still feeling awkward.

"Jerry, Sue, it's Robert. May I use the phone?"

Jerry appeared from the living room. "As long as you don't call Australia, you can use it anytime." He chuckled. "Call Emelia. We won't eavesdrop too much."

Robert smiled. "Thank you."

He dialed Emelia's number. After four rings, he heard her sweet voice. It was a balm to his heart.

"Em, if you're not swamped tonight, may I come over after supper so we can talk?"

"Mom wants you to come for dinner. I do too, of course. We can talk after."

"What time is dinner?"

"Six-thirty."

"I'll be there. I love you, Em."

"I love you, too. See you soon."

"See you soon." He listened until the click of the handset broke their connection.

Sue came around the corner. "Dinner for two here tonight. Give Emelia our love. We'll see you at six in the morning for breakfast."

"Yes, ma'am," he said, hugging her.

Showered, dressed in clean jeans and a nice polo, he arrived at Emelia's at six twenty-five. His heart beat faster than usual, and his palms were damp. He was nervous, though he'd never admit it. Emelia's mother had requested his presence, but seeing Emelia made it worth it.

She opened the door, and her beauty stole his breath. She kissed his cheek. The simple gesture lit up every sense. He followed her inside.

"Oh, good, you're here, Robert. We can eat," Henry rose from the couch and folded his newspaper.

"Peggy, Robert is here," he called toward the kitchen.

Peggy stepped out. "You two strong men can carry the serving dishes to the table."

Robert and Henry exchanged a glance, then did as asked. With the table set and the food on it, they sat. Henry gave thanks, and the dishes began to pass. Smiles surrounded the table, and Robert silently thanked the Lord for that, and for the glorious smell of fried chicken, mashed potatoes, gravy, and green beans.

His mouth watered when the basket of fresh rolls reached him. "Mrs. Norton, I mean Peggy, this is amazin'. Thank you for invitin' me."

Peggy smiled. "You haven't tasted it yet."

He dipped a roll in gravy and took a bite of chicken, groaning as he swallowed. "Premature thanks, maybe, but it's wonderful. Thank you, Peggy."

Henry chuckled. "Robert's right. My taste buds remind me to be thankful for you with every bite."

Robert noticed Peggy's pink cheeks and turned his attention back to his plate.

When the conversation shifted to wedding plans, Robert's focus drifted until Emelia said his name.

"Robert, don't you have an opinion?"

He scanned their faces. No one was smiling. Clearing his throat, he said, "I'll do whatever you tell me and be wherever you need me. All I care about is Emelia becomin' my wife."

Peggy frowned. "Do you know anything about wedding etiquette?"

"No, ma'am. I trust you, Emelia, and my mom will guide me."

Emelia tried to smile. "There are only two times I'd consider, Christmas or June, when my brother's home. Could the house be ready by Christmas?"

"I think I can make it livable. The kitchen appliances are the biggest hurdle. If we do a remodel and the owners don't keep theirs, I might get some, but it's not guaranteed."

Henry slapped the table. "Sounds like a wedding gift opportunity. Maybe we can team up with the Jacksons and help finish the kitchen."

Robert's brow furrowed. "What about Emelia's college? I can't afford her tuition." He looked at Henry. "Will you keep helpin' her?"

"We'll continue to support her education. As long as she keeps her grades up, her scholarship will cover most of it," Henry said, his pride showing.

Robert turned to Emelia. "Is a Christmas weddin' what you want?"

Emelia looked to her mom. "It gives us four months to plan. Is that doable, or should I wait until June?"

Robert fidgeted. Emelia's eyes sparkled as she smiled at her parents.

Henry's expression sobered. "Are you sure moving this fast is wise? You've only been dating since late May. We should all pray before making any decisions. Robert, talk to your parents, too."

"Yes, sir," Robert said, meeting Henry's gaze.

He turned to Emelia, whose smile had faded. "A few days of prayer will only strengthen our decision."

Then to her parents, he said, "I meant what I said. All I want is to marry your daughter. If the house were ready, I'd marry her today. I'll pray and seek counsel, because that's wise. But my future belongs to Emelia."

He stood. "I hope I haven't offended you. I'll pick Emelia up for dinner on Friday, and we have plans Saturday mornin'. Em, I need to speak with you."

He took her hand, and she followed him outside. At the car, he opened her door, then got in and drove. Silence filled the car. Emelia stared out the window.

"Em, I'm sorry," he said, eyes on the road.

Still silent, she finally asked, "Would you really marry me right now?"

"Yes, but I don't have a proper place for us."

"You're living at the Carters. Why can't I?"

He parked in the town square. "You could, but you deserve better."

She turned to him. "What I deserve is you. I'd love a Christmas wedding, but I'll be satisfied just becoming your wife. I'm as certain as you are."

He started the car again. "Let's talk to Jerry and Sue."

"Okay." She scrunched her nose. "Dinner Friday sounds good, but what are we doing Saturday?"

"I want to finish the bathroom. Jerry and Sue are choosing tile and want your opinion. It matters to me that you and Sue are happy with it."

Emelia smiled. "A shopping trip with them sounds fun."

"I'm glad. I didn't mean to spring it on you. I probably messed things up with your parents. I told them our plans and left with you without asking permission. That wasn't respectful."

Emelia laughed bitterly. "I walked out with you. I didn't ask either. Disrespectful or not, I hope they saw we're united."

At the Carter farm, they spoke with Jerry and Sue, who offered counsel, prayers, and assurances Emelia could live there once they were married. Sue encouraged her to call her parents, and Emelia did. They stayed for dessert, thanked the Carters, and headed back.

At her house, Robert parked. "Em, promise me you'll listen to them, and we'll both apologize."

Emelia frowned but agreed. He opened her door, and she took his hand as she stepped out.

Inside the house, Emelia's parents met them with scowls and shaking heads. Their expressions stopped Robert and Emelia cold.

"Robert, I wouldn't have believed it if I hadn't seen it myself. Emelia, you've never behaved like that. What were you thinking?" Henry's voice was stern, his hands animated.

Robert's head dropped. "Henry, Peggy, I was out of line. Disrespectful. I'm sorry."

Emelia's glare met her parents. "I promised Robert I'd apologize. I'm sorry. I'll try to be more respectful."

Peggy shook her head. "You said the words. It would help if you meant them."

Emelia let go of Robert's hand and sank into a chair. Robert followed her lead. The scent of fried chicken and fresh bread still lingered, and his stomach growled. Emelia's glare burned into him.

"Really, Robert?"

Her parents didn't react to their exchange. They sat on the sofa, facing them.

"Did either of you take what we said to heart?" Henry asked calmly.

Robert met his gaze. "Yes, sir. We agree prayer is important. Our commitment is firm, and wise counsel will help us stay grounded."

Henry nodded. "I'm glad to hear that."

Peggy forced a smile. "Emelia, I think we should talk about a wedding in early June."

Emelia crossed her arms. "No, Mom. I want a wedding between Christmas and New Year's, while James is home. If we can't manage that, Robert and I will elope."

Robert sputtered, speechless.

Henry leaned forward. "Son..."

Robert looked at him, still stunned. Peggy touched Henry's arm. "She must love you a lot to give up her dream wedding. She's imagined it for years."

Robert turned to Emelia. "You've dreamed of your weddin'?"

She nodded, rolling her eyes. "Yes." Then she smiled. "But I've learned the man I marry matters more than the wedding."

Robert grinned. "I don't care about a weddin'. I care about marryin' you."

Peggy raised her hands. "Do you even want a wedding, Emelia?"

Still gazing at Robert, Emelia said, "I'd love a small wedding between Christmas and New Year's. I want Robert, a dress, you two, James, Mark and Betsy, and Robert's siblings. If you want to add more, you can, Mom. But that's all I need. Honestly, all I need is Robert."

Robert couldn't look away from her.

"Wow," Henry said, breaking the moment. "I can see there's no discouraging you two. I'm no professional, but I've done a few projects. If you need help on weekends, let me know."

Robert stood. "Yes, sir. There's plenty to do. I'll let you know. Thank you."

He turned to Emelia. “I’ve got work tomorrow, and you’ve got school. Will you walk me out?”

She walked with him to his car, and he wrapped her in his arms.

“My parents are watching,” she whispered.

He chuckled. “I’m pretty sure they know I’m gonna kiss you.”

Emelia rose to her toes, eyes fluttering closed. He ran his hand up her back and into her hair, breathing in the honeyed vanilla scent before kissing the soft spot behind her ear. He feathered kisses along her jawline before capturing her mouth. He deepened the kiss slowly, savoring her response until breathlessness forced him to pull back, though he kept her close.

“I’d better let you go,” she said, stepping back.

He touched her cheek. “You should. I love you, Em.”

“I love you too,” she said, turning and walking toward the house.

Robert got in his car and started it. Emelia stood in the doorway, waving. He waved back and pulled away from the curb.

Chapter 15

Fall Festival

Emelia convinced Robert to come, even though he wanted to keep working on the house. The project could wait until tomorrow. Today, she wanted him to breathe, to laugh, to live a little. Watching his eyes soften as the music drifted over the crowd, she knew this was exactly what they both needed.

The square sparkled beneath rows of glowing string lights. The air smelled of barbecue, caramel apples, and fried dough—everything Emelia loved about fall. Red, yellow, and gold leaves drifted on the breeze, glowing like embers as they caught the light before scattering color across the brick walkway. Robert strolled beside her, his hand warm in hers. Solomon walked with them, while Lexi and Millie hurried ahead.

"Stay where we can see you," Robert called after them.

The girls slowed to a skip, their laughter trickling behind them.

After one slow walk through the festival, she nudged him toward Solomon. "Go have some fun. I'll keep your sisters out of trouble."

He grinned. "You sure you're up for that?"

"Positive," she said.

He planted a quick kiss on her cheek and disappeared into the crowd with his brother.

Emelia lingered with Lexi and Millie, weaving between tables lined with pottery, quilts, and painted wood décor. The girls had opinions about everything, what color matched her kitchen, and which wreath would look best for the wedding. Their laughter mingled with music and the hum of voices.

A cool breeze carried the scent of cinnamon and crisp leaves. Emelia paused at a carved wooden cross, brushing her thumb along the grain as she pictured it hanging by the door of their new home—the one Robert was remodeling board by board. The house could wait. Tonight was for remembering they were building a life together, not just a house.

Things grew interesting when Lexi and Millie asked, "When should a girl let a boy kiss her?"

Emelia stopped short. "Millie, you're eleven. That's way too young. Fourteen's still a bit early. Alexis, has someone asked to kiss you?"

Both girls shook their heads.

"We know you and Robert kiss," Lexi said. "We thought you'd know when we'll be old enough."

Emelia smiled softly. "Let's talk about this over something sweet. Darren's Diner booth has funnel cakes and strawberry lemonade. Sound good?"

"Yum," Millie said.

Grateful for the pause, Emelia led them toward the booth. *Lord, help me speak wisely,* she prayed silently. *I don't know what their parents have shared with them. Please guide me. In Jesus' name, amen.*

They found a table warmed by the late-October sun and shared one oversized funnel cake piled with cheesecake and strawberries. Lexi took the first bite before Emelia could sit down.

"So, what about kissing boys?"

Emelia rolled her eyes at Lexi's bluntness. *Must run in the family.*

"Your brothers made a pact," she said. "They promised not to kiss a girl unless they were in love and knew she was the one they wanted to marry."

Lexi scoffed. "Robert dated a new girl every month before you. Solomon doesn't date long either. I don't believe they haven't kissed those girls."

"Robert told me I'm the only girl he's ever kissed," Emelia said. "I believe him. You girls could make a pact like that and hold each other accountable."

Millie grinned. "You've kissed other boys, not just Robert. Right?"

Emelia lowered her gaze. "I have. I wish I hadn't. I thought those boys cared about me, but when a kiss was all I would give them, they broke my heart. Even boys from church aren't always pure in heart. I wish Robert were the only boy I'd ever kissed."

A throat cleared behind her. She turned. Robert stood with his arms crossed, Solomon beside him.

"Why are you talkin' to my sisters about kissin' me?" he asked.

Before she could answer, Lexi straightened. "Millie and I asked when we should let a boy kiss us." She pointed at Emelia. "She said you and Solomon promised not to kiss a girl until you were in love and ready to marry. Is it true you haven't kissed anyone, Solomon? And that Emelia's the only girl you've kissed, Robert?"

Solomon flushed but held her gaze. "I've never kissed a girl."

Robert lifted his chin. "Emelia is the only girl I've ever kissed."

"Because of your promise?" Millie asked, eyes wide.

Both nodded. "Yes," Solomon said. "That's why."

"Why did you make that promise?" Lexi asked.

Robert rounded the end of the bench and sat beside Emelia. "Lexi, kissing is part of love. And anything beyond hugs and kisses belongs inside marriage." His voice gentled. "When a man kisses a woman, sometimes his body wants more. I imagine that's true for women, too. Satan can use that desire to lead you down a road with consequences you don't want. Solomon and I made our pact to avoid that temptation with someone we didn't intend to marry."

Lexi twisted her hands in her lap, then looked at Millie. "I think we should make a pact, too. If we ever think about kissing a boy, we'll talk to each other first. Deal?"

Millie nodded. "Deal. That's easy for me. I don't like any boys, yet."

Lexi turned red. "Millie, that was our secret."

Emelia leaned closer. "Have you kissed this boy?"

"No."

"Has he acted like he wants to kiss you?"

"I think so. I'm not sure. No boy has ever liked me like Charlie does." Lexi's voice softened.

Emelia's stomach tightened. Robert's tone stayed even. "Charlie Hickum from church? He's sixteen. Dad and Mom are gonna blow a gasket."

"Dad's almost four years older than Mom. Why would two years matter?" Lexi asked.

Robert raked a hand through his hair. "Dad was twenty-three. Mom was nineteen. If she'd been fourteen and he'd been eighteen, it would've been a big deal. The younger you are, the more age matters."

"Lexi, be careful," Emelia said gently. "Your parents won't let you date for at least two more years."

Solomon nodded. "And if Charlie tries to kiss you, remember what Emelia said. She wishes she'd waited."

Lexi met Emelia's gaze. "I'll remember. I promise."

Solomon frowned. "If she gets in trouble and Mom and Dad find out we knew, we'll be in just as much trouble."

Lexi stood. "I get it. No kissing. Millie, I promise I won't kiss a boy—not even Charlie —unless we talk first. I need to be in love and ready to get married." She sighed. "That's at least four or five years from now."

Solomon stood and offered each sister a hand. "A ride on the Twister before we head home should help. Since Robert and Emelia are the only ones doing any kissing, let's leave them to it."

He led the girls toward the carnival rides.

Emelia exhaled slowly. Robert slipped an arm around her shoulders. "I'm sorry those boys hurt you," he said quietly. "Your heart is safe with me."

She leaned into him. "I feel safe with you because I know you love me."

They sat together, sharing the last bites of funnel cake and finishing their lemonades. The lights flickered across his face, softening the edge of exhaustion she'd seen earlier. After a quiet moment, Robert asked, "Will you ride the Ferris wheel with me? We could share a kiss at the top."

She kissed his cheek. "I'd like that. But you have to promise not to make the bucket swing."

Robert laughed, remembering. Emelia playfully swatted arm. "Don't you dare swing the bucket like you did at Six Flags!"

He grinned. "That was at the Labor Day youth retreat in Dallas last year. We were just friends. I didn't know sliding closer would scare you."

She narrowed her eyes. "You had to talk me into riding that Ferris wheel."

He kissed her temple. "We'd already ridden every roller coaster. You laughed through all of them. I didn't think you were serious about being afraid of the Ferris wheel."

"I don't understand it," she admitted. "I love roller coasters, but Ferris wheels scare me—especially when the bucket swings."

Her body trembled slightly against his side.

"Em, we don't have to ride it," he said softly. "Kissin' at the top isn't worth scarin' you."

She gave him a brave smile. "You'll sit right next to me. I trust you. I'm brave enough to want that kiss."

She slipped her hand into his and tugged him to his feet.

Robert chuckled. "You never cease to amaze me. It's gonna be a kiss to remember."

At the platform, after waiting in line, he asked, "You sure?"

She kissed his cheek and smiled. "I can do this with you at my side."

She settled onto the bench and patted the space beside her. Robert joined her, his hand finding hers.

"I'm the most blessed man in the world," he whispered.

Warmth rose to her cheeks. "I love you too."

When the Ferris wheel reached the top, Robert leaned in, and she met him halfway. The bucket rocked, and fear knotted in her stomach, but his steady hand and the warmth of his arm made it bearable. The kiss was a wonderful distraction, and when the ride carried them back down, she needed him to hold her steady until her feet touched the ground. She would always need him.

Chapter 16

Almost, But Not

Robert woke on Christmas Eve morning to the faint glow spilling from the closet's small window. He rolled over and checked the time on his alarm clock. Stretching, he smiled. *Emelia will be here tonight.* And in three more days, she'll live here—*my wife, in our home.*

A week earlier, he'd obtained permission from both the Carters and the Nortons for Emelia to stay at the Carter farm tonight so they could deliver the restored vanity to his parents' home before his sisters woke. They'd trusted him to be a gentleman, and he would be. They were both Christians. They knew what was sin and what was not.

He pulled his red sweater from the dresser drawer, then stopped, the weight of his thoughts pressing in. Laying the sweater across the bed, he drew a steady breath. It was time to be honest with himself and with God. He knelt beside the bed.

"Dear Lord, on this Christmas Eve morning, there are only three days left before we're married. Please help me keep my thoughts and desires in check and resist Satan. Forgive my sins—You know each one—and help me to forgive as You forgive. In Jesus' name, amen."

With his eyes still closed, he rested his forehead on his bed, breathing in the peaceful stillness until it settled in his soul. Rising, he dressed in black slacks and his red sweater, then grabbed his Santa hat from his bedside table. By nine o'clock, he was on the road, heading to meet the Carters for a late holiday breakfast.

As he turned onto the highway, he passed a familiar truck in the opposite lane. He squinted. "Was that Eddy's?" He shook his head and chuckled. "Nah. Couldn't be."

He enjoyed a leisurely breakfast with the Carters, then spent the rest of the morning and early afternoon browsing shops around the square until Sue found the *perfect* gift for Emelia. Later, they stopped at the local home improvement store, where Sue took the time to dream. His time was a small Christmas gift to give this couple who'd become family to him.

He looked at his watch and gasped. It was almost four. He said quick goodbyes to the Carters and drove to the Norton home. He couldn't be late. He was meeting Emelia's brother, James, for the first time and wanted to make a good impression. The evening's plan was simple: dinner, gifts, dessert, and family game time.

When he arrived, he donned his Santa hat and knocked on the door, expecting Emelia, but a tall man with a crew cut and familiar brown eyes opened it.

"You must be Robert. Come on in. Emelia's told me all about you. I'm James."

Though Robert stood six feet tall, James had a few inches on him. When he stepped inside, Robert offered his hand. James gave it a firm shake.

"Nice to meet you," Robert said.

James laughed. "The way Emelia talks about you, I half expected you to walk on water. Turns out you're just a regular guy."

Robert chuckled. "I'm as normal as they come. Your sister's the angel in this relationship."

James grinned. "That opinion's definitely skewed."

Peggy stepped out of the kitchen. "James, stop harassing Robert. You two can set the table and carry in the serving dishes."

Robert led the way, familiar with the routine. James lingered until Peggy nudged him toward the silverware and napkins.

"Bro, you're making me look bad," James whispered.

Robert winked. "Better you than me. Your spot in the family is secure. I'm still earnin' mine."

James clapped him on the back. Emelia entered with a tray of iced tea. "Mom's almost ready. Please bring in the dishes."

Once everything was on the table, Henry peeled off his apron and wiped his brow. Peggy kissed his cheek. "Merry Christmas, darling. Thank you for all your help. And thank you, Emelia."

Everyone took their seats. James looked to his father. "May I say the blessing?"

A knock interrupted. Peggy smiled with a twinkle in her eye. "Emelia, Robert, please answer the door."

Robert leaned close. "Why are we answerin' the door? I don't live here."

"We're doing what my mom asked," Emelia said, gesturing for him to open it.

Robert opened the door to find his parents standing on the porch. Emelia nudged him aside and let them in, though her eyes were as wide as his.

Back in the dining room, the table had grown. Two extra chairs and place settings had appeared. Something was up.

Robert sat, replaying the day. The Carters had invited him out for a late breakfast at the diner, then insisted he help them pick a last-minute gift for Emelia, followed by some browsing at the home improvement store before they parted ways. They'd gone home, and he'd come straight to the Nortons. *None of it seemed odd at the time, but now he wasn't so sure.*

Emelia's elbow nudged his arm. He looked around. Everyone's head was bowed. He quickly joined hands with Emelia and his father when James began the prayer.

"Dear Lord, we come before You with thankful hearts. Thank You for the gift of Your Son and His sacrifice. Please accept our repentance and help us forgive others as You forgive us. Thank You for blessing our family with growth and for providing a Christian man for my sister. Bless the hands that prepared this meal, and may it nourish our bodies. Yours is the kingdom, glory, and power forever. In Jesus' name, amen."

Amens echoed around the table. Dishes were passed, and plates filled. Robert smiled as he scooped lasagna onto his plate. Emelia filled his salad bowl and handed him his favorite blue cheese dressing. He grabbed two garlic-basil rolls and passed the basket. As he ate, he tuned out the conversation, studying the faces around the table.

Emelia squeezed his thigh. "Robert, stop ignoring me and everyone else," she said, her tone sharp.

He looked up, catching glares from both fathers, frowns from their mothers, and a scowl from James.

He set down his fork. "I'm sorry."

Emelia shook her head but said nothing more. Robert joined the conversation for the rest of the meal, and by the time they left the table, he felt forgiven. Or at least, he hoped so.

Everyone moved to the living room. Cleanup would wait until after the gift exchange. Robert and Emelia had joint gifts for her parents and James. He hadn't brought anything for his parents; he hadn't expected to see them until Christmas morning.

He leaned toward Emelia. "Was I supposed to bring our gift for my parents tonight?"

She rested her head on his shoulder. "No, my love. Your family is tomorrow."

He frowned. "Then why are they here?"

She shrugged. "I don't know."

When the gifts were exchanged, none were for Robert or Emelia. He looked between both sets of parents. "Thank you for our weddin'. I'm guessin' that's our gift this year."

His mother grinned and pulled a small, wrapped box from her bag, handing it to Emelia.

"Your gift is inside," came from five voices.

"Em, open it," Robert said, heart pounding.

She tore off the wrapping and lifted the lid. Inside were photographs. One showed a refrigerator, stove, and dishwasher in their kitchen. Another showed a washer, dryer, and utility sink in the laundry room. She handed the photos to Robert.

"Did you know about this?" she asked.

His mouth fell open. "No." He turned to the room. "I was only gone a few hours. How did this happen?"

"Sometimes it takes a village," his father said. "Solomon, Eddy, Henry, James, and I worked like a well-oiled machine. James painted the utility room wall first thing. With fans and heaters, it dried fast. We took the photos before hooking everything up so your mom could get them printed."

Mark smiled at James. "We sent him home once his muscles weren't needed. Henry left next, bringing back the butter Peggy sent. I worked as long as I could before picking up your mom."

He turned to Robert. "Solomon and Eddy finished up. Everything's installed and working. Your plumbing and electrical prep made it easy."

Emelia wiped tears from her cheeks. Robert blinked rapidly.

"Who all contributed?" he asked, voice shaky.

Peggy smiled. "Everyone your dad mentioned, plus Jerry and Sue. They kept you occupied and helped with time and money. Merry Christmas from your village. We love you."

A tear escaped Robert's eye. He swiped it away. "Let Emelia and me clean up dinner and get dessert ready. You've all done so much for us today."

Emelia stood. "And we won't take no for an answer. I don't even know how to thank you enough."

She turned away, wiping her cheeks. Robert joined her, wrapping her in his arms and guiding her to the kitchen.

"Em, we are so blessed," he said, resting his head on hers.

She nodded against his shoulder.

They stepped apart and began working.

After dessert and some light-hearted family board games, Emelia stifled a yawn. "Robert, we need to go. We still have things to do at the Carters," she whispered.

"Do you have your overnight bag packed?"

"I do."

"You grab it, and I'll make our excuses."

She slipped down the hall. Robert had only ever ventured as far as the bathroom, and now, standing alone, he shoved his hands into his pockets. Henry and Peggy's stares felt like weights. He pulled one hand free and ran it through his hair.

"Emelia's tired, and we've got a few things to finish up before we go to bed," he said.

Before we go to bed. The room suddenly felt ten degrees warmer. His face burned. *Why did I say that?*

James clapped him on the back, startling him. "Relax. We all know you're sleeping with my sister."

He barked out a laugh.

Robert's face went from warm to scorching.

"James!" Emelia's voice rang out, sharp and furious. She stood with her hands on her hips. "Robert would never. I would never. Not until after we're married. How dare you joke about something so serious?"

James only laughed harder.

Emelia turned to their parents. "Please tell me you don't believe that."

Her father stood speechless, but her mother stepped beside her. "You forgot what a terrible jokester your brother is. He warned us he'd pull something like this if either of you gave him an opening. Robert didn't just open the door—he tore it off the hinges."

Emelia's pulse slowed, but her cheeks still burned. She glared at James. "I wish I hadn't insisted on having my wedding when you could attend. You're mean. Just plain mean. I forgot how cruel your jokes could be."

She reached for her overnight bag, but James caught her arm.

"Let go of me!" she snapped.

"Emelia, please." His voice softened. "I didn't mean any harm." He released her. "I love you. I know you and Robert aren't sleeping together, and so do all the parents here. I spend most of my time around army cadets. The talk sometimes gets vulgar. I only meant to embarrass you a little, not hurt you. I'm sorry."

"It mattered to me that you'd be here when I got married," she said quietly. "Show Robert and me some respect while you're here."

James turned to both sets of parents. "I'm sorry," he said.

Mark nodded. "At least you warned your parents and my wife and me before you said something like that." He looked to Peggy and Henry, then to Robert and Emelia. "You're both Christians. We trust you."

Emelia exhaled, relief softening her shoulders as the others nodded in agreement. Robert hugged his parents. "Please tell Solomon and the girls how much we appreciate everythin'."

Emelia followed with her own hugs while Robert said goodbye to her parents. Then he clapped James on the back.

"No harm done," he said, picking up Emelia's small red case.

She eyed her brother warily.

"Come on, Emelia. Forgive me?" James asked.

"Maybe tomorrow." She hugged him anyway.

Emelia stared out the passenger window as they drove to the Carters'. She didn't speak until Robert's hand gently came to rest on her arm.

"My love, are you okay?" he asked, eyes still on the road.

She nodded. "Yeah."

"They all trust us. Even James. And the Carters do too."

Who is he trying to convince? Everyone knew the only place to sleep at Robert's was in his bed. *God, please let the Carters offer one of us their couch. What am I supposed to do if they don't?*

Her prayer was silent, but when Robert parked in front of the house and turned toward her, it felt like he'd heard it. She shivered.

He opened her door and helped her from the car. He kissed the soft underside of her wrist before letting go. "Go on inside, my love. I'll grab your bag and be right behind you."

Inside, Emelia paused in what would soon be their living room, her eyes drawn to the finished kitchen. The white appliances gleamed, the porcelain sink shone, and the light oak cabinets looked even more beautiful than they had in the photos.

Robert entered, carrying her overnight bag in one arm and slipping the other around her waist. He kissed her temple.

"It's your kitchen—go on, explore it. I'm gonna drop this in our room and then join you."

She turned sharply. "Are we sleeping together tonight?"

"There's only one bed," he said gently. "I don't know of anywhere in the Bible that says sleepin' is a sin. And that's all we'll be doin'."

Her brows drew together. "So, James was right?"

Robert stepped back, hands raised. "In a way, yes. But our parents, the Carters, and even James trust us to honor our Christian values."

She didn't respond. Instead, she walked into the kitchen, opening cabinets and the refrigerator. She ran her hand across the glass-top stove, peeked into the oven, checked the dishwasher, and admired the chrome faucet. In the mudroom, she found the washer, dryer, and utility sink. They were all pristine.

When she turned back, Robert stood in the middle of the kitchen, hands in his pockets. She approached slowly, stopping just short of him.

"We're not married."

His gaze stayed on the floor. "I know. But I thought you trusted me to be a gentleman."

"I do."

"Then what's wrong?"

"I'm going to be your wife. If I didn't desire you, I wouldn't marry you. Please tell me you feel the same." Her voice trembled with vulnerability, and pink crept onto her cheeks.

"You know I desire you," he said. "Sometimes I pull back from our kisses because I want more than kissin'."

She swallowed. "What if we want more than sleep tonight? It would be too easy. We're human. You should take me home. No, I'll call my dad or James from the Carters' phone."

She turned toward the door, but Robert stepped in front of her.

"If you really want to go home, I'll take you. I can sleep on the Carters' couch, and you can have our bed. But I'd love for us to surprise my sisters with the vanity in the mornin'. I can't do that without you. Please stay."

Her hands trembled. She clasped them together, blinking back tears. After a few steady breaths, she looked up at him. "I'm scared."

He gently untangled her fingers and held her hands. “I’ll keep you safe. Today’s the twenty-fourth. The twenty-seventh is just two more nights. We can wait. We’re strong enough in our faith to do what’s right. And if we feel weak, we’ll pray together. Okay?”

She stepped into his arms, resting her head against his chest. “Did you know there’s food in our fridge and freezer? The cabinets, too. We have pots, dishes, and silverware. Everything.”

“I had no idea. Show me, then let’s get some sleep.”

Warm tingling ran through her as he traced her jawline and smoothed her hair. When he released her, she led him into the kitchen.

“You explore. I’m getting ready for bed.” She covered a yawn and slipped into the bedroom, closing the door behind her.

Chapter 17

A Jackson Christmas

Robert woke on his side with Emelia tucked close, her warmth pressed against him. His arms already held her, and for a quiet moment, he just breathed her in, content. When she stirred and turned toward him, her lashes fluttered, eyes still heavy with sleep.

"Kiss me," she whispered.

He rolled her gently onto her back and propped himself on one elbow, his pulse quickening as he lowered his mouth to hers. The kiss was slow, tender—too good. Her hands slid up his shoulders, pulling him closer, and the ache that followed told him it was time to stop. He drew back, breath unsteady, her gaze still fixed on his lips.

"I'm sorry, my love," he murmured. "I can't kiss you anymore this morning. I'm feeling the temptation you were worried about last night."

Emelia sighed softly. "I feel it too."

They slipped from beneath the sheets and straightened the covers, trading small smiles across the freshly made bed.

"Thank you for being a true gentleman," she said.

"We were both exhausted. I fell asleep the moment you curled into me." He grinned. "The next two nights might be long ones now that I know what it feels like to wake up with you in my arms. I'm gonna miss you somethin' fierce." His smile turned playful. "Merry Christmas, my love."

"Merry Christmas," she echoed, her grin matching his. "You shower first. I'll start coffee and toast us each a bagel."

"Thanks, Em. I'll be quick. I'll get the vanity ready to load while you shower."

As the water warmed around him, Robert pictured her in the kitchen. In her nightclothes, with slippered feet, she brewed coffee and prepared breakfast. The image filled him with warmth and longing. *God, I want to be her husband. Please let the next two days pass quickly.*

When he stepped into the kitchen, Emelia handed him a steaming cup of coffee, doctored just the way he liked it. The scent of cinnamon-raisin bagels filled the air. One popped up in the toaster; she grabbed it and spread it with cream cheese.

"My love," she said softly, "I'm so grateful you honor the Lord. Because of your commitment to Him, you love, honor, and protect me. Thank you for this glimpse of what our marriage will be. In two days, I'll be the happiest woman alive."

Her cheeks were pink, her eyes radiant. Robert took the bagel from her and set it on a napkin.

"I love you so much. I'll be the happiest man when I'm your husband." He pulled her into his arms and kissed the soft spot beneath her ear. As he released her, his hands slid down her arms.

"Em, you've got goosebumps."

"That's your fault." Her brown eyes darkened as her smile grew.

He grinned so wide his eyes smiled. "I'm not sorry."

She giggled. "I pray in fifty years your touch and kisses still give me goosebumps."

He took both her hands. "Me too, my love. Let's pray before breakfast."

He bowed his head. "Dear Lord, thank You for this special woman. Please bless our weddin' and our marriage. Thank You for this glimpse of what's to come. Bless this food and Em's hands that prepared it. Thank You for our families and this home. Forgive our sins as we forgive others. In Jesus' name, amen."

After breakfast, they cleaned up together. Emelia headed toward the bedroom to gather her things, but Robert caught her gently by the waist.

"Thank you for makin' this the best Christmas ever," he whispered.

She turned in his arms, eyes shining. "It is the best Christmas ever."

She slipped away and closed the bedroom door behind her.

While she showered, Robert wrapped the mirror and tucked it safely into the back seat of the truck. He worked quickly. By the time she stepped out of the bathroom, dressed and ready to help, he had the vanity and bench prepared to load.

"I've got the mirror secured," he said, admiring her for a moment before snapping back to task. "Grab your coat and help me load the vanity. I'll wrap it in the truck bed while you finish getting ready."

Together, they carried the vanity outside, careful with each step.

While Emelia went inside, Robert wrapped and secured it in place, satisfied that, if by chance, his sisters were awake, they couldn't tell what the truck held.

Half an hour later, everything was ready to go, and he stepped back inside. When his eyes landed on Emelia, he stopped in his tracks.

Her long hair fell in soft curls over her shoulders. Her makeup was subtle, her lips glistening just enough to tempt him. Her sweater and jeans highlighted her every curve. The way her gaze met his warmed him from the inside out.

"My love, you're beautiful."

"Thank you, my love."

He offered his hand, and she took it. Together, they stepped out of the house that would soon be their home. Proud to have her on his arm, he walked her to the truck's passenger door and helped her inside.

"I hope you're ready for Christmas with my family," he said, starting the engine.

She smiled, eyes bright. "Ready."

"Next stop, the Jackson home."

Fifteen minutes later, Robert backed the truck into his parents' open garage, where his dad and Solomon waited. Before he and Emelia had even stepped out, the garage door was closing, and the tailgate was down.

"You guys clearly don't need my help." Emelia smiled. "Is Betsy up?"

"Yes," his dad replied. "She's in the kitchen. I'm sure she'd love your help with the cinnamon rolls."

Emelia slipped inside, leaving the men to their task.

Solomon elbowed Robert, eyebrows raised. "So... how was your night?"

Robert groaned. "We SLEPT well. To answer your real question, there was no hanky panky."

Their dad chuckled. "I'm proud of you, son. Now let's get this work of art inside so your sisters see it first thing."

"Please," Robert said with a sigh of relief.

Together, they carried the vanity into the house and placed it beside the Christmas tree. Just as they finished, Emelia and his mom emerged from the kitchen.

His mom's mouth fell open. "You two did such a beautiful job restoring this."

"She did most of the work." Robert nodded toward Emelia. "I was busy with the house, so I mostly advised."

Emelia shook her head. "You did the hard stuff. You took it apart, reglued the joints, and made it sturdy. I just made it pretty."

"You, my dear, can do things Robert can't." His mom laughed. "You rolled and filled the cinnamon rolls, and they're rising now."

His dad called down the hall. "Lexi. Millie. It's Christmas morning, and the cinnamon rolls are rising! There's a surprise under the tree. If you don't want it, I'm sure your mom will claim it."

Lexi came first, dragging Millie behind her. Their eyes landed on the vanity, and they gasped in unison.

"You bought it," Lexi whispered. "You really bought it. I can't believe it."

Emelia pulled them both into a hug, beaming. "Merry Christmas, sisters. Robert and I wanted this to be special for you."

Millie hugged her tightly, then ran to Robert. “Thank you, Bubba.”

Lexi stood frozen, tears spilling down her cheeks.

“Lex, what’s wrong?” Emelia asked gently.

“I was so mean to you. I was jealous. I’m sorry,” Lexi hiccupped.

Emelia turned to Robert. He stepped beside her and wrapped Lexi in his arms.

“We didn’t mean to upset you, sis,” he said softly.

Lexi buried her face in his chest, sobbing. “I was mad you didn’t notice how much Millie and I loved the vanity. I’m ashamed. You did notice. You bought it and made it beautiful.”

Robert sank to the floor with her still in his arms. “Emelia did most of the work. She made it beautiful. We both love you, Lex. You’ll always be our sister.”

Lexi’s tears slowed, her breathing steadied. She looked up. “I know that now. And if I ever forget, I’ll look at this and remember. I love you both.”

Robert took the tissues his mom offered and passed the box to Lexi. She dried her eyes and blew her nose.

Solomon sat beside them, coaxing Millie to his lap. Their mother smiled. “Since you’re all on the floor, are you ready for your stockings before my three girls and I finish breakfast?”

“Yes!” they all shouted. Robert and Solomon added fist pumps for good measure.

“I love Christmas mornin’ when all five of my kids are ready for gifts.” His dad handed out stockings, starting with Millie.

Each child received theirs in age order. When Solomon finished emptying his, Robert reached for the next one, but his dad shook his head.

“You’re still the oldest, Robert. This one’s for Emelia.”

Robert’s hand dropped to his lap. Emelia gasped. “Thank you. I didn’t expect...”

“You didn’t expect us to treat you like family,” his dad said warmly. “In two days, you’ll carry our family name. You’re our child as much as Robert, Solomon, Lexi, and Millie. We welcome you with open arms.”

Robert wrapped an arm around her shoulders and squeezed her. "Come on, Em. Open it. I want my stockin'."

Laughing, Emelia carefully pulled out each item. In the toe, she found a treasure, a silver brooch with pale blue stones. She looked up at Betsy in surprise.

"I hope that can be your 'something blue,'" Betsy said, her eyes misting. "My mother pinned it to a ribbon and tied it around my bouquet."

Emelia's fingers trembled as she held the brooch. A tear slipped down her cheek. "I'd be honored if you'd do that for me."

"I'd be honored to do it," Betsy whispered, blinking rapidly.

Solomon shook his head. "Wow. What a sappy Christmas."

"Solomon, hush!" Millie scolded.

Everyone laughed, and Robert finally got his stocking. "She gets Grandma's brooch, and I get Legos, kitchen gadgets, and socks. I guess I know who Mom loves most."

Betsy laughed. "I guess you do. Come on, girls. Let's check the rolls. We'll unwrap presents after breakfast."

The rolls were perfectly risen, soft and puffy. Emelia watched Betsy pull a small pitcher of cream from the refrigerator.

"Pour this over the top before they go in the oven."

Emelia nodded, careful not to spill the cream as she drizzled it over each roll. The scent of yeast and cinnamon already lingered in the air, and her chest swelled with satisfaction. Betsy opened the oven, and Emelia slid them inside, letting the moment settle deep inside her.

While the rolls baked, she helped pare fruit, the sweet juice slicking her fingers. Bacon crackled in the skillet, and sausage browned beside it. The kitchen buzzed with motion and warmth. Lexi and Millie joined in when the timer neared its end, scrambling eggs with practiced rhythm.

Then the ding. Emelia turned toward the oven, heart fluttering.

Betsy opened the door and smiled. "Emelia, these are beautiful. You did a wonderful job."

Heat rushed to Emelia's cheeks. She hadn't expected praise, but it felt like a hug.

Millie reached into the fridge and pulled out the frosting. "Momma, they smell so good. Can I help Emelia frost them?"

"Of course." Betsy stepped back.

Millie's fingers trembled just a little, so Emelia held Millie's hand steady while they spread the frosting together. Before they were finished, much of the frosting had melted into the swirls of the warm rolls.

Then Betsy called out, her voice bright and clear. "The cinnamon rolls are out of the oven!"

Emelia barely had time to step back before three Jackson men appeared, grinning like boys. Their smiles landed on the rolls, then on her. In that moment, Emelia felt like she belonged inside this family.

After a late breakfast, gifts, and rounds of Uno and Jenga sandwiched between snacks and his mom's Christmas brisket for dinner, Robert noticed Emelia stifling a yawn. He rubbed her back gently, leaning close enough for his breath to brush her ear.

"Think you can handle one more surprise today?" he whispered.

She smiled, soft and radiant. It made his heart ache in the best way. "I can for you, my love."

He scanned the room, then stood. "Guys, Emelia's tired. I think it's time we head out."

His parents nodded. "Merry Christmas." Lexi and Millie echoed the wish.

After slipping on his jacket, Robert helped Emelia with hers.

"Thank you," she said quietly.

He opened the front door. "Merry Christmas."

She paused, blinking back tears. "Thank you for making me feel like a real Jackson. Merry Christmas."

Hand in hand, they walked to the car. Robert opened her door and helped her in, then circled to the driver's side. As he drove, Emelia turned toward him.

"So where exactly is this last Christmas surprise?"

"It's at our house."

"Our house? Why not last night or this morning?"

He smiled. "It came with instructions. I promised my grandmother to give it to my intended two nights before our weddin', during a private moment."

She tilted her head. "You made a promise before we were even a couple?"

"I did. Trust me, Em. You'll understand soon."

She studied him for a moment, then nodded. "Okay."

At the house, Robert opened her door and helped her out. Her fingers slipped into his, and he felt her tension ease as they walked inside. He kissed her gently, then led her to the bedroom.

"Please sit, my love."

She perched on the edge of the bed, eyes steady on him. Robert knelt at the dresser, reaching deep into the bottom drawer. When he stood again, he held a worn, slender, white hinged box.

"My grandmother gave me this," Robert said, his voice low and reverent. "I don't know if it began as an engagement gift. It was first given to my great-great-grandmother, Navina Spencer, two nights before her weddin' by her intended, Alistair Jackson. She wore it on her weddin' day."

He smiled and kissed her temple. "It was later passed to my grandfather, Navina's oldest grandson, who gave it to my grandmother, Rose, in the same way. She wore it on her weddin' day. Before she passed, Grandma Rose gave it to me, her oldest grandson."

He looked into Emelia's eyes, then placed the weathered box in her hands.

"Tonight is two nights before we marry, and this is our private moment." When Emelia hesitated, he said, "It's okay. It belongs to you now. Please open it."

The hinges creaked as she lifted the lid. Her breath caught. Nestled in worn satin lay an oval emerald surrounded by diamonds, suspended on a gold chain.

"This is mine?" she whispered.

Robert knelt before her. "Yes. Please wear it on our weddin' day. It can be your something old."

Tears spilled as she traced the jewel with her fingers. "I'm honored. Will you put it on me?"

He kissed her cheeks, then fastened the necklace around her neck with care. She stood before the mirror, and he joined her, both gazing at the heirloom resting against her skin.

The sound of the front door opening broke the moment. Robert kissed her hair and went to see who had come in. He returned with Jerry close behind.

"Emelia, your dad's on the phone. He's upset and wants to speak with both of you."

Robert's stomach tightened. "Did he say why?"

Jerry shook his head. "He said it's urgent."

Emelia frowned. "Please tell him we'll be in shortly. I need Robert to help me take off this necklace and put it away."

Robert's hands moved gently beneath her hair, unfastening the clasp. He laid the necklace back on its satin bed, with gentle, respectful hands giving it the honor this treasure deserved.

Jerry's eyes widened. "That's a beautiful piece. Must've cost a fortune."

Robert shrugged. "I don't know. It's been in my family for five generations. It's Emelia's now, until it's time for her to pass it on."

Jerry nodded. "Sorry to interrupt. I'll let your dad know you'll be in soon."

When he left, Emelia ran her fingers across the chain and stones. "You've never called me your intended before."

Robert smiled. "It's what my grandmother always said. When I think of her, you're not my fiancée. You're my intended. I wish you could've met her."

He closed the box. "Go slip it into your purse in the car. I'll talk to your dad."

"No," Emelia said firmly. "He wants to speak to both of us. I'll put the necklace away, and we'll go together."

Admiring her resolve, he followed her to the car and then to the Carters' door. Robert and Emelia stepped into the Carters' home to find Jerry speaking into the phone in a low, calming tone. He turned as they entered.

"Henry, they're here now," he said, then covered the receiver. "Listen to him. Don't argue. Just tell him you're on your way home. It's in your best interest not to challenge his assumptions right now."

Robert took the handset and held it between them.

"We're here, Dad," Emelia said.

"Robert, bring my daughter home."

"We'll head your way as soon as we hang up."

"Good. We have a lot to discuss when you arrive. Goodbye."

They heard a loud thud, then nothing. Robert set the handset in its cradle.

Emelia blinked. "Wow. He's mad. I've never heard him slam the receiver like that. I'm not sure I want to go home."

Robert's brow furrowed. "Do you have any idea what we did to set him off?"

She shook her head. "None."

"Do you think your mom's upset too?"

"I don't know," she said quietly.

Robert led her into the living room, heart heavy. "Did Henry say what he's angry about?" he asked, voice tight.

Jerry and Sue exchanged uneasy glances.

"I'd rather not say," Jerry replied.

Emelia stepped forward. "Robert and I haven't done anything wrong. I need to know what I'm walking into. What did my dad say?"

Jerry hesitated, then looked at Sue before answering. "He thinks the two of you have been fornicating for months. I told him Sue and I have not seen any evidence of that."

Robert's jaw tightened. "We haven't. We both know intimacy belongs inside marriage. We would never dishonor God like that."

Jerry nodded slowly. “I told him the same, that he raised a Christian daughter who honors the Lord. But he wouldn’t hear it. Something’s turned in his mind. You need to go to him. Don’t react to his anger. Listen first. This is a misunderstanding. Help him through it. He’s a good man.”

Robert looked at Emelia. Her shoulders had relaxed, her eyes clearer.

“He is a good man,” she said. “Let’s go, Robert.”

Sue stepped forward. “I hope you know Jerry and I love you.”

“We do,” Robert said. “And we love you, too.”

Outside, Emelia led the way to the car. Robert kissed her gently, then helped her into the passenger seat.

As he started the engine, he prayed silently for peace, for truth, and for the grace to meet Henry’s anger with love.

Chapter 18

Emelia's Father

Robert parked in front of her house. Emelia sat beside him, wringing her hands in her lap with her gaze fixed on the front door. It was still her home, for tonight and one more, yet it no longer felt like a refuge.

He stepped out and came around to open her door. She couldn't move. His hand covered hers, stilling them.

He gently took her hand in his. "Em, we have to go inside and at least hear him out."

She leaned into his soft tug and let him help her out. As they walked the path, she stayed slightly behind him, her body tight with dread. At the porch steps, she drew a steadying breath and moved beside him. He shifted her hand to his other and rubbed her back.

"My love, God knows we've done nothin' wrong. We're right with Him. With God, we can face anythin'."

The door flew open. Her father stood there, face flushed. "Every date includes a trip to Robert's! This has been going on since September. Emelia, get in this house."

She froze. His tone was unlike anything she'd ever heard from him. Hearing Jerry's account was one thing, but hearing the implied accusation in her father's voice firsthand was another. Her breath caught. She couldn't move.

Robert's arm came around her, steady and strong.

"Em, we said we'd listen. But if you don't want to, we can leave."

Her father lunged forward and grabbed her arm. Pain shot through it, and she shrieked.

"Emelia, you are not going anywhere," he snapped.

"You're hurting me!" she cried.

Robert stepped between them, shielding her. James appeared behind their father and caught his wrist.

"Dad, I'm trained. I can make you let go, but I'd rather you do it willingly."

Her father exhaled sharply and released her. His shoulders sagged. Both men started to speak, but Robert quickly deferred.

"Dad," James said, his voice steady, "I've never seen you this angry. You're not a violent man. We all..." He glanced from Emelia to Robert. "...need to sit down and talk this through."

"Henry, James is right," her mother said, stepping forward. "Kids, come in and sit. I'll take Henry to the kitchen and fix something for us to eat."

Her mother took her father's hand and led him away. James motioned to the couch, and Robert guided Emelia inside. She sat close, trembling, struggling to steady her breath. Robert's arm stayed around her as James took a seat across from them.

"I'm sorry," James said, looking down. "I think this is my fault. When I joked about you two sleeping together, I planted a seed in Dad's mind."

He looked up, and she recognized the regret written on his face. "Emelia, he found your birth control pills. He said he trusted you both to behave like Christians last night, but he didn't. Then tonight he called Robert's parents and learned you'd gone to Robert's house. That's when he lost it. He believes you lost your virginity not long after you started dating."

Tears blurred her vision. Robert's arm tightened around her, grounding her.

"Your sister and I have not been intimate," he said firmly. "We've chosen to wait until marriage. God knows the truth. Emelia is a virgin. If your dad won't hear it, that's his choice. But we won't lie to please him."

He brushed her hair from her face. “Are you okay, my love?”

She met his eyes and drew a slow, steady breath. “I’m okay.”

“I’ll do everything I can to protect you. Do you want to stay?”

She nodded against his shoulder, then sat up. “I want to tell Dad everything, including the doctor visit and why I’m on the pills. Mom already knows because she was there.”

She wiped her cheeks. “We never meant to hide anything. I didn’t think we had. Dad can choose to believe us or not. But Robert spoke the truth. Our physical relationship is limited to hugging and kissing. It will stay that way until we’re married.”

James raised his hands. “I believe you. I never thought otherwise. I’m sorry for my part in this.”

Emelia looked down. “If Dad won’t believe us, I don’t want him to walk me down the aisle. James, if he holds onto this, will you escort me instead?”

James nodded. “Yes. If that’s what you want.”

He stood. “I’ll check on Mom and Dad.”

Once he was gone, Emelia leaned into Robert again. “How did things get this bad with my dad? I don’t want to lose him.”

Robert held her close, his cheek against her hair. “I don’t know. Maybe I shouldn’t have taken you to our house last night. I thought your dad and I had bonded while workin’ side by side on the house. I had no idea this was brewin’ inside him.”

She lifted her head, her heart heavy.

He tucked a strand of hair behind her ear. “You are your dad’s little girl. Could this be about his fear of losin’ you? Does he see me as takin’ you away from him?”

Her father’s voice cut through the room as he entered and sat across from them. “You’ve already taken Emelia.”

Her pulse jumped. “In a way, you’re right. Isn’t that what Genesis 2:24 says? ‘Therefore a man shall leave his father and his mother and be joined to his wife, and they shall become one flesh.’ But that doesn’t mean you stop being my dad. Robert and I will always need you and Mom.”

Her throat tightened as she glanced between her parents. Robert squeezed her hand. When her father’s mouth opened, she rushed to continue.

"You raised me to know the difference between sin and righteousness. You must know in your heart that Robert and I will *not* become one until after you present me to him on our wedding day."

Her father leaned forward, eyes hard. "Here's what I've seen. In August, he showed up anxious and agitated. You said everything was fine, and he gave me an itinerary that sounded innocent. That night, you denied anything beyond holding hands. But once Robert moved into the Carters' place, you started spending time there mostly alone."

His gaze shifted to Robert. "I tried to be okay with it. The Carters are good people. They wouldn't tolerate fornication if they knew it was happening. But his house only has a bedroom set, and I've heard both of you call it 'our bedroom.'"

He turned back to her. "You started kissing around the time you got engaged. I found your birth control pills, something neither you nor your mother mentioned. You've been on them for nearly two months. Why start that far ahead of your wedding if there's no physical intimacy?"

He looked at James. "You said you knew they were sleeping together last night. Then you brushed it off as crude military talk and teasing."

Then to her again: "Here's what logic tells me. He showed up in August because you were late, and he feared you were pregnant. After that scare, you abstained until you had a bedroom and time alone. This time, you were smart. Hence, the pills. I shouldn't have agreed to last night, but tonight was a bridge too far. My daughter shouldn't marry a man who's led her into immorality."

He shook his head, pinched the bridge of his nose, then glared at Robert. "I won't stop the wedding. But Emelia, you will stay home and only see him at the church building until then. After what you've done, you deserve the dignity of marriage even if it's to the likes of him."

Emelia's chest constricted. Her hand trembled in Robert's. "With Him, we can do all things," she whispered.

Robert drew a slow breath and met her father's glare. "Henry, your theory is well-constructed. I understand how you arrived at it. But it's completely false."

Her father laughed, short and bitter.

Robert didn't flinch. "Back in August, my parents were pressurin' me to go to college. My dad said I needed a degree before I'd have anythin' worth offerin' Emelia. I didn't want to make a mistake that would cost me the only girl I've ever loved. I needed to talk things through with her. That night, we started makin' plans. I told her I wouldn't kiss her until I was sure I loved her and was ready to ask her to spend her life with me. We were only holdin' hands then. Hand-holdin' has never caused pregnancy."

Before he could continue, Emelia spoke. "It's important to us that I finish my business degree before we start a family. So, we needed a form of birth control that would work for us after we're married. I went to the doctor with Mom and Robert. I wanted Mom's experience and Robert's support. The doctor said I should start the pills at least a month before the wedding, but starting sooner wouldn't hurt. I felt comfortable with that, and I started the next day."

Her father shrugged. "So, you could prevent pregnancy before marriage."

Her mouth fell open. Robert stood. "Henry, there's no way we can prove to you that we are not sexually active. Your daughter is a virgin. God knows I'm speakin' the truth. We have nothin' to be ashamed of, and no reason to repent."

Emelia rose beside him, voice trembling but sure. "I love my family. I love you, Dad. But this is how it is. Robert and I will not consummate our relationship until after we're married. I won't stay in a house where my father thinks I should wear a scarlet letter."

She turned to Robert and James. "My things are packed except for what I need for the next two days. Will you please load everything into the cars?"

"Emelia, you're staying here," her father growled.

Before Robert could move, James stepped between them and guided his father down the hall. Their mother followed, silent and shaken.

Emelia's shoulders sagged. "I'm thankful Dad didn't resist James," she whispered.

She led Robert to her room and pointed to the boxes. He carried them out one by one while she packed the last of her things. When James returned, he helped. When Robert left with the final box, James pulled her into a hug. Her tears came fast.

"I'm sorry, sis. Please forgive me."

"There's nothing to forgive," she said, though a sob broke through.

She wiped her eyes and turned to her closet, retrieving the one thing Robert couldn't see—the bag that held her wedding dress and accessories. She handed it to James.

"This goes in my car, out of sight."

He nodded and left with the dress. Emelia stepped outside to retrieve her purse from Robert's car. James met them there.

"Emelia, are you okay to drive?"

"I'll be okay," she said, surprised by the steadiness in her own voice. Then her chin dropped. "Because I fell in love, I've lost my dad. I should be so happy. It's Christmas, and my wedding is in two days. I've done nothing wrong, and yet I feel broken. I don't understand."

Robert and James wrapped her in their arms. James prayed.

"Dear Lord, please help Dad see the truth. Mom knows it, and deep down, Dad does too. Give Mom wisdom to guide him through this. Thank You for teaching me to guard my tongue and recognize the damage careless words can do. Please forgive me for the hurt I've caused my sister, my dad, and our family."

Emelia squeezed his hand as he continued.

"Give Robert and Emelia strength to endure this storm. Bless their relationship and their marriage. Please, Lord, help Dad find humility and offer the apology they deserve."

Silence settled around them, sacred and still. Then James cleared his throat.

"It's part of Emelia's dream to be walked down the aisle by her father. I'll do it if I must, but please don't let Satan take that piece of her dream away. Give her our father back. Forgive us our sins and help us forgive as You forgive us. Tonight, the second part is really tough. Please give us peace and understanding to follow Your example. In Your Son's precious name, amen."

Chapter 19

After the Storm

Robert carried Emelia's overnight bag into his parents' home. The sound of the door drew his mother from the kitchen with a dishtowel draped over her shoulder. She stopped mid-step when she saw them, her eyes widening and the lines around them deepening.

"Mark," she called down the hallway, "Robert and Emelia are here."

Her gaze flicked between them, a frown settling in. "Emelia, your dad called, looking for you. He wants you to come home." She stepped closer. "What happened? You two look... crushed."

Robert let out a strained laugh. "Yeah. Crushed is about right."

He guided Emelia to the sofa, but when they sat, she slipped from his arm and moved to the far end. His heart sank.

"Em?" he asked softly.

His father appeared beside his mother, taking in their faces. "What's wrong?"

Emelia's eyes dropped to her lap. Her voice trembled. "Robert, just tell them about my dad's accusations."

Robert met his parents' eyes, steady and unflinching. "Emelia and I haven't done what her dad is convinced we've done."

"What does he believe?" his dad asked.

Robert sighed. “The short version is he thinks we’ve been sleeping together for months.”

His mother looked at Emelia, then back to him. “And the long version?”

Robert turned to Emelia. “Are you sure you want me to tell them everything?”

Her face flushed, her hands twisting in her lap. “Yes. They should know.”

Robert nodded. “Do you remember that day in August when I left because you were pressurin’ me to go to college?”

They both nodded.

“Her dad thinks my anxiety that day was because Emelia might’ve been pregnant. At that point, we were only holding hands. He believes we abstained after that scare until I moved into the Carters’ place and had a bed and privacy.”

He glanced at Emelia and reached out, but she didn’t take his hand. “Do you want me to keep going?”

She nodded without looking up.

“Emelia, her mom, and I went to the doctor together. We decided not to start a family until after she finishes college. The doctor recommended starting birth control pills at least a month before the wedding. Emelia felt comfortable starting sooner, so she did. Her dad found the pills and assumed they were to prevent pregnancy before marriage.”

Robert shook his head. “He’s convinced we were intimate last night and tonight. He said, ‘My daughter shouldn’t be marrying a man who’s taken her down a path to immorality. But I won’t stand in your way. After what you’ve done, she deserves the dignity of marriage even if it’s to the likes of you.’”

His voice softened. “We promised each other we’d wait for physical intimacy until after marriage, and we’ve kept that promise.”

His parents shook their heads, their faces drawn with the same ache he felt in his chest. He reached for Emelia again, but she didn’t respond.

His mother stepped forward, her voice gentle. “My dear, you’ve done nothing wrong. Mark and I believe you. We trust you.”

His mom turned to his dad. "I'll go make up the guest room for Emelia. Robert can sleep in his old bed tonight. Mark, please get her bag and help me."

His dad nodded, then paused at the doorway. "I'll move my truck out of the garage and pull Emelia's car inside. There's no need for her car to sit out overnight."

His mom gave a soft smile. "Good thinking."

Emelia handed his dad her keys when he passed back through the living room. "Thank you."

With his parents gone, Robert slid across the couch toward Emelia. He started to wrap his arms around her, but she gently stopped him.

"My love, what have I done wrong?" His voice quavered. "I love you."

A tear slipped down Emelia's cheek. "You haven't done anything wrong. I just feel… overwhelmed. I know your touch won't hurt me, but right now, it feels like it might. I can't even tell you why. I need space. Time. Please, just for tonight, keep your distance."

Robert pulled back, his heart aching. "I will. But this is hard, Em. It feels like I'm losin' you. I need you."

She wiped another tear from her face. "I'm sorry."

He stood, hesitated, then turned back before heading down the hallway. "Do you still love me?"

Emelia met his gaze and nodded. "Yes."

He drew in a shaky breath. "Are we still gettin' married?"

She looked away, tears streaking her cheeks, and didn't answer. He turned and went to his old room.

Robert sat on the edge of the bed, elbows on his knees, head in his hands. Solomon sat up in his bed.

"Whoa, bro. What's wrong?"

Robert looked up. "She wouldn't let me touch her. Said she loves me, but when I asked if we're still getting' married, she looked away. She didn't say no, but it felt worse. Like I've already lost her."

Solomon moved beside him, offering a box of tissues. "She said she loves you. That's something. At the risk of sounding like Mom, give it to the Lord tonight and see what morning brings."

Robert took the tissues. Pulling out several, he mopped his face and blew his nose. “You do sound like Mom. But I don’t have any other choice.”

He peeled off his clothes, realizing he hadn’t brought anything to sleep in. He grabbed a pair of Solomon’s athletic shorts and a T-shirt. “Hope you don’t mind.”

Solomon nodded and settled back into bed. “You okay for now?”

Robert shrugged. “As okay as I can be. I’ll take your, or rather, Mom’s advice: ‘Give it to God and wait for mornin’. Pray for us, brother. I need Emelia. I love her completely. I can’t lose her.”

He climbed into bed and reached for more tissues.

God, I need these blasted tears to stop. I need Emelia more than I need air. She’s part of me. Please don’t take her from me. All I want is to comfort her, and for her to comfort me. Please let this be better in the mornin’.

He sighed, his heart heavy.

Forgive me, Lord, for bein’ angry with her father. I know I shouldn’t blame him, but I do. Forgive me for not seein’ how things might look, even though we did nothin’ wrong. A husband is supposed to protect his wife, and I’ve already failed her. Please help her forgive me. Yours is the kingdom, power, and glory forever. In Jesus’ name, amen.

He sank into the pillow, eyes finally dry, praying sleep would come.

“Where is Robert?” Betsy asked, her brows drawn.

Emelia met her gaze. “He went on to bed,” she said quietly.

“Oh, honey, are you alright?” Betsy stepped forward, arms open.

Emelia raised a hand to stop her. “Everything’s too much right now—touch, conversation, everything. I feel overwhelmed. I need some time alone.”

Betsy nodded gently. “Your room’s ready. Your bag’s on the end of the bed. If you need me, just say so. If you need Robert, you have our permission to get him. But if he’s with you, the bedroom door stays open. Mark and I will say a prayer for you. Don’t forget to say your prayers.”

With that, Betsy disappeared down the hall. A door clicked shut.

Emelia remained curled in the corner of the sofa, legs tucked beneath her, head resting against the cushion. She closed her eyes and drifted off. When she woke, the house was dark except for the faint light spilling from the guest room.

She stretched, stood, then moved toward the hallway. Before she reached it, Robert stepped into the living room, rubbing his eyes.

Her movement stalled.

His hands dropped to his sides. "Em, please. Can we talk?"

She nodded and stepped toward him. "I'm better. Will you hold me?"

He opened his arms, and she melted into them. They stood in silence, wrapped in each other's arms, until Robert gently pulled back.

"Let's sit in the kitchen."

His hazel eyes looked dull, more green than gold, and full of pain. She hated seeing it.

She followed him to the table. He filled the kettle, set it on the stove, and pulled down a box of jasmine tea, her favorite. Placing two mugs and a jar of honey on the table, he joined her there. Her heart sank when he spoke.

"I know you don't want to get married. At least not now. But I still love you."

Her breath caught, and tears welled. "I love you, too."

He blinked, then reached across the table and covered her hand with his. "I still want to marry you. Will you ever consider marryin' me?"

She grabbed a napkin, dabbed at her tears, and steadied her breath. "I can't get through this without you. I want to marry you. I don't want to change anything, my love."

Her voice quavered, but her words were clear.

The kettle whistled. Robert quickly lifted it off the burner before the sound could carry. He poured hot water into both mugs, handed her a tea bag, then added one to his cup. She stirred in honey and passed him the jar.

"Em," he said softly, "Why did you look away last night when I asked if we were still gettin' married?"

She reached for her tea bag, but her hand shook too much to grasp it. Folding her hands together, she whispered, "I don't know. I just couldn't."

Robert slid his palms across the table, open and waiting. Emelia met his eyes, then placed her trembling hands in his.

"Are we still gettin' married the day after tomorrow?"

She searched his face, every line, every shadow. She didn't know what she was looking for—only that she needed to see him.

"Yes," she whispered, just as his mouth and eyes began to sag. "I want you to be my husband. And I want to be your wife."

Her smile broke through, the first since Jerry had entered their home.

Robert moved to the chair beside her. "My love, I need to kiss you. May I?"

She leaned toward him. "Yes."

Their lips met, and she relaxed against him. Peace spread through her chest, quiet and sure. She resolved to cleave to Robert and stop letting her father's false beliefs define her feelings. She couldn't change him. Only God could.

When Robert pulled away, she drew him back. Kissing him felt like a lifeline—something that steadied what grief and tears could not.

When they parted, they drank their tea in companionable silence. They left the mugs and kettle where they sat, too drained to clean up. Robert walked her to the guest room door and softly kissed her goodnight.

She stepped inside, closed the door, and dressed for bed. Crawling beneath the covers, she whispered, "Thank You, Lord," and closed her eyes.

Chapter 20

One More Day

The next thing she knew, gentle knocking sounded on the door. Betsy's voice came through it. "Emelia, it's time to get ready to meet your mom and bridesmaids for breakfast."

Going to breakfast with a crowd of women who would see straight through any mask she tried to wear was the last thing Emelia wanted after the confrontation with her father and a night with little sleep. But she'd told Robert she wanted to go through with the wedding, and she meant it.

"Betsy," she called through the door, "I'll get dressed and be out as soon as I can."

"We don't have to leave for another forty-five minutes," Betsy replied gently. "May I come in and talk for a moment?"

Emelia's stomach twisted. She wasn't sure her nerves could take another surprise. *Please, Lord, no more bad news.* She crossed the room and opened the door for Betsy.

"Your stress is written in the tightness of your face," Betsy said softly.

She drew Emelia into her arms, rubbing slow, reassuring circles along her back.

"My dear girl," she murmured, "I spoke to your mother this morning. I assured her you're safe here with us. She told me she spoke with your father and made it clear there's no truth to his accusations."

Emelia lifted her head. "Do you think he'll apologize?"

"I don't know," Betsy said. "But your mother and I agree, he won't be allowed near you unless we believe he's truly contrite. You won't face any more of his baseless accusations."

The tension in her shoulders eased. "Did Mom say anything about James? If Dad won't walk me down the aisle, I'll need James to present me to Robert."

"She said James is firmly on your side, and he's told your father as much."

Emelia exhaled and leaned into Betsy's embrace. After a quiet moment, she lifted her head again. "I'd better get ready, or we'll be late for breakfast and the spa."

Betsy nodded and released her. "We'll see you in a little while." She stepped out and gently closed the door behind her.

The Jackson men had two tasks that day: move Emelia's belongings to Robert's home on the Carter farm and deliver the wedding décor to the church. Mark volunteered to start in the garage, removing the boxes from Emelia's car.

When he opened her car door, a dress bag lay discreetly among the boxes in the back seat. Curious but cautious, he unzipped it just enough to confirm what he suspected. It was Emelia's wedding dress.

He didn't understand the superstition, but he knew better than to let Robert lay eyes on it. The women would have his hide. With Robert busy unloading his car, Mark quietly slipped the dress bag into the guest room closet.

He felt like he was invading Emelia's privacy, but he couldn't risk sending anything wedding-related to Robert's house by mistake. So, he checked each box as he pulled it from the car, setting aside anything that looked remotely bridal and tucking it into the closet with the dress.

Once Emelia's car was empty and only the safe-to-move boxes remained in the garage, Mark opened the garage door. His boys had already loaded Emelia's things from Robert's car into the truck. He asked them to add the remaining boxes from the garage to the bed of his vehicle, confident now that nothing bridal would be moved to Robert's.

Since Robert didn't know where Emelia wanted her things, they stacked her boxes in the room that would eventually become the spare bedroom, where his sisters' vanity had stood just yesterday. With the last box set down, Robert reached for the light switch, his shoulders sagging under the weight of what had spoiled an otherwise perfect Christmas.

He sighed, then bowed his head. *Thank You, Lord,* he prayed silently. *She still wants to marry me.*

After his prayer, he turned off the light and climbed into the truck with his dad and brother. They headed back to the house to load the wedding décor from the garage and take it to the church. Once all the boxes labeled *wedding* were in the truck, Robert's breath caught. His chest tightened, and his heart pounded like a drum. *Panic attack?*

Gripping the side of the truck to steady himself, he forced the words out. "I was supposed to get the weddin' stuff from Emelia's house and take it to the church. How's that gonna happen? I'm sure I'm not welcome there."

He worked to slow his breathing. "I think I need to eat."

His father stepped beside him, wrapping an arm around his shoulders. "Don't worry about the Nortons. James will bring everything there to the church. I should've told you earlier. Let's stop at the diner and get some pancakes."

Robert leaned into his dad, letting the comfort settle his nerves. When his heart finally slowed, he climbed into the truck and rested his head against the seat.

As they pulled into the diner's parking lot, he whispered, "Why did Henry have to make this so hard?"

His dad and brother exchanged a glance, but neither answered.

She stood in awe as she entered the decorated Auditorium. The arch, wrapped in pine boughs and twinkling lights, stood proudly, poinsettias blooming at its base. Along the aisle, each pew bore either a pine wreath with a red satin bow or a poinsettia wreath with a green one. It was everything she'd hoped for—festive and beautiful.

In the Fellowship Hall, faux pine garland laced with white lights traced the room's perimeter. Each table wore a crisp white cloth, and at the center of each sat a silver tray with a candle surrounded by red and green Christmas balls. At each place rested a red or green votive candle, etched with their wedding date and a name card.

Relief settled over Emelia. The day had unfolded without a hitch. Even the wedding rehearsal went smoothly, despite her father's absence.

Emelia leaned against Robert, her body heavy with exhaustion. She hadn't done much physical labor, but the weight of her father's accusations and his absence had drained her. Robert stepped in, offering their excuses and leaving the rest of the family to finish. She was grateful.

He walked her to his car, his arm steady around her waist. When he opened the door and helped her in, she murmured, "Thank you for helping me call it quits for tonight."

"My love, you're dead on your feet," he said, pressing a kiss to her temple. "You've got to rest tonight, or you'll be too tired to enjoy our weddin'. Let's get you to my folks' so you can sleep."

At his parents' front door, Emelia kissed him goodnight. She didn't want to stop. The longer she kissed him, the longer he'd stay. With him, she felt safe, cherished. After everything that had happened, letting him leave was harder than ever.

When he finally pulled away, he kissed her temple, then her neck, and whispered, "Good night, my love" into her ear.

She watched him leave, then closed and locked the door behind him. In the quiet of the guest room, she readied for bed, then sank to her knees beside it.

"Dear Lord," she said, "I need Your help. I've always been my daddy's little girl. Please forgive Robert and me for anything that looked wrong. You know our hearts. You know we've honored You in our relationship. But my dad saw something different, something that hurt him. And our actions, innocent as they were, caused him pain."

Her voice trembled. "Please help him see us clearly. Help him trust the truth of our words and the integrity of our choices. I want my dad back, the one who loves me and believes in me. Before last night, he had never raised his voice or laid a hand on me. But last night, he did both."

She wiped her cheeks and drew a shaky breath. "Please help him repent and find his way back to You. Help me forgive him. I wish I didn't need to hear him say he still believes in me, but I do. I need to hear it. Please give him the strength to make this right. I need my dad. I need my family. And if it's Your will, Lord, I would love for him to walk me down the aisle tomorrow."

She exhaled slowly, her heart laid bare before Him. "I'm giving all of this to You, Lord. Not my will, but Yours be done. In Jesus' name, amen."

With her prayer spoken, she climbed into bed and drifted into dreams where everything was as it should be.

Robert stepped into the house that tomorrow would become his first home with Emelia as his wife. In the bedroom, he dropped his keys on the dresser and emptied his pockets, the weight of the day pressing heavily on his shoulders.

While he readied for bed, her father's accusations echoed in his mind. *How do I forgive Henry for Emelia's pain for the loss she feels, for the dreams he's shattered? How do I do any of that, Lord?*

He sat on the edge of the bed and reached for his Bible. Thumbing through its pages, his eyes landed on Luke 6:27-29. He read aloud, voice low and steady:

"But I say to you who hear: Love your enemies, do good to those who hate you, bless those who curse you, and pray for those who spitefully use you. To him who strikes you on the one cheek, offer the other also. And from him who takes away your cloak, do not withhold your tunic either."

Henry wasn't his enemy. At least, Robert hoped he wasn't. But tonight, it felt close. Still, the words pierced his heart. If he was going to marry Emelia tomorrow, he had to find a way to love the man who had wounded her so deeply.

He knelt beside the bed.

"God, You already know the pain Henry's caused. I'm still wrestlin' with anger, and I need Your forgiveness for that. Please quiet my fear of him. Help me be the man Emelia needs, the man who can walk with her through this rift in her family."

His voice softened. "More than anythin', Lord, let Henry see the truth. Forgive him for the assumptions he made. Help us forgive him. Emelia needs an apology, but I'm willin' to forgive him even if it never comes. Please let him show up for her tomorrow. Let him make things right."

Robert bowed his head to the mattress, words spent, heart aching.

"Holy Spirit," he whispered, "I know You understand even my grunts and groans. Please hear what I can't say. In Jesus' name, amen."

He climbed into bed and closed his eyes. Peaceful at last, he slept.

Chapter 21

Forgiveness and Dreams

Emelia, along with Robert's mother and sisters, left for the church at noon. Though the ceremony wouldn't begin until evening, she wanted time to inspect the décor in both the Auditorium and the Fellowship Hall one last time before settling into the Bride's Room. There, a photographer would capture the bridal party as they got ready.

She knew Robert and the other men wouldn't arrive until the ladies were nearly ready. She would pose alone and with the women in both the Bride's Room and in the decorated Auditorium.

Under the pine arch where she and Robert would soon exchange vows, Emelia stood for a solo portrait. But as the photographer adjusted her lens, movement at the back of the Auditorium caught her eye.

Her heart stumbled.

Her mother and Robert's entered, with her father walking between them.

Emelia waved off the photographer and sank onto the front pew, her pulse pounding in her ears. Closing her eyes, she focused on breathing. In and out. In and out. Both their mothers had promised they wouldn't let him come unless he was truly contrite. *Please, Lord. Let it be so.*

A pair of hands gently took hers. She opened her eyes.

Her father knelt before her, holding both her hands. Behind him, the two mothers stood silently, their expressions tender.

"I'm sorry, baby girl," he said, voice trembling. "I was wrong. My heart felt you slipping away, and I wanted to protect you. Hold on to you. But I shouldn't have jumped to conclusions. I've asked God to forgive me, and now I'm asking you. Will you forgive me for the horrible things I said and did?"

Tears welled despite her best efforts to hold them back. "Last night, I asked God to help me forgive you. I also prayed He'd bring you back to Him and to me." Her voice faltered. "Tonight will be my first time with Robert. What I need to know is, do you believe me?"

Her father lowered his gaze, then looked up again, eyes glistening. "I'm ashamed that I ever thought otherwise. Your mother and I raised you with Christian values. Abstinence until marriage is one of them. You're a Christian woman, and Robert is a Christian man."

He swiped at his wet cheeks. "Your mother, James, Robert's father, and Solomon spoke with me this morning. They prayed with me. I repented asking God's forgiveness and theirs. I believe you."

He reached up and gently wiped her tears. The father she'd always known looked back at her now. Relief washed through her, and she leaned down and wrapped her arms around him.

"Will you walk me down the aisle and present me to Robert?"

Tears slid down his cheeks. "It would be my honor." His voice quavered.

Emelia held his gaze a moment longer before he reached for her mother's hand and rose to his feet.

"Now," he said, glancing toward the back of the Auditorium, "I need to face Robert."

Emelia smiled through her tears. "He'll forgive you. He's a good man."

Her mother hugged her, then held her at arm's length. "Oh, honey, your makeup is a mess. Let's get you back to the Bride's Room and get it fixed."

"I'm sure it looks downright awful."

She laughed, wiping the last of her tears away.

"We'd better hurry." Betsy scooped up Emelia's train. "The photographer's waiting!"

With a giggle and a grateful heart, she let both mothers guide her back to the Bride's Room.

Robert arrived at the church with his father and groomsmen right on schedule. Solomon ventured ahead to make sure Robert wouldn't catch a glimpse of his bride.

"Coast is clear," he called out, loud enough to echo through the building.

Robert exhaled. The room designated for the men was one of the larger classrooms. His stomach growled at the sight of a snack platter on the corner table. He hesitated, nerves twisting, until he spotted his mom's cranberry-pecan chicken salad tucked between triangles of multigrain bread. *Worth the risk.*

He grabbed a small plate, just big enough for two sandwiches, and a bottle of sweet tea from the cooler. The other men followed suit, and his father led them in a quiet prayer before they ate.

Midway through their snack, the classroom door opened.

Robert's eyes widened. Henry.

He shot to his feet. "Sir, I don't think it's a good idea for you to be here today." He glanced at the others. "Please help him out before he upsets Emelia."

His father spoke before anyone moved. "Son, I think you should hear what the man has to say before you jump to conclusions." He stepped forward and took the garment bag from Henry's hands.

Robert gave his dad a wary look, then turned to Emelia's father. "Henry, this is your daughter's and my wedding day. It needs to be a good day. If you're not here to confess the wrongness of your accusations, acknowledge the truth, and ask God's and our forgiveness, then you need to leave."

Henry nodded slowly, ran a hand through his hair, and placed the other over his heart. "I repented and asked God's forgiveness earlier today. I apologized to Emelia moments ago. I'm truly sorry. Will you forgive me?"

Robert glanced at James, then at Solomon, and finally at his father. Each man nodded, and the tightness in his chest eased. His father added, "We prayed with Henry this morning. He's telling the truth."

Robert turned back to the man who would soon be his father-in-law. "Last night, I asked God to bring you back to Him, to Emelia, and to me. I asked for forgiveness for my anger and for the grace to forgive you."

With an exhale, he stepped forward and extended his hand. "I forgive you."

Henry took it, his grip firm and his chin tucked. "Thank you, son. Emelia asked me to walk her down the aisle. If that taints the ceremony for you in any way, I'll step aside and take the blame."

Robert shook his head, a smile breaking through. "Henry, you're forgiven. And I'm sure you gave your daughter the best wedding gift she could've hoped for today. She's told me more than once that walking down the aisle on your arm was part of her dream wedding. I'm thankful it's going to happen."

Chapter 22

A Joyful Beginning

Robert stood in front of the mirror in the Groom's Room, adjusting the cranberry red satin bow tie Emelia had chosen for him. The wedding was two days after Christmas—close enough, she'd said, to embrace the season's colors: cranberry red and evergreen.

He wore a black tuxedo and a crisp white shirt, but it was the cummerbund and bow tie that set him apart. What did it matter, really, if he wore holiday hues—as long as the day ended with her as his wife?

The other men in the room wore identical tuxes, their accessories in evergreen satin to match the bridesmaids. He pictured the procession—each man beside a woman in green—while he stood apart in red.

When Henry excused himself to check on his daughter, Robert noticed even his collar and pocket square were evergreen.

Surely, he wasn't the only one in red. Emelia must be wearing it too. She had to be.

All the pre-ceremony photos had been taken. Emelia, her bridesmaids, and both mothers were back in the Bride's Room. The mothers moved from girl to girl, inspecting every detail, from the red sparkly necklaces and earrings to the bouquets. Emelia laughed when they turned their attention to her, giving her the same loving scrutiny.

Her snow-white gown shimmered with rhinestones from neckline to waist. The satin A-line skirt skimmed the floor in front and trailed modestly behind. A penny rested in one of her cranberry-red satin pumps. Her lace veil trimmed in red satin and scattered with iridescent sequins was anchored by the tiara her mother had worn on her own wedding day. Emelia stood still as her mother fastened it into her long, dark chocolate curls.

Robert's mother gently adjusted the emerald necklace that had belonged to his great-great-grandmother. Then she wrapped the base of Emelia's bouquet—red and white poinsettias and pine sprigs—in red satin ribbon, tying a generous bow beneath the blooms. She pinned the silver brooch with blue stones at the center, just as her own mother had done for her.

Finally, both mothers stepped back, their eyes softening with pride as they took in the girls. "Betsy," Emelia's mother said, "it's time to let them know the bride is ready."

Emelia paced.

"Emelia, stand still." Deanna crouched to straighten the train. "You're going to step on this."

Emelia sighed. "I'm ready. I'm so ready to marry Robert."

Rising, Deanna studied her. "I hope I find someone to love the way you love him."

Emelia smiled, soft and sure. "You will. And he'll love you the way Robert loves me."

A knock sounded. A male voice called through the door, "It's time."

Deanna opened the door a crack. "Where's Robert?"

A male laugh, like Robert's yet subtly distinct, floated through the cracked door. Solomon obviously stood on the other side of the door. "Already at the front of the Auditorium. We need to line up and get this show on the road."

Then his gaze locked on Deanna's, and neither of them moved for a long moment.

Emelia giggled and nudged her friend. "Stop staring at Solomon."

Robert stood beneath the pine arch, shifting from foot to foot. To calm his nerves, he tried to picture the ceremony the way they'd rehearsed it yesterday, but the details, especially those concerning Emelia, were covered in a fog.

When the rear doors of the Auditorium opened, he stilled. His first steady breath came when his father appeared with Deanna, Emelia's best friend, followed by Solomon and Alexis, then James and Mildred.

Then he saw her.

His breath caught. Emelia was radiant. He couldn't move. Couldn't think.

His father's hand landed gently on his shoulder. "Breathe, son," he whispered.

Robert blinked, inhaled, and the fog receded.

As Emelia approached on her father's arm, his eyes caught the sparkle of his grandmother's brooch beneath her bouquet, the red satin ribbon wrapping the stems, and the strip of red along her veil's edge.

When he noticed the toes of her red heels with her next steps, he chuckled softly. *We match.*

He couldn't pull his gaze away. She was marrying him. It felt like a miracle.

Her father placed Emelia's hands in his. "Son, I'm trusting you with my girl. Make her your most important person."

Robert swallowed, his smile growing as he nodded. "I will, sir."

He reached out, his fingertips brushing the emerald on his great-great-grandmother's necklace. "You wore this down the aisle as my intended. When you walk back up, you'll wear it as my wife. Thank you."

Emelia's eyes sparkled, warming him from the inside out. "You're welcome. It's my honor."

He returned his hand to hers. From that moment on, she held his full attention. The ceremony passed in a blur, his eyes never leaving her. He knew he'd said "I do," and slid the ring onto her finger because he could see it there on her hand.

Then Emelia squeezed his hand. The press of a new ring against his skin startled him. She'd said her vows and slipped it on his finger without him even noticing. Laughter rippled through the guests.

The minister cleared his throat. "Pay attention this time, son. I now pronounce you husband and wife. You may kiss your bride."

Joy stretched across Robert's face. He pulled Emelia into his arms, dipped her, and kissed her with reckless abandon. She met him with equal fervor.

"Brother, if you don't stop soon, you'll be sent home without dinner or dessert," Solomon stage-whispered. "I'll gladly eat your cake."

Laughter spread through the crowd. Robert straightened, returning Emelia to her feet.

"I now present to you, for the first time, Mister and Missus Robert Jackson," the minister announced.

Faces burning, they hurried up the aisle to a wave of applause and cheers.

Once out of earshot, he leaned close. "If you want to cut out early like Solomon suggested, I'm not opposed."

Still pink from their kiss, Emelia's blush deepened. "I'm hungry. We also have photos, a toast, cake, and a garter and bouquet toss. After all that, we can go home."

The bridal party and parents exited next, forming a receiving line—parents on one side, bridesmaids and groomsmen on the other. Every guest received a handshake or hug before the group was ushered back into the Auditorium for photos.

When it was time for the combined family picture, Robert noticed Jerry and Sue were missing. Emelia insisted they be included.

He found them quickly. "Come on up here. You're our family too," Emelia said.

The photographer arranged the large group and snapped the photo. As everyone began to disperse, Robert's mother stepped forward. "I think we need one more," she said, smiling at Jerry and Sue.

The photographer frowned at her list. "Is this picture supposed to be here?"

Robert's mother nodded. "If it's not, that's our oversight. These two are like grandparents to Robert and Emelia. The bride and groom need a grandparent photo."

Under the arch, Robert and Emelia stood between Jerry and Sue as the shutter clicked.

Emelia's mother bustled her train to keep her from stepping on it, and together they headed to the Fellowship Hall to join their guests for dinner.

Emelia floated on air from the moment she'd been introduced as Mrs. Robert Jackson. *I'm Emelia Jackson.* Her cheeks ached from smiling, but she couldn't stop. When the last posed photo was finally behind them, she entered the reception on her husband's arm.

"We're married," she whispered.

"We sure are," Robert said, his smile unchanged since the minister had declared them husband and wife.

"Go on and eat," the minister chuckled. "I prayed over the meal while you were with the photographer. Couldn't have the natives getting restless."

The meal was simple and comforting—baked chicken with stuffing, mashed potatoes, green beans, and corn. Nearby, the cake table offered small treats and flutes of sparkling cider, ready for celebration.

Robert's father stood and raised his glass. "Everyone, get a glass of bubbly and join me in a toast to the bride and groom."

It took a few minutes for everyone to get their cider. Then Mark lifted his glass high. "I couldn't be prouder of these two young people who joined their lives today. Congratulations to my son and my new daughter. May God bless your life together."

Emelia's father stood and tugged his wife to her feet. "I second that. We're proud of you both. Congratulations to my daughter and my new son."

Cheers and clinking glasses filled the room.

When the noise settled, Robert and Emelia raised their glasses. "Thank you all for celebrating our marriage with us," Robert said. "Several of you have known us for most of our lives and helped shape who we are."

"We love you more than you know," Emelia added warmly. "Especially our families."

They stood by the cake, arms entwined as they sipped their cider. Then, with careful hands, they fed each other bites of cake—no smashing—despite the disappointed hisses from the guests, egged on by Solomon and Deanna's snickering.

Emelia sat and lifted her dress just above her knee. Robert knelt and removed the red satin and lace garter, then turned his back to the crowd of single men and slingshot it over his shoulder.

Solomon caught it.

"Brother," Robert said, grinning, "that means you'll get married next."

He helped Emelia onto the chair as the single ladies gathered behind her. Her mother handed up the bouquet minus the brooch. Emelia laughed. "I wonder who's going to marry Solomon," she teased, then tossed the bouquet behind her.

Robert helped her down. Emelia turned to see who'd caught it and gasped. Deanna held the bouquet high, eyes wide with surprise.

Emelia turned to Robert. "When they met, they couldn't take their eyes off each other. Hmm. I wonder."

He kissed her cheek. "Time will tell. But doesn't this fulfill our obligations for this shindig? I'm ready to take my wife home."

Emelia leaned into him. "I believe it does. I'm tired. Let's go home."

She smiled at the disappointment as it flickered across his face.

"Let's go home, my love," he said.

She nudged her mother. "We're ready."

To her surprise, her mother put two fingers from each hand in her mouth and produced an ear-splitting whistle—the same one she'd used to call Emelia and James home from the far ends of the neighborhood. It worked. Heads turned.

"The bride and groom are ready to leave," she announced. "There are bowls of birdseed packets in the foyer. Grab one and head outside to give them a proper send-off."

They hugged their parents and siblings. Robert's mother handed them food and cake to take with them. "I'll get the top tier of your cake in the freezer," Emelia's mother promised.

"The guests are lined up outside," the minister said.

Emelia lifted the hem of her dress as they ran through the birdseed shower. Robert helped her into the car, and they drove away with a *Just Married* banner on the bumper and tin cans clattering joyfully behind them.

Chapter 23

Married

Robert parked the car, aligning the passenger side with the walkway before shutting off the engine. He stepped out and circled to Emelia's door. She gathered the folds of her white dress, and he helped her out, catching the trailing fabric before it brushed the ground. Then he scooped her into his arms.

She grasped his shoulders. "Robert, I can walk."

"I know you can walk. But it's tradition. A husband's supposed to carry his bride over the threshold the first time she enters. And tonight, you're stepping into our home for the first time as my wife. So, you belong in my arms."

Once through the door, he set her on her feet. She stayed still, eyes wide. "Where did that come from?" she asked, staring at the sofa that hadn't been there before.

Robert chuckled as she took in the furnished space.

"When did this furniture get here?" she asked again. "It wasn't here when we left on Christmas."

"No, ma'am, it sure wasn't." He smiled. "I wanted it to be a surprise. I thought my wife deserved a proper place to sit when she had guests over—something outside the bedroom. It was delivered yesterday. Happy wedding. I hope you like it."

She bounced on her toes and turned to him. "Thank you. I love it," she said, wrapping her arms around his neck.

He held her close, lifted her chin, and kissed her gently. She melted against him, her breath mingling with his. When his lips brushed the curve of her neck, warmth spread through him, fierce and tender at once.

He drew back just enough to meet her gaze. Her cheeks were flushed, her eyes shining.

Then he lifted her again and carried her toward their bedroom. His pulse pounded with each step. She clung to him, her breath coming in quiet, uneven bursts.

At the edge of the bed, he set her down carefully. "Em, my love, what's wrong? Are you alright?"

She reached for his hand. "Sit with me."

He did.

Her voice softened. "Things are different now. I'm your wife. You're my husband. And there are... well... no limits anymore."

Her cheeks burned. He brushed his thumb across her knuckles.

"We can go slow," he said. "As much or as little as we want. We'll learn this part of loving each other together. I've never done this either. But I want to love you—physically, tenderly, completely. Please tell me you want that too."

"I do," she whispered. "I want to love you and be loved by you. I'm just nervous."

He smiled softly. "That makes two of us."

Emelia woke to her first morning as a married woman with one thought pressing on her heart: thanking the Lord for her husband. She slipped quietly from their bed, surprised when happiness filled her instead of the self-consciousness she'd expected. Pulling her robe closed, she moved with purpose, already knowing where she'd packed her prayer journal.

Settling at the small secretary desk Robert had placed just outside their bedroom, she opened her journal to a fresh page. With her favorite pen in hand, she poured out her gratitude.

Dear Lord,

This morning, my heart is overflowing with gratitude for the imperfectly perfect man You've given me. He is gentle, kind, and a man after Your heart. Last night I was nervous, but You surrounded us with peace and tenderness. By Your design, our first night together was filled with warmth, joy, and the wonder of becoming one. Thank You for the beauty of marriage and for the man I will love and honor for all my days.

In Jesus' name, amen.

Warm hands caressed her shoulders, and lips brushed just in front of her ear. "My love, what's got you up writing already this morning?" Robert murmured.

The tickle of his breath sent shivers through her. She turned, tilting her face toward him. His lips met hers, and her eyes drifted closed as she savored the kiss that ended far too soon.

"I woke up full of gratitude," she said softly. "Grateful to be your wife. I had to write my thanks to God."

He smiled, eyes tender. "I'm the one who's blessed. You are..." He looked around as though searching for a word, then gave a small shrug. "There are no words special enough to describe you."

He tilted his head. "Do you always write your prayers?"

"Only the important ones," she said. "When I'm really feeling something, I write. This morning, I was really grateful for you."

His mouth curved into that playful half-smile she knew so well.

"Em?" he asked.

"Em what? Robert, use your words."

He chuckled. "Since you're going to make me ask, may I read your prayer?"

She hesitated. "I've never let anyone read my prayers. But I'll let you read this one. It's about our first time. I'm not ready to share more than that."

She placed the journal in his hands. He read slowly, then again, before reverently handing it back. She tucked it into a cubby and closed the desk.

His whole face lit with joy as he scooped her into his arms. "My love, we've got some time before we need to leave."

He pressed kisses along her neck and collarbone. "Mrs. Jackson, would it be alright if we experienced a little more *joy and wonder* before we go?"

She pulled his mouth to hers, pausing just before the kiss. "Yes, Mr. Jackson. It's more than alright."

Robert kicked the bedroom door closed behind them.

Part Two

SOLOMON

SOLOMON

Chapter 24

Where is Deanna?

Each morning and night, Solomon picked up the red-trimmed lace garter he had caught at his brother's wedding and pictured the girl who had leaped for Emelia's bouquet—the one whose hazel eyes had locked with his before the ceremony.

He still saw her in that green satin bridesmaid gown, strawberry waves cascading over her shoulders. He remembered the faint strawberry scent when she leaned out of the Bride's Room to speak with him, her porcelain skin dusted with freckles, and those unforgettable eyes—golden-touched hazel that held him until Emelia nudged her and broke the moment. If not for that, the wedding might have started late.

And then Robert had to say, "Brother, that means you'll marry next," right in front of everyone. She had raised Emelia's bouquet like she had won the world's best prize, and Solomon had barely remembered to breathe. He had not seen her since.

Six months later, Deanna still filled his dreams. He had searched all spring, but she must have graduated with Robert and Emelia. She did not attend their church either. How had he not run into her again in such a small town? She was Emelia's best friend. Turning the garter over in his hands again before bed, he vowed to ask Robert about her at work tomorrow.

When Solomon arrived at the job site, Robert was nowhere to be found. He climbed from the truck he had bought after graduation and approached Eddy.

"My brother's a chronic early bird. Have you heard from him?"

Eddy shook his head, smiling. "Not from Robert, but I did hear from Conner."

"Conner Bard?"

"Yeah. Bard's Buildings. The big boss."

Solomon shoved his hands in his pockets. "I know who he is. What I don't know is where my brother is."

"Conner called Robert this morning and pulled him onto a new job. He wants him to run it. Conner called me because Robert won't be working with us anymore."

Solomon stilled, then grinned. "So Robert's a boss man now. Sorry for interrupting. Where are we starting today, boss?"

Eddy chuckled. "Drop the 'boss' part. The temporary walls are up. Let's knock out the one between the living room and kitchen."

By lunchtime, they had demolished the wall and begun clearing the debris.

"Do you know what Robert's got planned this weekend?" Eddy asked.

"He and Emelia are painting the spare room. He wants to lay the floor and trim it out so they can move in, then they plan to work in the primary bedroom," Solomon said, running a hand through his hair. "I'm tired just thinking about it."

Eddy laughed. "Tell him I'm free Saturday afternoon if he needs a hand. Let's eat."

Cleaning the site and preparing to install the new support beam consumed the afternoon.

After work, Solomon called his brother, wrapping up the conversation once he had secured a dinner invite.

"Mom, I'm going to shower, then head to Robert's."

His mother nodded. "Have fun."

At Robert's door, Solomon knocked. When it opened, Deanna stood before him. Their gazes locked. Neither moved. Neither spoke. His breath caught, his heart thudded against his ribs.

A throat cleared. They jumped. Robert stood behind her.

"Evenin', brother," he said. "Deanna, if you'll kindly step aside, I think Solomon will come in."

She stepped aside, and Solomon entered, though their eyes lingered on each other.

"Hey, Em, come look at these two. I think we've got a pair of love-sick puppies joinin' us for supper."

Solomon blinked out of his daze. "I'm sorry, Deanna."

She blinked back. "I'm sorry, too."

He knew he had stared too long, and the urge to reach for her was nearly overwhelming. He shoved his hands deep into his pockets.

"I'm going to see if I can help in the kitchen," he said, heading that way.

Robert opened the door. "Deanna, come outside with me. Emelia and I are picking paint colors for the new siding. We'd love your opinion."

Deanna narrowed her eyes and put her hands on her hips. "You're up to something, Robert."

Still, she followed him out.

Emelia finished paring a tomato and turned to Solomon. "Thank You, Lord. We need to talk."

He looked up, wary. "Why?"

She smiled gently. "Robert and I have known since our wedding that sparks fly when you and Deanna see each other."

Solomon rolled his eyes. "No kidding. I hadn't noticed."

"She was the youngest graduate in our class, three months past her seventeenth birthday. You turned eighteen last October, so you're older by four months."

He frowned. "So age isn't the problem. But you and Robert see one."

Emelia nodded. "Not a problem. But a barrier. Deanna isn't a Christian. We've invited her to church many times over the last six months. She's always declined. I've studied with her one-on-one, and Robert and I have studied with her together. I don't know where she stands. She said her family used to attend church when she was little, but it's been years. My guess? She's afraid her parents wouldn't approve if she came with us."

Solomon's shoulders sagged. He stared at the floor. "So, bouquet, garter, and sparks aside, you and Robert don't think I should pursue anything with her."

Emelia placed a hand on his shoulder. "We're afraid you'll both get hurt."

He lifted his head, squared his shoulders, and met her gaze. "Deanna's the only girl I've thought about for six months. I hear you. I appreciate the warning. But I need to find out for myself if there's a chance. I'm going to ask her out. Right now."

Robert led Deanna to the color swatches painted on the siding. She studied them slowly, thoughtfully.

"If it were my house..." She brought her finger to her chin. "I'd paint the doors light yellow, the body cream, and the trim either dark brown or dark gray, and add white accents around the doors and windows. But it's not my house. The choice belongs to Jerry and Sue, and to you and Emelia."

"Now that we're done with your little ruse, it's my turn." She turned to face him. "Why did you want me out of the house? More specifically, why did you want me away from your brother?"

Her tone softened, but she had a point to make. "For the last six months, you and Emelia have made sure Solomon and I were never here at the same time. Why?"

Robert exhaled, the truth weighing on him. "We hoped the attraction between you two would fade, or one of you would move on. But six months later, you're still drawn to each other like moths to a flame."

He met her gaze. "Deanna, you know Em and I love you. This isn't about you not being good enough for Solomon, because you are. But you're not a Christian. And Solomon needs a wife who'll walk with him in faith, help him raise his children in the church, and encourage him spiritually. Emelia and I have studied with you, hopin' to lead you to the Lord. Somethin' is holdin' you back. I wish I understood what it was."

She crossed her arms. "So unless I believe what you believe, you'll keep putting roadblocks between us."

Robert shook his head. "That's not it. Or maybe it is, unintentionally. What I'm sayin' is, faith is foundational in our family. It's not a small thing. It will be a stumblin' block between you and Solomon. Emelia and I were tryin' to protect both of you from that pain. We love you both. We didn't want either of you hurt."

He paused. "But if what happened at the door today is any indication, there's no stoppin' this train."

Deanna managed a half-smile. "Is that a warning or a blessing?"

"Neither," Robert said gently. "It's us gettin' out of the way."

Just then, the front door opened and closed. They turned. Solomon stood there, his presence steady and sure.

Robert gave Deanna one last look. "Emelia and I will keep you both in our prayers." He clapped Solomon's shoulder as he passed, then disappeared inside.

Solomon waited until the door shut behind his brother. "I'm guessing you got an earful from Robert, just like I did from Emelia."

"I did."

Their eyes met, and the air between them hummed.

"Before we start anything, I want us to be honest," he said.

She reached for his hand, then drew back at the sudden warmth. "Did you feel that?"

"Yes." He took her hand again, holding it gently.

She looked down at their joined hands. "Robert thinks you're looking for a wife."

His smile faltered. “Isn’t that the point of dating?”

“I suppose.” Her voice dropped. “But your brother and Emelia don’t think we’re a good match.”

Solomon’s smile returned, slow and certain. “Then it’s a good thing they don’t get a vote.”

When she didn’t look away, he stepped closer. *I promised I wouldn’t kiss a woman I’m not in love with, a woman I’m not sure I’ll marry. But I’m going to kiss this one if she’ll let me.*

Heart pounding, he closed the distance. “May I kiss you?”

She tipped her face toward him, lips parted slightly. That was all the permission he needed. He brushed his lips across hers, soft and careful. The moment flared bright and pure, a spark that settled deep in his chest.

He pulled back, searching her eyes for confirmation. She answered by drawing him in again, and this time the kiss deepened—slow at first, then sure. The world fell away, leaving only the warmth of her in his arms.

A throat cleared behind them. Solomon turned to see Emelia standing with one brow raised.

“Dinner’s ready, if you two are interested,” she said, turning back toward the house and muttering, “love-sick puppies,” just loud enough to hear.

Deanna laughed first. Solomon joined her, still holding her close.

“Robert’s going to give me an earful about that kiss,” he said, “but I’m not sorry. Not even a little. Unless you object, I see a lot more kissing in our future.”

Deanna rested her head against his chest. “You promise?”

“I do,” he said with quiet certainty. “Remind me later to tell you a story about another promise.”

He laced his fingers through hers as they walked toward the house.

Chapter 25

Connection

Dinner was warm and easy, the conversation congenial, and the food delicious, especially Emelia's chocolate cake. Afterward, Deanna followed Emelia into the kitchen to clean up. They kept their voices low as they worked, glancing now and then toward the living room where Robert and Solomon lounged with their feet propped up, deep in discussion about house projects and weekend plans. A far safer topic than the one unfolding between her and Emelia.

Emelia's expression was unreadable, her voice calm. "That kiss I saw earlier, it's a bigger deal than you realize."

Heat bloomed in Deanna's cheeks, mingling with the memory of Solomon's lips. "It was a great kiss," she said, trying to sound casual. "But it was just a kiss."

Who am I trying to convince, Emelia or myself?

Emelia shook her head. "Not for Solomon."

Deanna drew a breath, tamping down the flicker of defensiveness. "Seriously? Why?"

"Because you're the first girl he's ever kissed." Emelia's gaze didn't waver.

Deanna's jaw dropped. "No way. That kiss was... uh... spectacular."

Emelia giggled, handing her a second plate before stifling her laughter.

What's so funny?" Deanna asked, incredulous.

"That's exactly how I felt when Robert kissed me for the first time. He told me he'd never kissed anyone before, and I braced myself for awkward. But there was no learning curve. I accused him of lying."

She smiled. "He said, 'Just because I hadn't done it didn't mean I hadn't studied how it should be done.' I suspect Solomon studied the same material."

Deanna laughed. "Whatever it was, every guy should study it."

They shared a moment of laughter before Deanna's voice softened. "It was my first kiss too."

Emelia's head tilted. "Really?"

"You know how strict my parents are. No dances, no games, no dates. Boys asked me out, but I couldn't go. So yeah, it was my first kiss. And unlike Robert and Solomon, I didn't study anything. I hope I didn't disappoint him." She bit her lip.

Emelia took her hand gently. "If the way he looked at you during dinner means anything, he wasn't disappointed."

"I hope you're right."

With the kitchen clean and the last dish tucked away, Emelia rested her hands on Deanna's shoulders. "You're my best friend, and I love Solomon as much as I love my brother James. Be careful."

Deanna nodded. "I will. Please pray my parents let me date him. I've never had a boyfriend before." She sighed. "I've got a test tomorrow. I need to get home and study. Let me say goodbye to the guys."

She stepped into the living room. "Thanks for a lovely evening. I need to head home and study."

She leaned in and kissed Solomon's cheek. His eyes widened, and he caught her hand and stood. "I'll walk you to your car."

"Please."

As they stepped outside, he asked, "Homework?"

"Yeah. I'm taking a couple of summer classes."

"What are you studying?"

They reached her car, and instead of opening the door, Solomon backed her gently against it, a slow smile forming.

"I'm working on a degree in business and accounting," she said, her voice breathy as her hands found his chest.

He brushed a strand of her strawberry hair behind her ear. "My girl's in a hurry. Why?"

Her breath caught. "Your girl?"

"After that kiss, how could you not be?" he said, tracing her lower lip with his thumb.

"So, you're my boyfriend?" she asked, her fingers settling lightly at his collar.

He kissed her cheek. "Yes, ma'am. Now tell me, why the rush?"

She rested her head against his chest, listening to the steady beat of his heart. "I want to be a nurse. The business degree will help me pay for nursing school."

He lifted her chin. "Are you paying for school yourself?"

"Yes. I live at home, so no housing costs. My parents help that way. I've got a scholarship, and with my work-study job, I'm managing," she said, blinking.

He brushed a thumb beneath her eye, then paused. "Dee, are you crying?"

She blinked again. "Just a little."

He held her close. "I'm here. Let me help."

She rose onto her toes. "Kiss me goodbye tonight and call me tomorrow."

"Kissing you is the easy part. I don't have your number or your address."

"I'll give you both. But kiss me first."

He leaned in, resting his forehead against hers. "Of course."

Her eyes fluttered shut, lips parting in anticipation. His hands guided her gently, and when their lips met, she melted into the kiss. He tasted of chocolate, his kiss both firm and tender. She deepened the kiss, losing herself in the rhythm of their mouths until he slowed and pulled away.

"I don't think I can live without kissing you," he whispered, forehead still pressed to hers. "But I'd better let you study."

He stepped back, and she let him. "Is it awful that I want to kiss you more than I want to study?"

"Not to me. May I get the door for you?"

She nodded, stepping aside. Once inside, she pulled out a pen and notepad, scribbled her number and address on a page, and handed it to him. "You meant it, right? You'll call me tomorrow?"

He nodded. "Every word. "May I borrow your pen and paper?"

"I'll wait for you to call," he said. "I don't want to interrupt your studies, but if you need a break or reassurance, I'll be there."

He handed the pad back. She read his note:

I'll always be honest with you. You can trust me. If you need a break or have doubts, call me. I'll be there.

It was signed: *Love, Solomon,* followed by his number.

She placed her hand over his, then brought it to her heart. "Thank you, Solomon."

He closed her door gently. She waved, then pointed her car toward home.

Once Deanna was out of sight, Solomon stepped back into the house, bracing for the coming conversation. The pact he'd made with his brother years ago, no kissing until love and marriage were certain, Robert had honored. Tonight, Solomon had shattered it.

Robert stood waiting, arms crossed, jaw tight, lips pressed into a hard line.

"Solomon," he said, low but firm, "the way you're kissin' her is gonna get you in trouble. What happened to keepin' your lips to yourself until you were sure? Until you were ready to marry?"

Emelia glanced between them, her expression unreadable. "I'm going to get ready for bed. When you two finish this..." She gestured in a slow circle. "...Solomon, you can head home. Robert, please calm down before you come to bed."

She turned and disappeared into their bedroom, leaving the brothers alone.

Solomon lowered his gaze and shook his head. "There's something about Deanna. I felt it the moment I saw her. I can't explain it, but I know she's the one. Somehow, someday, she'll be my wife."

Robert uncrossed his arms, fists flexing. "You've seen her twice, Solomon. Twice. What you're sayin' makes no sense."

Solomon's mouth curved into a half-smile. "You don't have to like it, and I'm not accountable to you. Emelia trusts Deanna. They're best friends. I know I broke our pact, and I'm sorry. I want your support, but I'm going to keep seeing her—keep kissing her. We're a couple now. That's not up for debate."

Robert's posture softened, but concern lingered in his eyes. "She's not a Christian. Emelia and I have studied with her, prayed with her. She understands the gospel, even admits it, but she won't come to church or consider baptism. There's somethin' holdin' her back, somethin' she won't name. Can you build a life with someone who doesn't share your faith?"

Solomon's smile faded. "Your warning's heard. But Deanna's different. I'm drawn to her in a way I can't ignore. Scripture speaks to this in 1 Corinthians 7:13-16. How do you know I won't lead her to Christ?"

Robert nodded slowly. "We love her, Solomon. Em and I did our best to show her the way, and we couldn't reach her." He paused, his voice gentling. "Just don't rush it. Don't say 'I love you' until you're sure. Marriage is a lifetime commitment, for better or worse. Emelia and I will keep you both in our prayers."

He opened his arms, and Solomon stepped into them. They clapped each other's backs, and the tension eased.

"I love you," Solomon said as he stepped away.

"I love you too. I'll always be here for you," Robert replied.

At the door, Solomon paused, hand on the knob. "I know. But thanks for saying it."

Then he left, the night quiet around him as he headed home.

When Deanna arrived home, she headed straight to her room, determined to study. But before she opened her book, a knock sounded on the door.

"Come in," she called.

Her mother stepped inside. Deanna turned in her desk chair, smiling. "Hey, Mom."

Her mother returned the smile. "Judging by that grin, I'd say you and Emelia had a good visit."

"We did." She hesitated, then sighed. *Might as well get this over with.*

"You know Robert has supper with us, but tonight his brother, Solomon, was there, too."

Her mother's smile faded. "Solomon? How long have you known him?"

"I met him at Robert and Emelia's wedding. He was Robert's best man. That was about six months ago."

A deep frown settled on her mother's face. "You don't have your father's permission to date this young man. Have you been seeing him behind our backs?"

Straightening the hem of her blouse, Deanna met her mother's gaze. "I would never. Tonight was just happenstance. I went to see Emelia, and Robert had invited Solomon over. He's a good guy. He wants to ask me out. And I'd really like to say yes."

Her mother's frown held firm. "You know your father and I want you to focus on school. Dating can wait."

She dropped her head, fingers fidgeting with her blouse. "That only leaves me a few weeks in summer, two at Christmas, and one at spring break. So, even in college, I can only date a few weeks a year?"

Her mother tilted her head. "You're only four months past eighteen. There's no need to rush into dating."

"There's something different about Solomon," she said quietly. "I want to spend time with him. I want to date him."

Her mother nodded slowly. "Your father will want to meet him first. And your studies come first. If your grades slip, dating stops."

Deanna smiled and reached for the note Solomon had written. "Mom, he respects that I'm in school. Look, he asked me to call him when I need a study break. He said he wouldn't call, because he doesn't want to interrupt my studies."

Her mother's frown deepened as she pointed at the note. "'Love, Solomon? What's this?"

"He cares about me. He's kind."

Her mother's expression didn't soften. "I was never allowed to call boys. My mother said, 'Only loose girls call boys.'"

Deanna giggled. "Mom, it's 1982, not 1940. I think my reputation will survive a phone call. Did homes even have phones in the forties?"

Her mother laughed. "We did. I was born in 1940, but I wasn't a teenager until the fifties. We had a party line and a phone on the kitchen wall, just like ours."

The door opened, and her father stepped in. "I could hear you laughing from the living room. What's going on?"

Her mother turned to him. "Deanna ran into a young man she met at Emelia's wedding, Emelia's brother-in-law. She wants to date him."

Her father's frown was deeper than her mother's. He crossed his arms and widened his stance. "You're in school. You need to focus on your studies and forget about boys."

Deanna huffed. "I promise my grades won't suffer. Honestly, Solomon would be disappointed if I didn't put school first. Will you at least give him a chance?"

Her father didn't budge. "If he calls, you tell him he must talk to me before he takes you anywhere. When is this date supposed to happen?"

"We haven't set anything up yet," Deanna said. "Tonight, I'll call him during a study break. He doesn't want to interrupt me."

Her father shook his head. "Good girls don't call boys."

Deanna laughed again. "It's 1982, not the 1950s. How does calling a boy make me bad? Even back then, I'm sure no girl lost her virtue by dialing a phone. Wasn't that the whole thing? Good girls were virgins, bad girls weren't?"

Her laughter lingered, but her father's face turned deep red.

"Good girls save themselves for marriage," he said sternly. "Sex comes after marriage."

"I know that." She kept her tone calm. "My point is, phone calls are safe. It doesn't matter who makes them."

Her parents stared at her in silence.

She sighed. "I'll tell Solomon he needs to speak with you before we go out. But if I'm going to prioritize my studies, I need to study. Please trust me to do what's right."

Her mother stood and hugged her. "Be careful, my dear," she whispered, then slipped from the room.

Deanna stiffened, then met her father's gaze. His arms hung at his sides now, and a faint smile tugged at his lips. He stepped forward and hugged her.

"You're our greatest treasure," he said, pulling back. "Remember your values. Act wisely. We're only trying to protect you. I'll meet your Solomon soon enough."

He turned and left. Deanna watched him go, then turned back to her desk and opened her book.

An hour later, she had read her chapter twice and prepped her ledger notebook for entries. Her eyes blurred, refusing to focus—time for a break.

She picked up Solomon's note from her desk and headed to the kitchen. At the table, she reached for the phone, grateful she didn't have to share a party line like her mom had growing up. The thought of a nosy neighbor eavesdropping made her shudder.

She spun the rotary dial, one digit at a time, then sat again as the line rang.

"Hello," Solomon said.

His voice lit up her face. "Hi."

"Hey, Deanna. Thanks for taking your break with me."

"You're welcome. My eyes were crossing. I couldn't keep going until they rest a little."

She waited through a beat of silence. "You still there?" she asked.

"I'm here. I didn't know what to say." He exhaled audibly. "Did you tell your parents I want to take you out?"

His breath gave away his nerves. She hated to add to them. "I did. They said yes, conditionally."

"Conditionally?" His voice tightened a notch.

"Yes, but that's a big deal. They've never let me date while I'm in school."

He gasped. "Never?"

"No. I wasn't allowed to go to school events unless they were academic, math contests, science fairs, speech competitions. And my parents were always there. But now, we can date as long as my grades stay up, and you impress my dad."

She hoped he'd hear the joy in her voice.

"So I'm your first boyfriend?" he asked.

She heard pride in his tone. "Yes. My first boyfriend, and my first kiss."

He chuckled. "So we shared our first kiss tonight."

Her cheeks flamed. She ducked her chin instinctively, even though he couldn't see her.

"Dee, you still there?"

"Sorry. I was remembering our kisses."

"Mmmm," he murmured.

"I agree." She smiled. "Emelia told me you studied kissing techniques. I'm glad my lack of experience didn't ruin the moment."

Solomon laughed. "My girl's a quick study. The way you responded. I'd say your instincts are perfect."

She was sure the air conditioning was working, but it felt like summer heat had settled on her skin. *It's time to change the subject.*

"Do you want to make plans for this weekend?"

"I sure do. I'd love to celebrate the Fourth with you. May I buy you dinner from the food vendors in the park, take you to the carnival, and watch fireworks together Saturday night?"

His excitement was contagious. "I'd love that. I'll ask my mom if you can come for lunch and talk to my dad after."

Solomon groaned. "How tough is he going to be?"

She sighed. "I don't know. Probably pretty tough. You'll be the first guy to have that conversation with him. Just be your sweet, honest self. You'll be fine."

"I hope so. I really want to go out with you." He paused. "What if I don't pass muster?"

"You will," she said, trying to sound more confident than she felt.

"I appreciate your faith in me. I'm going to pray you're right."

"Sounds good." She groaned. "I should probably get back to the books."

"I'd love to talk tomorrow, but I've got church in the evening. I'm usually home by eight-thirty. Can I call you between then and nine?"

"I'll make it work."

"Talk to you tomorrow then."

"Can you call around six-thirty Thursday evening?"

"I'll try. I'm supposed to mow at Robert's while they prepare the spare bedroom for paint. I might be able to use the Carters' phone. If I haven't called by six-forty-five, can you try me between eight and nine?"

"I will."

"I miss you, Dee."

"I miss you, Solomon. Until tomorrow."

"Goodbye, my sweet."

She listened for the click before gently placing the handset back in its cradle.

Chapter 26

Study First, Date Maybe

On Thursday, Deanna met Emelia for lunch. She greeted her friend with a quick embrace, her heart light with good news she couldn't wait to share. They slid into their usual booth, already knowing what they wanted.

When the server arrived, Emelia ordered loaded baked potato soup with garlic knots, and Deanna chose creamy tomato basil soup with a grilled cheese sandwich. They both asked for sparkling blueberry lemonades.

After the server walked away, Emelia leaned in. "How did your test go this morning?"

Deanna sat a little taller. "I think I aced it. The instructor said grades will be posted tomorrow."

Emelia grinned. "Perfect. You can help me next semester when I tackle advanced financial accounting."

Their drinks arrived, bright and fizzy, and they sipped in companionable silence. When their meals arrived, Emelia offered a quiet prayer of thanks before they dug in. They spoke little until half their plates were cleared.

Emelia set down her spoon. "So, what happened after you got home? With your parents?"

Deanna's smile faltered. "They said I can date Solomon as long as my grades don't slip. But my dad insists on talking to Solomon first."

"Your parents have always made you put school first. I feel for Solomon, though. A one-on-one with your dad? That's intimidating. And I've known the man for years."

Emelia's calm tone didn't ease the tightness in Deanna's chest.

Deanna huffed. "I hate the words, 'Put your studies first.' I want the chance to fall in love."

"You should have that chance," Emelia said gently. She dipped her spoon into her soup. "Do you think you might fall in love with Solomon?"

Deanna set her spoon aside. Her gaze drifted, unfocused, her smile softening into wistfulness. "I've dreamt of him since your wedding. Last night, he said he missed me. And then, in my dreams, we talked and kissed all night. I know I barely know him, but my heart belongs to him."

Emelia's brows knit. "What if the conversation with your dad doesn't go well?"

Deanna's frown deepened. "It has to. I don't know what I'll do if it doesn't."

They ate in silence for a few moments, dipping bread and sandwich corners into their soups. Then Deanna's spoon slipped from her hand and clanked against the bowl

."I've never gone against my parents," she said quietly. "But if they reject Solomon on Saturday, I won't have a choice. I need this chance. I need him."

Emelia reached across the table and gently stilled Deanna's hands, which were worrying the edge of her napkin. "It's going to be alright."

Deanna met her gaze, pain rising. "You don't know that."

"I do," Emelia said with conviction. "Robert and I will stand with you, no matter what. You're not alone anymore."

Deanna exhaled, her shoulders relaxing. "Thank you. I couldn't ask for a better brother and sister."

"Do you think it would help if your date with Solomon was a double date with Robert and me?"

She hesitated. "I'm not sure. I just want time alone with him—space to really talk, without anyone else's input. You understand, don't you?"

Emelia nodded. "I do. Remember when Robert came to me and said he wanted his plans to be our plans? That conversation had to be just ours. It changed everything. We hadn't even kissed yet, but it made us a couple."

Deanna laughed softly. "You waited forever for Robert to kiss you."

Emelia smiled. "I did. But it was worth the wait. You and Solomon need that same space. Time to talk, to grow, to fall in love at your own pace. Robert and I will be here when you need us."

"Thank you." Deanna pushed her dishes aside and finished her lemonade. "I've got to get back to school and then to work."

They stood, paid, and hugged before parting ways. Deanna smiled, thankful for a best friend who felt like a sister.

After dinner, Deanna settled at the kitchen table with her business management textbook, determined to finish the chapter her instructor would cover tomorrow. She glanced at the clock. It read six-thirty-five.

Solomon, please call.

She was halfway through the next paragraph when the phone rang. Her heart jumped. Pressing one hand to her chest, she reached for the receiver with the other. "Hello?"

"Hello, my sweet. How did your test go this morning?"

"I think I aced it."

"I'm proud of you. Are you studying tonight?"

"I'm reading tomorrow's chapter now. I'll be done soon."

"How long do you think it'll take?"

"Maybe half an hour. Why?"

"I've got about fifteen minutes left in the yard. I'll finish trimming the bushes and trees tomorrow. Dee, please ask your father if I can come by at eight to speak with him?"

Her voice trembled. “Are you sure you want to do that tonight?”

“I hear the worry in your voice. I’m nervous too. I want this done before Saturday. I want your parents to know that you matter to me, and I want what’s best for you. I want to celebrate your accomplishments with you. Please, Dee. Ask him.”

“Okay,” she whispered. “I’ll go ask.” She gently set the receiver down.

In the living room, her father sat in his favorite chair, book in hand. She drew a breath to speak, but he looked up first.“

I heard the phone. Solomon, I assume.” He gestured to the chair beside him. “Sit, my child.”

Deanna obeyed, her shoulders sagging as she sank into the seat. “Solomon’s still on the line. He wants to know if he can come over at eight to talk with you.”

Her father’s mouth flattened into a line. “What’s his hurry?”

“He’s nervous.”

A low growl rumbled from his throat. “If he’s here at eight sharp, I’ll speak to him. If he’s late, the answer is no. No dating.”

Deanna nodded quickly. “I’ll tell him.”

He waved her toward the kitchen. “Go. Tell the boy eight sharp.”

She rose. “Yes, sir.”

Deanna returned to the kitchen and picked up the receiver. “Solomon?”

“I’m here, Dee.”

“My father said he’ll speak with you at eight. He’s a stickler for punctuality. If you’re late, he said, ‘The answer is no. No dating.’”

Solomon chuckled. “My dad always says, ‘On time is five minutes late.’ Don’t worry, my sweet. I’ll be early. See you soon.”

The line clicked before she could say goodbye. She stared at the receiver before returning it to its cradle. She sat down and tried to focus on her reading, but the words blurred. After fifteen minutes of rereading the same paragraph, she closed the book.

Solomon, I needed to read my chapter.

She carried the book to her room and tucked it into her backpack. Lying on her bed, she closed her eyes and let her thoughts drift. Soon, she imagined herself in a white dress, standing before a church full of people, Solomon's arms around her as the preacher declared, "I present to you, Mister and Missus Solomon Jackson."

"Deanna," her father said.

Her eyes snapped open. He stood in the doorway. She sat up. "Dad?"

He crossed the room and crouched beside her, his tone gentle. "Why is your young man coming to speak with me tonight?"

"He's nervous. He wants you and Mom to know I matter to him, and he wants what's best for me."

Her father smiled. "I like a young man who takes the bull by the horns. If he shows up on time, this may be a good conversation."

He left her alone with her thoughts. She checked the clock. Seven-thirty already. At her dresser, she refreshed her hair and makeup, then smiled at her reflection. "On time is five minutes late. I'll have to work on that."

She joined her parents in the living room. The television was off, as usual. Suggesting entertainment would only earn her one of two replies: *There are better stories in books,* or *Your time would be better spent studying.* She'd grown weary of hearing that.

Maybe I should wait to get my nursing degree.

The thought startled her, but she tucked it away.

The doorbell rang.

Her father checked his watch. "It's not eight yet. Maybe your Solomon is early. Please get the door."

Deanna peeked through the peephole. Solomon fidgeted but straightened when she opened the door. She gave him a warm smile and gestured him inside, saying nothing of the nerves she'd seen.

Her parents stood. She turned to them. "Solomon, these are my parents, Ephraim and Lydia Keaton."

Solomon shook her father's hand, then her mother's. "It's nice to meet you both."

Her mother smiled. "May I get you a glass of sweet tea or water?"

"Yes, ma'am. Water, please."

"Son, have a seat. Let's talk," her father said, gesturing to the chair across from the sofa.

"Ephraim, let me get the drinks before you dive in," her mother said.

"Yes, dear."

"Deanna, come help me in the kitchen."

"Yes, ma'am."

In the kitchen, her mother handed her a plate. "Relax, child. He'll be fine. Fill this with the peanut butter cookies I baked this morning."

Deanna obeyed, wishing she could hear through the wall. Her mother took the plate. "Go on to your room. I'll come get you when they're finished."

Back in her room, Deanna sat on her bed, nerves twisting inside her. *It feels like I threw Solomon to the wolves.* I wish I were beside him to support him.

Twenty minutes passed before her mother returned. That was a long talk. When she entered the living room, her father and Solomon were laughing. Relief bloomed in her chest, though she couldn't help rolling her eyes at their ease.

She walked to Solomon and whispered near his ear. "Things went well?"

He nodded. Her father stood. "I like this one, Deanna." Then to Solomon, he said, "You may visit until nine. After that, I expect you to go home."

Solomon rose and shook his hand again. "Understood, sir."

Her parents hugged her. "Let's give them space," her father said, guiding her mother down the hallway.

Deanna blinked after them, then shrugged. Solomon stepped behind her, kissed her cheek, and whispered, "Come, my sweet. I'll tell you everything."

They sat on the couch. Deanna's eyes were wide, her voice lost. Solomon rubbed gentle circles on her back.

"I didn't realize you were this worried," he said. "You didn't think your dad would let us date."

She stayed silent, lips trembling. He kept rubbing her back, offering quiet comfort until she finally spoke.

"He... he's never let me d-date. Is... is this even real?"

"Yes, Dee. It's real. We can date. We'll take it slow. I won't call in the evenings unless you're free. Your parents said you can call me during study breaks. I can take you out on Friday or Saturday, not both. I'm thinking Saturdays, so we'll have more time."

He paused, watching her blush. "I didn't ask your dad this, but on the days you work and study at the college, I could bring dinner. We could eat together before you hit the books. Would we have to tell him?"

Deanna leaned against his shoulder. "It all sounds good. I won't tell him, if you don't."

Solomon chuckled. "No, ma'am. I won't."

They talked quietly, Solomon sneaking kisses to her hair, her cheek, her temple. Each kiss sent warm shivers through her. His spicy pine scent wrapped around her, and she nestled closer.

At eight-fifty-five, Solomon released her hand and stood.

"We have five more minutes," she whined.

He smirked. "On time is five minutes late. I'd better stick to that with your dad. Will you walk me out?"

She smiled. "Yes. I know a spot where we won't be seen."

Taking his hand, she led him outside. "I'm glad you parked by that big tree. We can stand between it and your truck. No one will see us, not from the house or the neighbors."

Solomon chuckled. "So you want a goodnight kiss."

"Are you saying you don't?" she teased, hands on her hips.

He gently lifted her hands to his shoulders. "It was all I could do not to kiss you senseless on the couch. My patience is hanging by a thread. Yes, I want to kiss you."

She melted into his arms. Her fingers slid around his neck and into his light auburn hair, and his hands tangled in hers. Their lips met, and with each stroke, each touch, her blood sizzled with electricity.

Solomon pulled back. "If I don't leave now, your parents will be suspicious."

He kissed her cheek and stepped away. Though the July night was warm, she felt cold without him and hugged herself. Back on the porch, she checked the ground to be sure her feet were still touching it.

She waved as Solomon drove off, then went inside. The living room was empty. In the kitchen, she poured a glass of water, then returned to her room. She pulled out her textbook and sat at her desk.

I need to see Solomon. I will keep my grades up.

Just as she'd thought, it took half an hour to finish the chapter. She went to bed, hoping to dream of their goodbye kiss beneath the tree.

Chapter 27

In A Heartbeat

On the way home from Deanna's, Solomon sat waiting for the light to change from red to green at the intersection on the south side of town. His mind wandered to their kiss—each one better than the last, leaving him wanting more. Double-checking the light, he watched it turn green. Moving his foot from the brake to the accelerator, he proceeded. Halfway through the intersection, he felt the crash more than he heard it. His truck spun out of control.

When his truck came to a stop, Solomon's heart raced, and his breathing quickened. He tested his limbs and head, giving thanks for the movement everywhere, despite the limited motion and pain in his left arm and shoulder, and his throbbing head.

He assessed his surroundings and determined it was safe to exit the truck. Releasing his seatbelt, he slid out. The driver's side of his pickup's bed was crushed and pulled away from the cab. His eyes landed on a lifted red truck with a mangled bumper and smashed grille. Its driver slumped over the steering wheel.

He flagged down a bystander. "Please, as fast as you can, go to the gas station on the corner and call 911."

He watched the young man sprint away, then went to check on the other driver. The first-aid certification he'd earned through his job at Bard's Buildings would be used today. He stepped up on the running board of the man's truck and tapped on the window. The man's eyes opened.

"Help me," he said.

"Help is on the way," the man who'd gone to call 911 said between breaths. "The guy at the gas station had already called."

"Thank you."

He turned his attention back to the other driver. "Please don't move, in case something is broken. I'm going to open this door and check your vitals. Help is on the way. I'll stay with you until it's here."

Opening the door, he did a brief assessment. The man's color was good. His skin was warm but not clammy. His pulse and respirations were steady.

"I'm going to open the other door so it isn't so warm for you. I'll be right back. Stay still. It shouldn't be much longer," Solomon said.

While he accomplished the tasks, he prayed silently for the other driver and thanked the Lord for their survival. He returned to wait beside the man.

"I think I would feel better if I sat up. Please help me?" the man asked.

Solomon heard sirens coming closer. "Do you hear that? That's the sound of help. I was taught to keep the injured person in the position I found them in as long as their vitals are good and there is no danger. That's the case here."

The flashing lights stilled.

"The paramedics are here. They'll help you move safely." Solomon waved his right arm. "Over here!" he called.

When the medics approached, Solomon stepped aside, letting them assume care. The female paramedic stopped him when he started to walk away.

"Is there anything we should know about your friend?" she asked.

He shook his head. "I don't know him. I made sure he didn't move and was safe. He seems okay. He wants to sit up, but just in case he's injured, I asked him to stay still."

The paramedic nodded. "What you did was the right thing. Why are you here?"

"I'm here because his monster truck hit my pickup. By the looks of things, he didn't even slow down." Solomon nodded, then resumed walking away.

"Sir," she called after him. He stopped and turned back to her. "If that's your truck over there, you're not going anywhere in it. Judging from the way your left arm is hanging, you have injuries that your adrenaline is masking. Let me help you."

Solomon groaned. "I'm fine, really."

"If that's true, I'll only be wasting about fifteen minutes of your time." She stepped closer, pinning him with her gaze.

He groaned again. "I can tell you aren't going to let this go. Lead the way."

With him sitting in her rig's doorway, she assessed him. She touched the lump on his collarbone, causing him to flinch and moan. He groaned when she tried to move his left shoulder. The tenderness as she pressed on his belly surprised him. She shook her head while making notes.

Her gaze speared him. "You need to go to the hospital and get checked out. Your clavicle is likely fractured, and your shoulder separated. The tenderness in your abdomen could be due to seatbelt bruising, but it may also indicate an internal injury. I'm going to wrap your left arm to immobilize it and prevent further damage. Go to the ER."

"I don't have to go in this ambulance, do I?" he asked, frowning. "My dad or brother can come."

She nodded. "Stay here so I can keep an eye on you until someone comes. I'll send an officer over to notify them for you. While you wait, he can get your statement. I need to help my partner. Stay put."

"Yes, ma'am."

Solomon gave the officer his father's name and phone number, listening as he radioed dispatch to notify Mark Jackson and relay the contact information. The officer then took Solomon's license and insurance card and transmitted the details.

"Was the number you gave me your current phone number?" he asked.

Solomon nodded, grimacing at the increased pain. "Yes, sir."

"And your address is the same as the one on your license?"

"Yes, sir."

The officer handed back the documents. "Tell me what happened in your own words."

Solomon described the accident. The officer asked him to repeat a few details while jotting notes, then confirmed with dispatch that Mark Jackson had been notified and would take his son to the local emergency room.

"Your dad's on his way. If I need anything else, I'll be in touch." He offered a polite smile and a curt nod.

Solomon returned both, careful not to jar his head or body. As the officer walked away, exhaustion hit him like a wave. He leaned his head against the ambulance door and closed his eyes. He must've dozed off, because the next thing he heard was his father's voice.

"Son. Son!"

Solomon opened his eyes to see his dad standing in front of him.

"An officer and a paramedic pointed me your way." He reached for Solomon's left arm, then paused. "I see why they said you need to go to the hospital."

Solomon followed his gaze and saw the wrapping. "The medic said it's possible my collarbone's fractured and my shoulder's separated. She wrapped it so I wouldn't make it worse. It's really sore."

His dad stepped closer and gently took his right arm. "Let's get you into my truck."

Solomon nodded, grateful. "Can you help me move my stuff from my truck to yours?"

He looked at his pickup, heart sinking. He probably wouldn't drive it again. A tear slipped down his cheek before he could stop it. "What happens now?"

"I've already arranged with the officer to have your truck towed to a body shop. I'll call the insurance company once we're at the hospital. Now, tell me what I need to grab."

Solomon did his best to direct him, though his thoughts were foggy and his body felt weary. His dad's arms were full when Solomon murmured, "I'm sorry, Dad. We need to go."

His dad gave him a once-over. "I agree. Lean on me."

Solomon gripped his dad's shoulder with his good arm as they walked to the truck. He leaned against the side while his dad emptied his arms, then his dad helped him into the passenger seat. As the door shut, Solomon rested his head against the headrest and closed his eyes.

"Are you making any calls besides the insurance company?" he asked quietly.

His dad glanced over, eyebrows raised, then turned back to the road. "Yes. I'm callin' your mother. She and your sisters are worried sick. She'll update Robert and Emelia."

Solomon's chin dropped. "I'm sure they're all worried. But I need one other person to know what happened. Could Mom or Robert call Deanna? I don't want her to panic or feel hurt if she hears about this secondhand. I wish I could call her myself."

He shifted, pulling his wallet from his back pocket and slipping out the note with Deanna's number.

"I didn't know you were seein' anyone," his dad said, eyes still on the road.

"I was on my way home from Deanna's when that truck ran the red light. I met her at Robert's wedding. She's Emelia's best friend. I asked her dad for permission to date her tonight. She's important to me." He kept his eyes shut.

His dad didn't respond, but Solomon felt the truck slow and turn. He opened his eyes to see the ER parking lot. His dad pulled into the spot closest to the entrance.

"Stay here," his dad said. "I'll get a wheelchair."

"I can walk," Solomon protested.

His dad gave him a sharp look. "You may be able to walk, but you were unsteady gettin' to the truck. I'm gettin' a wheelchair for both our sakes."

Solomon knew better than to argue. When his father returned, a nurse followed with a wheelchair. His dad helped him out of the truck and into the chair. Solomon didn't understand how he'd felt strong enough to help the other driver, yet now he was weak, aching, and exhausted. His shoulder throbbed, his head pounded, and his lower abdomen was sore. He still didn't believe he needed to be in the hospital, but everyone else sure did.

The nurse wheeled him into an exam cubicle and asked him to change into a gown. Solomon waved off the offer of help, but as he reached for his boot, pain shot through his left arm, stealing his breath and spreading across his chest and neck. His face went pale, and his dad steadied him.

"I think you do need help changin'," his dad said gently. "Let me help you, son."

Solomon saw only love and compassion in his father's face and nodded, though humiliation welled up. He offered a silent prayer.

God, You've shown me how life can change in a heartbeat. A grown man should be able to dress himself. Help me accept this lesson in humility and be thankful for my dad, who loves me enough to help me in my time of need. In Jesus' name, amen.

Once his boots and socks were off, Solomon looked up. "Dad, thank you for loving me enough to take care of me."

His dad's face held concern, but the corners of his mouth lifted. "Kiddo, no matter how big or old you get, I'll still be your dad, and I'll be here when you need me. I'm so thankful I still have you to love." He sniffled and swiped his cheek. "Now let's finish up and get you in that bed."

He let Solomon do what he could and helped with the rest. Once Solomon was clothed in the hospital gown — if such a thing could be called clothing — his dad eased him onto the bed and covered him with a sheet and a blanket.

Solomon rested his head back and closed his eyes. The darkness helped. *Maybe I do need to be here.* Then Deanna came to mind.

"Dad, are you still here?"

"Yes."

"Do you have that piece of paper I had in the truck?"

"I do. It has your girl's address and number."

Solomon sighed. "Please make sure someone calls her."

"I will. As soon as the nurse comes back, I'll call your mom. She'll handle the rest. I think I need to stay here with you."

Just then, the nurse returned. "Sir, you can use the patient's phone for local calls. Dial nine for an outside line."

"Thank you," his dad said.

The nurse, Baxter, according to his name tag, handed him a clipboard. "Please fill out the pertinent information. Admissions will be in shortly."

He turned to Solomon. "Can you tell me your name and date of birth?"

Solomon answered.

"Any allergies, latex, medications, foods?"

"No known allergies," his dad said, eyes on the form.

Baxter nodded and began his assessment, checking vitals and asking about pain. He asked Solomon about his shoulder. When Solomon reported pain while trying to change, Baxter made a note and left the shoulder alone. He examined his head for abrasions and pressed gently on his abdomen. Solomon assumed Baxter wrote every grimace and groan in his chart.

Setting his notes aside, Baxter shone a light in Solomon's eyes and asked him to follow it. Then he tested limb strength, avoiding the injured arm.

"This next part may seem silly, but go with it," Baxter said.

Solomon grimaced. "Can I do it with my eyes closed? These lights feel like a jackhammer in my skull."

"Absolutely. Is your headache worse than before?"

"Yes. About seven and a half now. Closing my eyes helps."

Baxter dimmed the lights and made a few notes. "Here's the silly part. Remember these three words: apple, truck, dog."

Solomon nodded slowly.

"Who's the president?"

"Ronald Reagan."

"What state are we in?"

"Missouri."

"What day is today?"

"Thursday."

"Who is this man with you?"

"My dad."

"What were the three words?"

"Apple, truck, and dog."

Baxter smiled. "Good news! You're fully oriented, and your memory's intact. The doctor will be in shortly. I'll let him know you need something for the headache. Anything I can do before I step out?"

"No, thank you," Solomon said, his eyelids already heavy. For now, he was safe and grateful.

Chapter 28

In the ER

Solomon's eyes were closed, his dad sitting quietly beside him, when the metallic clicking of the curtain startled them both. Solomon cracked his eyes open just enough to see a man in a white coat at the foot of his bed, then closed them again.

"I'm Dr. Gannon, and you must be Solomon Jackson. Nice to meet you." The doctor pulled the curtain closed behind him. He held Solomon's chart in one hand. "Your vitals look good, breath and heart sounds are normal. Mind if I take a quick listen?"

"I don't mind," Solomon murmured, eyes closed again.

After a few moments with the stethoscope, Dr. Gannon nodded. "Sounds good. I take it your head's still hurting. Can you describe the pain, where it is, what it feels like, and rate it from zero to ten?"

Solomon groaned softly. "It's better with the lights dimmed and my eyes closed. If I stay still, it's about a six. Less jackhammer now, more like a slow, steady drumbeat. It fills my whole head."

"Do you remember hitting your head?"

"No, sir. I don't remember anything that would've caused these injuries. I felt fine right after the accident. I helped the other driver until emergency personnel arrived. It wasn't until the paramedic insisted on checking me that the pain set in. Why don't I remember getting hurt?"

"Adrenaline masks pain. That's likely what happened." He glanced at the chart. "Which shoulder is it?"

Solomon opened his eyes to a slit. "My left. But shouldn't you already know that?"

Dr. Gannon smiled. "Just confirming. I'll check it."

"Please don't. When I tried to remove my boots, the pain shot through my arm, chest, and neck. I don't want to feel that again."

"Fair enough. I still need to take a look."

Dr. Gannon carefully opened the shoulder of Solomon's gown, touching the lump on his collarbone, commenting on the bruising and the unnatural slope of the shoulder. Solomon groaned, and tears slid from his eyes.

"I'm sorry that hurt so much." The doctor handed him a tissue and closed the gown over his shoulder. "May I check your abdomen?"

"Do you have to?"

"I do, but I'll be gentle."

Solomon lifted the blanket with his right arm. The doctor held the blanket and pulled his gown back just enough to expose his abdomen. "You've got some significant bruising," he said, pressing gently. Solomon winced and moaned.

"The tenderness is mostly where the bruising is, but it radiates a bit. I suspect seatbelt trauma, though we'll check for internal injury."

Solomon's dad leaned forward. "So what does all this mean? How are you gonna help my son?"

"First, I'm ordering pain medication."

"Thank you, Lord," Solomon muttered.

"I'm sorry you're hurting so much. It'll start getting better from here. We'll draw labs, give you pain meds, and send you to radiology for CT scans, head, left shoulder and clavicle, and abdomen," Dr. Gannon said, speaking to Solomon.

"I'm confident you have a concussion and some shoulder damage. We need to rule out internal injury. The scans and labs will guide treatment. The lab tech is waiting, so I'll step out."

"How long before the pain medicine comes?" Solomon asked.

"I'm ordering them stat. The nurse should be in shortly after your blood is drawn."

"Stat means quick?"

"Stat means quicker than quick." Dr. Gannon winked at Solomon. "I'll see you once I have your results." He held the curtain open for the lab tech, then slipped out.

After the labs were drawn and the pain meds kicked in, Solomon drifted off.

"Knock, knock," came a voice from behind the curtain. "Radiology. May we come in?"

His dad stood and opened the curtain. Two men entered, raised the bed rails, and unlocked the wheels.

"Name and birth date?" one asked.

Solomon stated both.

"Ready to go?"

"Dad," Solomon murmured.

His father moved to his side, squeezed his right hand, and kissed his forehead. "How long will the scans take?"

"About an hour. We'll bring him back when we're done."

"I'll be here when you get back. I love you, son."

"Thanks, Dad. I love you, too."

When Solomon returned to his ER cubicle an hour and a half later, both parents were waiting.

"Mom, you're here."

"Yes, I am. Your brother and sisters are, too. You are so loved, my boy."

"I love you, Mom." His voice cracked. "Does Deanna know what happened?"

His mother nodded. "She does. I spoke with her and her parents."

He wondered how that conversation had gone, but he didn't have the energy to ask. *Deanna knows.* "Thanks, Mom." He closed his eyes and let the world fade.

He stirred when his mother gently took his hand. "The doctor's here."

His dad's voice was tight with urgency. "We need to know what's wrong. What did the tests show? Do you have a plan?"

Dr. Gannon turned to Solomon. "Ready for the rundown?"

Solomon opened his eyes.

"Your labs are normal. There are no signs of internal injury. The abdominal tenderness is likely deep bruising from the seatbelt. You have a grade-two concussion, a separated shoulder, and a fractured clavicle. I hope the fracture will align when your shoulder is reset. If it does, immobilization should allow it to heal. If not, it'll need to be realigned surgically with a plate and screws. An orthopedic surgeon will evaluate the scans and speak with you in the morning."

"How long will he be in the hospital?" his parents asked together.

"At least through tomorrow. It depends on how the shoulder and clavicle respond. I'm less concerned about the concussion, but he'll need to avoid bright lights, reading, watching television, and using a computer if you have one, and anything that strains the brain for a couple of weeks. A neurologist will review the head scan and see you before you're discharged."

Solomon's frown deepened. "I won't be able to drive or work. Watching fireworks with my girl on the Fourth is out, isn't it?"

"I'm afraid so. I'm sorry, Solomon." Dr. Gannon held his gaze and offered a small, sincere smile. "I'll keep checking in while you're here. Your nurse can reach me if you need anything. I wish I had better news." He slipped out through the curtain.

Solomon turned away.

"Are you okay?" his mother asked, gently rubbing his arm.

"No. I'm not," he said quietly.

His dad leaned in. "Son, you're gonna be alright. In a few weeks, you'll be back to everything you love. All this will be in your rearview mirror." He paused, voice trembling. "I'm so thankful you're here, that you'll recover."

Solomon turned toward them. "I'm thankful I'm still here."

His mother leaned over and hugged him gently. "Are you up to seeing your brother and sisters? Dad and I will step out so they can come in."

He tried to smile. "I'm really tired."

"Just a quick hello? They're worried sick. I'll make sure they keep it short."

"Okay."

Robert came in first, with Millie at his side. After five quiet minutes and hugs, they left, and Emelia and Lexi took their place. Five minutes and shared embraces later, they promised to return tomorrow once he'd had a chance to rest.

Solomon closed his eyes as the curtain fell shut. When it opened again, he assumed it was one of his parents. He didn't stir until the soft scent of strawberries and vanilla surrounded him, and soft lips brushed his.

"Deanna," he whispered, lifting his right arm to hold her close for one more kiss. When he let go, she raised her head, tears slipping down her cheeks.

"I can't imagine losing you," she said.

He reached up and gently wiped her tears with his fingertips. "I'm going to be fine. But I won't make our first date."

A soft smile curved her lips, and Solomon returned it. She settled into the chair beside his bed.

"My parents didn't want me to come with your mom tonight," she said. "But I had to see you, touch you, kiss you, know you were okay. I've never defied them before. Home won't feel the same when I go back."

"Dee, I'm sorry. I didn't mean to cause trouble between you and your parents." He reached for her hand. "But I'm so thankful you're here. Is there any chance you can stay?"

He didn't expect her to say yes, but he hoped.

His mother's face appeared through the curtain. "The nurse just told me there's a room ready for you on the orthopedic floor. She wants to know if someone's staying with you tonight. I'll stay if you want."

"I want Deanna to stay. Can she, Mom?"

"I told her parents I wasn't bringing her home tonight." She turned to Deanna. "Do you want to stay?"

"Yes, ma'am. I want to stay with Solomon," Deanna said, fingers fidgeting with the hem of her blouse, her lower lip caught between her teeth.

Betsy smiled. "I'm thankful for your willingness to care for my boy. Deanna, please, call me Betsy. I think we need to be friends."

"Oh." She turned back to Solomon. "I'm sorry I didn't answer you. Yes, Deanna can stay."

Deanna rose and hugged her. "Thank you, Mrs. Jackson. I mean, Betsy."

She returned to Solomon's side, and he grinned from ear to ear. "Thanks, Mom."

"I'm thankful you'll be in Deanna's loving care. Dad and I will be back in the morning after we drop the girls off at summer school. It's their last day." With that, his mom disappeared through the curtain.

Chapter 29

A Room

By the time Solomon was settled into his room on the orthopedic floor, it was just past two in the morning. Another hour crawled by before the nurse tech finished taking his vitals and the new nurse completed her assessment. Solomon rested his head against the pillow, closed his eyes, and groaned.

"What's wrong? Are you hurting? What can I do?" Deanna asked, her voice laced with concern.

"I'm hurting a little more," he admitted. "Probably from all the jostling during the move and the exam. If it doesn't ease up soon, I'll ask for something."

He opened his eyes and found hers. "I told your dad I'd never interfere with your studies. They're supposed to come first. How will you make it to class tomorrow? If you miss it, our gooses are cooked. Your parents will never let me take you out."

Deanna's gaze dropped to the floor. A moment later, she lifted her head, squared her shoulders, and met his eyes with quiet resolve. "I'm dating you. I won't let them keep us apart."

His head throbbed, but he couldn't look away from the woman who had just transformed before him. Her words stirred something deeper. *Am I in love with her already?*

"Are you sure you want to take that kind of stand?" he asked gently. "Shouldn't we try to please them?"

She shook her head. "If I don't stand up to them now, they'll keep us apart. I don't want to lose you. I..."

He reached for her hand. "I don't want to lose you either. I do, too."

A giggle slipped out as she squeezed his fingers. "We should try to sleep before someone else comes in."

"Yeah. Move your chair closer. I want to fall asleep holding your hand."

She pulled the recliner next to his bed, gathered the pillow and blanket from the counter, and made up the chair. He watched her with a full heart.

"Dee," he said softly, "before you settle in, please kiss me."

She sighed. "I wish I could kiss you goodnight every night."

Her cheeks turned the prettiest shade of pink he'd ever seen. "I wish you could, too."

She leaned over and touched her lips to his. The kiss was gentle, but he wanted more. His hand slid into her hair, drawing her closer. He teased her lips open and deepened the kiss, breathing in the strawberry scent of her hair. With her fingers in his hair, his pain faded into nothing.

She pulled back too soon. "I promise we'll kiss again," she whispered.

"Please, Dee. Kiss me again. I need you," he said, fingers threading through her hair.

"You need me?" she squeaked.

"I need you. I want you. I..." He waited for her eyes to meet his. "It feels fast, but I think I love you."

She brushed her lips against his. "I think I love you, too," she whispered, then let him kiss her the way he wanted.

When they finally broke apart, both were breathless. Deanna traced his face with her fingertips. "Sweetheart, you need sleep. They'll wake you in a couple of hours, if not sooner. I should catch a few winks, too."

She slipped from his one-armed embrace, trailing her hand down his arm until their fingers intertwined. It was awkward, but she managed to climb into the chair and pull the blanket over herself without letting go.

"Sweet dreams, my sweet," Solomon murmured, closing his eyes.

Soft, whistling snores soon rose from the chair. They were the sweetest sounds he'd ever heard. Her music lulled him to sleep.

A knock on the hospital room door, followed by a lab tech's voice, pulled Solomon from sleep.

"I guess the vampires around here have to get their job done before sunrise," he muttered.

"And we have to see to get our blood," she replied with a straight face, flipping on the overhead light. "Name and birthdate, please."

The brightness stabbed at his eyes, and his head throbbed instantly. He snapped his eyes shut. *I need pain medication.*

She cleared her throat. "Mr. Jackson, I can't use this arm because of the immobilizer on it. I need to use your right arm to draw your blood."

She glanced at the recliner beside his bed. "Your wife is still sleeping."

"Dee," he said softly. The vinyl crackled, then silence.

"My sweet, I need you to wake up."

"I'm not ready," she mumbled.

"I'm sorry, but the lab tech needs the chair moved so she can draw my blood. You can go back to sleep right after."

The chair squeaked and thudded as she adjusted it. He imagined her rising, hair tousled, rubbing her eyes. He longed to see her, but the pain kept his eyes shut tight. The scrape of the chair told him she'd moved it.

While the tech drew his blood, he heard Deanna settle back into the recliner. Despite the pain, her presence brought a smile to his face.

"All done," the tech said, bandaging his arm. "Anything I can do before I go?"

"Yes, two things. Please turn off the light and ask my nurse to bring pain medicine. My pain level's about an eight."

"You got it," she said.

Wife. With the lights off, Solomon opened his eyes and looked at Deanna, curled in the recliner. She'd come despite her parents' objections, stayed by his side, and slept in a chair just to be near him. *That's what a wife would do.* The title was premature, but it felt right.

Just as the thought settled, another knock came.

"I have your pain medication," a voice called.

"Please come in," he said, grateful.

The nurse entered, and before she could speak, he blurted, "Solomon Jackson. October third, nineteen sixty-four."

"Is your pain still an eight?"

"Yes, ma'am."

He used the bed control to raise the head of the bed, wincing as his shoulder protested. It was less painful than trying to sit up. After swallowing the pills, he lowered the bed again.

"Thank you," he said, grimacing.

"The orthopedic surgeon is reviewing your chart and scans now. He'll be in shortly." Her expression softened. "I hope you're not a breakfast person. He's ordered you NPO."

"NPO?" Solomon frowned.

"It means nothing by mouth. No breakfast."

The door opened, and a man in scrubs and a surgical cap stepped inside, nodding to the nurse. "Please stay while I go over the treatment plan with him," he said. She nodded and remained.

"Deanna, my sweet, I need you to wake up." With the lights still dim, Solomon could see her clearly. He watched every movement until she reached his side and took his hand.

"Name and birthdate?" the doctor asked.

Solomon gave the information, and the man introduced himself. "Dr. Cutter. I know, it's a fitting name for a surgeon. Believe me, I've heard it all."

Even half-awake, Deanna responded with a soft laugh. "I bet you have."

Dr. Cutter smiled. "Now that we've got that out of the way, when was the last time you ate?"

"Dinner last night, around six thirty."

"And the last time you drank anything?"

"I took pain meds around five this morning. Just enough water to swallow the pill."

"That's fine." He turned to the nurse. "Sally, please get the consent forms while I explain the procedure."

Dr. Cutter outlined the plan much like the ER doctor had, with one key difference. "Your clavicle is broken and needs realignment to heal properly. Once it's aligned, I'll secure it with a titanium plate and screws. This will stabilize the area and allow the bone to heal correctly. Then I'll restore the shoulder joint. Physical therapy starts next week."

"I work in construction, mostly home renovation. How long before I can go back?"

"It depends on your healing. Recovery usually takes three to six months. Given the physical demands of your job, I'd lean toward six. You'll need full strength to avoid reinjury."

"Three to six months?" Solomon frowned. "That's a long time off work."

Dr. Cutter's expression shifted, stern, like his minister's when he spoke about the consequences of sin. "You're young, Solomon. Eighteen. If you don't respect your limitations while healing, this injury could affect you for the rest of your life."

"He'll do everything he's supposed to," Deanna said firmly. "I'll see to it."

Dr. Cutter chuckled. "Well, okay then. The boss has spoken."

Solomon looked at her. This side of Deanna was new, and he liked it. He reached for her hand, and she nestled hers inside his. The door opened again, and Sally returned with a clipboard.

"I'm going to write your pre-op orders," Dr. Cutter said. "Sally will take good care of you until I see you in about an hour."

Sally reviewed the form, listing potential complications. Solomon's eyes widened. Deanna squeezed his hand.

"Relax, sweetheart. All surgeries carry risks. If you don't sign, your shoulder won't get fixed. I'm sure you want more than one usable arm."

"And without surgery," Sally added, "you'll be in constant pain."

Solomon raised his right hand in surrender. "I get it. The greatest risk is not having the surgery. Give me the pen. Let's get this show on the road."

After he signed, Sally took his water cup away. "Is there anything I can do before I go?"

Solomon hesitated, then blushed. "I need to go to the bathroom. Could you help me?"

"I can." She set the form aside. "You know this adventure will increase your pain."

He nodded, grimacing. Sally helped him to and from the bathroom, then settled him back in bed. "If your pain doesn't settle, let me know," she said before leaving.

Deanna's gaze followed him until he was settled back in bed. *Was she watching so she can help me later?*

"You should call your parents," she said.

Solomon glanced at the clock, grateful he could see it in the dim light. "Almost eight. They'll be here any minute. Robert's already at work. Mom will figure out how to let him and Emelia know."

Deanna nodded, and her stomach rumbled.

"You're hungry," Solomon said.

She smiled. "Only a little."

"My sweet, get yourself some coffee and something to eat. Just because I can't eat doesn't mean you shouldn't."

She looked in her purse, then back at him. "I can't."

Solomon resisted the urge to shake his head. "Get my personal belongings bag from the closet. There is cash in my wallet in the back pocket of my jeans. Take it and put it in your purse."

Her mouth fell open, but she did as he'd asked. "I'll keep it safe."

"Deanna, I want you to use that money to take care of yourself. You're taking care of me. Let me take care of you."

"You trust me to spend your money?"

"If I didn't trust you and your judgment, we wouldn't be together. I trust you, Dee."

He reached for her hand. When she took it, he pulled her close, guiding her mouth to his. He poured everything he felt into the kiss, and she gave just as much in return. When she broke the kiss, she laid her head on his shoulder.

"You can take care of me," she whispered. "I'll do my best not to disappoint you."

He lifted her chin to see her eyes. "My sweet, you won't. Please, go feed yourself."

Her eyes darkened to a deep green. "I'm not leaving you until they take you for surgery."

His parents entered the room. "Surgery?" his mother asked.

Solomon gently released Deanna's hand, and she stepped back. "The surgeon came earlier. He's going to place a plate and screws in my collarbone to hold it together. It's too misaligned to heal on its own. Then he'll repair my shoulder. I signed the consent form."

Before they could respond, the nurse entered. Solomon immediately gave his name and birthdate.

She held a vial and syringe. "This will help you relax. They'll be here to take you to surgery in about fifteen minutes. Are you ready?"

"Is anybody ever really ready for surgery?" he said, his voice dry.

Sally drew the medication into the syringe, connected it to his IV port, and slowly administered the drug. Solomon felt the warmth spread through him, his words began to slur. "Thank you."

"I'll see you when it's all over," she said with a kind smile.

Chapter 30

Surgery

The medicine made Solomon happy. He laughed at everything but was too impaired to answer his parents' questions. Deanna sighed and stepped in, doing her best to fill in the gaps. The fifteen minutes passed quickly as she and his parents talked quietly.

The transport team arrived. Solomon perked up and rattled off his name and birthdate. "How come nobody can remember who I am?" he asked, puzzled.

Deanna took his hand. "They know who you are. It's just how the hospital makes sure they've got the right person," she said gently.

"What body part is Dr. Cutter repairing?" one of the men asked.

"My left shoulder. I want to move it again. Duh."

The team chuckled. "That pre-op med really kicked in," one of them said with a grin.

Solomon's dad stepped forward, placing a firm hand on the bed. "Dr. Cutter?"

The men nodded. The same one replied, his tone steady. "Yes, sir. He's the best orthopedic surgeon in the area. His name gets reactions, but he's excellent. Your son's in good hands."

"It's time to say goodbye," another said.

Deanna leaned in and kissed Solomon's lips. His mother kissed his cheek. His father kissed his forehead, then let go of the bed. "We'll be praying, son," he said softly.

"We'll bring your husband and son back to you in a couple of hours," one of the men assured them. "If anything changes, someone will come let you know."

"Bye," Solomon shouted as they wheeled him away.

Once the door closed, Betsy turned to Deanna, eyes wide. "Husband. Is there something else we need to know?"

Deanna's chin dropped. "No, ma'am. I'm sorry that man said that. I promise it was just an assumption."

Betsy softened and pulled her into a hug. "Not your fault. Thank you for taking care of him last night."

Deanna's stomach growled.

"We probably have time to grab something while he's in surgery," Betsy said. "Have you eaten?"

They headed to the cafeteria. Mark and Betsy got coffee, and Deanna picked up food and coffee. At the register, she pulled Solomon's wallet from her purse, took out cash, and paid. She tucked the change back into the wallet, catching Betsy's gaze as she returned it to her purse.

At the table, Deanna sat across from them. As she reached for her fork, she hesitated, then tucked her napkin into her lap, hiding her trembling hands.

"I'm sorry for whatever I've done wrong," she said, her voice shaking.

Mark's expression was firm. "Why do you have Solomon's wallet?"

She swallowed. "He wanted me to get breakfast before Dr. Cutter came in. I didn't have any money. He told me to take it from his pants pocket and use it. He said he wanted to take care of me while I was taking care of him."

Betsy nodded slowly. "So he knows you have it."

Deanna wadded the shredded napkin in her lap and placed it on the table. A tear escaped despite her efforts to hold it back. She wiped it away with the napkin scraps and exhaled.

"Yes, ma'am. Solomon knows. He said if we can't trust each other, we shouldn't be together. He trusts me to use his money wisely." She steadied her breath. "He trusts me. Mr. and Mrs. Jackson, I won't take advantage of his generosity. I promise."

Mark's face softened. "That's good enough for us. And please, call us Mark and Betsy."

He bowed his head and prayed over her meal. Then he stood. "I'll get you some napkins that aren't in pieces."

"Thank you." The tension in her shoulders finally eased.

Deanna's gaze followed him the whole time. Betsy reached across the table and gently covered Deanna's hand. "I'm sorry we upset you. If something bothers us, we'll talk to you, and we'll listen."

Deanna nodded, offering a weak smile. "Thank you."

Mark returned with fresh napkins just as syrup dripped from a bite of pancake. She wiped her chin and hurried through her meal. They refilled their coffee cups and returned to Solomon's room.

Sally entered just after they arrived. "Dr. Cutter asked that you wait in the surgical waiting area. He wants to speak with you when he's finished."

They each drew in a sharp breath. "Has something gone wrong?" Betsy asked, alarmed.

"No, nothing's wrong," Sally reassured. "I didn't mean to worry you. I'll have a tech walk you down."

"Thank you," Mark said.

In the waiting area, Deanna struggled to stay awake. Her sleep had been shallow and brief. Her head bobbed until a call for the Jackson family snapped her upright.

They were led into a consultation room. Deanna was grateful Mark and Betsy would hear the news directly from Dr. Cutter. The surgery had gone exactly as planned. The tightness in her chest eased, and breathing came easier.

"When Solomon's awake enough, he'll be brought back to his room," Dr. Cutter said. "A neurologist and I will see him tomorrow. If recovery goes well, he'll be discharged then."

Back in Solomon's room, Betsy looked Deanna over. "You haven't even changed clothes today."

"No, ma'am. Maybe later, while Solomon's resting. I'll put on my sleeping clothes and still have something clean for tomorrow," she said, stifling a yawn.

"You're staying again tonight?" Betsy asked, one brow raised.

"Yes, ma'am. I promised him I would. I won't let him down. I'll let my parents know."

Betsy hesitated. "Are you sure that's wise? They may not take it well."

Deanna nodded. "I know they won't. But I've never been allowed to make my own choices. This is my line in the sand. Solomon wants me here, so I'll be here. He's worth the consequences."

Mark and Betsy encouraged her to nap while they waited. She curled up in the chair, and Betsy draped a blanket over her. With most of her stress gone, sleep came easily.

When Solomon was wheeled into the room, Deanna woke. He was awake and alert. But a flurry of activity, including the nursing assessment, post-op vitals, and visits from Robert, Emelia, and his sisters, wore him out. He fell asleep mid-sentence. When he snored softly, everyone cleared out, asking Deanna to give him hugs and let him know they were praying for him.

She closed the door behind them and walked to his bedside. She kissed his cheek and whispered, "I love you." He wouldn't remember, but she wanted him to hear it.

A dietary attendant arrived with a tray. After Deanna confirmed Solomon's name and birthdate, he left it on the bedside table. "If he wakes up, he may want something to eat," he said before leaving.

Deanna used the room phone to call home. Her father answered, and as expected, he disapproved.

"Dad, Solomon wants me here. I'm staying. I'm not asking, I'm telling you, so you won't worry."

She repeated herself for clarity. "I am staying."

Her father grumbled but didn't threaten to come get her. "I love you, Dad. Please tell Mom I love her, too. I'll call tomorrow when I know more. Bye."

Sleep mattered more than a shower, clean clothes, or food. She pulled the recliner close to Solomon's bed, grabbed the blanket, and curled up. The moment her eyes closed, sleep took her.

Chapter 31

Going Home

Other than a few brief awakenings for vitals, an antibiotic added to his IV, and an early morning blood draw, Solomon slept straight through the night, or at least as far as he knew. He vaguely remembered asking for pain meds and something about telling Deanna to eat his dinner. How much do I remember, and how much did I dream? It was all a little foggy.

Still, he felt better this morning. His head ached, and bright lights made it worse, but his mind was clear. What surprised him was the absence of shoulder pain. Then he realized he couldn't feel his left side at all. There was no sensation from his neck to his fingertips.

He turned his head and saw Deanna asleep in the chair beside him. Her presence was a balm to his soul. *She stayed.* But panic crept in. *Did I have a stroke?* His heart pounded and breath quickened.

"Deanna, please wake up," he said, louder than intended.

She sat up, eyes wide. "Are you okay? What do you need? I'll call the nurse."

He forced himself to calm down. "I can't feel anything from my neck to my fingertips on my left side. Did I have a stroke during surgery?"

Deanna took a breath and exhaled slowly. "You're fine. They performed a nerve block to numb the area and prevent pain for a couple of days. The feeling will return in about two to three days."

"Oh." He paused. "Wait. I remember asking for pain meds last night."

"You did. You told the nurse your head was pounding and rated it a seven."

Relief washed over him. He closed his eyes and relaxed into the bed. "I'm so happy you're here."

She rubbed his upper arm gently. "I'm happy to be here."

He sighed. "What's wrong, Deanna?"

"Nothing you need to worry about. I have finals next week, but I can study at your side just as well as I can at home. I'll need to leave to take my tests and go home at night once you're discharged, but until then, I'll be here. I promised you I'd stay. Trust me to keep that promise."

Her voice was steady and sure. It didn't match the restrictions her father had laid out before the accident. Maybe things had shifted. Whatever the reason, Solomon was grateful.

"Dee, I trust you. Please, kiss me, my sweet."

She leaned in and gave him a brief kiss. "If you'll be okay for fifteen minutes, I'm going to shower and change."

Solomon raised an eyebrow. "I don't think I'll survive fifteen minutes without you unless you kiss me again."

"Sol. O. Mon."

"Dee."

"You drive a hard bargain."

She kissed him again, but he wanted more. He pulled her close with his good arm, slid his hand into her hair, and deepened the kiss. Her lips, her scent, the warmth of her touch, he was lost in it. When she finally pulled away, she smiled.

"Will that hold you for fifteen minutes?"

He sighed. "I suppose so."

"I'll be quick," she said with a laugh.

She was showered, dressed, and back at his side when his parents arrived. His dad carried a backpack.

"Any word from the doctors?" his dad asked.

"Nope," Solomon said, eyes still closed.

A knock sounded. "Dietary. Are you ready for breakfast?"

"Yes, please come in," Solomon said, smiling. "I'm hungry."

After confirming his name and birthdate, the attendant placed the tray on his table. "Do you have everything you need?"

He nodded.

Once the door closed, Betsy turned to him. "Did you eat anything yesterday?"

"They brought a snack after you left, but he didn't eat it," Deanna said. "He slept most of the evening. I woke him for dinner, but he wasn't interested."

Solomon chuckled. "I was nauseous and groggy. Did I tell you to eat my dinner?"

"You did," Deanna said. "The nurse said it was fine. They keep snacks on the floor if you wake up hungry. I ate your dinner, and it was pretty good."

He considered that and smiled.

She handed him his fork. "You said you're hungry. Please eat."

"Have you had breakfast, dear?" Betsy asked.

"No, ma'am."

Another knock. "Come in," Solomon said.

His nurse entered with a tray. "Dietary had an extra. I thought you might like some breakfast."

Deanna smiled. "Thank you for thinking of me."

"You're welcome. Would you like coffee?"

A few minutes later, the nurse tech returned with coffee, milk, and sugar for everyone. Solomon and Deanna ate while his parents sipped their coffee.

After half an hour, Solomon's headache returned. He pressed the call button.

"How may I help you?" came through the speaker.

"Please tell my nurse I need pain medication. My head's at a six and climbing."

He closed his eyes, mouth tight, rubbing his right temple. His left arm was useless, and he hated it.

Deanna touched his arm briefly, and he knew she saw his pain. The room quieted, and he was grateful.

A knock. "Come in," Deanna said.

His nurse entered. "Name, date of birth, and pain level?"

"Solomon Jackson. Ten-three-sixty-four. Pain's at a seven. Thank you for coming so quickly."

He raised the bed, took the pills, and Deanna handed him water. She took the empty cup from his hand.

"I'll check on you soon. Anything else?"

"Please help me with the trays," Deanna said, picking up hers. The nurse grabbed Solomon's, and Deanna followed her out.

Betsy came to his side. "Your Deanna's taking good care of you. Is there anything your momma or daddy can do?"

"Just knowing you're here and love me is enough." He paused. "How are Lexi and Millie handling all this, and Deanna?"

Betsy didn't answer. "How serious are you and Deanna?"

Solomon opened his eyes. His dad stood beside her. "Very. She's the one."

"How long have you been datin'?" his dad asked, rubbing his chin.

Solomon resisted the urge to shake his head. "Does it really matter?"

"You should know the woman you marry well before you marry her."

Solomon blinked. *How well do I know her?* He began a mental list: patient, unselfish, determined, kind, trustworthy, smart, gorgeous. She smells delicious, kisses like heaven, and has the softest skin. *At least I started with her character.*

"I know her well enough. And since we're not getting married tomorrow, I've got time to know her better."

But then he heard Emelia's voice in his mind: *She's not a Christian.*

He closed his eyes. *Dear Lord, please don't let my faith be a stumbling block for us. Help her open her heart to You. I love her. Not my will, but Yours. In Jesus' name, amen.*

He released a shuddering breath. *Not my will but Yours.* It was the scariest prayer he'd ever prayed. He remembered Jesus in Gethsemane: *"O My Father, if it is possible, let this cup pass from Me; nevertheless, not as I will, but as You will."* Jesus had accepted the cross.

Solomon knew he had to accept God's will even if it meant walking away from Deanna.

Please don't let it come to that. Please.

"Solomon? Are you okay?" Betsy asked.

"I'm sorry. I was... thinking."

A slow smile spread across her face. "Thinking is good."

Deanna opened the door to Solomon's room and stepped inside. Three pairs of eyes landed on her, and she froze as the door clicked shut behind her. *They trust me,* she told herself sternly, shaking off the discomfort.

"Both your doctors are at the desk," she said. "Dr. Cutter will come in first. Dr. Wang, the neurologist, said she's seeing another patient before she comes in."

Solomon motioned her over, and his parents stepped back to make room. She moved to his right side and took his offered hand. He pulled her close and whispered, "Are they still calling you my wife?"

"Yes. I don't know what to do about it."

Solomon shrugged. "Do you mind their assumption?"

Deanna frowned. "It feels like I'm lying."

He squeezed her hand. "A glimpse into our future?"

Her lips curved slowly. "Maybe."

"If we stepped outside, would it be easier for you two to talk?" his father asked, brows furrowed.

Deanna tried to pull her hand away, but Solomon held tight. "No, Dad. I'm sorry. We'll stop whispering."

Betsy's arms remained crossed. "That better not have been about Solomon's health."

Deanna turned toward them, chin tucked, bracing herself. "The nurses and doctors have assumed Solomon and I are married. It makes me feel dishonest, but I don't know how to justify being here if I say I'm just his friend."

"You're not just my friend," Solomon said, loud and clear. "You're my girlfriend. And I love you."

She flushed from head to toe. Even looking at the floor couldn't hide the heat in her cheeks.

"Deanna, look at me." Solomon tugged gently on her hand.

She lifted her chin and met his gaze. His eyes were soft, but brighter than usual—a blue rather than blue-gray. "I love you," he said again, this time softly.

His right arm slid up her left, across her shoulder, and into her hair. He pulled her lips to his and kissed her, brief, sweet, and unashamed. When he released her, "I love you" ghosted from her lips.

Solomon's grin said he'd heard her or read her lips. But before she could process it, a knock sounded, and Dr. Cutter entered.

Solomon's parents stood beside Deanna at the bedside. Dr. Cutter checked the dressings over the three small puncture sites and palpated the shoulder joint. "Wiggle your left fingers," he said.

Solomon couldn't.

"Good," the doctor said. "The nerve block's still working."

He continued with post-op instructions. "As far as I'm concerned, you're ready to go home, but Dr. Wang has to clear you, too. Your nurse will bring prescriptions, instructions, and follow-up appointments. I look forward to seeing you in my office instead of here. Any questions?"

No one spoke. Dr. Cutter shook Solomon's hand and left.

Dr. Wang entered as Dr. Cutter exited. Petite and focused, she performed a standard neuro exam, skipping strength tests on Solomon's left arm. He chuckled through the memory questions and repeated the three unrelated words she'd given him.

"Do not be around fireworks tonight," she said firmly. "Promise me that, and I'll write your discharge orders."

"I promise. Why do light and sound make my head hurt so much?"

"Because you have a concussion. Your brain is bruised and slightly swollen. The more stimulation it gets, the harder it has to work, and the more it hurts. Protect it from light and sound, move slowly, and it will heal. If symptoms worsen, come back to the ER. I want the next time I see you to be in my office."

Solomon refrained from nodding. "Yes, ma'am."

"Any questions?" she asked.

"No, ma'am," Betsy said. Mark and Deanna shook their heads.

With the doctors gone and discharge assured, Solomon revisited his earlier question. "How are Lexi and Millie handling all this, and Deanna and me?"

Deanna's mouth fell open. "Your sisters may have a problem with me?"

"When Robert got serious with Emelia, Lexi was moody and jealous. Millie came around faster. Lexi didn't want to share her big brother. I just want to be prepared."

His parents shrugged. "Once they knew you'd recover, they haven't said much," Betsy said.

Mark chuckled. "You're takin' care of Solomon, which means they won't miss the carnival or fireworks. That makes you their favorite person."

He looked at Solomon's hand wrapped around Deanna's. "Young lady, you're good for my boy. You've taken care of him and made the rest of our lives easier. We're grateful."

Deanna blushed, eyes dropping to the floor. She swiped at her eyes, swallowed, and looked up. "I couldn't have been anywhere else."

Chapter 32

Home

Between the bright sunlight that his eyelids didn't fully block and the movement of the car, the jackhammer was back at work inside Solomon's head. He leaned heavily on his dad as they walked into the house. By the time he sat on the edge of his bed, his vision swam, and a wave of nausea hit hard.

"Dad, I need to lie down." Pressing a hand to his stomach, he inhaled through his nose and exhaled slowly through his mouth.

His father propped pillows behind his back and placed an empty trash can beside the bed. *God, please, I don't want to throw up.* Then his dad closed the blinds, drew the curtains, and turned off the light.

Solomon kept his eyes shut and focused on breathing. After several long moments, the nausea eased. "Dad, are you still here?"

"Yes, son."

"My stomach feels a little better. Could you ask Deanna to bring me some ginger ale and sit with me?"

His father touched his right shoulder, and Solomon leaned into it. "I'll get her and the soda." His dad's hand lingered for a moment before he stepped away and left the room.

It felt like a long time before the door opened again. Soft footsteps crossed the room.

"It's so dark in here," Deanna said gently. "I can't see where to set your drink. May I open a curtain or turn on a light?"

Solomon groaned. "You can try opening a curtain a little, just enough to see. My head's pounding, and I'm afraid to open my eyes."

Deanna moved slowly, feeling her way through the room until her hand met the desk. She set down the drink and turned. "Am I next to you?"

She jumped when his hand brushed her leg. After a sharp breath, she whispered, "I am."

Leaning over the desk, she found the curtains and opened them just a crack. The sliver of light revealed Solomon propped against the headboard, pillows stacked behind him.

"Are you upright enough to drink? Your mom sent a straw if you need it."

He opened his eyes and reached for the glass. "Straw, please."

While he sipped the ginger ale, she pulled out the desk chair and sat. "I have finals Monday and Tuesday. I love you, Solomon, but I have to ace those tests. My parents can't have any reason to use them against us."

Her gaze moved to the sliver of light, and she frowned. "It's too dark in here for me to study. If you're okay for a few minutes, I'll talk to your mom."

He squeezed his eyes shut and rubbed his temple. "I'm okay for now. If I can have some pain medicine, please bring it when you come back."

"I will."

"I love you," he called softly as she left.

In the kitchen, Deanna found Betsy. "Betsy," she said gently.

Betsy turned, her expression alert. "Is Solomon alright?"

"His head's really hurting. The nurse noted when he could have more pain medicine. May I check?"

Betsy pointed to the envelope on the table. "Go ahead."

Deanna pulled out the medication list and scanned it. "He can have some. Do you have a sleep mask?"

Solomon's mother studied her. "I do. Why?"

"I have finals coming up. Solomon needs the room to be dark, but I can't study in the dark. I'm hoping a sleep mask will block enough light for him so I can study. If not, I'll have to stay home."

"My mask will work for him," Betsy said firmly, handing her the bottle of pills. "I'll grab it."

Deanna stopped her. "I don't even have my books. Once Solomon's settled, could you or Mark run me home? I'll grab my things and drive back."

Betsy nodded. "Just let us know when you're ready. Lexi wants to help. She will sit with him while you're gone."

Deanna returned to Solomon's room and gave him the pain medicine. After he swallowed it, she kissed his cheek. "Once you're resting, I'll run home. I'll be back soon. Lexi will be here if you need anything."

"I don't want you to leave," he said, his voice soft and pouty.

She smiled, shaking her head at her big, strong guy. "I won't be gone long. Your sisters need time with you, too. And remember, I'll be going home at night now that you're home, and I'll be away on Monday and Tuesday mornings for my tests. You're not alone. Your parents, your sisters, your brother, and Emelia all want to help."

"I know," he murmured. "But they aren't you."

She kissed his cheek again. His right arm caught her as she bent over. "A real kiss, please."

She obliged him, then settled beside him, resting her hand in his. Warmth and comfort filled her, and she hoped he felt it too. Thirty minutes later, he was asleep. She kissed his cheek once more and slipped from the room.

In the hallway, she spotted Lexi at her bedroom door. The fifteen-year-old came straight to her and wrapped her in a hug.

Lexi looked her in the eyes. "You love my brother."

Deanna's eyes widened. She inhaled sharply and exhaled slowly.

"It's okay," Lexi said with a smile. "I'm not going to go all crazy jealous like I did with Emelia. She's a good sister and takes care of

Robert. You've shown me you will take care of Solomon. I think you'll make a good sister. Millie agrees, so you're good with us."

Deanna stood speechless until Lexi let her arms drop.

"Okay, sis," Lexi said. "What do I need to do to help Solomon while you're gone?"

With a smile, Deanna guided Lexi away from the bedroom door. "Dark. What can I do in the dark?" Lexi asked.

"Not much, unfortunately."

"He must be bored stiff."

"He might be once he feels better. Your mom has a sleep mask. If it works, you and Millie can take turns reading to him."

"Why can't he read?"

"Right now, it's better to rest his eyes and keep things quiet. His brain is injured and needs time to heal. That means minimal visual and auditory stimulation."

"How long will that last?"

"The doctor said if his pain and dizziness improve in a week, he can start increasing exposure. But recovery's different for everyone."

Mark stepped into the hallway. "Have you got Lexi squared away on what Solomon needs while you're gone?"

"He needs dark and quiet," Lexi said brightly. "I'll do what he asks."

Deanna nodded. "If you're ready to run me home, I'll grab my bag and purse."

Chapter 33

Bravery

Mark walked Deanna to her front door, where her parents waited. Their hostility didn't surprise her. Mark extended his hand. Her father hesitated, then shook it.

"This is Solomon's father, Mark Jackson," Deanna said with a forced smile. "And these are my parents, Ephraim and Lydia Keaton." She stepped past them and turned back to Mark. "Thank you for bringing me home. Please let Solomon know I'll be back as soon as I can."

"Thank you for letting your daughter stay with my boy," Mark said, shaking both her parents' hands. "She's been a great help to him, and to all of us."

Her parents nodded, and Mark left.

To avoid confrontation, Deanna went straight to her room. She checked her backpack, her books, and study supplies were all there. She zipped it, slung it over her shoulder, and headed back through the living room, hoping for a clean exit.

"Where do you think you're going, young lady?" her father's voice boomed.

She turned, face calm. "Back to the Jacksons'."

Both parents stood with arms crossed. Her father's tone was firm. "You have finals Monday and Tuesday. You missed class on Friday. You're staying home."

She shook her head. "I can study at the Jacksons'. There's a desk by Solomon's bed. I'll be home each night and return in the morning to help him. I'll get A's in both classes. Our deal was that if I kept my grades up and got a job after graduation, I could live here."

Their expressions didn't change, but she kept her voice steady. "Solomon is important to me. I promised I'd help him recover, and I intend to keep that promise. I'll see you tonight after his family gets back from the carnival."

"Deanna," her mother warned.

She held up a hand. "Stop. You're not going to change my mind. Unless you plan to stop me physically, I'll see you later."

"Young lady, you know our rules," her father said.

"I know what they used to be. But they're going to change because I'm changing. I'm an adult now. I'm making my own choices."

She rushed out, flung her backpack into the passenger seat, and slid behind the wheel, locking the doors with trembling hands. Her heart thundered. Breath ragged, she started the car and sped away. When distance finally gave her space to breathe, she pulled beneath a tree until she stopped shaking. Only then did she turn toward the Jacksons'.

She arrived in time for Solomon's family to leave for the carnival. Though disappointed to miss their first date, she reminded herself that she still had Solomon—and that mattered most.

She knocked. Emelia opened the door.

"What are you doing here?" Deanna asked.

Emelia hugged her. "Robert and I wanted to see Solomon before we go. I'm sorry you two can't go."

"Me too," Deanna sighed.

Emelia took her backpack and held her close. "You've been so good to Solomon. You're a treasure. I hope he knows how lucky he is."

Deanna laughed. "Not long ago, you and Robert didn't think we should date."

Emelia laughed too. "Even friends and family can be wrong."

Betsy stepped into the room. "You girls sound like you're having fun. Emelia and I put plates in the fridge for you and Solomon if you get hungry."

"Thank you. How is Solomon?"

"Better. His head's not hurting as much. When does the nerve block wear off?"

"I'll check the paperwork, but I think he's supposed to start taking pain meds routinely tomorrow. Has he said anything about feeling in his fingers?"

Solomon's mother pursed her lips. "I haven't asked. He hasn't mentioned it."

"I'll find out. If the feeling's returning, I'll have him take a pill before I leave tonight."

Betsy gasped. "Does he know you're not staying?"

She smiled, then sighed. "He does. But I don't think he's happy about it. I'll be back in the morning so you all can go to church."

Betsy touched her arm. "You're so good for him. I'd keep you here if I could."

If my parents won't let me stay at home, maybe Mark and Betsy will let me stay here. The thought startled her, but she hoped it didn't show.

"I'd stay if I could. My parents didn't want me to come back, but I promised Solomon I'd help him through his recovery. They'll be mad for a while."

When Emelia placed a hand on her arm, Deanna steadied.

"One way or another, this will be alright," Emelia said gently.

Betsy added her hand. "Mark and I are here for you. You can talk to us anytime. No judgment."

Deanna placed her hand over theirs. "Thank you. Emelia, you can tell them what it's like for me. I can't talk about it now. I need to see Solomon."

"Go to him, dear. He needs you, too," Betsy said.

Emelia picked up her bag and led Deanna to Solomon's room. "I'm sorry your parents are making this hard," she whispered.

Deanna reached to knock, but Emelia opened the door.

Robert grinned. "Congratulations, Mrs. Jackson. Welcome to the family, sis."

Deanna gasped. Emelia shook her head. "Robert, you promised you wouldn't tease her."

"Oh!" Deanna giggled and looked at Solomon. "You told them about the hospital staff assuming we were married."

Solomon's smile was wide. "I did. Come here, Mrs. Jackson, and kiss your husband."

Near the door, Deanna sank into the chair by the desk at the end of Robert's old bed. "I'm glad you're feeling better."

Emelia cleared her throat. "Come on, troublemaker. The others are ready to go."

Deanna darted from the room and found Lexi and Millie with their parents. "Thank you, girls, for taking care of Solomon while I was gone."

"Solomon said you have two big tests next week. We love our bubba. Can we help again?"

Deanna looked to Mark and Betsy. "If it's alright with you, I'd appreciate it."

"It's fine with me," Betsy said.

"See you when you get back," Deanna said.

She returned to Solomon's room. Mischief danced in his eyes. "You really are feeling better."

"I know you need to study, but come here and let me hold you and kiss you before I have to put this confounded thing back on," he said, waving the sleep mask.

"That confounded thing must help, or you wouldn't consider putting it back on."

"Lexi had me wear it while she read to me. It was nice."

"You don't have to sound so begrudging. I'm glad it was nice."

She sat beside him. His fingers slid through her hair, then skimmed her arm, making her shiver. When his lips met hers, warmth flooded her. Her stomach flipped.

He broke the kiss. Sprinkling kisses along her jawline to her ear, he whispered, "I can't believe how much I've missed you."

She curled up beside him, her head on his shoulder, his arm around her. "I was only gone a little over an hour," she giggled.

She reached across him and touched his left fingers. His brows furrowed. "That feels weird."

Her eyebrows lifted. “You felt that?”

“Kind of. Like you were touching me from a distance.”

“Did you see it or feel it?”

“I felt it.”

She smiled. “I’ll get you pain medicine before I leave, and again in the morning. Tomorrow morning marks forty-eight hours since the nerve block. Dr. Cutter said it would last between forty-eight and seventy-two hours.”

Solomon frowned. “So tomorrow I get shoulder pain on top of my headache. Great.”

She placed her hand on his. “He said the block would get you through the worst of it. Maybe it won’t be so bad.”

“I can only hope. No, more than hope. I’ll pray for that,” he said, still frowning.

Deanna snuggled closer. “Please pray.”

Solomon’s jaw went slack. “You want me to pray?”

She looked up at him, their eyes meeting. He kissed her temple.

“Yes,” she whispered. “I want you to pray.”

He began praying, but before he finished, her soft, whistling snores filled the room. He smiled, completed his prayer, and let her musical breathing and strawberry scent lull him to sleep.

He woke with his right arm tingling, completely asleep. “Dee,” he said, hoping to rouse her.

It took effort, but he extracted his arm from beneath her. The movement stirred her, and she grabbed his arm to keep from falling off the bed.

“Is everything alright?” she asked.

He smiled. “Yeah. My arm went to sleep. And I need to go to the bathroom.”

She swallowed hard. “I can help you get there and back, but I’m not comfortable helping once you’re inside.”

It was the first time he’d needed the restroom without a nurse or family member nearby. He exhaled slowly. “If I can’t manage, you may have to help. For the record, I'm not comfortable with that either."

They made it to the bathroom and back without incident. Solomon silently thanked the Lord for elastic-waist pants and boxers. Deanna helped him arrange his pillows so he could sit up. He watched her pull out her book and notebook, settling in at the desk next to his bed.

He couldn't help watching her. Something magnetic drew him in. *She's a beautiful sight to behold.*

Before long, his headache worsened. He slipped the sleep mask over his eyes, blocking the room's light. Deanna studied silently. The only sounds were the turn of a page or the scratch of her pen. Sounds he wouldn't have noticed under normal circumstances.

He must have dozed off, because the sound of the front door opening and closing woke him. His family was home. Moments later, Lexi and Millie bounded into his room.

"Will it make your head hurt to look at what Millie and I won at the carnival?" Lexi asked.

"Lexi, please turn off the overhead light," Deanna said.

Lexi flipped the switch. "It's off."

Deanna pointed the desk lamp away from Solomon. "I think you'll be alright without the mask for a few minutes."

Solomon removed the mask. "Be quick, girls. I want to see what you won."

They showed off their stuffed animals and told him how they'd won each one. When they finished, he slipped the mask back on and rested against his pillows.

Deanna turned off the desk lamp. The chair scraped as she pushed it back. She stood, and he heard the squeak of her shoes as she stretched. Then her lips touched his briefly.

"I turned the lamp off. You can take off the mask if you want. I'm going to get your medicine." Turning to his sisters, she said, "You girls should stay and visit while I'm gone."

Solomon removed the mask. His eyes adjusted slowly. A soft glow lit the wall between the door and the desk.

"Hmm. Mom must've plugged in the old nightlight," he muttered, his gaze drifting to the sway of Deanna's hips as she left the room.

Lexi and Millie laughed at his lopsided smile.

"Give me a break, girls. I like her a lot."

Lexi shook her head. "You don't like her. You love her."

Solomon started to shake his head, then stopped. "Yes. I love her. Now come hug your brother and show me those stuffies again."

Deanna returned with a prescription bottle and a glass of ginger ale. He glanced at the desk. No glass. He'd been so absorbed in watching her that he hadn't noticed her pick it up. *How did I not see that? Lust, that's how. Dear Lord, please forgive me.*

She dropped a pill into his hand. He grabbed the glass and chased the pill down.

She hugged Lexi and Millie.

When Lexi stepped out of her embrace, she smiled. "Mom said we can take turns sleeping in Robert's old bed in case Solomon needs something."

"Solomon said you took good care of him while I was gone. I'm sure you'll do great at night, too," Deanna said, smiling.

Lexi nudged Millie toward the door. "We need to go so Deanna can kiss Solomon goodnight."

"My girl is beautiful when she blushes," Solomon said, winking. "I'd really like that goodnight kiss."

She brushed a kiss across his lips.

Solomon sighed. "Really? That's all I get?"

She winked and giggled. "Yep. I'll see you tomorrow."

"Dee," he called after her.

She turned.

He smiled. "Sleep well, my sweet. You've earned it. I'll see you tomorrow."

"Sleep well." She blew him a kiss.

When Deanna entered the house, she was relieved to find the living room empty. She hurried to her room and collapsed into bed, hoping for her first uninterrupted night of sleep in three days.

She woke early to an alarm she didn't remember setting. Her parents usually slept in on Sundays. *If I hurry through showering and dressing, maybe I can leave before they're awake.* She moved fast, clinging to hope.

But when she stepped out of her room, dressed and ready to go, her father was already seated at the table, and her mother was setting down a serving dish.

So much for a clean escape.

Her father gestured to her chair. "You can at least take the time to have a meal with your parents."

Her shoulders slumped. She sat. "Did you set my alarm last night?"

Her dad nodded. "We did."

"Why?"

"We wanted to talk to you."

She groaned. "What is there to talk about? I thought I was clear yesterday."

Her father served himself pancakes and passed the plate to her. The quiet routine of passing food and condiments continued until all three had filled their plates.

She took a bite. "Yum. Mom, these are amazing. You should make them more often."

Her mother smiled. "Thank you, dear."

They ate in silence until her father finished. "Deanna," he said. "Your mother and I talked. As long as your grades don't suffer, we'll let you come and go with some restrictions."

She braced herself. *Here comes the but.*

"You're home every night by midnight. If exceptions arise, you speak to us directly. No messages through someone else. If we don't agree, you'll follow our decision without argument."

She shook her head. “No. I can’t agree to that.”

Her father’s expression hardened. “Then I hope you have somewhere else to live.”

She looked at her mother, who was quietly wiping tears with her napkin.

“I can’t control the world,” Deanna said firmly without raising her voice. “Cars break down. Accidents happen. How can I promise to get your permission in advance for something unplanned? And what is important to me may not matter to you.”

She set down her napkin and stood. “I’ll do my best to be home by midnight. I’ll keep you informed of any changes. If I can’t reach you myself, you may hear from someone else. I won’t make promises I can’t keep.”

Her father rose and walked to her mother. “Her terms aren’t far off from ours.”

Her mother hiccupped through her tears. “I’m not ready to lose our little girl.”

Her father looked at Deanna. “I don’t like the woman you’re becoming. I’m not sure Solomon or his family are the influence you need. But I won’t upset your mother. As long as you maintain your grades, finish your degree, and secure a job or continue your education, we’ll try it your way. For now.”

His posture radiated disapproval, but Deanna couldn’t stop smiling. She threw her arms around them. “I love you. Thank you.”

She headed for the door, but her father cleared his throat. “Where are you going?”

Grinning, she turned. “To the Jacksons. I’ll be there every day for the foreseeable future, except Monday and Tuesday when I ace my finals.”

She nodded curtly. “I know you don’t like Solomon or his family. I do. I promised him I’d help with his recovery. If anything changes, I’ll let you know.”

Chapter 34

Small Steps

Betsy greeted Deanna with a motherly hug as the girls dashed off to brush their teeth before church. "Go say good morning to Solomon, then bring his plate in. Have you eaten?"

Deanna sagged, and Betsy steadied her as the morning's tension seeped away. "At home." She drew a breath. "Has he had any pain medication?"

He hasn't asked," Betsy said, shaking her head. "Breakfast just wrapped up—he's probably waiting on you."

Deanna grabbed the bottle from the counter and headed toward Solomon's room. On the way, she knocked on the girls' door. "How'd last night go with your brother?"

"He slept like a baby piglet," Lexi giggled. "Didn't wake me once."

Deanna smiled. "He does snore a little. Thanks, Lexi."

Before she turned to leave, both girls wrapped their arms around her.

Millie looked up, eyes wide and earnest. "We love you."

Deanna hugged them close. "I love you, too."

The simple exchange filled her with warmth as she continued to Solomon's room.

She opened the door gently. "Will you be okay with a little light?"

"Deanna."

The tenderness in his voice made her heart skip. She stepped inside and closed the door.

"How are you feeling? Head or shoulder pain?"

"I could use a pill," he said, sitting up, "but I need you more than medicine." He held out his arm.

She moved into his embrace, kissed him softly, then pulled back. "Tell me what hurts and how much."

He sighed. "As you wish, Nurse Keaton. My left arm's still numb, so no shoulder pain. Head's at a seven. It was five and a half before I sat up."

She giggled. "Then you've earned a pill. Let's get that pain down."

She dropped one into his hand and handed him his drink. "You'll have to report back in thirty minutes."

Grabbing his plate, she turned to leave.

"Dee," he called after her.

She giggled and kept walking.

Solomon heard his family leave for church and prayed Deanna would return soon. When the door opened, there she was. His girl. He stared at her without shame as she stepped toward him, slow and steady, her gaze locked with his. When she reached his bedside, she surprised him.

"Where's your Bible?"

"Why?"

"Emelia says she and Robert read a chapter of the Bible daily. I know you never miss church unless you can't go, like today. I thought you might want me to read to you. And maybe we could pray again. But only if you want."

Her voice softened with each word, her eyes dropping to the floor. The night light cast a gentle glow, enough for him to see her and reach for her hand.

"Dee, look at me."

She did.

"I'd like that. Are you sure?"

She swallowed. “I want to. I understand the importance of your relationship with God. I don’t want you to lose that because of me. I love you.”

“I love you too. My Bible’s in the drawer.”

She pulled out the worn leather-bound book. “Where should I start?”

He placed his hand over hers. “Matthew. Will you read me a chapter daily?”

“I will.”

He slipped on his sleep mask, knowing she’d need the light. He’d heard the genealogy of Christ countless times, but her voice, soft and melodic, made it feel new. As she moved into chapter two, he silently thanked God for her willingness to step out of her comfort zone for both of them.

When she finished the passage about Jesus returning from Egypt to Nazareth, she paused. “That’s two chapters. Want me to read more?”

“One more, please.”

She began chapter three. He heard the hesitation in her voice as she read about John the Baptist, but she didn’t stop. She read through Jesus’ baptism and God’s blessing on His Son. When she finished, the drawer squeaked open, followed by the soft thud of the Bible and another squeak as it closed.

Her hand found his. “Who was John the Baptist?”

Solomon felt the weight of her question. He’d grown up in church. These stories were second nature for him, but for her, they were new.

“Jesus’ cousin. If you want to read his story, it’s in Luke chapter one.”

He smiled, hearing her retrieve his Bible again.

“Where’s Luke?”

“Matthew, Mark, Luke, and John.”

“I’ve got it,” she said, and began reading.

When she closed the Bible, she whispered, “Wow.”

“That’s a good way to sum it up. Sit next to me and I’ll pray.”

She settled beside him, resting her head against his chest. He kissed the top of her head and began.

"Thank You, Lord, for the blessing of Deanna at my side, reading Your words to me. Help us hide Your words in our hearts. Give us wisdom from what we've shared, keeping You at the center of our love as it grows." He kissed her temple. "Help me be the man You want me to be, and the man she needs."

She cleared her throat. "Help me."

His heart leapt at the simplicity of her request. "Help us both. Forgive our sins and help us forgive others. In Your Son's precious name, amen."

He held her close until she pulled away.

"I've got to get A's on my finals."

"I know. Can you do two more things for me before you settle in to study?"

"Of course. What do you need?"

He removed his sleep mask. "Okay, three things. Turn out the light. I need to go to the bathroom. And while I'm in there, will you make the house as dark as possible? I want to walk through it while it's quiet and my head isn't hurting much. I need you beside me in case I get woozy."

She flipped off the light. "Let's do it."

He moved through the house without any wooziness—a small but welcome victory.

When his family returned from church, they had lunch. Deanna settled in to study while Lexi and Millie took turns reading to him. After dinner, his headache returned. He asked for another pain pill. Deanna took his left hand, and he gripped hers.

"Sweetheart, it's almost time for me to go. I won't be back until after my final in the morning. You're holding my hand with your left one. That nerve block's wearing off. If your shoulder starts hurting, you have to tell someone. It's Millie's turn to sleep in here. Wake her if you need to. Please, please, don't be a tough guy. I don't want you suffering."

"I promise I'll ask for the medicine when I need it. Just let me hold you and share a good kiss before you go."

She smiled at the pleading in his voice and settled beside him. His arm wrapped around her, pulling her close. She sighed, and he thoroughly kissed her. She gave as much as he did, and he held her until he had to let go.

She traced his lips with her finger. "I love you so much."

"I don't want you to go."

"I have to. Because I want to keep seeing you and caring for you."

He nodded. "I feel better when you're here. I miss you when you're gone. Because I love you, go my sweet."

She kissed him one last time and left the room. He listened as she said goodbye to his family.

"Millie. Lexie. Betsy. Solomon gripped my hand with his left one tonight. Please check his pain level. His shoulder's going to start hurting soon."

His mom answered, "We'll make sure he doesn't try to tough it out."

"Thank you. I'll see you tomorrow."

Chapter 35

Pushing for Normal

The days at home passed, thanks to Deanna and his family, but the nights dragged. His sisters stayed with him, and he loved them, but they weren't Deanna. He missed her with a quiet desperation. In the hospital, she'd been his anchor, his calm. Now, her nightly absence left him with a lingering emptiness until she returned.

Monday morning came, and she didn't. *She has a final,* he reminded himself. *She'll come when she can.* Still, he was restless, cranky, aching in heart, head, and shoulder.

When Deanna finally arrived with lunch, his heart rejoiced. But his pain flared when he tried to sit up. He'd let it get out of hand. He eased back against his pillows.

"My sweet, lunch smells amazing, but I need three things before we eat. Please kiss me, then bring me a pain pill and some ginger ale."

Her lips met his, just for a moment, and his world righted itself. When she returned, she held the rest of his relief in her hands. He swallowed the pill and drank half the glass.

"Thank you."

"You're welcome." Her smile bloomed. "I think I aced my final."

"Yay!" He reached for her, and she stepped closer. "I missed you." He traced her jawline with a finger. "Did you miss me?"

She closed her eyes and breathed. “Sweetheart, I miss you every moment we’re not together.”

“Me too.”

“Knock it off, you two,” Millie teased from the doorway. “Whatever smells so good is getting cold.”

“You hungry, sis?” Deanna asked.

“Nah, I already ate.” With another giggle, Millie disappeared.

Deanna held up forks and chopsticks.

“Forks,” he said.

She helped him sit up, and he gave thanks for the meal, his family, and, most of all, Deanna, before they began to eat. By the time lunch was gone, the pain in his shoulder and head had eased.

“I feel better. I’d like to walk like we did yesterday.”

“Did you use the ice on your shoulder this morning like you were supposed to?”

He dropped his gaze. “No. I hate messing with those ice packs.”

“Solomon! Before we walk, you will ice your shoulder.”

“Yes, Nurse Keaton.”

“If I’m only your nurse, the kissing stops now. Nurses aren’t that familiar with their patients.”

“Then you’re definitely not my nurse.”

She moved to his side and kissed him deeply. “Remember that next time you’re tempted to call me nurse.”

“Yes, ma’am.”

“I’ll be back with the ice packs.”

When she returned, he let her adjust them until they stayed in place. “There has to be something designed for shoulders that makes this easier.”

“Maybe. We’ll ask the doctor or physical therapist.”

He groaned and settled in for twenty minutes of immobility. She curled against his chest until the timer went off. Silencing it, she kissed him.

“I’ll take the ice packs back and get your mom and the girls to help close the shades. I’ll be right back.”

He walked through the house until exhaustion sent him back to his quiet, dimly lit room. Deanna fluffed his pillows and settled him in bed. He slipped on his mask.

"Please read to me before you dive into your studies."

"Your Bible okay, or do you have something else in mind?"

He nodded toward the desk. She retrieved his Bible. "Matthew four?"

"Yes, my sweet."

"Satan Tempts Jesus," she read aloud.

She tilted her head and frowned. "Jesus was tempted?"

"Yes," he said softly. "Three times. First, with physical need, He was hungry. Second, with pride and divine protection. Third, with power and worldly authority. And He overcame Satan every time."

He let the silence settle.

"He didn't fight with clever words or strength of will. He used Scripture. His Father's words. The ones you're about to read. That's how He stood. That's how we stand."

He turned toward her, even though he couldn't see her.

"When we fail, and we do, He doesn't turn His face. He intercedes. Not because we've earned it, but because He already paid for it. He knows what it is to be human. He knows what it costs to stand. And still, He stands for us."

He returned his head to the pillow, and she read. By the time she finished the chapter, he was softly snoring.

Stepping into Solomon's room Tuesday afternoon, Deanna felt a rush of joy. Her last final was behind her, and seeing him sitting up without his sleep mask made the victory complete. His smile lit the room.

"My sweet, you aced your final today, too!"

Her smile burst forth. "I'm pretty sure I did. But the grades from yesterday's final were posted. My name was at the top, the highest score in the class. An A for sure."

Sighing, her smile softened. "And best of all, no more studying for four whole weeks."

"I'm so proud of you." He opened his arm to her.

She moved into his embrace. His kiss sent warm tingles down to her toes, and fireworks exploded behind her eyelids. When he pulled back, she rested her head on his chest, content to be close again.

He nuzzled her hair, and she smiled. She loved the way it tickled and soothed her all at once.

"You really like my hair's strawberry vanilla scent, don't you?"

"I love that your hair looks and smells like strawberries." His fingers ran through the length of it. "Speaking of strawberries, are you hungry?"

"Yeah." She hummed.

She pulled back to see him more completely. "Your pain is better. What magic happened this morning while I was at school?"

He sighed. "Mom gave me a pain pill earlier, and Lexi helped me ice my shoulder this morning. It still hurts, but it's tolerable. My head's better. I've been to the bathroom without dizziness or turning off the lights. It made my head ache a little, but once I was back in here with the low light, it settled."

She studied him carefully. "Promise me you'll tell me if the pain starts to increase."

"I promise. Please, let's go eat lunch in the kitchen."

"I'll be right back," she said, turning toward the door. But he caught her hand.

"I need to turn the lights off."

"No, Dee. I want to try it with normal light. If it's too much, I'll ask you to turn them off, or we'll bring our meal back in here."

She hesitated. "You're sure?"

He nodded and stood. "I'm sure."

They ate in the kitchen with the lights on. He didn't complain, but between bites, he closed his eyes, shielding them with his hand. Still, he insisted on helping her clean up. Back in his room, he sank onto the bed and closed his eyes.

She sat beside him. "Solomon, if you don't want the narcotic pain medication, I can get you some Naproxen that Dr. Cutter prescribed for milder pain. You can have it twice a day. I don't like you suffering in silence."

"Okay. I'll try the Naproxen for my headache." He rubbed his temple.

She returned with the medicine and a glass of water, handing them to him. "Sweetheart, I see you're getting better, but you can't force your recovery. You'll only slow it down."

He groaned. "I know, but I'm so tired of this room and this bed. I want to do regular things. I don't want to live in the dark. I want to use the bathroom without turning off the lights. I want to dress myself. Eat with my family. Take you on a date. I hate all of this." He slipped the sleep mask back on.

She nearly laughed at the way he shoved it on, like he could hide behind it. But she didn't. Instead, she took his hand.

"This isn't forever. Every small improvement is still an improvement. You're tolerating the low light in here. The dizziness and nausea are gone. You've got feeling back in your shoulder, and the pain's manageable. Those are victories. And bigger ones are coming."

He removed the mask and turned toward her slowly. "What do you mean by bigger ones are coming?"

She smiled. "Thursday, you see Dr. Cutter. And Friday, you start physical therapy."

She gasped. "I'll be right back."

"Where are you going?"

"I need to talk to your parents. You're going to need very dark sunglasses to tolerate the bright sunshine."

She was out the door before he could respond.

She found Betsy in the laundry room and explained. Betsy agreed immediately.

"The girls and I can go shopping for them this afternoon."

"Thank you," Deanna said, turning to leave.

"Deanna," Betsy called. She turned back.

"Thank you for anticipating my son's needs. Mark and I will go with you and Solomon to his appointment on Thursday. Are you okay taking him to PT on Friday without us?"

She looked down, then met Betsy's gaze. "I'm here to take care of him. Whatever he needs."

Betsy nodded. "Just remember, Mark, the girls, and I are here to help. He isn't your burden alone."

She blinked several times. "He won't ever be a burden. I love him."

Betsy hugged her. "I know. It shows in everything you do for him."

When Deanna returned to Solomon's room, he was already settled against his pillows. She pulled his Bible from the drawer and read him another chapter from Matthew. His breathing deepened as she read, and by the time she reached the end, he was asleep.

Chapter 36

Finding a Routine

The next day, Solomon insisted on joining every family meal, even though the light and noise made his headache throb harder each time. Despite the mounting pain behind his eyes, he craved normalcy more than relief.

"You can be such a stubborn man," Deanna huffed.

He met her gaze, willing her to understand. "Dee, I need something to feel normal. Right now, family meals are all I've got."

She hesitated, eyes darting to the window. "Please let's eat our meals in your room tomorrow, and on Friday. You'll be exposed to so much light and noise Thursday at the doctor's, and again Friday at PT."

She blinked, turning away. Something in him tightened.

"Deanna."

She looked back, eyes glistening.

"I'll eat in here tomorrow and Friday," he said gently. "I'll wear the sunglasses. I'll speak up if I need meds. I won't suffer in silence."

Her shoulders eased. "Thank you. I hope you know I want you to get better. I love you."

"I do know, my sweet. I love you, too."

He patted the bed beside him, and she sat. He kissed the moisture from beneath her eyes and pulled her close. "Don't leave me," he murmured, half-smiling. “I’m sure Mom would let you stay in the guest room.”

She pulled back with a huff. “Solomon, we’ve been over this. My parents will kick me out if I don’t come home every night.”

He shrugged. “Problem solved.”

“Drop it!” She shook her head. “It isn’t going to happen!”

Before he could reply, his mom appeared in the doorway. “Everything alright in here?”

“Sorry for being loud,” Deanna said. “Solomon was being a pain.”

“In pain or being one?”

Deanna grimaced. “Being one and wouldn’t let it go.”

“Sounds familiar. Solomon, behave.”

He hissed like a deflating balloon. “Yes, Mom.”

She left, and he turned back to Deanna, guilt tugging. “I’m sorry. You spoiled me at the hospital. Now I miss you when you’re gone. Is it so terrible that I want you with me?”

“It’s not terrible,” she said softly. “It’s just impossible.”

“I get it.” He sighed. “I’ll man-up and let it go.”

She leaned in and kissed him. “Sorry, I raised my voice. Does your head hurt more?”

He moved his head slowly side to side. “It’s okay for now. I’ll ask Mom or Lexi for a pain pill before bed.”

She nodded and kissed him again. “Don’t forget the ice.”

“I won’t.”

As she started to rise, he held her hand. “Dee, I love you. I’ll never be sorry for wanting you at my side. Someday, we’ll make it happen. Just the two of us. Married for real.”

Her breath caught. “Married. Someday.”

He nodded, kissed her once more, then let her go.

Thursday morning, Deanna found Solomon still asleep. She tiptoed from his room, drawn by the sweet, fruity scent wafting from the kitchen.

Betsy stood at the stove, stirring a pot. "It's strawberry-blueberry compote."

"You enjoy cooking," Deanna said, inhaling deeply.

Betsy laughed. "I enjoy creating delicious things that make people happy—but not the cleanup."

Deanna smiled. "Your food makes me happy; I'll handle cleanup. What else are you making besides that fruity magic?"

"Cinnamon biscuits are in the oven, eggs are ready to scramble, and sausage patties are on a plate. Do you want to fry the sausage or scramble the eggs?"

Deanna looked down, hesitant. "I don't know how to do either."

Betsy placed a gentle hand on her shoulder. "No worries. I'll teach you."

Under Betsy's quiet guidance, Deanna scrambled the eggs while Betsy fried the sausage. Cooking together felt unexpectedly comforting.

"When you need a break from Solomon, or while he's sleeping, come spend time with me," Betsy said warmly. "We'll cook together. I'll teach you anything you want to know."

A soft warmth bloomed in Deanna's chest. "I'd love that. I want to learn how to cook for Solomon."

Her cheeks flushed, and she turned away.

Betsy giggled. "No need to be embarrassed. Solomon likes to eat. You'll need to know how to cook for my boy."

The words settled deep. Betsy saw her as Solomon's future wife. Her heart skipped. *I wish my parents heard and understood my heart's desire. Solomon is lucky.* Her breath caught. *Solomon would say he is blessed. I am blessed to be with him and his family.*

"Thank you, Betsy. I'll come find you every chance I get."

"That's my girl."

Solomon wore the sunglasses on the drive to Dr. Cutter's office, grateful for the shield. He lifted them for a glimpse of sunlight. It sent pain stabbing through his skull. Dropping them back in place, he sighed and leaned into the seat.

"Thanks for the sunglasses," he murmured.

Inside, he reached for them again.

"The lights in here are pretty bright," his mother warned.

His hand dropped. *I probably look blind.* His smile faded.

He could faintly see Deanna's smile. "Sweetheart," she said, "this season won't last forever. And the glasses are short-lived."

He shrugged his good shoulder. "I know. Doesn't mean I have to like it."

In the exam room, Dr. Cutter unfastened the immobilizer from Solomon's shoulder.

"I'll support your arm," he said. "Move it slowly when I direct. Stop at the first sign of pain, and I'll guide it back."

Solomon inhaled, then exhaled. "You want me to move it?"

"Yes."

"What if I mess it up?"

"I won't let that happen."

To his surprise, the slow movement, stopping at pain, felt good. Encouraged, he moved as far as he could.

"You're ready for physical therapy tomorrow," Dr. Cutter said. "I'll send my notes. Take a pain pill about an hour before. The first session is just an evaluation, but they'll ask you to push into the pain a bit. They need to see your limits so they can stretch them."

"So, I have to hurt to heal." Solomon grimaced.

"I wouldn't have put it that way," Dr. Cutter said, "but yes."

He pulled out a cloth sling. Solomon's eyes widened.

"No more immobilizer," the doctor said. "Wear this sling all the time, except during PT, when exercising, bathing, and dressing for the next two weeks."

He turned to the family. "Who's helping him with exercises?"

"Me," Deanna said.

"Mrs. Jackson, beware..."

Deanna blushed. "We're not married..."

"Yet," Solomon blurted.

Her blush deepened. "I'm Deanna Keaton. You can call me Deanna."

Dr. Cutter chuckled. "Beware, Deanna. He won't like the exercises. They'll hurt. But without them, his shoulder will stiffen, and his recovery could stall or cease."

Her gaze locked on Solomon. "He'll do them. Faithfully."

"Yes, ma'am," Solomon said, trying to sound convincing.

Dr. Cutter smiled. "I like her. How's the pain medication holding up?"

"He's got thirty-five of the fifty left," Deanna said. "I've been giving him Naproxen when it's mild."

"Perfect. Keep him on the Naproxen twice a day. It'll help with inflammation. I don't see any swelling. Still using ice?"

"Yes, sir," they said together.

"Twice a day," Deanna added.

"Any questions?" Dr. Cutter asked.

Solomon's father spoke. "How long for full recovery?"

"If he weren't in construction, I'd say three months. But with those physical demands, closer to six before he's back without restrictions or risk."

Dr. Cutter scanned the room. No one spoke.

"Stop at the front desk and schedule a follow-up in two weeks."

Chapter 37

CHALLENGES

Physical therapy tested more than his shoulder. It tested his grit, his patience, and his relationship with Deanna.

By the end of the first session, Solomon was drained. The therapist sat him down and applied ice packs to his shoulder. Relief washed over him, a hush after a storm. The therapist explained he could ice as needed, not just twice a day, but never more than twenty minutes on, followed by at least twenty minutes off.

Then came the handoff. A printed sheet of exercises with pictures and step-by-step instructions landed in Deanna's hands.

"He needs to do these twice a day, every day," the therapist said.

Deanna nodded, her expression calm. Then her gaze met his. The weight in her gaze sent chills through him. He blinked, seeing this side of her for the first time. *She's shouldering this responsibility because I can't.* He'd thank her later. Right now, he was too tired, too sore, and too aware this was only the beginning.

The first two weeks went smoothly. The exercises were gentle, designed to coax movement and healing. He tolerated them well, even joked through a few. Deanna was steady and encouraging, but firm when he tried to skip a rep. He loved her for it. He had to ask for her and God's forgiveness when the pain caused him to snap at her.

Then came the follow-up with Dr. Cutter.

"You're doing well," the doctor said, examining his shoulder. "You can lose the sling, but be careful. Now we shift to strength and flexibility. Keep following PT's lead, and respect your limits."

Solomon nodded, absorbing the shift. No more sling. No more passive healing. This was the part where he had to push.

"I'll see you again in six weeks," Dr. Cutter added. "Unless something comes up."

Solomon left the office, shoulder aching, resolve tested.

As they walked toward the truck, Deanna glanced up at him. "You okay?"

"Yeah," he said quietly. "Just realizing this isn't only about my shoulder."

"It never is," she said. "We'll take it one step at a time.

He smiled and nodded. "We'll both need lots of patience, plenty of perseverance, and a bit of grace."

After seeing Dr. Cutter, Solomon and Deanna headed to the neurologist's office. In the exam room, the nurse checked his vitals. Then Dr. Wang entered, clipboard in hand and a warm smile on her face.

"Tell me about your symptoms," she said.

"I'm tolerating low lights all the time now," Solomon replied. "And I can handle normal lighting at home for longer stretches. The dizziness and nausea are gone. I haven't tried reading or watching TV yet. I still have a mild headache, but it's manageable without meds."

Dr. Wang nodded, jotting notes. "Ready for another round of fun words and silly questions?"

"Go for it."

He answered everything correctly and remembered all three words. She glanced at the sunglasses resting in his lap.

"Bright lights are still a problem?"

"Yes, ma'am."

"That's normal at this stage. You were wise to protect yourself, especially from the sun. Your symptoms are improving as expected. I don't need to see you again unless something changes. If it does, I want a call right away."

Deanna nodded. "Yes, ma'am," Solomon said.

Dr. Wang shook their hands and left.

Back in the car, Solomon leaned back with a sigh. "At least that's one less doctor."

"You're not out of the woods yet," Deanna said gently. "You still have to respect your symptoms. If the light triggers a headache, you need to back off."

He turned to her, voice soft but firm. "Let me celebrate this small victory. I promise I'll be careful."

Her expression softened. "I'm sorry. I didn't mean to be a wet blanket. You're right, we should celebrate. How about ice cream before we go home?"

He grinned and fist-pumped. "Yes!"

She smiled, eyes warm. "I love you."

Each morning, Deanna arrived early. They shared breakfast with his family, then she handed Solomon his pain pill. Without fail, he prayed aloud, including a request, both earnest and playful, that she would let him skip his exercises. She always reminded him, gently but firmly, that prayers were answered according to God's will.

After breakfast, she read to him, usually from his Bible, sometimes from novels she brought from home. Then came the part he dreaded: the exercises.

Midweek, he whined through the first two again. Deanna pinched the bridge of her nose, eyes closed, summoning what patience she had left. When she looked up, her lips were pressed thin.

"Do you want to get better or not?"

His brows furrowed. He opened his mouth, then shut it again, a grimace flickering across his face. "Yes. I do. This is the hardest, most painful work I've ever done."

His gaze drifted upward, and she knew now that he was searching for strength beyond himself. He didn't cry, but the tears hovered. Progress was coming, but today the price was too high.

Encouragingly, she said, "Solomon, just two more exercises, then you can rest and ice your shoulder. You know what Dr. Cutter and PT said. If you don't push through, you won't recover."

He moved through the next exercise slowly, deliberately. His breath caught with pain, but he didn't stop. She saw the war in his eyes, his desire to heal battling the fear that he wouldn't regain what he'd lost.

When he finished the last exercise, she kissed him.

"I'm proud of you. My brave, strong man is getting better," she said softly. "I already see more range of motion. I know it hurts, but it's helping. I see it."

He hung his head. "Dee, I hope you never know what this feels like. I'm skipping tonight. You're not talking me into it."

Before she could respond, he stomped down the hall and disappeared into his room. She stood there stunned, her heart aching. She hadn't expected gratitude, but she hadn't expected a tantrum either.

She walked into the kitchen, blinking back tears. Betsy looked up from the mixing bowl.

"Need a break?" she asked gently.

Deanna nodded. "I do. I just... I need a minute."

"Let's bake cookies," Betsy said. "His favorites. You stir, I'll measure."

They worked in quiet rhythm until Mark appeared in the doorway.

"Deanna, you want me to check on him?"

She hesitated, then nodded. "Please. Just... don't push him. He needs ice and space."

Mark returned twenty minutes later, wordless, and began helping with lunch prep. Deanna didn't ask what Solomon had said. She wasn't ready.

When lunch preparation was done, Betsy went to get Solomon. Deanna stayed behind, setting the table with his sisters. Her heart was heavy, but her resolve hadn't wavered.

She loved him. That hadn't changed.

But love didn't mean enabling. It meant showing up, even when he didn't want her to. It meant holding the line when he wanted to quit. It meant believing in his healing more than he believed in it himself.

His voice came from the hallway, low and uncertain.

"Where's Deanna?"

Betsy answered gently, and Deanna caught the tremor in his voice. He was afraid, not of her, but of losing her.

She turned toward the doorway, waiting.

He would come.

And when he did, she'd be ready with cookies, milk, and grace.

After lunch, Solomon trudged back to his room, and Deanna stayed behind to help Betsy and the girls clean up. She let him stew a little longer, choosing peace over confrontation. When the dishes were done, she curled up on the sofa with Lexi and Millie to watch a television show, something she'd never had the chance to explore at home. The colors, the stories, the laughter. It was a world she hadn't known she'd missed.

When the show ended, she sighed. "Thanks, girls, for the break. I'd better go deal with your brother."

Lexi tilted her head, her gaze steady. "We're sorry he's being a grump. But he's hurting a lot. We hear him groan in his sleep. He's going to get better, but right now it's hard for all of us."

Deanna placed a hand over of theirs and smiled. "It is hard. Solomon will be kinder as he heals. I love him, and I want to be his primary caregiver, but it's not easy. You helped your brother today by helping me laugh. Thank you for being here for both of us."

The girls nodded solemnly.

Deanna stood, then paused. "Want to help me get cookies and milk ready for Solomon?"

They jumped from the sofa, racing her to the kitchen.

With a tray of cookies and two mugs of milk, Deanna walked down the hall and knocked softly on Solomon's door. "May I come in?"

"Yes, please." His voice was small and meek.

She stepped inside and set the tray on his desk. Before she could speak, he did.

"I'm sorry for being so cranky this morning. I love you, Dee."

"I love you, too. I'm not angry or hurt. But I can only help as much as you let me. I won't push harder than you want anymore."

"I need you to push me. I can't do this alone. Please, Dee, I need you."

"I know you need me. But do you want this from me? Your dad offered to help with your exercises until school starts."

Solomon blinked, then said quietly, "Dee, I want you every minute I can have you."

She nodded. "Then let's adjust. We'll break your exercises into four sessions, only half of them each time. You'll rest and ice after every round. The only downside is you might need more pain meds."

He exhaled. "I'm already taking Naproxen routinely. I'll only use the narcotics when I absolutely need them—no more than twice a day. I want to reduce them to once before bed. Could I try regular acetaminophen during the day?"

"You can, but if it doesn't help enough, you'll have to wait six hours before taking the stronger meds since they also contain acetaminophen."

"It's a risk I'm willing to take if you'll take it with me."

"I'll do what you want."

"If the acetaminophen doesn't help enough, would you help me ice more often?"

"I can do that."

He looked at her, eyes steady. "Deanna, I want to heal. I want to be your husband. I want to be my brother's business partner. I need this shoulder to be strong. I can't let any of you down."

Her heart ached at the weight he carried. "Sweetheart, I know these exercises are new and painful. It will get better. Right now, it's baby steps and pain. But I have faith that you..."

"Dee?"

She hesitated. *Do I really believe this?* "I have faith that God will help you do this."

His eyes widened. "Are you saying you believe in God?"

She broke a cookie into pieces, staring at the crumbs. "I'm not sure what I believe. But I know you believe God will get you through this."

"I do. I believe He'll be with me through every painful step."

She handed him a whole cookie and a mug of milk, then popped a piece of hers into her mouth.

"My sweet, thank you for hanging in with me. I want you, I need you, and most of all, I love you."

A knock interrupted them. Mark poked his head in. "What's the verdict? Am I helping with exercises, or are you hanging in, Deanna?"

Solomon grinned. "She's hanging in with me. Thanks for being willing, Dad."

Solomon hadn't liked last Sunday or this one. Now that his concussion symptoms had resolved, he'd resumed going to church with his family. His dad helped him with exercises before the service, and Deanna arrived after church to help him with the early afternoon session. He knew it was a concession she made for her parents. They wouldn't approve of her attending church with him.

God, things would be so much better if I could marry her. Please, Lord, make it happen soon. Forgive my impatience. I trust Your timing. Thank You for the decrease in my pain, even with the exercises. In Jesus' name, amen.

This was the last Sunday before school started. *More time alone. More time without Deanna.* He sat at the table, Deanna at his side, and a plate of food in front of him that would've tasted better without dread dulling his appetite.

"Sweetheart, are you feeling okay?" Deanna whispered.

"I'm not very hungry, but I'm fine," he whispered back.

She tilted her head, squinting slightly. She saw more than he said. She always did, but there was nothing he could do about it.

Once the table was cleared and the food put away, it was time for the family meeting. He already knew what was coming: a new care schedule that meant less time with Deanna. He didn't want to hear it.

It has to happen. She has to graduate. Dad and Mom have to teach. Lexi and Millie need their education. I'm better.

None of it eased the ache in his chest.

His father prayed before they began. "Dear Lord, we come before You asking for Your guidance in Solomon's recovery. Bring him comfort as we return to our schools. Give us wisdom and patience with each other. Thank You for the blessing of Solomon's progress and the young woman standing at his side. Bless us to go forward according to Your will. Forgive us our sins and guide us to forgive others in like fashion. Yours is the glory and power forever. In Jesus' name, amen."

His mother turned to Deanna. "Please go over the proposed schedule with us."

Deanna cleared her throat. "Since he's doing well with the four-times-a-day schedule, I'd like to continue it. Mark, can you get him through the morning exercises before you leave for school?"

His dad nodded. "I'll make it work."

"As soon as I finish my classes, I'll come get him lunch and help with the midday exercises. While I do homework, Lexi and Millie, do you think you can help him with the after-school session?"

The girls nodded. "If you show us what to do, we'll do it," Lexi said.

"I'll show you during today's session. I'll help with the nighttime ones before I leave. And none of us, including you, Solomon, can forget the importance of icing after each round. You'll need to ice as needed between sessions. Will you do it?"

"Yes, I can do it myself if it's needed." He frowned. "I sound like a group project."

Deanna giggled. "You kind of are," she teased.

She sobered. "The physical therapist is starting him on weights and resistance bands. We'll get the instructions at his next appointment. He'll need progressively heavier hand-held weights and wall-mounted resistance bands. Mark, Betsy, can you pick those up in the next few days?"

His parents exchanged a glance. "We'll stop by WXY Sporting Goods tomorrow and get what we can," Betsy said.

Solomon slumped in his chair, lower lip jutting out like a toddler's. He sucked in a breath and let it out in a huff.

"If anybody cares, I hate this. I know it has to happen, but I hate it. Excuse me." He stood and walked to his room.

Deanna followed. "Solomon?"

He held the door open for her. "I'm sorry. I know I'm acting like a child."

She placed a hand on his good shoulder. "I love you."

He shook his head. "I know you love me. And my family loves me. None of you would go to all this trouble if you didn't. But I'm jealous. You all get to go back to school and return to normal. I'm stuck here. Alone."

She stepped closer, her gaze steady.

"At least I don't have to wear the sling anymore," he said. "But I still have to be careful. I can't do much without risking injury."

He traced the outline of her face with his fingers. "I already miss you."

She stiffened beneath his touch.

"I promised I wouldn't pressure you about your home situation, and I won't. But you're my lifeline, Dee. I can't do this without you. I miss you terribly when you're gone."

She closed her eyes. "You know there's nothing I can change."

"Deanna, look at me." He waited until her eyes met his. "You can't change it now, but as soon as I can make it happen, I promise you it will change. I'll be there to help you."

She sighed. "I know."

He wrapped his right arm around her, pulling her close. He kissed her until the ache in his chest eased, then pulled back.

"Better?" she asked.

He hummed. "Better."

Chapter 38

Dreams and Decisions

By December, Solomon was mostly pain-free. He'd graduated from needing help to managing everything on his own. Not that Deanna's parents knew. Some truths were easier left unspoken.

On the second Saturday of the month, he attended Deanna's graduation with both families. He wasn't surprised she finished top of her class with her degree in business. What caught him off guard was her decision to take a job rather than pursue nursing school. She'd always dreamed of becoming a nurse.

When he asked why, she dodged the question. He prayed he wasn't the reason. He wanted her to chase her dreams.

A week into the spring semester, Deanna burst into the Jackson house, her smile lighting the room. Solomon jumped to his feet, grinning as she flew into his arms.

"The job placement office set up an interview with the electric company," she said breathlessly. "They offered me a full-time position in accounting. The salary's better than I imagined, and the benefits are amazing. There's even a savings plan to help employees further their education. Later on, I can use it for nursing school."

He picked her up and spun her around. "I'm so proud of you."

"When do you start?"

"Next week. Don't you have your final appointment with Dr. Cutter tomorrow?"

He kissed her cheek. "I do. If he releases me, we'll have a lot to celebrate."

She nestled into his chest, resting her head on his shoulder. He breathed in her strawberry-vanilla scent, felt the silk of her hair, the softness of her skin. She fit against him like she'd been made for him.

I told her I loved her in the hospital. I had no idea how much deeper that love would grow.

He tightened his hold, buried his face in her hair, and whispered near her ear, "My sweet Deanna, I love you so much."

He nosed her hair aside and kissed gently around her ear and down her neck. She sighed and turned her head. The sparkle in her eyes was all the invitation he needed. He kissed her, savoring the moment, until his father cleared his throat.

"I know you two kiss," his dad said, voice stern but eyes twinkling, "but do I have to witness it in my living room?"

"Sorry, Dad," Solomon said.

His dad chuckled. "No, you're not."

Then came the shift. His father's smile faded, and Solomon braced.

"Son, all your mother and I ask is that you don't compromise your Christian values. You're both adults. The decisions are yours. Just weigh the consequences."

"Dad, Deanna has exciting news."

His father raised a brow. "Anything you want to share?"

"I landed a job at the electric company," Deanna said, spinning beneath their joined hands. "It's a great opportunity."

His father's smile returned. "Congratulations. You look thrilled."

"I am. Are you and Betsy coming to Solomon's appointment tomorrow?"

"Nah. We're sure our boy's healed. All the doc's gonna do is kick him to the curb with a letter that says, 'Get your bum back to work.'"

Deanna laughed. "I see where Robert gets his bluntness."

Solomon felt a flicker of panic. "I've got less than a thousand dollars left from the insurance check after paying off my truck. I need a vehicle to get to work."

His dad chuckled. "Welcome to adulthood. It ain't all fun and games. Your mom and I talked about it."

Solomon frowned. "You and Mom talked about my need for a vehicle?"

"Yep. Neither you nor Robert used your college funds. We don't want you taking out a loan. Consider using some of your college fund to buy a vehicle. You can repay the trust over time."

Solomon exhaled. "You're sure?"

His dad nodded. "We are."

Then his father paused, eyes widening slightly as if seeing something beyond them. "When you and Robert are ready to launch your business, you can use your college funds as seed money. It's not college, but it's your future. The money was meant to give you a future."

Solomon let go of Deanna's hand and hugged his father. "God blessed us with the best parents. Thank you."

His dad clapped him on the shoulder. "I love you, too, son. If Deanna has time, you might want to look at vehicles today. Use your cash to hold one, and we'll go with you to pull the rest from your trust."

Solomon turned to Deanna, fingers intertwining with hers. "Do you have time to go shopping with me?"

"Sure do. Let's go."

"You should be buying that girl's gas," his dad called as they headed for the door.

Solomon gave him a thumbs-up and closed the door behind them.

As Deanna drove, Solomon stared out the passenger window. "Dee, let's go to the big park, and up to the overlook on the hilltop."

She glanced at him, then turned her eyes back to the road. "Okay, but why?"

She swallowed her panic, keeping her expression neutral.

His gaze didn't shift. "There's something we need to talk about."

Her breath caught. *He doesn't need me anymore. Hasn't for a while.* Fear crept in, but she drove to the park anyway.

At the top of the hill, she parked. Solomon turned to her, eyes serious.

"Deanna, this has bugged me since your graduation. Why are you working instead of continuing school and chasing your dream of becoming a nurse? I don't want you giving up your dream because of me."

His eyes dropped to his lap.

She smiled softly. "I still want to be a nurse. And when the time comes, I know you'll help me make it happen. This job gives me a way to save for it. But right now, I want to be part of your and Robert's dream like Emelia is."

"You'd be part of it with or without a job. Don't wait because of me. Because of my dream."

She leaned in, conviction filling her voice. "Listen to me, sweetheart. I do want to be a nurse. But through your recovery, I learned something important. I loved being your caregiver. It changed me. My dreams shifted. You matter more to me than a degree, and I learned a lot about patience."

She smiled again. "May I borrow some of your words?"

His brows drew together. "I guess."

"Thank you." Her smile widened. "All things come in the Lord's time. You, Robert, and Emelia are already deep into your dream. Now your parents are helping, too. Let me be part of it. My job lets me contribute to our dream and save for mine."

He reached for her hand. "Deanna, I love you. I'm thankful God blessed me with you."

She laid her other hand over his. "And I'm thankful for a man I can trust with my dreams."

After riding with Solomon while he test-drove several trucks, they headed back to her car. His heart wasn't in it, she could tell.

"Are you sure you're ready to do this today?" she asked gently.

He opened her door, then climbed in beside her with a sigh. "I'm not even sure what I'm looking for. Robert still drives a car. We need to talk to Robert and Emelia. Are you up for going over there?"

Deanna ran her hands along the steering wheel, blinking back the sting in her eyes. "You're buying a vehicle with money your parents saved their whole lives for you. Robert and Emelia are your family. Maybe I shouldn't be involved in this decision. I'm not your family."

Solomon traced her jawline with the pad of his thumb. "Are you tired of me?"

A tear slipped free. "Of course not."

He wiped it away. "Where is this coming from? Surely you know how much I love you."

She drew a breath to steady the storm inside. "I want you to be well and get back to your life. But when that happens, I won't have a reason to spend every spare moment with you. And come Monday, we'll both be working full-time." Her voice cracked. "You won't need me anymore."

"Deanna, look at me."

She met his gaze.

"I've needed you since the moment our eyes met in the doorway before Robert and Emelia's wedding. I love you more than I know how to say or show. I want you in my life. For the rest of my life. I'm not making any big decisions without you."

She swiped at her cheeks, unable to stop her tears. "You want me just the way I am? You want to know what I think and feel? You trust me to help you make decisions?"

He rested his hand on her shoulder. "I value you. And I trust you."

Her sobs came harder. “I know my parents love me in their own way. But they want me to be a certain way. I tried so hard to please them, but it was never enough. They’re always disappointed.”

Solomon rubbed gentle circles on her arm. “Dee, my sweet, you are the best. I love you. I want you. I need you. I am overjoyed with you.”

She looked at him through dripping lashes, took a deep breath, and let it out slowly. “You promise?”

He reached out with both hands, and she placed hers in his. “I promise.”

“I love you, Solomon. Am I really enough?”

He smiled. “No, you’re not enough. You’re more than enough. You’re my everything.”

She leaned into his touch. “You‘re my everything.”

He leaned across the console and held her. In his arms, she let herself feel the full weight of the possibilities of a life with this man. And in that quiet moment, she prayed her first prayer.

Let me be brave, Lord. Help me do what I need to do to be part of Solomon’s life. He says I’m enough, but I’m not Yours. Robert and Emelia showed me what I need to do. It’ll put more distance between me and my parents. They’ll like Solomon and his family less. They’ll even start to dislike Emelia. I know I need to choose You, Lord... but I’m scared. Amen.

Solomon pulled back just enough to see her face. “Are you okay, my sweet?”

With his hands on her shoulders, he held her at arm’s length, eyes searching hers. Her heart pounded. He was waiting for an answer. She took a breath and let it out.

“Will you take me to church with you on Sunday?”

His eyes lit up. “Absolutely. And every time the doors are open, if you want to go.”

He brushed a kiss across her cheek. “Do you have tissues or napkins somewhere in the car?”

“Under your elbow,” she said, pulling down the visor and peeking into the mirror. “I think I need several.”

He handed her the pocket-sized pack from the console. “You’re still beautiful.”

She playfully slapped his arm, then gasped. "That's your left arm. I'm so sorry."

He laughed. "Relax, I'm fine."

She gave him a half smile and a wink. "You are."

She busied herself with drying her face, cleaning up her smeared makeup, and avoiding his gaze. When she finished, she handed him the tissues, used and unused. He caught her eye, raised an eyebrow, and said, "Fine."

"You sure are." She smiled and started the car. "To Robert and Emelia's."

"Yes."

Chapter 39

Wise Counsel

Solomon knocked and nudged open the door. Deanna caught his arm.

"They're married," she whispered.

He grinned. "They promised I'd never find them naked outside their bedroom."

Her blush bloomed, and he couldn't help but smile. "Come on in. I promise it's alright."

Robert stepped in behind them. "I thought I heard a car. We're eating with the Carters tonight. There's plenty. Sue said to tell you to join us. Follow me."

"Will I be welcome?" Deanna asked.

Robert frowned. "Why would your girl, my wife's best friend, ask that?" He turned to her. "Of course you're welcome. You're family. Don't ever ask that again."

Leading them up the three outside steps, Robert opened the door to the Carters' side. The table was full, except for three empty chairs. He took one, next to Emelia. The place settings made it clear that this was planned.

Deanna hesitated. Solomon touched the small of her back. "Relax," he said softly, guiding her forward.

Sue smiled. "We had an inkling you might show up."

"Dad called Jerry," Robert said. "Wanted to talk to Em and me. We buzzed over and spoke with him and Mom."

Solomon trod carefully. "What did they talk to you about?"

Robert gave a half smile. "We know about the seed money."

Solomon nodded, his shoulders relaxing. "I see the doctor tomorrow. If I'm cleared, I'll need to buy a vehicle. Can we talk after dinner?"

"Sure. Jerry's input might help, too."

Solomon caught Jerry's eye. Jerry nodded. "I'm good with that. I need all the good advice I can get."

Sue laughed and covered her mouth. Jerry raised a brow.

"What?" she said.

"Susan," he warned.

"I'm sorry, but if the boy wants good advice, I'm not sure he's going to get it from you and Robert."

Emelia and Deanna laughed.

Solomon chuckled. "I'll give them a chance. If they fail me, I'll come straight to you."

After dinner, the guys bundled up and stepped outside. They wandered the yard in silence until Jerry broke it.

"The gals are still in my side of the house. I'm cold. Let's talk inside yours."

Back inside, jackets and boots shed, Solomon finally spoke. "I feel like I'm taking from our future business by using part of my trust to buy a vehicle. Are you okay with that?"

Robert and Jerry slid into the bench at the table.

"Sit down, bro," Robert said. Solomon did.

"Dad said you'd repay the trust monthly. You'll replenish it and save a boatload of interest. Emelia and Deanna can figure out a fair rate and even amortize the interest if you insist," Robert paused and shrugged. "I don't care about the interest, but if it helps you sleep, pay it into the trust. Em and I are good with Dad and Mom's plan. Smile, brother, this is a sweetheart of a deal."

Solomon managed a smile. "What kind of vehicle should I buy? A used car or a pickup? Something new? Or something utilitarian with racks and toolboxes?"

"If you can wait until Saturday, I'll go with you. I wouldn't buy new. Maybe something two or three years old. Starting the business is still a couple of years off. Too soon for a work truck."

Then Robert tilted his head and looked at him square-shouldered.

Solomon scoffed. "Glad you think so, because I think I need to buy Deanna a ring and ask her father's permission to marry her."

Robert gasped. Jerry smiled. Solomon rolled his eyes.

"That woman put up with me during the worst six months of my life. No matter how crabby I got, she was patient. She coaxed me through PT, figured out a schedule that made it bearable. She got this cranky, whiny man through his recovery."

He paused, lost in the memory. Jerry nudged him.

"You got more to say, son."

"Yeah. I wouldn't have done those exercises on my own. Without her, I'm afraid my shoulder would still be messed up. And after everything, she still says she loves me. She's a saint."

Robert shook his head. Jerry and Solomon looked at him.

"You've met her parents, right?"

"Yes." Solomon's brows furrowed.

"Do you think her father will give you permission to marry her?"

"I don't know. I hope so."

"You're the best thing that's ever happened to Deanna, according to my wife. But neither of us thinks her parents will say yes. What's your plan if they say no?"

Jerry frowned at Robert. "Your brother's a good man. If Deanna were my daughter, I'd be proud to have him as a son. I don't understand the problem."

Solomon traced the wood-grain pattern on the table. "I think I do. Deanna had a meltdown today. Said she's never been good enough for her parents. They're always disappointed in her. They've done a number on her."

He looked up and squared his shoulders.

"She was afraid I wouldn't need her anymore now that I'm healthy. I told her nothing between us is going to change. I love her. I trust her. She matters to me in every way. She's my everything, and she's perfect for me just as she is."

Silence settled. Solomon's finger still roamed the woodgrain.

"If her parents say no, I'll ask her anyway. And pray she says yes."

He looked up, smiling. "She asked if I'd take her to church on Sunday. Robert, she wants to come to church."

Jerry smiled. "You do need a ring for that girl's finger."

"I second that," Robert said. "And I know exactly where to take you. Two important missions on Saturday."

Jerry stood. "Should we go check on the ladies?"

Deanna and Emelia helped Sue clear the table and put away the food. Once that was done, Sue tried to shoo them out.

"I'm letting these dishes soak," Sue said. "Jerry will help me in the morning. You girls should go on. I'm sure you have catching up to do."

Emelia met her gaze. "It really bothers me to leave you with the mess. With Deanna here, we can knock this out in minutes. Let us help. We'll catch up while we work."

Deanna smiled and nodded. "I've missed you. We're staying."

Deanna rinsed dishes and handed them to Sue, who loaded the dishwasher. Emelia wiped down the counters, stove, and table. When the kitchen was clean and the dishwasher hummed, Emelia pointed at the clock.

"See, only fifteen minutes."

Sue smiled. "Point taken. You can help when you eat with us, unless Jerry's here. No offense, ladies, but I prefer my husband."

Emelia laughed. "I get that. My time with Robert matters, even if we're just doing chores."

Deanna sighed. "I'm really going to miss my time with Solomon."

Emelia's brows shot up. "You two looked pretty cozy. Why would you miss him?"

"If he's cleared tomorrow, he'll go back to work Monday. I start my new job at the electric company on Monday."

"Ahh," Sue said. "Back to real life. You'll miss each other, but you're so in love. You'll make it work."

Emelia nodded. "I stacked my classes on Tuesdays and Thursdays with a night class."

She giggled. "I got into the electric company's paid internship program. I'll be working with you on Monday, Wednesday, and Friday."

Deanna's eyes widened. She grabbed Emelia, and they jumped, both of them squealing.

Sue leaned against the counter, smiling. "I'm so thankful to have you two in my life. Your joy does my heart good."

When Deanna's shoulders slumped, Sue's smile faded, narrowing her gaze on Deanna. "I sense you're worried. Let's sit in the living room. You can tell this old lady all about it."

"Yes, ma'am." Deanna followed her out of the kitchen.

Sue motioned Emelia to follow as well. Deanna sank into the sofa, and Sue sat beside her. Emelia settled on the opposite couch, facing them.

Deanna leaned forward, elbows on her knees, face in her hands. "I'm going to lose Solomon, and there's nothing I can do."

Sue placed a hand on her back. Emelia's voice was gentle. "Why would you say that? That man loves you with his whole heart."

"I know. He told me I'm more than enough. That he's overjoyed with me." Her voice cracked, but she didn't raise her head.

"So what's the problem?" Emelia asked.

Deanna lifted her face, swiping at her spilling tears. "My parents. Solomon won't ask me to marry him without their permission. They won't give it. They don't like him. They'll say he isn't good enough. No degree, no future. And Solomon will walk away."

Sue pulled her into a hug. Emelia knelt in front of her.

"Deanna," Emelia said, "Jackson men are stubborn. Solomon will fight for you. Let him show you how deeply he loves you. He'll contend with your parents. He'll honor your love. Don't give up hope. Love him."

Deanna twisted her lips, trying to believe. Emelia looked earnest, still on the floor, gaze staying on Deanna. "How did you get so much time with Solomon? Your parents never allowed that before."

When Sue handed her a tissue box, Deanna wiped her face and took a breath.

"I told them Solomon mattered to me. I promised to help him through recovery. I refused to bow to their will. I said I'd return to their rules if my grades dropped. I studied every chance I got at the Jacksons and went home each night to sleep. My grades never dropped."

She turned to Sue. "With my parents, only A's count. I can live at home as long as I'm in school or working. I'm so thankful I landed a job so quickly."

She paused and shrugged before continuing. "My dad said he doesn't like Solomon. He thinks the Jacksons are a bad influence. I know he'll turn Solomon down flat and humiliate him in the process."

She looked from Emelia to Sue. "I love him so much. No one's ever made me feel as valued as he and this family have. The thought of losing him, and all of you, makes me feel sick."

Tears spilled again. Sue pulled her close and rubbed her back.

"Trust us. Trust Solomon. We'll love you no matter what your parents say or do. You'll always have a place in our hearts, and in our home."

Though Deanna's weeping ceased, Sue continued to hold her at arm's length.

"You're a wonderful person," Sue said. "Smart. I heard you graduated top of your class. You are valued. Don't listen to anyone who says otherwise, not even your parents. They're wrong. And Solomon knows it."

Emelia stood from the floor and hugged her. "Trust Solomon. Trust us. We love you."

Deanna smiled through tears. "I stood up to them once. If I have to, I'll do it again. You'll be my safety net if it goes bad?"

Sue nodded. "Absolutely."

Deanna sighed. "I don't know how to thank you. I've never had this kind of love and support before."

The back door opened. Three sets of footsteps approached.

"There's my girl," Jerry said. "Thanks for helping, Sue. This old man is tired."

Robert joined Emelia. “You girls have a good visit?”

Emelia glanced at Deanna. “We did,” she said softly.

Solomon held out his hand. “Ready to take me home, my sweet?”

She met his gaze. “I am. It’s been a long day.”

Chapter 40

A Ringing Release

Solomon endured one final scan, then followed Dr. Cutter into the exam room. When the doctor tested the strength and mobility of his shoulder, Solomon moved through every one without pain. From the corner chair, Deanna watched silently, her focus unwavering. He could feel her taking mental notes.

When the exam ended, Solomon sat beside her as they waited for the verdict.

Dr. Cutter placed the scans on the light box, displaying the pre-op, post-op, and that day's images, while pointing out the changes as he went. "Your clavicle's fully healed. If the screws and plate aren't bothering you, there's more risk than benefit in removing them. You have full mobility, no pain, and solid strength. Are you ready to return to life without restrictions?"

Relief swept through Solomon. "I'm so ready. Thanks, Doc."

Dr. Cutter clapped his shoulder. "I only need to see you if there's a problem. I hope I never see you again."

"Same here," he chuckled. Standing, he reached for Deanna. "Come on, my sweet. Let's celebrate your new job and my return to the old one."

She took his hand. As they stepped into the hallway, Dr. Cutter called out, "Stop at the front desk and grab your work release."

Outside, the late January sun warmed his skin. Solomon paused beside her car, took a deep breath, and pulled her into his arms.

"I feel free," he murmured. "No more fear with every move. I can't thank you enough. You're just as responsible for my recovery as the doctors and therapists. I love you so much."

He kissed the top of her head.

Her arms tightened around him. "I love you, too."

He stepped back and gave her a soft kiss. "Let's eat. Then find someplace I can kiss you the way I want."

He opened her door and waited until she was settled. As he climbed in, she turned to him.

"We both like Italian. How about Mama Mia's on Main Street? The veal parmigiana for two sounds good."

Solomon grinned. "Sounds great to me."

On Saturday, Robert and Solomon first stopped at the pawn shop where Robert had purchased Emelia's engagement and wedding rings.

Solomon frowned. "Umm." He hesitated. "I thought we were buying rings?"

Robert guffawed. "When I wanted to ask Emelia to marry me, Eddy told me about this place, and I had the same reaction. Eddy assured me I'd find somethin' here, and I did. Trust me."

Solomon nodded, rolling his eyes. "I sure hope you're right."

Robert led the way to the jewelry cases and pointed to one full of wedding and engagement rings. Solomon scanned the display, then glanced at Robert. "Thanks, bro."

"Hello, Joe. Jim."

Solomon looked up when his brother spoke.

"Solomon, this is Joe, the owner, and his son, Jim," Robert said.

Standing behind the jewelry case, Joe asked, "How long ya been married now, Rob?"

Robert smiled. "Thirteen months. Emelia loves her rings." He held up his left hand. "Mine's good, too."

Jim smiled. "So, this guy looks like he may be your brother. His turn to belly up to the altar?"

Robert laughed. "Belly up to the altar? I haven't heard that one before. Yes, this is my brother, Solomon, and he is ready to take the marriage plunge."

Joe clapped Jim on the back. "Nice to meet ya, Sol. Jim will take good care of you. Since Rob here brought his brother to us, make him a good deal."

"What's her ring size?" Jim asked.

Solomon shrugged. "I don't know."

Robert shoved a piece of paper into Solomon's hand. "Emelia got the info for me."

Dazed, Solomon unfolded the paper and handed it to Jim.

Jim read it aloud. "Size six. Do you know your ring size?"

Solomon pulled his class ring off his right hand and transferred it to his left. He started to remove it, but Jim stopped him. "Point your fingers at the ground and shake your hand really hard."

Solomon's brows drew together, but he did what Jim requested.

Jim looked at his hand. "The ring is still there. That's a good sign. Now, take it off." He held out his hand

"Give him your ring," Robert said.

Jim reached under the counter and pulled out a sizing rod. He dropped Solomon's ring onto it. When it stopped, Jim turned it so Solomon could read the number. "Nine point five."

"Matching wedding bands, or a woman's wedding set and a man's band?"

Solomon shrugged and looked at Robert.

Robert glared. "I'm not marryin' her. What do you want?"

Jim smiled and laughed. "I'll pull out some size six wedding sets for her, and we'll go from there."

When Jim set the fourth set on the counter, Solomon's breath caught. Without asking, he removed the rings from their box and slid them onto his pinky. "I can see these rings on Deanna's hand."

His hand shook when he slid off the rings and returned them to the box. He knew nothing about gold or diamonds. He saw two silver bands, one with a round sparkly stone surrounded by six smaller sparkling stones.

"Good choice," Jim said.

He pulled some white gold wedding bands in Solomon's size. "Which one do you see on your finger?"

Solomon picked up a band with silver on the inside and edges, along with a band of what looked like wood in the center and slid it on his left ring finger. "This looks like a carpenter's ring."

Jim chuckled. "It's actually called a carpenter's band. The set you picked out for Deanna is fourteen-carat white gold with a total of two-thirds of a carat of diamonds. The band you chose for yourself is ten-carat white gold with a Carpathian wood inlay."

Solomon drew in a breath and blew it out. "That sounds like I'll be spending a fortune if I buy those rings. I may need to sit down before you give me a price."

Jim looked at Robert. "You are an evil man."

Robert threw back his head and laughed. When he quieted, he said, "Put my brother out of his misery."

Jim looked up the rings in the ledger, punched several buttons on the ten-key, then met Solomon's gaze. "How does two hundred and seventy-five dollars sound?"

Solomon looked at Robert. "Is this some kind of a sick joke?"

Robert shook his head. "Give him the wedding ring spiel."

When Jim finished, Solomon said, "Oh."

He pulled out his wallet and handed Jim the cash.

"Take him to Glitter & Gold and get those rings checked and cleaned," Jim said to Robert, handing Solomon his receipt.

"Why did they call you Rob and me Sol?" Solomon asked as they headed to Glitter & Gold.

Robert shrugged. "My guess is nicknames are their thing. They know their stuff and make good deals. I can live with Rob for the money they've saved me."

When they entered Glitter & Gold, the man behind the counter greeted Robert by name. "Did you bring your wife's rings in for their six-month checkup?"

"No, but Em and I do need to get that done. Mr. Owen, this is my brother, Solomon, and he just purchased some rings from Joe and Jim."

"I'll check them out for you. I'll tell you if they need any work and give you an estimate. I gave your brother a round-figure appraisal on the rings he bought. I do that for free. If you want an itemized appraisal, I charge twenty-five dollars for that. As I check them, I will tell you what I see."

Solomon set the small sack on the counter and pulled out the two velvet ring boxes. "Please do for me what you did for Robert."

Mr. Owen gave Solomon a more detailed description of Deanna's rings than Jim had.

"The prongs on the diamonds show some wear, but I wouldn't recommend repairing them yet. I want to check them again in three months just to be safe. Did they mention anything about the cut of the center diamond?"

Solomon shook his head. "No."

"It's a rose cut. I rarely see stones like this anymore. It's a remarkable piece."

I bought my sweet a rose. He smiled.

Then he removed Solomon's ring from its box and gave it a thorough examination. "This is a sturdy ring of ten-carat white gold. Ten-carat gold is harder than fourteen-carat. The wood will require some maintenance along the way, but I can take care of that for you when I check the prongs on your girl's rings. I don't get to see a carpenter's band very often. Are you working with your brother?"

Solomon smiled. "Yes, sir. I'm still learning everything. But I'll be with him when we open our own business."

Mr. Owen wrote on a piece of paper, folded it, and slipped it to Solomon. "I told your brother this same thing. Wait until you are at home and alone to look at that. You're in for a pleasant surprise."

Back at the car, they slid inside. Robert buckled his seat belt and started the engine. "How much of the remaining insurance money do you have left?"

"A little more than five hundred," Solomon said.

"Connor called me yesterday and told me he has a new hire and wants to start him out workin' with Eddy. You and I are goin' to be workin' on projects together for the foreseeable future. If you're not opposed to stayin' with Em and me, you and I can ride to work together."

You can postpone buyin' a vehicle until a few paychecks are in your account. We can look for trucks then."

"I'd really like to take Deanna out on some real dates. Are you and Emelia opposed to my borrowing a car to do that until I buy something?"

Robert smiled. "We can work that out. Let's go talk to Dad and Mom."

Chapter 41

Big Moves

At their parents' home, Solomon found his mother busy in the kitchen. He walked up behind her and gave her a gentle squeeze.

"Something sure smells good."

"It sure does," Robert said. "I hear a saw out back. What's Dad up to?"

"He's cutting shelves for the girls' room. They're running out of space. You boys needed so much less than they do," she grumbled. "Are you boys staying for dinner?"

"We actually stopped by to talk to you and Dad," Solomon said.

"He should be in soon. I don't hear the saw anymore. This sauce is ready to simmer. Now's a good time."

"Holler when he's in. I'm going to see the girls," Solomon said.

"Right behind you, bro," Robert added.

"Okay, boys," their mother called after them.

Solomon knocked on his sisters' bedroom door.

"Come in." Lexi's voice carried through the door.

Robert was beside him when he opened it. "Whoa!" they said in unison, eyes wide.

Lexi and Millie jumped up to hug them. When they stepped back, Lexi planted her hands on her hips.

"You guys need to chill. We're just rearranging and organizing a little."

"A little?" Robert said, aghast.

"It looks like something blew up in here," Solomon added. "You girls need more space."

Millie mirrored Lexi's stance. "We're getting more room. Dad's making us shelves. Go on, we've got work to do."

Solomon and Robert shook their heads.

"Can't argue with that," Solomon said.

Lexi slammed the door in their faces.

Chuckling as they walked back toward the kitchen, Solomon said, "Mom and Dad may jump at the chance to give those two more space. If I move out, they can have separate rooms."

"Maybe," Robert said.

Solomon tapped his chin. "Lexi and Millie each have their own beds. Maybe we can move our old bedroom furniture to your house."

Robert stopped him. "Cart before horse, brother. We need to talk to Dad and Mom first. They may think we're nuts."

"Boys," their mother called.

"I guess we're about to find out," Solomon said.

They joined their parents at the kitchen table.

"What's up, boys?" their dad asked.

Solomon swallowed. "I'll be right back. I have something to show you."

He returned with a small bag, pulled out the velvet boxes, and opened them. "I spent some of the insurance money today."

As his parents looked at the rings, he added, "Dee and I looked at trucks this week. I didn't find anything worth buying. Robert has an idea."

Robert groaned. "I guess that's my cue. Our boss called last night—Solomon's workin' with me for the foreseeable future. Emelia and I talked about his transportation. We think he should move into our spare room. When he was helpin' us, it was easier to keep up with the chores the Carters can't handle. We're strugglin' now. He and I can ride to work together, and he can postpone buyin' a vehicle until he finds one he's comfortable buyin'."

Their mother frowned, eyes glassy as she held the open ring boxes. "I'm losing my boy."

Their dad chuckled. "We're not losing a boy. We're gaining a bedroom and a daughter."

"Mark!" She playfully slapped his arm. "I'm not ready for the bright side right now."

Solomon looked between them. "Mom, I just bought the rings. I haven't talked to her parents or proposed yet. I don't think our engagement will be short. Don't worry about me living with Robert and Emelia. Emelia will make sure you see us as often as you'd like. May I have some of the furniture in my room?"

His father rubbed his chin. "Is Robert's dresser still empty?"

Robert and Solomon exchanged a glance.

"You emptied it when you packed for me," Robert said.

Solomon nodded. "Then it should be empty."

His mom's lips twitched, and he could tell she was resisting a smile. "I already miss seeing Deanna every day, and now I'm going to miss you, too. What I won't miss is Lex and Millie arguing over everything. Take everything except the empty dresser."

"At least you're smilin' now," their dad said, giving her a side hug.

Robert laced his fingers and set his hands on the table. "Givin' the girls separate rooms is gonna cause more arguments. They'll both want the vanity."

Solomon's eyes widened. "Oh! We're going to need another vanity, or we'll start a teenage war."

Their dad stood, kissed their mom, and jingled his keys. "Let's go solve this problem."

When they returned from the antique mall, a restored vanity sat in the bed of their dad's truck. Their mom appeared in the garage doorway.

"How much did that set us back?"

"When Robert bought the vanity for the girls for Christmas, they said they could get four or five times what he offered. I offered a hundred. We settled on a hundred and ten," their dad said, chuckling. "And there's no work to do. A small price to prevent arguments."

His mother nodded. "Deanna's picking up Emelia, and we're all having dinner here. Solomon, you and Robert are packing up that room and loading everything on your dad's trailer. Tomorrow after church, we're getting the girls sorted. I need peace around here."

His dad sighed. "Who gets the new vanity? Asking them will start another fight."

His mom nodded. "Lexi. The one in that room stays. It's one less thing to move, and she already claimed the boys' room. Millie's okay with that. No boat rocking. Please."

She turned to her sons. "You boys get to clean that room once it's mostly emptied. Lexi and Millie want to paint. You're going to teach them how once they choose colors."

Robert and Solomon groaned and headed inside.

Before packing, Solomon detoured to the kitchen, slid the ring boxes back into the bag, and tucked them under his socks in the dresser drawer.

"I don't see any need to empty this. Let's secure the drawers before we move it."

Robert nodded. "Sounds good to me. Less packing and unpacking."

After a couple of hours, the room was packed and dinner was ready. At some point, Emelia and Deanna had arrived and were already knee-deep in the chaos of the girls' room.

"It's amazin'. It's quieter with four girls than with two," Robert said as they approached the open door.

Emelia stuck out her tongue and put her arm around Deanna. "We added the necessary maturity. Something you two will never supply."

"If you mature ladies want to join us, Mom says dinner's ready," Solomon said, muffling his laughter.

Following the smell of garlic and fresh bread, Solomon and Robert were nearly run down as the four girls barreled past.

Solomon peeled himself off the wall, eyebrows raised. "My guess is they're hungrier than we are."

He offered Robert a hand up. "Remind me not to stand between them and food."

They laughed all the way to the kitchen.

Chapter 42

Big Decision

The weekend was a whirlwind. By Sunday afternoon, Solomon and Deanna had unpacked and arranged everything in his new room at Robert and Emelia's. They fell onto the bed, savoring the last few quiet minutes of rest before church.

Robert and Emelia drove with the Carters in Emelia's car. Solomon followed in Robert's car with Deanna beside him.

He'd driven her to church Wednesday night and again that morning, but tonight felt different. She wrung her hands in her lap, eyes fixed on the window. Solomon reached over and covered her hands with his.

"My sweet, what's wrong?"

"There's something I need to do. It's a big deal. I'm nervous," she said, still watching the passing trees.

"You know you can talk to me about anything."

"I love you. You and your family have changed my life." She turned to him. "But this thing, I need to do it on my own. For me. Not for you."

His hand stayed over hers, the other steady on the wheel. "You're trembling."

"I told you it's a big deal."

"But you can't, or won't, tell me what it is?"

"This one thing has to be my decision alone."

He pulled his hand away as they turned into the church lot. After parking, he rounded the car to help her out, but she didn't take his hand. His smile faltered.

"You have to trust me," she said. "I have a meeting with someone. I'll join you in the Auditorium."

Solomon's mouth gaped as she walked away. Then he jogged to catch up with Robert and Emelia.

"Do you guys know what's going on with Deanna?"

Emelia shook her head, brows drawn. "No. Where is she?"

"She said she had a meeting and would join me later."

They settled into their usual pew. Solomon scanned the Auditorium. The youth minister was the only one missing.

"Could she be meeting with Brother Walker?"

Robert and Emelia exchanged a look.

"You don't think..." Emelia trailed off.

Robert shrugged.

"Think what?" Solomon pressed.

"We have a guess," Robert said, "but it wouldn't be right to share it. We could be wrong."

Solomon scoffed. "I'm not sure I like either of you right now."

During the opening hymn, Deanna slipped into the pew beside him, calm and smiling. Solomon stared at her, determined to uncover the mystery after service. She entwined her fingers with his and whispered, "I love you."

The rest of the service blurred as his mind raced through worst-case scenarios. When the invitation hymn "Why Not Now" began, Deanna held his hand through the first and second stanzas. When the third verse started, she inhaled sharply and let go.

She stepped into the aisle.

"Deanna?" he whispered.

He started to follow, but Robert grabbed his arm.

"She needs to do this on her own."

Solomon shoved the songbook into its holder and stood, gripping the pew so tightly his knuckles turned white.

"I should be beside her," he said through clenched teeth.

Brother Bassing stepped forward. "Deanna came forward this evening requesting baptism. She has studied extensively with

Robert and Emelia Jackson and has counseled with Brother Walker. Deanna, tell us what you believe."

My hand should be holding hers. I should be giving her strength.

He held his breath.

Deanna's shoulders rose and fell, again and again. Robert kept a firm grip on Solomon's arm.

"I believe that Jesus Christ is God's Son," she said, voice trembling, "that He died on the cross as a sacrifice for my sins and rose again on the third day. He ascended to heaven and sits at His Father's right hand."

Emelia and Solomon's mother stepped forward and led her into the dressing room beside the baptismal.

Solomon startled when a hand touched his shoulder. Robert released him.

"Come with me," Brother Walker said. "She wants you to baptize her."

Solomon followed him to the men's dressing room.

In the Auditorium, the singing continued. Solomon changed into the chest waders Brother Bassing always used, tightening the straps and rolling up his sleeves. The youth minister turned on the baptismal lights and opened the door.

"You'll be there to help her in when she's ready," Brother Walker said.

"I've been baptized. I've witnessed baptisms. I've never baptized anyone," Solomon admitted, voice shaking.

"You know what to do. Confirm her confession, cover her nose and mouth, and dunk her." He handed Solomon a white handkerchief. "As long as you don't drown her, you can't mess this up."

Solomon sighed and took the cloth. He climbed the steps and descended into the water.

On the other side, Emelia held Deanna's hand as she climbed up. Solomon took both her hands and guided her down into the waist-deep pool.

"I've got you," he whispered.

She nodded. "I'm ready."

"Do you believe that Jesus Christ is the Son of God, who died on the cross, was raised on the third day, ascended into heaven, and sits at His Father's right hand?"

"That is what I believe."

"Upon that confession, I now baptize you in the name of the Father, the Son, and the Holy Spirit for the remission of your sins."

He placed the handkerchief in her hand and guided it over her nose and mouth. Leaning her back, he fully immersed her, then lifted her again to her feet.

Turning her toward the congregation, he said, "I present to you our new sister in Christ, Deanna Keaton."

He helped her up the stairs. Emelia met her at the top and led her into the dressing room, closing the door behind them.

Solomon exited on his side. Brother Walker clapped him on the back.

"You did good. I'm proud of you."

Inside the dressing stall, Deanna changed out of the wet garment, hung it over the door, and watched it disappear. After drying off, she wrapped her hair in a towel and got dressed. Her smile bloomed when she stepped out and saw Emelia had laid out powder, blush, mascara, a brush, and a comb.

"Thank you."

"You didn't think your best friend would let you meet your new family without freshening up, did you?"

"But you didn't know. Honestly, I didn't know for sure until after I spoke with Brother Walker tonight."

Emelia waved a hand over the items. "These aren't anything special. Just what I keep in my purse for those just-in-case moments."

Deanna's eyes dropped to Emelia's purse hanging from a hook. "You're the best."

Emelia grabbed both her hands and bounced. "We are sisters," she squealed.

They squealed together, "We are sisters."

Letting go, Deanna quickly combed out her hair and dabbed on a little makeup. "Good?"

Emelia beamed. "Great. Time to meet the family."

When they opened the door, the congregation was still singing. The hymn warmed Deanna's heart, and the song leader ended the verse with a gentle, "Welcome, sister."

Brother Bassing asked Brother Walker to lead the closing prayer, gestured for Deanna and Emelia to sit in the front pew beside Solomon, and moved to the back.

After the prayer, Emelia hugged Deanna and stepped away. Solomon stayed at her side.

"I'm so proud of you, my sweet," he said, slipping an arm around her waist.

Everyone had stayed to witness her baptism. One by one, her new Christian family welcomed her with hugs and handshakes. When the last person headed up the aisle, Deanna leaned into Solomon.

"That was a lot."

He held her from behind. "What you did tonight was a lot. Let's go home."

They walked toward Brother Bassing, who hugged Deanna and shook Solomon's hand. "See you two on Sunday."

When Solomon parked Robert's car at the Carters', Deanna stilled, her gaze on him. "I wish this were my home."

"I want that, too." He laced his fingers through hers.

She sighed, her whole body sagging. "I changed my life tonight, and my parents will never understand. My baptism is one more thing I can't tell them. I do want to see Robert and Emelia before you take me home."

Solomon nodded. "I'll make you a cup of tea. After you drink it, I'll take you."

He softly squeezed her hand, then got out. Her eyes stayed on him as he rounded the hood and opened her door. He helped her out and led her inside.

She leaned on the kitchen counter while Solomon filled Emelia's tea kettle and placed it on the stove.

"What are you guys doing?" Emelia asked, joining them.

"Solomon put water on for tea. We thought we'd visit before he takes me home."

Feeling safe and accepted in this house, Deanna let her shoulders sag and her frown show. "I wish I didn't have to go home. I'm so tired of never being good enough and having my every action judged."

By the time she finished, Robert had joined them. Emelia pulled her into a hug, and Solomon and Robert wrapped their arms around them both.

"I love you guys so much," she said when they let go.

"We love you, too." Emelia pulled her basket of teas from beneath the counter and set it down.

Deanna peeked inside. "I'll have Emelia's favorite, Jasmine." She licked her lips.

Solomon chuckled. "I'll have that one, too."

Emelia pulled out chamomile. "This is for Robert and me."

She and Deanna giggled at Robert's expression.

"Chill, my love. I'll put honey in it. You know it helps you sleep."

"It's not bad with honey, but I'd rather have the Red Zinger."

Emelia handed him a bag of Red Zinger, and Deanna grabbed mugs from the cabinet. When the pot whistled, Solomon poured the water, and the girls added the tea bags and honey. Robert added cream to his.

They settled in the living room. When her cup was empty, Deanna picked up Solomon's and took them to the kitchen. When she returned, he stood.

"It's time for me to go home," she said, frowning.

She was enveloped in another group hug by the people she loved most. When they released her, Solomon took her hand, and Emelia rested hers on Deanna's shoulders.

"Sis, I'll see you in the morning. You're in our prayers."

Robert nodded, and Emelia dropped her hands. Deanna smiled and waved as Solomon led her out.

At the passenger side of the car, he took both her hands. "I hate that you're so unhappy." He kissed the tip of her nose.

"I'm not always unhappy. You..." She dropped her head to his chest. "You make me happy."

Solomon lifted her chin. “You make me happy, too.” He kissed her.

She took control of the kiss, pouring everything into it. They held each other tightly, mouths moving with reckless abandon. When Solomon pulled back, they both gasped for air.

After a few breathless moments, he tugged her gently away from the door. “My sweet, I’d better get you home.” He opened it for her.

Once she was settled, he got in on the other side.

“Why are you looking at me that way?” he asked.

“Sweetheart, sometimes I can’t take my eyes off you. You’re a sight to behold and beautiful on the inside, too. God truly blessed me when He brought you into my life.” She rested her hand on his arm. “I love you.”

“My sweet, please tell me you know I love you and feel exactly that way about you.”

“It’s hard to believe anyone feels that way about me, but the more you say it, the more I believe it.”

He leaned across the console and kissed her cheek. “Then I’ll keep saying it. Let’s get you home. We both have big days tomorrow.”

Chapter 43

Expectations

Solomon entered the house and went straight to his room. He pulled the wedding set from his sock drawer and stared at it, praying that Deanna's new relationship with the Lord would silence the dream that haunted him.

It replayed in his mind.

He and Deanna were at the big park on the south side of town, sharing a picnic supper. When he kissed her, a voice whispered through the trees, "She's not a Christian." Soft at first, then rising until it filled the air. He looked one way and saw a shadowed form glowing faintly red; the other, a figure clothed in light, hands marked by sacrifice. Both repeated the words, steady and sure.

As the sound swelled, Deanna faded away, gone. The figures reached for him from opposite sides—one burning, one blinding. A searing pain tore through him as they pulled in opposite directions, the voices rising until they drowned out his scream.

Each time, he woke with his heart pounding. The words still echoed in his mind.

The dream first interrupted his sleep on the Saturday he bought the rings and returned as recently as last night. But things were different now.

Deanna *is* a Christian.

He exhaled slowly. It's time to put this diamond on her finger.

Her birthday was just over two weeks away. He'd propose then.

In the meantime, he enlisted Emelia's help to get Deanna out of the house. He needed to speak with her parents without her knowing.

Nearly a week passed before Emelia convinced Deanna to spend Saturday with her. Once the girls set their date, Solomon called the Keaton home and arranged a time to meet.

When Saturday came, he paced until Emelia left to pick up Deanna. He kept pacing long after she drove away.

Robert stepped into the living room. "Solomon, let's put your nervous energy to use. Help me assemble this shelving unit for Emelia's books. By the time we finish, it'll be time for you to go."

Solomon nodded. He took the box knife from Robert and opened the packaging while his brother sorted the parts. An hour later, the bookshelf stood at a ninety-degree angle to Emelia's desk, giving the illusion of an office.

"Thanks for the distraction."

Not wanting to leave Ephraim Keaton waiting, Solomon arrived a few minutes early. He wiped his sweaty palms on his jeans and knocked.

Mr. Keaton opened the door. Mrs. Keaton stood beside him.

"Come in," she said.

Solomon stepped inside and swallowed hard. Their unsmiling faces made him more nervous than he'd been on the porch. Mr. Keaton gestured toward the sofa. He and Mrs. Keaton sat across from him.

"What is this about?" Mr. Keaton's tone and expression were stony.

A lump rose in Solomon's throat. He swallowed twice before he could speak.

"I..." He swallowed again. "I'm in love with your daughter."

"And?" Mrs. Keaton prompted, her lips as tight as her husband's.

"Deanna loves me."

Their silence pressed down on him. He sat up straighter, drew a breath, and spoke.

"We want to spend our lives together. I will care for her, provide for her, respect her, and love her. May I have your permission to marry her?"

Mr. Keaton threw back his head and laughed. "You have the potential to do everything you said, except provide for her. Our daughter deserves better than a man with no education and no aspirations. No, you may not marry our daughter."

Mrs. Keaton stood and opened the door. Mr. Keaton gestured toward it.

"Your time with Deanna ends now. See yourself out. Don't darken our door again. Don't call. Your phone calls are unwelcome."

Solomon's mouth fell open, but he stood and walked out. The door slammed behind him.

He got in Robert's car and drove, stunned and numb.

God, what happens now? I know Deanna loves me. You know I love her. A question surfaced. How do I see her? How do I talk to her?

He managed to park and return to the house before his composure cracked.

He stomped inside, wound so tight he could barely breathe.

Robert held up his hands. "They said no."

Solomon glared. "Not only did they say no, they said I'm too inadequate ever to see or speak to her again."

He deflated. "I love her. And she loves me."

Robert guided him to the couch and sat beside him. "Do you still want to marry her?"

Solomon let his head fall against the back of the sofa. "Yes. But how do I even ask her if I can't see or talk to her?"

He threw his hands in the air and stood. "Never mind. I'm going for a walk."

Two hours later, when Emelia arrived home, Solomon hadn't returned to the house. Robert stood at the back door, shoulders slumped. She dropped her purse and crossed the room.

"The shelf looks good, my love."

He didn't respond.

"What's wrong?"

"Solomon left to go on a walk over two hours ago. It's cold out there."

Emelia turned him toward her. "Let's see what Jerry thinks we should do."

He led the way to the Carters' side of the home. He opened the door, and Emelia called out, "Jerry? Sue?"

"In the living room," Jerry boomed.

When they rounded the corner, there Solomon sat, feet up in the recliner.

"I should ring your neck, brother," Robert said. "I thought you were out in the field somewhere freezin'. We came in here to see if we should form a search party." Moving to Solomon's side, he clapped his shoulder. "I'm glad you're okay."

Solomon sat up. "I'm sorry. I got cold fast. Jerry saw me wandering and brought me in. I'm not okay, though. I'm worried about Dee. Her parents don't know she's been going to church with us. She won't understand why I don't show up tomorrow."

Emelia studied him, his eyes red and swollen. "They didn't mention you when I dropped her off. I thought they were keeping quiet so they wouldn't spoil your proposal. I'll call her."

She stepped into the kitchen and dialed. Mr. Keaton answered the phone.

"Hello, it's Emelia. May I speak to Deanna?"

"Hey, girl. Just checking on you."

"Why? You just left."

"Any chance you want to ride with us tomorrow?"

"I can't. I was going to call Solomon and let him know. We're going to Springfield to see my grandparents."

"I'll let him know for you."

"Thanks, Emelia. Give him my love. I miss him."

"I will. See you Monday."

"See you Monday."

Emelia returned and sank onto the sofa between Robert and Solomon, frowning. "She doesn't know what happened. She's going with her parents to visit her grandparents tomorrow."

Everyone sat quietly, looking at one another. Solomon nodded and seemed to deflate further.

"She said she loves you," Emelia added gently. "She was going to call you, so I just bought her parents time before they have to tell her she can't see or speak to you."

Sue leaned forward. "You've known them for a long time. Do you know why they want to control her?"

Emelia sighed. "My guess is its insecurity. Her dad works in a factory, her mom at a big-box store. Neither went to college. I think they want to ensure better for her."

She continued, settling her hand in Robert's. "In high school, they didn't let her do anything but study. No dating. Nothing less than an A was acceptable."

"It's still like that," Solomon muttered. "And I'm apparently an F."

Emelia glared. "To Deanna, you're an A-plus."

He wiped a tear. "With her parents' stranglehold on her, does what she thinks even matter?"

"She stayed with you in the hospital—risked being kicked out. You matter to her. You're the love of her life. I believe she'll stand up to them."

Emelia suddenly brought a hand to her mouth, eyes wide. "What if they kick her out this time?"

Robert squeezed her hands. "Cart before horse. We'll figure it out."

Jerry and Sue nodded. "We'll take care of our girl."

Emelia reached for Solomon's hand as he looked around the room. He shook his head, but his shoulders lifted a little. "My heart is still broken. But you give me hope."

Chapter 44

A Leap of Faith

When Deanna and her parents returned home Sunday night, she went straight to the kitchen and the phone, her father hot on her heels.

"Who are you calling?" he demanded.

She paused, brows furrowing. "Solomon. Just to talk before bed. Why?"

His expression hardened. "You will not call him. You will not see him again."

Deanna frowned, temper rising. "Why?"

His face reddened. "Because he's not good enough for you. Your mother and I are done watching you waste your time. It stops now."

She picked up the receiver. He snatched it from her hand.

Her mother entered. "I heard your father tell you no."

Deanna squared her shoulders. "I love Solomon. I will see him. I will talk to him. If you make me choose, I choose him."

Her mother glanced at her father, then back at Deanna. "If you want to wallow in the mud with someone beneath you, we won't stop you."

Then her mother lifted a stack of flat packing boxes and a fresh roll of packing tape. "You need these."

Deanna gasped.

"You can pack your things and go," her father said. "We spoke to Officer Charlie. You're a legal adult. We can't keep your car or belongings, but we can tell you to leave."

Deanna stared at them, stunned. "You asked our neighbor how to get rid of me? That's low. You've always run my life. I was never enough. If I got an A minus, or worse, a B plus, you crushed me with your disappointment. You made me believe I deserved it. I worked myself raw trying to be good enough, and I never was. I didn't have a life because you convinced me I shouldn't have one."

Her voice trembled. "Emelia is my only friend. I don't know how she tolerated you. I'm blessed she married Robert. They led me to Solomon and the Jacksons. They showed me real love, acceptance, and worth."

She lifted her chin. "I'll pack fast. I don't want to be here. When I drive away, I won't come back. There are people who truly love me. And since you're done with me, I'll share the best thing I've ever done. I was baptized last Sunday night."

Her parents' mouths fell open. Deanna snatched the boxes and tape from her mother and marched to her room.

Once inside, she assembled the boxes, then pulled out her luggage and carefully wrapped her few breakables in her sweaters. One by one, the closet and dresser emptied until nothing of hers remained.

She stared at the bare room. "Why couldn't they love me? Why was I never enough?" she whispered. Then she lifted her gaze. "Lord, thank You for the family and friends who love me just as I am. Thank You for Solomon."

In the bathroom, toiletries, makeup, and hair supplies filled the last box. Moments later, every box was in her car. With her luggage rolled behind her, she walked out of the house without a word.

Her car was packed to the brim. She wiped a tear and backed down the driveway. She wasn't ready to face Solomon. Maybe Mark and Betsy would let her stay.

"God, please. I need a place tonight."

She parked in front of the Jackson home. Her stomach churned. She shut off the engine, gripped the keys, and stepped into the cold February wind. Shivering, she knocked.

Betsy opened the door, smiling warmly. "Deanna, what a wonderful surprise. Come in. Solomon's not here."

Mistake, mistake, mistake, her mind screamed. But her stomach growled louder.

Betsy helped her out of her coat and guided her to the kitchen. "You must be hungry. I'll fix you a plate."

Deanna sat as Betsy placed fried chicken, mashed potatoes with gravy, peas, and buttered rolls before her.

"Thank you," she whispered.

Betsy paused. "You're always welcome here. I can see something's wrong. I'll listen when you're ready. With or without my son, you're family. Now eat. It'll help."

Deanna took a few bites. She tasted the love in each one. *Thank You, Lord.* Her stomach settled. She ate in silence.

When she finished, she cleaned up, started the dishwasher, and joined the family in the living room. Mark waved her over. The girls scooted apart.

"Sit with us, sis," Lexi said.

Nestled between them, soon she was laughing at Blair Warner's snootiness. When the episode of *The Facts of Life* ended, she felt steady enough to speak.

"Girls, may I talk to your parents privately?"

Lexi and Millie headed down the hall. Deanna smiled when they separated.

"Do they like having their own rooms?" she asked.

Betsy chuckled. "They do, but I like the peace it brought to this house even more."

Mark nodded. "Much more."

Deanna took a breath. "My parents kicked me out tonight. I need a place to stay."

Betsy took her hand. "The guest room's ready."

"I backed my truck out of the garage. Your car should be inside with Betsy's. Want me to move your things to the guest room?" Mark asked.

Deanna blinked. "How did you know?"

Mark opened the front door. "Betsy saw your loaded car."

She turned to Betsy. "Why didn't you say anything?"

"I knew you'd tell us when you were ready. We know there's more, but it's your story to share. You're safe here. Loved. Always welcome."

When Deanna stood, her knees buckled. Mark steadied her, guiding her back to the sofa.

"Just my luggage from the trunk and the bathroom box from the front seat," she said.

Mark handed her purse to her, and she gave him her keys. He stepped outside.

Betsy moved beside her. Deanna met her gaze, and the tears came.

"They said I couldn't see or speak to Solomon. That he's beneath me."

Her breath hitched. Betsy covered her hand.

"I love him. Even if they hadn't told me to leave, I couldn't have stayed. I can't be without him."

Betsy squeezed her hand. "Sweetheart, he loves you, too. You should talk. Let's call him. You'll both sleep better."

"Robert, I need your keys." Solomon pushed through the door.

"Bro, where's the fire? It's almost nine." Robert gasped. "Wait. Jerry said it was Mom on the phone. Is somethin' wrong? Is everyone alright?"

Solomon sighed. "Our family is fine. It's Deanna. She's there. Mom said we need to talk and told me to bring the ring."

Robert's eyes widened. "Em! Bring me my keys. Solomon's about to propose!"

Emelia's delighted shriek echoed from the bedroom.

Solomon's heart surged with hope for the first time since yesterday's brutal confrontation with Deanna's parents. He grabbed the small bag from his sock drawer. Emelia met him in the living room, dropping the keys into his hand.

"Be careful," she said. "And I want every detail when you get back."

He parked Robert's car at the curb and frowned at the sight of his dad's truck in the driveway. Inside, the house was quiet. No sign of Deanna. His father sat in the living room.

"Dad, why's your truck in the drive?"

Without a word, his father walked to the guest room and slipped inside. Solomon stood alone, tension rising.

"You guys are killing me," he muttered. "What is going on?"

When he turned, there she was. His Deanna stood in the hallway, radiant, hair and makeup flawless, dress hugging every curve. He swallowed hard, stunned by her beauty. His family scattered, leaving them alone.

He stepped forward. She met him halfway.

His fingers traced the outline of her face. "You're so beautiful," he whispered. "I didn't think I'd ever see you again."

Her smile bloomed slowly. "I couldn't let that happen."

He pulled her into his arms. "My sweet, I love you so much."

He ran his fingers through her hair, inhaling its strawberry-vanilla scent. "I love that your hair smells like it looks. I love your softness, your heart, and most of all, I love that you love me."

Her eyes shimmered. "I do love you, Solomon. I can live without a lot of things, but not you."

He held her close, then kissed her, slowly, reverently. When she pulled back, he kissed the tears on her cheeks and led her to the sofa.

When she sat, he turned away, pulled the pouch from his pocket, and fumbled for the right box. He opened the box when he knelt. Her gasp filled the room.

"Yes," she said before he could speak.

He laughed softly. "I had something planned."

"I still want to hear it," she said, gaze flicking between his face and the sparkling diamond.

Her joy lit up the room. He kissed her quickly, then took her hand.

"Deanna Keaton, you are the most beautiful woman I've ever known. Your outer beauty is stunning, but your heart takes my breath away. I want to spend my life loving you, building a home, a business, and a family. When we're old, I want to sit beside you, rocking away our days. Will you be my wife?"

She squealed. "Yes, yes, a thousand times yes!"

He slipped the ring on her finger and sat beside her, brows raised. "Why are we in my parents' living room?"

"My parents kicked me out tonight. They said awful things about you. I didn't know how to talk to you. I didn't even know if I'd be welcome here."

He took her hand again. "Dee, stop. You have nothing to be sorry for. They said plenty of ugly things to me. None of it changed how I feel about you, and it never will."

He kissed the ring on her finger before bringing his gaze back up to hers.

"As your future husband, I want to share everything. Our burdens and our victories. You can always talk to me. And I'll always talk to you, even if you don't like what I say."

When she swatted his chest, he grinned.

His mother peeked in. "The suspense is killing me."

He chuckled. "No, it isn't. She squealed. I know you heard."

The family poured into the room. Lexi and Millie rushed to see the ring. Deanna held out her hand, and they oohed and ahhed.

"For a guy, you have good taste in jewelry," Lexi teased.

"Don't ever stop being ornery, Lex." He smiled.

His parents admired the ring again, and his mother hugged Deanna, eyes misty. "You should call Robert and Emelia."

Solomon shook his head. "Mom, we all have to work tomorrow."

He turned to Deanna. "Speaking of tomorrow, where are you staying tonight? Where's your car?"

"I'm in the guest room. My car's in the garage."

"You'll be safe here. Walk me out?"

She slipped her hand into his. At the door, he helped her with her coat, then put on his own. At the passenger side of the car, he kissed her. *His fiancée*. His heart soared.

"I'll see you tomorrow. I want you to stay with me. Please think about it."

She ran her hand down his cheek. "I can't. We're not married."

"You can have my room. I'll take the couch. I want you near me."

She kissed him softly. “I’ll think about it.”

He stepped back, shooing her toward the house. “It’s cold. Go inside.”

He watched until the door closed behind her, then climbed into the car, his heart joyful.

Chapter 45

Steps Toward Forever

When Deanna arrived at work on Monday morning, Emelia was waiting by her desk."Let me see the ring."

"Let me get my coat off and put my purse away."

"If I have to wait, hand over your lunch. I'll stick it in the fridge."

Deanna passed her lunch to Emelia, who returned moments later. Deanna held up her left hand.

Emelia gasped. "Girl, it's lovely."

Deanna smiled. "Only because a lovely man put it there."

"Did I sound like that when Robert proposed?"

"Exactly like that."

Their boss passed by. "Time to get to work, ladies—but first, Deanna, show me the lovely ring your lovely man gave you."

Deanna held out her hand. Her boss nodded. "It's beautiful."

They eyed the mountain of receipts and expense reports on their desks and got to work. They couldn't take their morning break together, but shared lunch. After Emelia prayed, they unpacked their meals. Deanna fussed with hers, arranging everything just so.

Emelia narrowed her eyes. "That's procrastination if I've ever seen it. Spill."

Deanna blurted, "Solomon asked me to come stay with him."

"I know. Jerry, Sue, Robert, and I are fine with it as long as you and Solomon stay celibate until you're married."

"He said he'd sleep on the couch and give me his room. I don't feel right taking it."

"That's his choice. Besides, you'll be living with us after the wedding anyway. We can't afford unnecessary expenses while starting a business. The sooner we pool resources, the faster we reach our goals. Are you on board?"

Deanna inhaled sharply. "This is getting real."

Emelia pressed her palms to the table. "Life has a way of doing that. Are you ready to start your real life with us as a family?"

Deanna swallowed. "I am."

After work, Deanna returned to the Jackson home. Solomon's parents and sisters greeted her warmly.

"Welcome home," Betsy said. "Your fiancé, Emelia, and Robert are joining us for dinner. Come help me in the kitchen."

When Deanna entered the kitchen, she found dinner nearly finished. Betsy gestured toward two cups of steaming tea."Sit with me."

Deanna sat, shoulders slumping. "Am I in trouble?"

Betsy waved her off. "Of course not. I just wanted you to know we trust you—all four of you. We're okay with you living with Robert, Emelia, and Solomon. So, how soon do you want to get married?"

Deanna sighed. "I always pictured walking down the aisle on my father's arm, in a white dress, to my groom. That picture's been shredded. I'd still love the dress, but as long as I get to be Solomon's wife, even that doesn't matter. A year-old piece of frozen cake would be nice to share on our first anniversary, though."

Her voice faltered. The dream she'd held for so long was gone.

Betsy pulled her into a hug. "We'll do our best to make some of your dreams come true."

Deanna sniffled. "It'll be okay. I get to spend my life with Solomon. That's what matters most."

"Drink your tea, sweetheart. I'll finish the salad. We'll talk more at dinner."

Solomon arrived with Robert and Emelia just as Lexi and Millie placed the final setting on the dining table. His dad emerged from the kitchen with a pan of lasagna. His mom followed with a bowl of salad. Behind them, Deanna carried the large breadbasket—the one used on holidays—filled with garlic knots.

"Lexi, I forgot the Italian dressing," his mom said. "Please grab it for me."

Once everyone was seated, they joined hands and bowed their heads.

His dad prayed.

"Dear Lord, we come before You with humble hearts. Comfort Deanna as she mourns the loss of her relationship with her parents. If it's possible, open Ephraim's and Lydia's hearts and give us the chance to lead them to You. Bless Solomon's and Deanna's upcoming union. Guide us as we help them prepare for their life together. As we go forward as a family, grant us wisdom and patience. Bless this meal and the hands that prepared it. Forgive us our sins as we forgive those who've sinned against us. Yours is the power and glory, forever. In Your Son's precious name, amen."

"Amen," echoed around the table.

Solomon lifted his head. Deanna's whispered amen drew his attention. He laid his hand over hers, silently asking if she was all right. She nodded and passed him the breadbasket.

Serving dishes were passed and plates filled. For a few quiet minutes, everyone simply ate.

His dad looked at him. "Your mom and I reviewed both college funds. They're healthy." Then, to Robert, he added, "I know you and Emelia have been pinching every penny. How's your savings?"

Robert glanced at Emelia. "We have enough to pitch in."

Solomon braced himself. He'd drained nearly everything after the accident.

His mom turned to him. "There's good news. Our insurance agent called. Their attorneys negotiated a settlement that included medical costs, lost wages, compensation for the truck, and for your pain and suffering. They'll subtract what they paid for the truck and issue a check for the difference. They'd like you to come by tomorrow to review the numbers."

He blinked. "Will your medical insurance need to be paid back? What about what you guys paid yourselves?"

His mom shook her head. "Our insurance would've paid no matter how you got hurt. And as for what we paid, that's water under the bridge. We love you. We'd do it again."

His dad added, "We're praying the settlement helps you and Deanna. She was with you every step."

He nodded, swallowing past the tightness in his throat. "She was with me through it all."

Emelia leaned forward. "Are you saying they can afford a wedding?"

"I don't want a big wedding," Deanna said softly. "Just a dress, a cake, a bouquet, all of you, ending with Solomon as my husband."

Solomon's heart swelled. His parents, Robert, and Emelia, exchanged glances, then spoke together. "We can do that."

Deanna turned to Robert. "Do you think Jerry would walk me down the aisle?"

"I think he'd be honored," Robert said. "Jerry and Sue love you."

His mom clapped her hands. "Ladies, Saturday, we're going dress shopping."

Deanna yawned. "Tonight, I need sleep."

Solomon leaned toward her. "Dee, are you coming home tonight?"

"Tomorrow. I'm sorry. I just can't tonight. We'll move my things after work."

He kissed her forehead. "I get it. It's been a long couple of days. Robert and I will be here after work."

Emelia grinned. "Deanna, I brought tiramisu. You can't skip your favorite dessert."

Deanna giggled, and Solomon smiled at the sound. She turned to Emelia. "You're right. May I have a small piece, please?"

After dessert, Deanna thanked everyone and apologized for not helping with cleanup. His mom waved her off.

Solomon walked her down the hall and pulled her gently into the guest room, leaving the door open. He wrapped his arms around her. "I love you, my sweet."

She tipped onto her toes, and he met her halfway. Her lips were soft, tasting of cocoa and cream. He could've kissed her forever.

But that would come soon enough.

He broke the kiss, keeping her close. She rested her head on his chest, and he stroked her hair. After a quiet moment, she looked up.

"If I stay here, I'll fall asleep standing. One more kiss, then you have to go."

He kissed her again, lingering for a long moment before letting her go. "Good night, my sweet. Don't forget to say your prayers."

He closed the door behind him, a smile pulling on his face.

Chapter 46

Bound by Love

During lunch the following day, Solomon drove to the insurance office, sandwich in hand. He thanked the Lord the morning job with Robert had been clean, with no grime or sweat. He arrived five minutes early and chuckled. That was rare for him lately.

The receptionist greeted him and directed him to the agent's office. After a quick handshake, the agent waited until Solomon settled into a chair, then handed him the offer.

Scanning the pages, he was grateful he had picked up some legalese reading remodeling contracts at Bard's Buildings. Conner Bard insisted his employees read them to avoid job-site misunderstandings. Solomon hated reading them but was thankful now because the language was familiar.

His eyes widened at the final number of the settlement offer. Still, he couldn't help but wonder why Deanna's value as his caregiver wasn't mentioned. He leafed through the papers one more time. It wasn't there.

"This all sounds good," he said, "but I have one question. My parents had to work, so a young woman came daily to help me. Is there any way to include compensation for her care?"

The agent frowned. "I don't see any documentation for a caregiver. Let me call the attorney."

He placed the call on speaker. "Mr. Dansbury, you're on with me and the insured, Solomon Jackson."

"How can I help?" the attorney asked.

The agent explained Solomon's request. Mr. Dansbury confirmed there was no documentation and outlined what would be required.

"How soon?" Solomon asked.

"Tomorrow. The settlement needs to be finalized by week's end."

Solomon hesitated. "If it's finalized this week, when will I see the money?"

"They have thirty days to cut us a check," the attorney said. "Then our company processes it, which could take another thirty days, then a check will be sent to you minus what you've already received for the loss of your vehicle."

"So, two months."

"Yes, sir," the attorney said. "Just get us that documentation."

"I will. Thank you."

The call ended. Solomon stood and shook the agent's hand. "I'll be back tomorrow. If I can't get the paperwork, I'll sign it as is."

"See you then."

A heaviness settled in his chest. *Dear Lord, grant me strength, wisdom, perseverance, and patience. In Jesus' name, amen.* He prayed that same prayer over and over throughout the day.

That evening, he and Robert headed to his parents' house to move Deanna to the Carter farm. She and Emelia were already there. Robert cleared boxes from her car so Solomon could ride with her.

While Robert rearranged the load, Solomon sat with Deanna, Emelia, and his mom, explaining the possible reimbursement for Deanna's help during his recovery. The women agreed to prepare the documentation.

Then the ladies sent him and Robert ahead to the Carters with instructions to unload Deanna's things into Solomon's room, then return with enough pizza for everyone.

"Emelia, I can't leave. You forgot something," Robert said.

She kissed him.

Solomon turned to Deanna. "Your turn?"

When she kissed him, he smiled.

"My boys and girls, don't forget those goodbye kisses. Research shows they strengthen marriages and lengthen lives." His mom beamed at them.

Deanna grinned. "Yes, ma'am."

At the farm, Solomon and Robert unloaded the car and rearranged the living room, sliding one of the twin beds between the wall and the back of the sofa.

"That was a great idea," Solomon said. "I'll sleep better in my bed than on the couch."

Robert shrugged. "Credit goes to Emelia."

Solomon laughed. "Of course it does."

The next morning, Robert sent Solomon straight to the insurance office with the caregiver documentation as soon as it opened.

The agent scanned the papers. "This looks like exactly what we need."

"Please keep me updated on the settlement."

"As soon as the revised document is ready, I'll call you in to sign."

They shook hands, and Solomon headed back to work, grateful that one more piece of the puzzle was in motion.

After midweek service, Deanna sat quietly beside Solomon and his family in Brother Bassing's office. Her heart thudded while Solomon described their living arrangements. He had moved his bed to the living room, hers was in the bedroom, and they'd all set boundaries. She nodded when needed, offering her own affirmations. Every word felt like a thread stitching together the fragile fabric of trust they were trying to build.

Brother Bassing listened intently, but his expression remained unreadable. When they finished, he leaned forward, folding his hands. "Scripturally and personally, I see nothing sinful in your setup," he said. "But to outsiders, it may invite gossip and misinterpretation. I'll perform your wedding ceremony on the condition that you commit to regular marriage counseling until the ceremony. And if you're willing, I'd like to visit your home."

Her breath caught. *A home visit.* She glanced at Emelia, who didn't miss a beat.

"Would you and your wife join us for Sunday dinner?" Emelia asked.

Brother Bassing raised a brow. "You do know we have three children?"

"We live in part of the Carter home," Robert said. "There's plenty of space and room outside for the kids to run."

He smiled, picked up the receiver, and dialed. After a brief call, he nodded. "We'd be glad to come. And if gossip gets out of hand, I'll do two things: confirm to anyone who asks that you're living scripturally, and preach a sermon on the evils of gossip and the one who is without sin casting the first stone."

Relief washed over Deanna. Not only had he accepted their arrangement, but he was willing to defend it. She hadn't realized how heavy the fear of judgment had been until it began to lift.

The months leading up to the wedding had both flown by and dragged on, depending on how overwhelmed she felt. Solomon's twentieth birthday had passed quietly, a small reminder of how far they'd both come since his accident just over a year ago. But this first Saturday in October wasn't about survival—it was about joy.

With her hand tucked into the crook of Jerry's elbow, Deanna stood in her simple white satin gown, a sheer veil draping her hair and falling to just above her feet. Her white-tipped fingers tightened around her sunflower bouquet, and her white-tipped toes peeked through her Cinderella-inspired heels.

Jerry nudged her toward the chapel doors of the Northside church of Christ. She drew a steadying breath and stepped toward Solomon—the best man she'd ever known. She was ready to be his wife.

As she entered the chapel, her eyes swept the room. She came to a complete stop when she spotted her parents.

Her legs froze. She looked between Jerry and her father, who was already stepping forward.

"I've been talking to them," Jerry whispered. "Your dad would like to walk you down the aisle, if you'll allow it."

"Jerry, please don't leave me," she whispered.

"I won't."

Her father stopped beside her. "Your mother and I should've trusted you. We're sorry. May we share your wedding day?"

She looked toward Solomon. His gaze met hers—steady, familiar, full of grace. Just like the first time they'd locked eyes at Emelia and Robert's wedding. He gave a small nod, his eyes encouraging her to forgive.

She drew a breath, then turned to her father. When he offered his arm, she placed her hand inside it. Flanked by both men, she walked down the aisle.

At the altar, Jerry kissed her cheek and clapped Solomon on the back. "I love you both," he said, then stepped aside.

"Who gives this woman to be wed?" the minister asked.

"Her mother and I," her father replied, kissing her cheek. Then he met Solomon's eyes with a nod and a quiet smile. "Take good care of her, son."

He placed Deanna's hand into Solomon's and joined his wife in the pew.

Deanna looked up at Solomon. His gray-blue eyes had deepened to a bright blue, sending butterflies fluttering through her chest and making her heart flip.

As he pushed a lock of hair off his forehead, his Adam's apple moved up and down in his throat.

He pulled in a breath. "You look amazing."

She handed her sunflower bouquet to Emelia and turned back to Solomon. He stood before her in his tailored black suit, white shirt, and black tie, with a sunflower on his lapel.

"You're so handsome."

When his hands returned to hers, their gazes locked again. Her legs turned to jelly, and the strength of Solomon's grip steadied her. A moment later, she stood strong.

She was grateful they'd chosen a simple ceremony with traditional vows. After they said "I do," they lit a candle together, the single flame symbolizing their union, just as the circles of their rings spoke of never-ending love.

Returning to Brother Bassing, they bowed their heads as he prayed over them. Then he smiled.

"By the power vested in me by the state of Missouri and the good Lord above, I now pronounce you husband and wife. You may kiss your bride."

Deanna stepped joyously into Solomon's arms, the world narrowing to just the two of them. Their kiss was everything she'd dreamed it would be—deep, sure, and full of promise.

When Solomon pulled back, Deanna saw Robert directly over his brother's shoulder. "That's enough, bro. You've got the rest of your life for that."

She laughed. "We should've known you'd return the favor."

The minister turned them toward their family. "I present to you, for the first time, Mister and Missus Solomon Jackson."

The reception was simple and sweet, just like Deanna had hoped. A two-tier cake, homemade meltaway mints, nuts, and sparkling cider. She and Solomon toasted with their arms entwined, then fed each other cake, laughing through the crumbs. Since only Solomon's sisters, Eddy's children, and the minister's kids were single, they skipped the bouquet and garter toss without regret.

Leaving the church beside Solomon—**her husband**—her heart fluttered. He drove the truck he'd bought with part of his settlement, another symbol of how far they'd come. Yesterday, they'd stored the twin mattresses in his parents' garage and placed a king-size mattress on the tied-together twin frames.

"Are you ready for our wedding night in our bed?" he asked.

Her cheeks warmed.

He smiled. "Yeah, me too. We'll learn together." He kissed her hand, and her heart melted.

"I love you," she whispered.

Back at the Carter farm, she and Solomon had just changed out of their wedding clothes when Robert and Emelia arrived.

"Mom sent dinner," Robert announced.

They ate together, laughter filling the room. Then Robert, ever the dramatic brother, stood and—reminiscent of Old Testament unions—declared, "Solomon, you may join Deanna in your room tonight."

Deanna ducked her head, face hot. Solomon playfully slugged Robert's arm and stood, tugging his wife gently to her feet.

"I don't have to be told twice," he said, grinning. "Help your wife with the dishes tonight."

She followed him to the bedroom she'd been staying in—the one he'd vacated for her months ago. Now it was theirs.

"My sweet," he said. Pausing in the doorway, he scooped her into his arms. "This is the first night of the rest of our lives."

He closed the door behind them. Her heart whispered, *Thank You, Lord.*

Chapter 47

The Dream Becomes Reality

Three and a half years after he first asked Emelia out, Robert finally felt things coming together. After their honeymoon, Solomon and Deanna settled into married life easily. And the foursome spent another year scrimping, saving, and getting the Carter farm in order. Robert earned his national contractor license over two years ago, and Solomon's was six months old. Now Robert was working toward his real estate license, the last piece of the puzzle. It was time.

In mid-November they sat around the kitchen table after dinner. Robert swallowed hard. "I think it's time to get our dream off the ground," he said. "Ladies, how's our budget and savings?"

Deanna laid out the numbers, steady and thorough. Emelia followed with her savings records.

Solomon chuckled. "The settlement from my accident helped a lot."

Robert clapped his brother's shoulder. "It sure did. I just wish that wasn't how you had to contribute."

Emelia cleared her throat. "If we're serious, we need to look for a foreclosed property or one being auctioned for back taxes. Ten thousand max, or we won't have enough left to remodel."

Robert nodded. "Let's vote. Are we ready to start looking?"

Four raised hands. Four voices said, "Yes."

"I'll start after Thanksgiving," Robert said.

The day after Christmas, he sat beside Solomon on the couch, flipping through real-estate ads and auction notices. One listing caught his eye.

"Hey, guys, come look at this."

Emelia and Deanna leaned over the back of the couch. Solomon turned off the TV and joined them.

"This one goes to auction December thirtieth," Robert said. "We can't walk the property or look through the windows until the day of the sale. Even then, we can't go inside. Cash is due at the time of sale. It's a risk, but it could be worth it."

Emelia tapped her chin. "We can't walk it yet, but we could drive by and see what we can see."

Robert turned to Solomon. "What do you think?"

Solomon jingled his keys. "Let's go."

With Robert and Solomon up front and the girls in back, they took Solomon's truck to the house. Deanna spotted an alley behind it.

"Good eye, my sweet," Solomon said.

Emelia jotted notes about the front and sides. Solomon asked if they were ready to check the back. Emelia read her list aloud.

"Add the cracks in the walkway," Robert said.

Solomon drove around to the alley and parked. Everyone called out observations as they spotted them.

Emelia groaned. "Whoa, guys. I can't write that fast."

"Sorry, my love. Read what you've got, and I'll fill in the gaps. Solomon and Deanna will help."

Robert added three items. Solomon had nothing more. Deanna pointed out the sagging garage door.

Emelia frowned. "I can't believe you all missed the damage to the pad between the garage and alley."

Robert laughed. "We make a good team. What one of us misses, another sees."

Solomon exhaled. "We need to take this list to the auction. If we can look through the windows, we'll add anything new. Based on what we've seen, do you think it's a good risk?"

Robert reached for the list. Emelia handed it over. "Pencil?"

He scribbled rough repair costs and worst-case estimates for the interior before passing it back.

Emelia and Deanna added the numbers, plus the ten thousand for purchase.

"We'd have a small contingency fund," Deanna said. "You should go to the auction, but if you see something awful inside, walk away."

Robert looked at Solomon, then at their wives. "We go on the thirtieth. If it looks okay, we bid. No more than ten thousand."

Solomon fist-pumped, and the girls nodded. "Yes!" Solomon said.

December thirtieth was bitterly cold. The turnout was small. Robert carried ten thousand in his wallet and kept his hand over it like a shield. He and Solomon re-inspected the property. Through the windows, they saw abandoned furniture and trash but no signs of water or structural damage.

They registered. Robert held paddle number ten. The bidding started at three thousand and crept upward. He stayed silent until "Going once."

"Four thousand," Robert called.

"Going, going, gone," the auctioneer said. "Sold to paddle number ten."

Robert turned to Solomon, stunned. "We bought our first house."

The next eight months were tough—pizza dinners, cold sandwiches, late nights, and long weekends. Between renovation work, the farm, and their regular jobs, exhaustion became a constant companion.

But when they listed the house in August and it sold within two weeks, Robert couldn't stop grinning. Even after listing below market, they'd cleared nearly fifty thousand.

"Our mission is to serve the Lord by improving our town and helping our neighbors," he had told the realtor.

After a couple of weeks to breathe, Robert dove back in. Within the next year, they'd bought, renovated, and sold two more homes. The following year, three. Each new project taught them more than the last.

By the time Robert added his real estate license, he finally felt they were doing what God had called them to do.

Thanksgiving evening, a little more than six and a half years after Robert first shared his dream on his graduation day, they sat around their parents' table eating apple strudel and pumpkin pie.

Robert smiled. "Dad, Mom. I have an announcement."

"Let's hear it, son," his dad said.

Robert caught his mom's expectant expression. He knew she wanted a grandchild.

"I'm sorry, Mom. Emelia's not pregnant."

His mom frowned, but everyone else laughed.

She shook her head and laughed with them. "So what is the big announcement?"

Robert sat straighter and squared his shoulders. "We're opening an office," he said. "Jackson Home Design and Sales."

Solomon grinned. Emelia and Deanna beamed. And something swelled deep in Robert's chest.

This was only the beginning.

Robert and Solomon made their dream a reality while honoring their mission to serve the Lord by improving their town and helping their neighbors.

Years later, that same mission and legacy live on in the contemporary Christian novel *When Wounds Heal* and its sequel, *When Love Overcomes*, featuring Jedidiah—a young man recovering from childhood abuse—and Solomon and Deanna's daughter, Maggie, whose quiet strength and faith shine through both stories.

Coming soon, the final installment of Jedidiah and Maggie's journey in *When God Leads.*

Leave a Review

Did you like this book?
Please leave a review on Amazon
(https://www.amazon.com//dp/B09MSY4C5V/)
Thank You!

For more about Denice and her stories, follow her on social media or her website:

- Facebook-Page:
(https://www.facebook.com/denice.perkins.author//)
- Facebook-Group:
(https://www.facebook.com/groups/566822318311404)
- Instagram:
(https://www.instagram.com/deniceperkinsauthor/)
- Amazon-Author-Page:
(https://www.amazon.com/stores/Denice-Perkins/author/B09NGNNKSD)
- Website::
(https://deniceperkinsauthor.com/)

More by Denice

If you enjoyed this story, I'd love to invite you to continue reading the *When God* series, stories of faith, healing, redemption, and the families God builds along the way.

If you haven't already, you can read Jedidiah's story from the beginning in *When Wounds Heal.*

When Wounds Heal on Amazon (https://www.amazon.com/dp/B09NGKK96F)

When Wounds Heal

Beaten. Broken. But Never Truly Alone

After enduring seventeen years of cruelty at the hands of his drug-addicted parents, Jedidiah longs to give and receive love he isn't sure exists.

The deaths of his parents leave him abandoned and scared. His neighbors give him a home, care he craves, and take him to church. Their minister brings him a Bible, filling him with anger. He can't bring himself to believe in the God who allowed him to suffer.

When Jedidiah meets Maggie, whose steadfast faith and kindness awaken hope in his heart, she offers love, belonging, and the future he desires. Building a life with her means confronting bitterness, forgiving the God he blames, and believing he is worthy of redemption.

But when his past collides with the future he longs to build, Jedidiah must decide whether fear will define him or whether he will risk everything to move forward in faith.

Jedidiah and Maggie's story continues in:
When Love Overcomes on Amazon (https://www.amazon.com/When-Love-Overcomes-Ejected-Embittered-ebook/dp/B0DJPJ2BQ8/)

When Love Overcomes

Ejected. Embittered. Embraced by Enduring Love

Twenty-year-old Jedidiah Matthews has a life he once only dreamed of: a roof over his head, an engagement, and progress toward his High School Equivalency Diploma. But his hard-won stability is shaken when he recognizes a young woman from his past, a fellow victim he cannot fully remember. He knows one thing: she was pregnant when he left high school, and the child may be connected to him in ways he cannot recall.

Nineteen-year-old Maggie Jackson is thrilled to be engaged to the boy she once watched run track. She wants to stand beside Jedidiah, but his past has already tested their relationship. When a child not yet three years old is linked to that past, Maggie realizes that doing what is right may mean becoming a mother before she becomes a wife.

Together, they must decide whether they are ready to become the family a vulnerable child now needs.

Coming Soon: The final chapter of Jedidiah and Maggie's story

When God Leads

Challenged. Changed. Choosing to Trust Together.

The final chapter of Jedidiah and Maggie's story. As they face new responsibilities, lingering doubts, and unexpected changes, they begin to discover that God's plans for their future may be bigger and more challenging than they ever imagined.

Note of Gratitude

To every reader who opened *When Wounds Heal* and *When Love Overcomes* and asked, "How did it all begin?" this story is for you.

Your love for Jedidiah, Maggie, and the Jackson family made me want to return to the very foundation —the dream that started it all. *When It Began* was written because you cared enough to ask for more. That is the greatest gift a writer can receive. Thank you for investing your hearts in these characters and their journey. You are true blessings.

My deepest thanks go to my husband, whose unwavering support and encouragement make every page possible.

To my family, my church family, and my critique partner, Andy, thank you for your constant prayers, feedback, and belief, which sustain me through every draft.

To my editor, Lara, your insight, patience, and professionalism bring clarity and strength to every story. You make me a better writer, and I am grateful for all you do.

A special thank-you to my local ACFW chapter, MozArks, for your support and encouragement. Over the past two years, you have championed me through podcasts, book purchases, your time, and, most importantly, your prayers. You have given me the courage to trust God and keep writing.

I pray these stories continue to lead hearts to Christ.

About the Author

Denice Perkins is a proud wife, mother of three, and grandmother to fifteen. Her days are filled with writing, reading, gardening, baking, cooking, crafts, and often chauffeuring grandkids to school, scouts, or dance. Family is her heart, and she treasures being present for all of life's little moments.

Born in California and a Missourian by choice, Denice has lived just outside a small town in the Missouri Ozarks since her parents moved there when she was sixteen. She met the love of her life shortly after high school graduation and married him a year and a half later. Decades later, they're still in love. Her husband, an avid hunter, fisherman, and jack of all trades, keeps life interesting.

Denice has a background in marketing, journalism, and healthcare. She's worked in newspaper advertising, business management, and dental assisting, before earning her nursing degree and spending many years caring for others. Now retired, she's devoted to mastering the craft of storytelling.

A committed Christian, Denice serves faithfully at her local church and writes fiction rooted in Christ-centered values. Her greatest hope is to lead people to Christ through storytelling.

Recipe

Betsy's Christmas Cinnamon Rolls

In the Jackson family, these cinnamon rolls are a cherished Christmas morning tradition. Betsy passed the recipe down to her daughters—teaching Alexis and Mildred as they grew in her kitchen—then to Emelia on her first Jackson Christmas, and finally to Deanna as she learned to cook at Betsy's side. Now, this treasured recipe is shared with you.

These from-scratch cinnamon rolls are soft, gooey, and irresistibly rich. The secret? A pour of warm, heavy cream over the risen rolls just before baking creates a caramel-like sauce that seeps into every layer.

Ingredients:

For the Dough:

- 1 cup warm milk (about 110°F / 43°C)
- 2 tsp active dry yeast
- ¼ cup granulated sugar

- 1 large egg, lightly beaten
- ¼ cup unsalted butter, melted
- 3½–4 cups all-purpose flour
- 1 tsp salt

For the Filling:

- ½ cup unsalted butter, softened
- 1 cup packed brown sugar
- 2 tbsp ground cinnamon

For the "Secret" Cream Pour-Over:

- ¾ cup heavy whipping cream, slightly warmed

For the Cream Cheese Frosting:

- 4 oz cream cheese, softened
- ¼ cup unsalted butter, softened
- 2 cups powdered sugar
- 1 tsp vanilla extract
- 1–2 tbsp milk or heavy cream (optional, for consistency)

Instructions:

1. Prepare the Dough

1. Activate the yeast: In a large mixing bowl (or the bowl of a stand mixer), combine the warm milk, granulated sugar, and yeast. Let sit 5–10 minutes, until foamy.
2. Mix the dough: Add the beaten egg, melted butter, salt, and 2 cups of flour. Mix on low speed (or by hand) until combined. Gradually add remaining flour until a soft, slightly sticky dough forms.
3. Knead and rise: Turn the dough out onto a lightly floured surface and knead 5–7 minutes, until smooth and elastic. Place the dough in a greased bowl, cover it with a towel, and let it rise in a warm place for about 1 hour, or until it has doubled in size.

2. Assemble the Rolls

4. Roll out the dough:

Punch down the risen dough and roll into a 12×18-inch rectangle.

5. Add the filling:

Spread softened butter evenly over the dough. In a small bowl, combine brown sugar and cinnamon, then sprinkle evenly over the butter.

6. Roll and cut:

Starting from a long edge, roll the dough tightly into a log and pinch the seam to seal. Slice into 12 equal pieces using a sharp knife or unflavored dental floss.

7. Second rise:

Arrange rolls in a greased 9×13-inch baking dish, leaving slight space between each. Cover and let rise 30 minutes, or until puffy.

3. Bake and Finish

8. Preheat the oven to 350°F (175°C).

9. Add cream:

Warm the heavy cream slightly (10–15 seconds in the microwave). Pour evenly over the tops of the risen rolls, letting it seep into the gaps.

10. Bake:

Bake 25–30 minutes, until golden brown and most of the liquid has been absorbed.

11. Prepare frosting:

While baking, beat cream cheese, butter, powdered sugar, and vanilla until smooth. Add milk or cream as needed for the desired consistency.

12. Frost and serve:

Cool rolls 5–10 minutes before spreading or drizzling with frosting. Serve warm and enjoy!

A Note from Denice

This recipe can easily be multiplied.

Our family grew from five to eight, then to twenty-three, and will soon be twenty-four. With gratefulness, we include those who have become family by choice. At times, our gatherings reach thirty or more, because all we love and all who love us are always welcome. Count your blessings every time you need twelve more cinnamon rolls.

www.ingramcontent.com/pod-product-compliance
Lightning Source LLC
LaVergne TN
LVHW020532100826
845148LV00010B/1434

9798985279276